Ellen Wiles was born in 1981 and grew up in Reading. After doing a music degree at Oxford, she did a Master's in Human Rights Law, and then became a barrister at a London chambers, disappearing off periodically to work, including on The Bushmen Project in Botswana and with Karenni refugees in a camp in Thailand. After scribbling fiction on the side for a while, she did a Master's in Creative Writing, and eventually quit the law. She is the author of *Saffron Shadows and Salvaged Scripts: Literary Life in Myanmar Under Censorship and in Transition* (Columbia University Press, 2015), which includes interviews with Burmese writers and new literary translations. She is currently doing a PhD in Literary Anthropology, researching live literature, and directs an experimental live literature project. She lives in London with her husband and two small children.

The Invisible Crowd

HQ
An imprint of HarperCollins*Publishers* Ltd
1 London Bridge Street
London SE1 9GF

This edition 2017

1

First published in Great Britain by
HQ, an imprint of HarperCollins*Publishers* Ltd 2017

ISBN:
HB: 978-0-00-822881-1
TPB: 978-0-00-822883-5

MIX
Paper from
responsible sources
FSC™ C007454

Printed and bound in Great Britain by
CPI Group (UK) Ltd, Croydon, CR0 4YY

The Invisible Crowd

Ellen Wiles

ONE PLACE. MANY STORIES

Someone has flung rainbow pepper on the air.
The hummingbirds are migrating, each alone:
Blossomcrown, Coppery Thorntail and Flame-Rumped Sapphire.
RUTH PADEL, *THE MARA CROSSING*

All across the country, people said that
it wasn't that they didn't like immigrants.
ALI SMITH, *AUTUMN*

Prologue

We're clinging to each other, fistfuls of flesh and bone, and battering rams are smashing over our heads leaving us stingy-eyed, breathless, a woman and her child are clinging to one of my legs each, everyone is clinging to someone or something, and I almost envy the two tiny babies slung tight to their mothers who don't have a clue what this chaos is about, who don't understand the enormity of this terror, because there are way too many of us piled in here, we've created a death trap for each other, we know this, but we need each other too, we're all we've got left, and this might be the last group of faces I'll ever see, and I've never seen a group of faces so petrified, and I've seen a lot of petrified faces, and there's another one approaching, oh God, it's coming, it's coming, and we're rising, rising up – up and up and up – and this wave is taller than the tallest cliff and my stomach clenches and our boat is vertical now and I'm clinging on with all my strength and we're going to flip backwards and this is the end… but then we dip forward, just a little… and then we're nearly horizontal again – we're floating on nothingness, we're flying – and then we SLAP down on the water, and my brain explodes through my skull and the water is roaring and children are shrieking and women are wailing and men are sobbing, and I look beyond the boat and there's still nothing but this vast purple-grey sky bleeding into a desert of wetness you can't drink, with a furious monster thrashing underneath the surface, waiting to devour us, and why couldn't it have chosen a group of people who've had an easier life? – and now the child who's got hold of my leg has vomited in my lap but it doesn't matter, because we're rising again, oh God, we're rising, up and up and up and up…

Chapter 1: Jude

YK (Eritrea) v Home Office. That's all you have so far. It's 8 p.m. already, and you're supposed to submit the skeleton argument tomorrow. You were all set to leave chambers at 6 p.m., for once, when your clerk phoned. You so nearly didn't pick up, but the receiver tugged at your hand like a magnet.

'Brief's just come in for you, counsel's sick – skelly's due in the morning, papers being biked over now, all right?' he barked.

It wasn't really meant to be a question. But you still could have said no. You had the right to say no. You should have said no. But if you want to get decent work at the Bar you have start out as a Yes person, and as your old supervisor kept telling you, he got his breakthrough case by stepping in at the last minute. You trill your fingernails on the desk.

Back home, Alec will be listening to his final story before lights out. You're a terrible mother! You should be the one reading him *Burglar Bill*. He'll move onto books without pictures soon, and before you know it he'll be off to uni. You should be spending this precious time cultivating his language development, guiding him through important moral lessons like if you burgle tins of beans and bedpans from people's houses you have to give them back, or just feeling the warmth of his little body snuggled against yours… But unless you have a career you can't even pay for the nursery fees you need so that you can *have* a career… oh, wait…

Anyhow, your papers will arrive any minute. You'll do the speediest prep possible, enough to wing it, then you'll jump on the Tube, and in half an hour you'll be back in your kitchen, making a cup of peppermint tea, then sitting on the edge of Alec's bed, touching your lips softly onto his apricot cheek, watching his silhouette gently rise and fall with his breath, letting yourself indulge in a moment of utter peace. And then you'll crash. Meanwhile…

You write the initials YK in your blue notebook, italicize them, doodle some flowers around them, and fill out the acronym in your head: *Yoghurty Koala. Yielding Kipper. Yesterday's Kleenex.* Your friends are probably all out having fun right now, on a night out at that new Brazilian place you had to pull out of last time because you were working, or seeing whatever the new film of the moment is… you're so out of the loop. None of them have procreated yet, or become obsessed with a futile desire to change the world. As a result, all of them appear to have managed to achieve a sane work–life balance involving that mystical thing called down time. You wouldn't change Alec for the world, of course. But why were you so obsessed by getting into human rights law? Why? The fees have got so low for publicly funded work that you won't make enough from this case to cover the weekly food shop. *Come on, YK. Yowling Kitten. Yachting King. Yossarian Killer.*

Your clerk finally lumbers in with two large boxes and dumps them on your desk. 'Enjoy. I'm off home,' he says, as if you'd be thrilled. This will take hours just to skim-read. You're tempted to throw them out of the window and jump after them – or at least just disappear from chambers for a while. You're so drained, and all you've got is a Snickers for dinner, and you're becoming a stranger to your little boy, not to mention his daddy, and right now you feel less like a human rights warrior and more like a masochist… You manage enough grace to say 'bye' but your clerk is already out of the door. His feet thump down the stairs, two at a time. You pull out the first file, and just after you extricate it from the box, it bursts. White sheets drift over your desk and across the floor like snow.

Max would love you to quit the Bar! He says it's not worth the stress. If you did quit you could start your own business, like screen-printing pretty muslin cloths, that idea you had when Alec was a baby – there's clearly a market among new mums who want to look artsy while mopping up sick – or maybe just trade barrister for barista, and get a no-stress nine to five in a hipster coffee shop. You'd probably make more money, in the short term anyway, and the pay would be regular. Or else, you and Max could shove all your stuff into storage and migrate somewhere exotic like Zanzibar, teach English, and sip coconut water as Alec splashes through turquoise waves and rides on dolphins.

You pull down a new ring binder from the cupboard, gather up the papers, stick them back in again, in order, which eats up at least fifteen minutes, then start to flick through. So, YK is a male... arrived from Eritrea a year ago... university... government job... writer... conscript... prison break... desert... boat... cabbage truck... and you share a birthday! Seriously, 2 March 1975 – what are the chances? Could he have been born at 8.20 a.m. as well? For your last birthday, Alec made his first ever card for you – a portrait of Mummy in crayon that looked like a warped tomato on stilts with spaghetti on top – and while you were blowing out the candles on Max's home-baked chocolate and raspberry cake, YK was probably... being smuggled through France? Cakeless and cardless, at any rate.

You go through his witness statement again, more slowly, and find you're gnawing your knuckles. This isn't a case you should be skim-reading. The reason you wanted to do this job is because people like YK have had the worst luck thrown their way, and all they get in return for escaping to a supposed safe place is a sea of newspaper headlines branding them liars, scroungers and criminals. At a moment as crucial as a tribunal hearing they need someone who will not only expend time and effort to put their case, but will actually care: that's you. That's why you're still here, when you could be reading *Burglar Bill* or ordering a caipirinha (probably not simultaneously). But, first things first, where is Eritrea exactly? Might be nice at least to locate it within the continent before you attempt to persuade a judge not to send someone back there.

The internet informs you that it's a moon-shaped sliver of coastline in East Africa, with mountains inland and coral reefs along the coast. Should be lush. But apparently it's an 'open prison'. Ethiopia is its next-door neighbour but also its worst enemy since they split up… after a *thirty-year-long* war. And then another war over the border… So in 1990, when you were on a camping holiday with your parents in the Lakes, pretending you were a *Swallows and Amazons* character, YK was stuck behind a front line. And in 1998, when you were doing your law conversion course and trying to get your head around trusts and torts, he was being conscripted. In 2001, when you were starting pupillage in the beautiful surrounds of Temple, his government announced the end of the free press. And in 2003, when you were stressing about leaving your beautiful baby boy in nursery so you could go back to your sought-after job after your maternity leave, he was being tortured in an underground oven.

After a bit more research, you find yourself clicking into a few diaspora blogs, expecting a barrage of outrage against the government, but while you do find a lot of that, you find a lot of defenders as well. It's like going down a rabbit hole into a world of patriotic passions, fierce emotions and vicious insults. But you've got to crawl out: you're seriously pressed for time now. You need to focus on the law, the expert reports, the evidence. You unwrap your Snickers, take a large bite, and read on.

If what he says is true, YK has lived a more terrifying life than you can contemplate enduring and remaining sane. But as you read his rejection letter from the Home Office, go through his witness statement again and note down questions you want to ask, a cynical voice in your head can't help asking: how much is he exaggerating? He claims he was imprisoned for writing articles criticizing the regime… but would he really have dared to do something *that* risky in a country *that* repressive? There's less press freedom there than in North Korea. And then to stage a prison break near a militarized border – is that even possible? It's ironic that the more oppressive the country, the harder it is to make any stories of resistance sound credible in a tribunal, when, if they were true, the case for asylum would be all the stronger. YK has also got zero hard evidence from Eritrea to back up what he says, which of course makes sense if he had to flee, but never helps with credibility. Also, could his journey really have been *that* hair-raising? And why didn't he just seek asylum here sooner? Plus, you bet in person his English will be rubbish and he won't remember what his solicitor put in his statement and he'll come across as stilted and awkward and the judge will make him squirm.

You plough on, sticking Post-it notes on pages of the file and making lists. YK has got some good character witnesses, like Molly Muldoon, his English teacher, and Nina Lambourne, a friend who claims she trusts him enough to let him babysit her daughter... Doesn't that name ring a bell? Oh, and she's Molly's daughter. So how come she became friends with him? Not relevant, not relevant...

Your eyelids start dragging. You yawn, check your watch. It's late. Coffee is essential if you're going to get through this. You get up, stretch, and walk along the deserted corridor to the kitchen.

The ceiling light sputters and flickers as the kettle crackles. You've pretty much planned your argument now, and bullet-pointed the facts you need to prove. But it's funny – although you're frazzled, it's at moments like this that you wish your job went further, that you could know more, understand more. Sure, maybe it is a big enough challenge to take a mountain of legal documents and adapt them into a convincing account of someone's life constructed solely from words and facts that can be evidentially proven and are appropriate to the context, and tessellate all that into a persuasive argument about legal merit. It's a high-stakes brainteaser. But however well you solve that puzzle, and however well YK performs as a witness, at the end of the hearing he'll still be a mystery to you. You'll never know the truth. *Truth.* Well, you will have a handle on the kind of truth that the law demands – a cluster of facts weighty enough to tip the case over the balance of probabilities – but what you'd love to get a sense of is the truth of what it has felt like to be YK, Yonas Kelati, the living, breathing human being, your birthday twin. At least solicitors get to spend time with their clients, taking statements. Barristers barely get to meet them, usually. You wish you could dive inside the pages of these case files and swim around underneath the text to find out what your life would have been like if you and YK happened to have been switched at birth.

You pour out hot water, stir in two spoons of instant coffee with two heaped spoons of chocolate powder, splosh in the last of the communal milk, and sit down on the spare chair by the photocopier. After the first hot, bittersweet sip, you close your eyes. Imagine if, instead of meeting YK at the tribunal hearing, you could meet him for a coffee – not a vile mocha like the one you've just made, but a nice cappuccino in your local café with the comfy armchairs – and introduce yourself, not as his barrister, but just as Jude, a random British woman who happens to be exactly the same age. After some small talk you could mention that you'd be interested to know more about him and what led him here, and let him tell his story in his own words, while you probe subtly for details along the way, as any friend might do, allowing the conversation to branch and spiral beyond that square box labelled legal relevance.

Imagine if you could do the same with the other witnesses too. You could invite them each to tell you how they got to know YK, and find out what they really think of him. Yes, that part would be like when you were introduced to Max's friends and family: you thought you had the measure of your boyfriend, but they gave you a clearer sense of who he was before you came along, and illuminated quirks of his personality. The way Max knocks on his teeth with his fist while trying to make a decision, as if he were asking his inner oracle for permission to enter? His circumspect dad does exactly the same. By the end of a marathon of chats and coffees you'd be bouncing off the walls, but you would also be able to adapt all the sterile witness statements in this ring binder into something resembling stories.

You could go further, and adapt YK's story into a third-person narrative like the kind you normally get in an asylum judgment, but more red-blooded and visceral. You'd go way beyond that *Miller v Jackson* judgment you learned about at law school, where Lord Denning started off by waxing lyrical about a summertime cricket match, in order to cement his legal argument about nuisance. You'd go the whole way, turning law into literature. But how would that help YK? You could kidnap the immigration judge listed for YK's hearing, borrow her robes and pose as her while you read out your own prose to the tribunal, and conclude triumphantly that the appeal has succeeded… Oh, except you'd have to be there to listen to the judgment, as YK's barrister. And you'd probably end up jailed yourself.

Anyhow, you've finished your drink, so it's time to stop fantasizing and get back to work. But, when you sit at your desk again, your fingers seem to get a will of their own and start typing words into an online search box: *Eritrean restaurant London*. Your mouse clicks on a link. The food looks pretty good – lots of big pancake-type things and curries. You imagine taking YK and your solicitor there after the hearing to celebrate your win, and inviting him to choose the dishes… It'll probably never happen. There probably won't be an appropriate moment to ask, and anyway he might have no interest in getting to know you, might not care at all that you share a birthday, might not want to let you into any more details about his parallel, polar-opposite life. But you can at least make it a belated New Year's resolution to step away from Pizza Express and drag your family along to eat some authentic Eritrean food one day, if you ever get time off work, to close your eyes while chewing, to immerse yourself in the new flavour sensations on your tongue…

Chapter 2: Yonas

It was the ninety-third morning. Yonas picked up a shrimp, tore off its head, pulled off its tail, eased away its leg-fringed shell, then tossed the shell in a bucket to the right, dropped the flesh onto the pile to the left, and grabbed another, then tore off its head, pulled off its tail, and on, and on… until his numb fingertips fumbled, and a shrimp dropped to the floor. He stopped and stared at it for a moment. Lying there. Taunting him. He felt like lying down on the floor and curling up next to it. As he finally bent to grasp it, his spine made a cracking noise and a twinge spiked across his lower back. He straightened up, tentatively, stretched his arms and felt his shoulders crunch. The others were all hunched over cockles, mussels, oysters and crabs, and he imagined the whole lot of them solidifying and being found in here one day by a bunch of archaeologists, frozen in time like statues in a derelict church, with rotting shellfish strewn around their feet.

His stomach growled, reminding him that, by some miracle, he was still alive. Before he knew it he would be free to go out to a restaurant to eat a tasty meal with a bottle of beer on the side, and even some fresh fruit afterwards if he felt like it. What he would give right now for the zingy fragrance of a mango, fresh from the garden, newly sliced, glistening gold and dripping with juice! Saliva gushed around his tongue.

He blew pointlessly on his fingers, and turned the next shrimp around in his palm, picturing the beast when it was still alive, pottering along the seabed, waving its whiskers, unaware that it was about to be scooped up and boiled. He broke the shell open and extracted the flesh. When it dried, its colour would intensify and it would shrink into a crescent bead. He could string a collection into a necklace for little Lemlem... but she wouldn't be so little any more. It had been over a year since he'd seen her running around on those chubby legs. How great it would be to hear her voice chirping down a phone. Better still, to have her run through the door squealing *Uncle Yonas!*, reaching her arms out to be picked up, tossed in the air and spun around...

A sharp slap on the back of his head jarred his neck, and grey sparkles danced before his eyes. 'Get on with it,' Aziz barked.

Yonas felt like jumping up, kicking his stool away, chucking his entire bucket of shrimp shells over Aziz's ugly, balding head, then roaring: *You get on with it! We're out of here!*

But Gebre was hissing at him: 'Eh! M*elehaye!*' his face peeking around a mountain of scallops. 'While you were daydreaming over there I started my fourth bucket. I'm being tipped for promotion.' He flicked a shell into the air so it spun down and landed with a clink.

Yonas laughed, as much in surprise as at the joke. He couldn't remember when Gebre was last in a good enough mood to banter, but then one of them had always tried to pep up the other if they were down. 'No chance, my friend,' he retorted. 'You're the donkey to my racehorse.'

'There's only one donkey in here,' Gebre said, 'and I'm talking to him.'

'If you weren't the donkey you'd have noticed that my shrimps are a quarter the size of your scallops so my buckets take way longer to fill. Which means I can take time out and still go faster than you.'

Gebre cackled. 'Listen, one of your shrimps is about the size of your—'

But Aziz was approaching Gebre from behind now, and before Yonas had time to gesture a warning, his friend had been yanked around. 'What did I tell you,' Aziz snarled, snout to nose, then let go suddenly, so that

Gebre nearly toppled. Then he looked over to Yonas. 'Stop slacking, both of you, and get on with your fucking work,' he said, and skulked off to his den again, mumbling something that sounded like 'fed up with managing reprobates'. A piece of paper taped to his door stated OFFICE NO ENTER in unequivocal red marker.

Gebre's face crumpled into its default frown, his liveliness fading as quickly as it had appeared. He absently gnawed at a well-chewed fingernail, then got back to his shelling. *We have to get out of here*, Yonas thought. It was crazy to have been in the UK all this time and still to have no sense of what this country was actually like.

Their arrival felt like yesterday and for ever ago. Yonas remembered so clearly when they first walked in, both of them so weak they could barely stand, but still vaguely elated at having survived, together, through everything. When he registered how dank and eerie the factory was, Yonas's first reaction was to think he must be hallucinating, that in his fatigue he'd dreamed up some kind of ghost story set in Victorian Britain. He'd uttered a staccato laugh – but the sound had reverberated back at him, and a couple of the other workers had glanced up, confused. The place was dimly lit, with only narrow shafts of daylight struggling through boarded-up windows, and the workers wore glazed, otherworldly expressions. The ceiling was high, and charred remains of timbers were dotted along the wall where the first floor must once have been. The kitchen on the back wall consisted of a big vat perched on a tiny gas burner, like an oversized owl on a twig. The bathroom comprised two industrial sinks with a hosepipe shower, and the toilet was in a shed outside with no lock. Sharing it between nineteen other men meant it was never free when you needed it. But at least there was a toilet. Yonas thought back to those interminable days in the lorry through the Sahara, how he'd had to close off the top of his throat and breathe through his mouth so that he couldn't smell the foul cocktail of piss and shit and vomit, and later the sickly sweet infusion of decomposing human flesh. Yes, this place might be an improvement, but that didn't make it endurable. This was the UK, after all.

On the very first morning in the factory, when they could have slept for another twenty-four hours, they hauled themselves up, stiff as rusted robots, and Aziz put them straight to work. New crates of shellfish were delivered before dawn, and they all had to be rinsed, the bad ones discarded, the rest graded and sorted, then shelled or polished, cooked up or chilled, potted or packed, and finally re-loaded into the crates and lugged back outside for collection. Buckets and tools had to be emptied and cleaned, stray shells and seaweed fronds swept up, floors mopped. It wasn't as if Yonas hadn't anticipated some drudgery when he first got here – they had to pay back the smugglers after all – but he hadn't expected to be stuck in a place this grim without any pay at all. So much for his university degree. If it weren't for that stupid war, he might be at work right now in a warm office, with his own desk under a fan, wearing a thin, crisp shirt, writing something, coming up with new ideas… The only thing going for this place was the hope that they'd end up with papers, a ray of light that was diminishing daily. Ninety-three days…

The shrimp shells started to cut into Yonas's scarred finger pads, and pinkish blood began seeping out. The point of a headache drilled into his skull. It was so damply cold here, he felt like mould was growing into his bones. He jiggled his feet and waggled his fingers in an attempt to get some feeling back.

A rumbling came from above: rain dancing on the roof. Drips began to splat on the floor in syncopated rhythms, and the radio crackled into 'Billie Jean'. Yonas looked over at Gebre, trying in vain to catch his eye, hoping for a sign that he too was remembering his attempt to moonwalk all the way to school.

That evening it was Yonas's turn to make dinner, and Aziz, with a vindictive look in his eyes, paired him up with Samuel, who never seemed to utter more than a monosyllable. Yonas surveyed the ingredients glumly. 'Well, there's not much oil left,' he said, 'so how about we boil the pasta and potatoes, put chunks of that plastic cheese on top, and steam those reject mussels?'

Samuel nodded blankly.

'We'll get about two runts each from that lot if we're lucky,' Yonas added.

Samuel just stared at the reject mussels, expressionless.

'I'd give anything for a big, tasty lamb zigni stew with rice right now, and some herbs and spices, and vegetables – wouldn't you?' Yonas persisted. 'If you could eat any other dish in the world, what would it be? Come on. Your favourite! You must have one.'

Samuel thought, long and hard, or so it appeared. Then he just shrugged.

Yonas tipped potatoes from the sack into buckets, got two nail-brushes, told Samuel to scrub one bucketful, and started on the other. Dirt clouded into the water and embedded under his fingernails. He considered his chances of supplementing the mussels with some of the scallops that were intended for customers, and glanced over at Petros who was on enforcement duty, looking bored. After a few minutes his bulbous head began to nod. Yonas trod softly over to the scallops, and reached for a handful.

'Er, we're not allowed those ones,' Samuel said dozily.

Yonas only just managed to snatch his hand back before Petros sat up to see what was going on. 'I'm going to take a leak,' he said, and walked outside.

Once he got through the door he punched his fists at the dark and yelled, 'GET ME OUT OF HERE' – noiselessly, and to nobody in particular. He took a few deep breaths before going in again.

Once dinner was ready, Yonas banged the ladle on the vat lid. The others mooched over, collected plastic bowls, and held them out. He swallowed his own gloopy portion as fast as possible, as most of them did, and watched Gebre pick listlessly at his. Just before bed, he beckoned Gebre outside.

'It's time,' he said. 'Let's cut our losses and go.'

'What, now? In the dark?'

'Harder for them to find us.'

'What about our papers?'

'We're never getting papers – we've been slaving here for three months now. We must have earned enough to pay off our debts. And I feel so guilty about Melat: the police will be onto her about me and she'll be hounded for diaspora tax, and Sheshy needs prosthetics and Lemlem needs school fees. . . I've got to wire them some money.'

Gebre looked away, then down at his feet. 'I know, but Blackjack promised we'd get papers, and that must take some time.'

'Ninety-three days?'

'Maybe. And anyway, if we leave with nothing, and it's too late for asylum, we'll just get locked up then sent back. I'd rather kill myself.'

'Hey, stop that! Look, we've done amazingly to make it here, but now it turns out we're being used, we just have to keep going a bit longer, and then we can make a life for ourselves. A life where we at least get to earn money and have a bit of freedom and self-respect. Also, don't we owe it to all the people who didn't make it here to *do* something with this chance? Remember—'

'Don't make me.'

'Okay, but—'

'Aziz will kill us. He's got a gun, Rashid said.'

'I doubt it. He'd have waved it in our faces by now if he had. I reckon he's just blustering. Anyway, he can hardly leave the factory with no one except Petros in charge and come on a wild goose chase for us, can he?'

'He can call Blackjack.'

They had only met Blackjack once, when he came to do an inspection, a white guy dressed all in black, with sunglasses when there was no sun, his only decoration a fat gold watch. He had effected a miracle transformation on their boss when he stepped in the door, turning Aziz from a glowering tyrant into a smiling sycophant.

'I bet he's posturing too. Playing the tough guy.'

'He scares Aziz though.'

This seemed true. 'Still, I doubt he would waste his time sending people after us,' Yonas said.

'But we've got no money. We don't even know where we are…'

'We can find a way! I'm pretty sure we're north of London, just from reading the local newspaper. And once we call Auntie, she can direct us.'

'But if we just had our papers…'

'Gebre, that's not going to happen! And this place is making you more depressed by the day. You know you're like a brother to me – I don't want to sit here and watch you morph into a mollusc. Worse, into Samuel.'

This at least produced a flicker of a grin. 'Two more weeks then?'

Yonas sighed. 'Okay. If you insist. But let's sneak out on a Friday during free time to plan a route, okay?'

Back inside he grabbed his sleeping mat, rolled it out, lay down, pulled his blanket over his head, and willed himself to go to sleep quickly to avoid Rashid's tank-engine snore.

Drifting off, he pictured himself hand in hand with Sarama, sneaking off from the barracks, clambering up the mountain path, turning down a goat track and pushing through bushes until they reached their secret spot, where they fell on each other, where nothing else mattered, and then lay there, warm and entangled, looking up at the wide sky, azure and beautiful above the filth as if the war didn't exist, as he stroked her hair and touched her dimpled cheeks…

He was woken by moaning in his left ear. In the dimness he saw Gebre's head rolling from side to side, arms poker-straight, forehead crumpled. The moan grew louder, Gebre's body jerked, and he shocked himself awake. Yonas reached out and put his hand gently on his friend's arm in the dark. The skin was clammy. Gebre twitched, froze, then curled into a foetal position. Yonas resigned himself to wakefulness for a while. He rummaged around in the dark until he felt his little wooden rooster, extricated it from his pocket, held it lightly between his fingers, then enclosed it tight in his palm. He wondered whether underneath Rashid's snores he could hear the sea, or whether it was only the shushing of the others' sleeping breath.

Another drizzly morning followed, with no visible chink in the cloud. The new crates were filled with crabs, piled and twisted together. Some were dead or not far off, but many were still alive, moving their pincers feebly, waving for help. One was valiantly attempting to clamber to the top of the pile. It struggled upwards, slipped back, and climbed up again. It was as if it had already seen the vat inside. *It's too late for you, my friend*, Yonas told it. The crab pawed vainly at the crate wall.

Chapter 3: Joe

Oh go on then, I'll have a coffee. Which type, did you say? Just normal, like, milk and two sugars. Americano? If you say so.

So, you want to know about how I met that African lad. I don't know, that's got to be one of the oddest things that's ever happened to me. For starters, in that neck of the woods you don't come across many people, you know, that colour… or anyone, like, it's just fields and that. And he sprung me out of the blue… what-d'you-call-it… ambushed me! It were outside this old farm building down a track off Blithe Lane.

Things had been a bit fishy with that place for a while. In more ways than one. Ha! Anyway, it used to be a little arable farm, but it got a bit run-down, and I remember folks saying the farmer were in debt, and then there were a fire – that some said weren't an accident – and then he sold the fields off. Not long after, we heard he'd passed. But he were a loner type, Bill Hardy. No one really seemed to know him personally, and apparently his son lived abroad, so I didn't know what were going on for a while, but it seemed like the farm business had folded cos I'd pass the track on me route and the buildings down there just looked empty. But then one day I spotted some lights on, and I thought, hmm, what's going on there then, and a couple of weeks later I got told it were back on me route. Sure enough, when I drove down, a couple of big rubbish sacks were out waiting for me, and I saw some movement in one of the windows. The sacks stank of fish, and I thought, well, this ain't farming again is it – what are the new folks up to? I decided to mind me own business and just chucked the sacks into the truck. But a few days later, I were about to pick up some more when this bloke came out.

Now this weren't our African lad, not yet – this one were a chunky Paki-looking bloke, and that threw me too, you know what I mean, around here! I said hello, and asked what were planned for the farm now. He looked kind of nervous, said summat about getting things set up for a new farm and retail business. And then he went: 'It would be good for people who ask if you can say that is what we are doing,' and held out twenty quid! Said he'd really appreciate it, and looked right in me eyes. Nowt like that happened to me before, I can tell you.

'So… you'd sort me out like this next week and all?' I asked.

'Every week,' he said. 'I can leave money under there.' He pointed out a lump of rock close to the rubbish sacks.

I were a bit torn then. I mean, I were pretty sure it must be summat dodgy. But the wife and me were under pressure with money and that, what with me son being expelled and me daughter dyslexic and there being no work for young'uns round here these days. Not to mention she's a stickler for the accounts, the old lady, and so I have to give her every penny and I'm only allowed three pints a week. So an extra few quid weren't going to do me any harm.

And it weren't as if I knew what were going on exactly. I mean, this bloke could've been planning to set up summat legit soon enough. Anyway, I were only a bin man so who were really going to ask me anyway?

And he kept his word. Every week, cash were under that rock like he said. I could even get rounds in for the lads down the pub. I took to joining them earlier, got me pool skills up to scratch, and after a month or so I were king of the table for winner-stays-on for the first time ever! I saved up a bit and got meself a nice bottle of Scotch and a flask to keep me goin' on a chilly morning on the round.

Didn't get away with it for long though. That's marriage for you! One day, when I got back late from the pub, Jill were waiting in the kitchen, hands on her hips, and she went: 'What's got into you, Joe? You never used to stay out till closing.'

'Leave it out, will you,' I said.

'I hardly see you any more,' she said, *nag nag nag*. 'And you always come home smelling of whisky these days. I don't like it and I don't know how you're paying for it.'

'Aw come on, it's just the odd nightcap, love. Don't start naggin' now, will you?'

Should've known that'd wind her up. 'I'll say what I like!' she said. 'Go on, tell me, how can you be affording whisky every night when you always used to moan about how much I let you take out of the kitty?'

'The lads are a generous bunch,' I said.

'Come off it, Joe, they're as tight as you.'

'Well if you must know,' I said, 'I've got nifty on the pool table. Found meself on a winning streak.'

'Oh pull the other one,' she said. 'I used to thrash you at pool, and I've got the hand–eye coordination of a… I don't know. A penguin.'

'Penguins don't have hands, Jill.'

'Exactly,' she said, all smug.

'Well,' I said, 'why don't you join the lads at the pub tomorrow then, and see me skills for yourself?' I wished I hadn't said that, soon as it came out me mouth. Knowing Jill, she would and all and I'd get all nervous and fluff it up. But luckily she said she'd got better things to do.

Anyway, I'd got to the point where I'd almost forgotten there were anything unusual about that building, and it were just a normal drizzly morning when I were driving up the track and in me mirrors I saw summat moving in the bushes and then pop out – guessed it were a deer or summat – but it were that black African lad! And he jumped on the back of me truck, quick as a flash. Nearly give me the fright of me life! It were like seeing a ghost… but the opposite colour – ha! Anyway, I braked, opened the door, and looked out at him. 'All right there?' I asked. He got off, and I thought he might make a run for it, but he walked towards me. He were wearing worker's overalls and they were right filthy. He were youngish, thirties I'd say, pale brown skin, tall and skinny as a rake with matted hair and a beard, and I wondered if he were one of them jihad terrorists about to hijack me or summat. But then I thought, they're normally Arabs. And then I thought, Why would a bloke do summat like that out here to a bloke like me? He didn't say a word at first, just stared, and I couldn't tell if he were scared or crazy. I wondered if he'd escaped from some loony asylum or if he were illegal, one of them that are supposed to be all over the shop. So I told him I'd better be on me way.

But he burst out: 'Wait! Please wait. Sir, I'm lost, can you please take me to the train station?'

I'd never been called *sir* in me life, and it were such an odd thing to hear, it made me laugh. But how could you get lost trying to get to the train station out here? And why did he jump on the back? Didn't sound right.

'Not on my route,' I told him. 'Sorry. And I'd better be going, so if you could move aside…'

'Please,' he said, and there were this look in his eyes, this desperation. 'You can drop me anywhere.'

Now, normally I do like to pick up the odd hitchhiker. Used to hitch meself back in the day. But no one'd ever hitched a ride in me rubbish truck before! Most folks who walk past it hold their noses, and folks wrinkle their noses up at me when I'm in me work gear in a shop or summat – and I'm used to that now. But he didn't seem to mind. Probably smelled himself but I'm immune to that. I could've told him just to get out the way again, but I remember what that were like, when people told me to move it when I really needed to get somewhere and I could see they had room. But then I thought, if I take this lad along, I might stop getting the weekly tip. But then another part of me felt bad for taking it in the first place.

So then I thought, what the heck, and told him to hop in. As we got further up the track I noticed he kept on looking in the rear-view mirror, like he were spooked. And when we got to the main road he went, 'Thank you, you've saved me.'

I wished he hadn't said that. I said it weren't a problem. But then I couldn't stop meself asking what country he were from.

Oh Lord, now, what were it he said? To be honest I hadn't heard of the place. It were in Africa, close to Ethiopia, I remember that much, and I felt bad then. 'I remember those pictures on the telly in the eighties,' I told him. 'Kids with bellies popping out.' It were horrible, that famine, horrible. I hadn't thought about it for a while. 'Were it like that in your country?' I asked him. He said that they used to be the *same country* in the eighties. News to me! Geography were never me strong suit. Well anyway, then I felt all right, like I were actually doing a good deed by giving this poor lad a lift, like I were finally doing something for all them starving kids, not just watching them on telly and donating a couple of quid to Bob Geldof and feeling pretty useless. And then he asked me if I knew London.

'Not well,' I told him. 'Too hectic for me down there. I've got a brother who lives in the East End though. Moved there not long ago and got himself a job. Place called Canning Town. Haven't visited him yet. Should get round to it. So – what brought you to England then?'

'Just to live,' he said. I guessed then he were after benefits, like they say, you know, and fair play, in a way – I mean, I suppose you would be, coming from somewhere like that. But he added: 'And work.'

'Oh right,' I said. 'What kind of work?'

'Anything,' he said. 'If it pays some money. Even cleaning toilets would be good just now.'

'Well, who knows,' I said, 'you might even find a bin man job, there's worse things!' And he laughed. 'You go for it, lad,' I said. 'So, when d'you get here then?'

He took a while to answer, till I thought maybe he hadn't heard the question. Then he said, 'Not long ago. Actually I already started work, but I was working for a bad man.'

I didn't like the sound of that. 'Long flight to get here, was it?' I asked him, to change t'subject.

He laughed. 'I didn't fly,' he said. 'First we had to walk through the desert for four days with no food. We only survived because we came across a shepherd's water container in a valley so we could drink, and the hyenas decided not to eat us.'

I looked at him, and nearly laughed, like – you *what?*

'Then, for some time we were living in a lorry, a bit like this one,' he said. 'But stuck inside a box on the back, with no room to sit down, and it was as hot as an oven – and the smell was worse than this.'

'Ha!' I laughed. 'Come on now. Not many folk would say that about a rubbish truck smell.'

'Maybe they haven't smelled—' then he stopped.

'Smelled what?! Dead people?' I laughed at me own joke, even though it were a bit dark, like.

But he weren't laughing. He looked out the window. Didn't deny it. I mean, he could have said he were just being *polite* about me truck or summat! I felt queasy all of a sudden. This were creepy, like. Were he saying they'd been *murdered*, these dead people he were travelling with? Were *he* the killer? Were he about to finish me off and all? Me heart started going then, nineteen to't dozen, I tell you. Tricky thing to hijack though, a rubbish truck. I mean, you'd get spotted pretty quick, wouldn't you? Couldn't get up much of a speed. And this lad seemed polite, anyway, not like a killer. Maybe there weren't actually dead people in a lorry with him – maybe he just didn't *say* there *weren't*. If you know what I mean.

'We came in a boat, for the last part,' he told me.

'Who's we then?' I asked. 'Did you come with family?'

'With a friend,' he said, 'who is like my brother.' But he didn't tell me nowt more, and to be honest I'd heard enough. Can of worms, I'd got to thinking.

'Well, you're probably doing the right thing, heading to London now,' I said, trying to sound cheery. 'Tough to get any kind of work round here these days, so no point you hangin' around. I'm sure you'll settle into the Big Smoke, no worries.'

I switched on Radio 2. There were Bryan Adams on, and then Bob Dylan – 'Like a Rolling Stone', you know the one. And then your lad started singing along! He knew the lyrics – I mean, word for word. I had no clue they listened to that sort of thing in Africa! Thought they were more into drumming or reggae or whatever. But anyway it were quite funny – I ended up joining in, and we were there driving to town, the two of us, singing like we were a couple of mates who'd just left the pub on New Year's Eve. And I thought: this lad is all right!

Soon enough we got to the station. 'Here we are then,' I said.

He were about to get out, but then he stopped and asked for me phone number. Pulled a crumpled piece of newspaper out of his pocket for me to write on.

I weren't keen about that. I mean, I had started to warm to him a bit, but once you write stuff down and give out your details – you know? But he said he didn't know anyone in the UK yet, and maybe we could meet again some day as he'd like to say thanks. Just so bloody polite! There were loads of reasons to say no. But then he'd come from that country with the starving kids, and he'd travelled all the way here on his tod, in some kind of grave on wheels – and the lad knew all the bloomin' words to 'Like a Rolling Stone'! So I scribbled it down.

As I drove off down the road I kicked meself. Not literally. But I just felt like I'd been a softie, and I started to get worried about what might happen. For all I knew he could be a criminal. I could've aided and abetted. But I tried to put it all out of me mind and think of it as a good deed. And that were that, for a long while anyway. The twenty-quid notes kept on coming, and I stayed king of the pool table for a month, till some young upstart came along. Assumed I'd never hear from the African lad again. And after a week or two of having strange dreams with corpses stuffed like sardines in the back of me rubbish truck, things went back to normal and I very nearly forgot all about him.

Chapter 4: Yonas

On Friday morning, Yonas went outside to collect the new deliveries and jogged on the spot for a minute, trying to pump some blood back into his toes. Beyond the fence, a pinkish sky illuminated the scattering of copper and mustard leaves among the dense bushes. Some were already forming a squidgy layer on the cracked concrete. As he looked up the track, his feet itched at the prospect of getting out. Only a few hours to go before the scoping walk.

He reached out to pick up the topmost crate of scallops, and its newspaper lining caught his eye.

TORTURED ASYLUM SEEKER FRAUDULENTLY CLAIMED £21,000 IN BENEFITS WHILE EARNING £2,000 A MONTH

£21,000? That sounded like a lot! Even £2,000 sounded like a lot. Could this story be made up? But this was the UK, and newspapers here were regulated – didn't they have a duty to present facts? Still… He tore out the headline carefully, put it in his pocket, and lugged the crate inside.

For the rest of the morning he worked faster than usual, with jiggling feet. In anticipation of the walk he thought back to his military service days, how impatiently he'd look forward to striding out of the barracks, up that long, stony path all the way up to the Eye, a hole in the rock that was big enough to sit in, to curve your spine into its shape, smoothed by the weather and the years and countless other human forms, and rest for a while, absorbing the rippling mountainscape, free for a precious moment just by rising above it all. When the wind was easterly the Eye would emit a low wail, like a giant flute.

At noon, Aziz started caterwauling his call to prayer and pulled out the frayed carpet, marking the start of free time. While he and the other Muslims prostrated themselves, everyone else sat around and played mancala games or snoozed. Yonas leaned against the wall preparing to read his saved sheets of newspaper, but Osman's wheezy cough sounded beside him. 'Yonas, can you help practise my English?'

'Sure,' he said, swallowing his irritation. 'Take a seat. Why don't you start from here, the bit about the football team?'

Osman stumbled along, tracing his finger at a snail's pace underneath the words. He was a cute kid, seventeen at most, and the only other person in the factory who showed any interest in reading, in finding out more about this country they were in, anticipating more than mere survival. Meanwhile Gebre was watching a mancala game with a vacant expression. Yonas chipped in now and then to correct Osman's pronunciation or explain a definition, and time dawdled on. But finally prayers were over, Petros went out, and Aziz retreated to his den, from where a rhythmic snore signalled the start of his nap. Yonas told Osman to carry on reading while he went to the toilet, got up and went out, nudging Gebre on his way.

As planned, Gebre followed him. 'Okay, let's go!' Yonas whispered.

But Gebre shook his head. 'I've been thinking – it's too risky. If we're going for good on Monday, let's just figure out a route then, on the fly.'

He had a point. But Yonas wanted so badly to get beyond the fence. 'I think we should plan,' he said. 'But I'll just go solo if you don't want to.'

He crossed the yard, clambered over the gate and started up the hill. But then he heard footsteps. He turned with a flicker of panic – but it was Gebre, after all! Yonas grinned, held up his palm for a high-five and they carried on side by side. The sun was struggling through thick swathes of cloud and the wind strengthened as they climbed. It felt so good to be moving. 'So, we'll get to a higher point,' Yonas said, 'and work out a direction, some landmarks, sketch out in our heads a rough route that seems like it's away from main roads with foliage to hide in… We'll travel mainly at dawn and dusk, find odd jobs, dry places to sleep, and then once we get to London—' He stopped. Grabbed Gebre's shoulder. Yes: footsteps again. They turned, expecting to see Petros with a snarl on his face.

'Osman!' Yonas laughed incredulously. 'What are you doing?'

'I want to come,' the kid said. 'Where are you going?'

'Just for a walk. But if Aziz finds out…'

'I don't care.'

'You should,' Gebre said.

'You can't stop me.' For a moment, Osman looked exactly like Yonas's little brother Tekle, with those stubborn, pleading eyes, those puppy eyebrows.

'Come on then!' Yonas relented, and jabbed Gebre in the ribs. 'Race you to the top!' To his surprise, Gebre took off as if he'd got new batteries. Yonas pounded behind, energy streaming into his blood, laughter making him gasp for air. His feet thundered, his stiff, cold muscles came painfully to life, his arms pumped like pistons, his lungs were about to explode, his whole body was on fire, but he carried on regardless.

When they finally made it, panting, to the crest of the hill, they were struck in the face by a blast of salty wind. Blood thumped in Yonas's temples as he let out a whoop. Gebre bent forward, hands on his knees, puffing steam into the air. Osman, wheezing, finally made it to join them. About a mile down the slope ahead, and stretching out indefinitely, was the sea.

It wasn't bright blue or gleaming like the Red Sea, or violent and terrible like the Mediterranean. It was a soft, deep grey flecked with white foam like a scattering of goose feathers. A few birds hovered over it, frolicking in the wind, making light of its huge scale, a scale that brought back the terror… and yet, from this safe vantage point, the sight was liberating. Reaching out his arms like a champion sprinter, Yonas flung back his head and inhaled into parts of his lungs he had forgotten existed.

Gebre stood with his feet wide, hands on hips, shaking his head, a smile transforming his face. 'It is good to be out of there,' he said.

Yonas nodded sagely. 'I told you so.'

'All right, all right, you didn't paint this view.'

'I made this whole sea out of my saliva,' Yonas said. 'You should start worshipping me like I deserve.'

'Idiot', Gebre said, shoving him gently, then flopped down on the ground. Yonas copied, feeling almost drunk on the lightness of laughter and the weight of his body on the earth and the intense, sharp scent of damp grass.

Eventually he sat up, and leaned on his elbows. The sky to the south was blue-green, like the inside of a duck egg shell, and splashed with drifting clouds, but to the north a malevolent purple mass was forming. He closed his eyes, and let the wind pummel his cheeks. Feeling his sweat cool, he shivered, rubbed his arms and sat up straight. 'Okay – we're supposed to be planning a route here, and then we should head back,' he said, and began to scan the inland horizon. There was no sign of a town; the only buildings visible were an industrial-looking complex and some clusters of houses in the distance. Yonas figured if they followed the coastline southwards for a while they would be able to get quite a long way unnoticed, before working out a way to call Auntie. Gebre was still lying down with his eyes closed and a serene look on his face. Yonas cast around for Osman. He looked behind, and either side – and then spotted him, running down the hill ahead, at full pelt towards the sea.

He grabbed Gebre's arm. 'Look! Osman – he's running off!'

Gebre jerked upright, then they both scrambled to their feet. 'Osmaaaaan!'

'He can't hear. But they might hear us at the factory if we yell any more. We'll never catch him and get back on time...'

'*Donkoro*. I knew something like this would happen,' Gebre groaned. 'We shouldn't have let him come.'

'Maybe he's got the right idea,' Yonas said. 'Come on, let's go too – screw it!'

'We can't. We agreed two weeks. And my photo's still in there.'

'What? The one of your parents? Why didn't you bring it?'

'It's all I've got left. I have to get it.'

Yonas reached into his pocket and ran his finger over the crown of his wooden rooster. 'It's just a piece of paper,' he protested weakly. 'And if we go back without Osman, Aziz will go nuts…'

'We'll get back in time – he won't know we left. And Osman will turn around any minute. Come on.'

Gebre set off. Osman's figure was already just a speck on the horizon. Yonas followed.

When they slipped into the factory again, there were a few raised eyebrows among the other workers but nobody said anything. Aziz re-emerged from his nap, dinner preparation started as normal, and nobody seemed to notice anyone was missing. But then Rashid came up behind Yonas. 'Where's Osman?' he whispered. Yonas mimed zipping his mouth.

It was only a few minutes before Aziz clocked his absence. 'Osman!' he bellowed. He looked around and turned on Rashid. 'Where's the boy?' Rashid shrugged, and Aziz spat at his feet. 'Fetch him now. I need my laundry.'

'Sir – I think he's on the toilet,' Yonas improvised. 'I'll check and get your laundry.' He went outside, ran around the side of the building and peered up the track. No sign. It was starting to rain. Of course Osman wasn't coming back. Yonas felt a burn of envy. If he'd been stronger-willed, less sentimental, and said he was going to leave regardless, maybe Gebre would have followed. His friend's photo, a small sepia one of his parents on their wedding day, was about to disintegrate anyway – it'd got all damp and bent in its ripped plastic wallet so that you could barely make out their faces. Yonas had to stop himself kicking the bins in frustration. He walked back inside. 'The laundry is still wet,' he said to Aziz. 'I couldn't see him out there.'

28

Aziz pursed his lips, and looked around. 'If he is not back soon, there will be trouble. If anyone knows anything, they need to tell me. Right now.'

They all feigned concentration on their tasks.

'Nobody?' Aziz's tone was cajoling. Then he slammed his hand down and roared, 'ENOUGH. Stop what you are doing, all of you. Look at me.'

They all looked. Aziz pivoted his head like an owl, meeting every set of eyes in turn. Fatally, Rashid scratched an itch.

'You,' Aziz barked, and grabbed him by the hair. 'Where – is – Osman?'

'I don't know. I think… he might have gone for a walk,' Rashid croaked.

'A *walk*? Where? When?'

'Not long… I am not sure, I did not see… I know nothing.'

'You obviously *do* know something, dog breath.'

Yonas nearly laughed, despite the situation; that was a new one.

'No, not me, sir.'

'Who is going to tell me, then?' Aziz said, looking around.

There was no response.

'Right, Petros. Go and hunt for him. If you do not find him in fifteen minutes I will tell Blackjack to get his men on the case.'

Petros nodded and went out, while Aziz stayed, glaring, as if he could shoot truth-forcing rays at them from his pupils.

After a while, Petros returned, shaking his head, which prompted Aziz to go into his den and make a phone call to Blackjack in such a loud, portentous voice that Yonas reckoned it was fake, but couldn't be sure. They ate dinner in silence. Cleared up in silence. It started to rain. Yonas wondered if Osman had found a town by now, a friendly English person to talk to, a bed to sleep in. But rain was now battering the windows. He was more likely to be shivering under a tree. He'd survive though, wouldn't he? If anyone from here deserved to, it was that kid.

But just as they were about to roll out their sleeping mats, the door squeaked open, and there he was. *What are you doing?* Yonas wanted to shout. *Turn around, run away!* But Osman stood still. His wet hair glistened and his eyes were black mirrors. It might have been a trick of light and water, but he seemed to be standing in an aura, like an icon.

'Osman,' Aziz said, his voice all smug, the purr of a cat dangling a mouse.

'I… I am sorry, sir, I just wanted to have a walk, to get exercise, I got lost…'

'You know the rules, Osman.'

'But sir, I just went out because it was free time – I was always going to come back…'

'Come here.'

Osman walked forward, then stopped a couple of metres in front of Aziz, looking down at his shoes. Rainwater dripped around his feet. Yonas saw Aziz's arm tense up, ready to swing, but then he seemed to get an idea.

'Please,' Osman said, hopefully.

Aziz bent down to pick up a metal bucket, grasped it with both hands, and slammed it down hard, on each of Osman's feet, so that he yelped with pain, crouched, then fell heavily.

'That will teach you to go walking,' Aziz said. 'Now, you four,' he said, pointing, 'pick Osman up and carry him outside so he can think about what he's done. Everyone else, stay where you are. Samuel, bring that rope. Tie up his ankles, then string them to the tree, from that fat branch.'

Yonas screwed up his eyes. Rashid had told him just the other night how Aziz and Petros had threatened to string him upside down once, because he'd demanded to know when his debt would be paid off. Yonas had seen the technique used in prison; when they did it to Abraham, another political prisoner, it made all the veins explode in his eyes and forehead, turning him into a bloodthirsty monster. More memories bubbled up. Being whipped like an ox while lugging stones in the heat; his head being pushed into a bucket of water until he saw sparkles and was sure he was drowning; and, the worst, the helicopter position…

'I am sorry, I will never do it again, please, I am sorry,' Osman was sobbing, even as the rope was being tied, even as his thrashing body was left to swing from the branch like a pendulum.

Aziz barked to the rest of them to get to bed, and walked implacably towards his den, as if they'd all just wish each other a pleasant good night and settle down.

'You're not just going to leave him there?' Yonas said. He dumped his sleeping mat and ran towards Aziz, grabbing his arm. 'Look at him, he's only a kid, he's been punished enough – you've probably broken all his toes!'

'Get. Off. Me.' Aziz snarled the words, wrenching away. Then he plunged his hand down into his shirt, fumbled awkwardly for a minute somewhere above his gut, his face reddening with the effort, until he pulled out a pistol, black and shining. So, it did exist. He lifted it slowly, and advanced a step towards Yonas. 'You do as you're ordered,' he said. 'I'm the one who decides punishments around here.'

Yonas stayed still a moment, feeling oddly calm. This was it, one way or another – there was no way back now. No way he could live any longer under this bastard's orders. Torture was the main reason he'd fled all the way here – it wasn't supposed to happen in the UK! And he wouldn't take it. If Aziz didn't shoot him first, he would be out of this place, by tomorrow morning at the latest… It occurred to him that he had never stood so close to Aziz for so long before. He took in the saggy eyelids, the tousled eyebrows, the beige, blotchy skin, the browning teeth. This was a man who was disillusioned with life, who seemed to have no family and no friends, who lived in shoddy enough dwellings here himself, and whose sole aim seemed to be to wield the little power he'd been given. Yes, he was capable of shooting. But he probably didn't want to. None of the other workers were saying a word in Yonas's defence, but he could feel them all, silently rooting for him. Yonas turned away from Aziz, and started to walk back towards his sleeping mat, expecting any second the sound of a gunshot, searing pain. None came. But instead he heard another strangled sob from Osman. Fury bubbled up, and he turned back to Aziz again. 'So string *me* up there instead,' he challenged in an unnaturally loud voice. He felt everyone else go still, and wondered what the hell he was doing.

Aziz looked confused for a second, then laughed snidely, took a handkerchief from his pocket and began, ostentatiously, to polish the muzzle of the pistol. 'Since you asked so nicely, I *will* string you up, *as well, next* to Osman. . . if you say *one more word*. I'm giving you a chance, here. A last chance. If you've got any sense you'll shut your mouth, and get to bed.' He didn't sound entirely convincing though – a bit like a cross parent who has just refused to tell another story but is now conceding. Yonas told himself to stand his ground a few moments longer. Aziz put the handkerchief away, and then, remarkably, his shoulders seemed to sag as he tucked the gun back into its pouch and looked away. 'Right, Petros,' Aziz said, 'give the kid five more minutes, then if he apologizes – like he means it – he can come down.' With that, he went into his den and slammed the door.

A couple of the others came over and patted Yonas on the back, but he was still seething at their collective gutlessness. 'Come on, Petros,' he said, 'make it a quick five minutes', and was met by an unsurprising glare. But about two minutes later, Petros summoned a few of them outside to support Osman's body while he cut the rope, then slouched off.

They carried Osman inside, laid him down gently on his mat and gathered around. He seemed to be unconscious. Was he dead? His eyes were bright red, devilish, his face greyish-purple and blotchy, his skin cold to the touch. Salim grabbed his wrist, held an ear to his chest. 'Yes – he's got a pulse!' he said. 'Osman?'

But Osman didn't utter a sound. They all began tenderly stripping him, and putting on dry clothes. His feet were swollen and bloodied, and a couple of his toes pointed in odd directions. Yonas reached out to try to straighten them, which must have been agony, but Osman barely reacted. After a few minutes he coughed, as if he were coming to, but he still didn't seem to be hearing anything they were saying, just closed his freakish eyes and groaned a little.

'You will be okay,' Yonas told him. 'A friend of mine came through the same thing.' Tenderly, they wrapped him in blankets.

'We can keep an eye on him during the night,' Yonas offered, and he and Gebre put their mats down either side of him, and lay down, both facing him, like anxious new parents caring for a baby. Yonas began humming a lullaby his mother used to sing. It didn't seem to have any effect on Osman, but made Yonas feel a bit calmer. Gradually, the skin of Osman's palms warmed, and eventually he took a long breath, like a sigh, that turned into a husky, open-mouthed semi-snore.

A while later, when it sounded like most of the others were asleep, Yonas leaned across and whispered, 'Gebre, that was the last straw. We're out of here, tomorrow morning. I've got an idea. Involving rubbish. It might be genius. You just need to follow me outside when I say, okay?'

Gebre was silent. He wasn't asleep though – Yonas could see his eyes glinting in the moonlight.

Chapter 5: Quentin

BARE-FACED CHEEK: FURY AS GERMAN NUDISTS ARE ORDERED TO COVER UP AFTER A MIGRANT SHELTER ARRIVES NEAR THEIR LAKE

Long black, please, extra shot, extra hot, no sugar.

So, this Mr Kelati of yours. Well. I wouldn't say I *know* him exactly, but what I *do* know is that he managed to sneak into this country and turn my life into a train wreck. Talking of trains, that's where I first came across him, joyriding – though he didn't exactly look joyous. Look, I'm sure he's had a tough time of it. I don't doubt that. But so do thousands of others. My point is that asylum seekers should go through the proper processes if they want to live here, not sneak in illegally and then use public transport without paying and work tax-free and do God knows what else. Otherwise we can't know who genuinely deserves protection under the Refugee Convention. Which is very unfair to all the genuine refugees. As well as to British people. That's my opinion. I know, I know: you don't want my opinion, you want the story.

So, I was with my campaign manager, Alice, en route back to London from Grimsby, where I was Conservative candidate. It was a while before D-day, but you need to start canvassing early: a fact Nina, my wife, struggled to understand. I know it's not easy looking after a child by yourself, but I would usually only go off for a few days at a time, which lots of mothers manage fine, and Nina is as capable as anyone – except her anxiety was taking her totally off piste. She'd started claiming she couldn't cope and I didn't care enough and I was never around and our abysmal parenting was going to ruin Clara's life. Which was baloney, but she wouldn't listen. I told her we could pay for some extra childcare if we had to, and she should try going back to her CBT therapist, but she bit my head off. I said she should at least spend more time on her painting, which she says is her best therapy; the problem is she gets herself into a catch-22 situation whereby she needs to go to the studio but is too stressed out to leave the house, and blames it on housework and childcare, even on the days Clara is in nursery.

I've always tried to be patient, but it's hard if you're constantly being deluged with someone else's worries or pestered for reassurance or blamed, especially when you've got a lot going on yourself. Not to mention the fact that, after I accepted the candidacy, Nina decided she actively disliked *all* party politics and refused to speak about my work at home. Point-blank! So I was expected to gag myself against any mention of the work I was doing at the most important point in my entire career, but constantly tell Nina not to worry about ridiculous things in a patient voice that implied she wasn't in fact being ridiculous? It didn't exactly motivate me to rush back home when I had a constituency to convince, put it that way.

But I digress. That day, Alice and I were on our way back to London, as I say, and I had a vile hangover, but Alice had scheduled a review discussion en route. So I bought myself a long black at the station, and once we were on the train I pulled out my notebook. We talked about how the trip had gone, how the campaign had progressed, what had worked well or less well, and how we might adapt our approach, and, inevitably, we got onto immigration.

It had never been a policy priority for me personally before, not really, but this phase of the campaign had made me realize I just had to take it seriously and focus on it if I wanted to engage the constituents. It was a huge deal for them. Their biggest worry. People were already concerned about all the Eastern Europeans in the mix offering labour for peanuts, and what with illegal immigration stepping up too and asylum seekers swarming in, they felt like they were being invaded. And I needed to up the ante – my UKIP counterpart was wielding all kinds of extreme language, and he was becoming far more popular than anyone had predicted.

Alice and I had always seen eye to eye on pretty much everything. But that morning she said that, in her view, a lot of the headlines I was regularly quoting were more media hype than fact and I should 'maybe chill out a bit'. I told her she risked being naïve, and while I appreciated her playing devil's advocate, I ultimately needed her to endorse the approach I was taking, and in fact strengthen it, and that what I was saying was actually *more* considered and moderate than it necessarily *needed* to be to make the point. Basically, genuine refugees are fine, but illegal immigration and bogus asylum seekers are major problems that have got to be tackled. She apologized then, and stroked my knee, which I quickly moved away, beginning to be irritated. (Alice is an unusually tactile person, but I'd told her several times before that physical contact like that between us in public was inappropriate. She's not at all unattractive, so I knew people would jump to conclusions.) I took a break and made my way along the corridor to find a Gents.

I admit I did then start to wonder whether Alice was partly right, and whether I could moderate my tone a bit, if not my fundamental stance. I mean, the evidence of the impact of illegal immigration wasn't yet clear – how could it be, if these people are under the radar? – though the constituents were convinced. But I had to take a line. Voters like a strong line. I just wished Nina would let me run this kind of issue by her. I've always been open to talking about *her* work, about the arts scene, all that. My head was pounding, and I was reprimanding myself for letting Alice persuade me into that last bottle of wine the night before, wishing I'd got the evening train home so I could have read Clara a bedtime story and played a bit of piano – and that was when I saw him. Your Mr Kelati. Standing in the toilet doorway talking with the conductor.

It didn't look friendly, so I intuited pretty quickly what was going on. I took a few steps closer to try to hear what they were saying; having just come from that conversation with Alice I was particularly intrigued to see someone like him in the flesh, caught in the act. He looked like a tramp, quite frankly, smelled like one too, and had a heavy African accent. As I was trying to overhear, it occurred to me to snap a photo of the two of them, thinking I might blog about it as part of the public conversation. I still couldn't quite make out the words, but then I saw him wince and clutch his stomach, which looked *entirely* fake to me, and I managed to capture it in another shot, but the conductor seemed to be developing a sympathetic look on his face. And then, to my disbelief, he patted the guy on the shoulder and began to turn away, with no ticket or anything being handed over! So I snapped once more, then cleared my throat and said, 'Excuse me, but as a paying customer I'd like to check that appropriate action is being taken if people are travelling without tickets.'

'Well, I've dealt with it *appropriately*,' the conductor said, rather abruptly. 'So please go ahead and enjoy your journey.'

'But I didn't see a ticket,' I persisted, and then asked the guy to show me his ticket. My head was exploding and I thought there was a good chance I might be physically sick, but I also felt that I was now engaging in a tiny act of heroism on behalf of the constituents that I could tell Alice about.

Anyway, the conductor obviously felt his pride was at stake. He said, 'Hang on – what right have you got to make demands? Are you police?'

I contemplated pretending I was for a second. 'I'm the Conservative Parliamentary Candidate for Great Grimsby, and I'm asking this as a representative of people who are deeply concerned about illegal migration and its consequences,' was what I said. I expect I sounded deeply pompous but it was true.

He rolled his eyes and told me to 'drop it'.

'Excuse me?' I said. 'I'm perfectly free to ask a question if I want, like any other conscientious citizen. But if you're unable or unwilling to answer me, I've got a photo of your exchange—'

'Oh, do what you like with your photo,' he said, and proceeded to call me the f word, before shoving past me into the next carriage to check more tickets! Unbelievable. When I turned to your guy, he was gone too. of course he was.

At least the loo became free eventually. I locked the door behind me and sat on the lid, looking at the photo I'd taken, zooming into the guy's face, then out, and wondering how best to encapsulate what I wanted to say about the incident on my blog without sounding too sensational. It's a lot of pressure on a candidate, in this day and age, being expected to blog all the time, and make sure you say the right things in the right words. I wasn't being an arse by publishing his photo, was I? No, I thought – this was exactly my point about the difference between illegal scammers and genuine refugees that I had been trying to make, and a photo can say a thousand words. So I went for: *Came across this illegal immigrant on the train without a ticket today. It brought home voters' rightful concern about the rising influx.* That was about as measured but proactive, clear and firm as I could make it. Then I realized that wording might make me sound as if I hadn't *already* been on the case, so I changed *brought home* to *reminded me of.*

If I hadn't looked at the photo and thought about the exchange at such length so I could write about it, I would never have recognized the guy the next time I saw him. I didn't spot him when we changed trains, and it's frankly bizarre that I came across him again at all, never mind in my *mother-in-law's kitchen*! I haven't even got to that bit yet.

In hindsight I do feel like a bit of a numpty about that whole encounter, which was probably tied up with my elephantine hangover, and election stress, and my discomfort over Alice boundaries – which I should have nipped straight in the bud – and with Nina censoring me at home. If only I'd just stayed back, watched from a distance and called 999, I could've got the police to anticipate him in London at the station and they could have investigated properly. I can tell from your expression that you think that's vindictive. But remember, other passengers had paid, and this guy was travelling illegally. Likewise, he could just have claimed asylum when he got here, but he chose not to. And his illegality didn't stop there, did it? But anyway, I bungled it, so he continued on his merry way.

Chapter 6: Yonas

The toilet door snapped shut and Yonas let out a long breath. The space was tiny, but for a train toilet it was amazingly clean. It barely even smelled of toilet. He looked cautiously into the tiny mirror above the sink – then jerked away. Surely that bearded scarecrow wasn't really him. He splashed his face, reached for the snail of toilet roll, dabbed a soft wad of it against his cheeks, stuffed some in his pocket for later, then sat down on the toilet lid to think. He failed to stop himself replaying Osman's ruby-red eyes, those crooked toes…

Slowly and smoothly, so that he could barely feel it, the train moved off. The glass of the little window was clouded. Yonas managed to shove it open an inch, then leaned onto the edge of the sink and stared out of the gap at the receding station. Rows of neat houses passed by, more and more quickly, before all the buildings petered out, giving way to rolling green fields and low, misty skies, leaving Osman and Gebre behind.

Yonas dropped his head to his knees and groaned. What was Gebre thinking, staying on? They'd gone through so much together to get to this country. Why did it have to end with an argument?

'Okay, we need to leave in five,' Yonas had whispered. 'Ready?'

Gebre had followed him silently outside. 'I don't know what your genius plan is,' he said when they were round the corner, 'but we can't leave Osman. He's still not speaking and he can't walk – it's our fault.'

'It's not our fault!'

'It kind of is. We can't abandon him.'

'He's in a bad way, but he'll recover – Abraham did, remember? And if we get out of here we have a chance to rescue him; we can report Aziz, and that way Osman might be taken to hospital, or a safe home of some kind – he's only a kid, they'll go easy on him.'

'So how would we report Aziz, then? By turning ourselves in?'

'There must be a way.'

'Osman wanted to come with us.'

'Well, he can't now,' Yonas found himself snapping. 'Look, the others are taking care of him, and Aziz will leave him alone after this. Plus, if we leave it'll teach the bastard that torture doesn't work.'

'It could make him do it more. To the others.'

'Well then, the same could apply to us. We need to *survive*, Gebre. I have to earn some money to send to Melat… Look, here's the plan – we hitch a ride on the rubbish truck. If it works we'll be miles away in minutes. And it's about to arrive – have you got your photo?'

'We can't get on a rubbish truck in daylight! The driver will see us.'

'He might not. We've done much riskier things. Gebre, I cannot stay one day longer with that monster. And we don't have to – we're not in prison any more.'

'Well, I don't like it either, but I'm not going to run off now and get into more trouble just because you've suddenly decided it's time. I'm done with your reckless plans – if it wasn't for you we wouldn't have got ourselves into prison in the first place.'

'But… Gebre, it was a joint project! We had to tell the world…'

'No, you came up with the idea, and I followed, like always. Well, not any more.'

'But we got all the way here, didn't we? Come on, the rubbish truck will be here any second! We're not seriously going to split now?'

'If you won't wait, then go. I've always dragged you down anyway.'

'No...'

But Gebre had already turned his back and walked inside. Yonas wanted to yell at him to come back, but that would alert Aziz, and he could already hear the rumble coming down the track.

Bang bang bang. Yonas jerked up straight. The handle of the train toilet door rattled, and then... nothing. After a few seconds, he relaxed a little and listened to the gentle chunters and rumbles of the train as it grunted towards his new life. So, he and Gebre were apart. For a while. But Gebre would follow soon. It would be easy enough for them to find each other – he had memorized Auntie's number too. And maybe he would bring Osman along, fully recovered, and Yonas and Auntie could help them both get settled. In the meantime, there was no point regretting the decision to go. The deed was done and it was just too painful to dwell on separation from Gebre, just as it was on leaving Melat, leaving Eritrea – he had to focus on the now, on the near future, on survival practicalities. Top priority: getting off the train without getting caught, and then getting some coins together to phone Auntie. From her house he would be able to phone Melat, tell her he'd made it, and find out how they were all doing. He might even get time to tell her a bit about what England was like, about these scenes out of the train window, rolling velvety hills, plump clumps of trees, cotton-wool sheep swimming in verdant grass...

But she would ask after Gebre. What would he say? She was a bit like a big sister to him too, ever since his father was disappeared all those years ago. The train shuddered past an old church spire, a farm, some glossy black cows, a sports car whizzing along a perfectly tarmacked road...

Yonas wished he could tell Gebre how simple it had been to escape after all. More than that – when 'Like a Rolling Stone' came on the radio, while he sat there in the truck next to Bin Man Joe, as if he were getting a lift from an old friend, it had felt like fate, like it was meant to happen exactly that way, almost like his father was sitting in the back, singing along out of tune, getting ready to tell his son for the hundredth time how, when he was studying in America, every student knew the lyrics to Bob Dylan's songs, because they meant freedom... If only he could tell his father that he'd finally made it to the UK! Even fifteen years on, he couldn't shake the ridiculous idea in the back of his mind that his parents might both reappear one day, open a door when he least expected it, laughing as if they had been playing an attenuated game of hide and seek all this time. He leaned his forehead against the window and felt it judder, bouncing his brain around in his skull, and it took him back to that trip on the steam train to the beach at Massawa with his family when he was little, how he'd craned out of the window in awe at the rugged brown mountains and the dazzling sapphire skein of the Red Sea…

This train will shortly be arriving at Doncaster. Change here for trains to London King's Cross.

Yonas leapt up from the toilet seat and stood, poised for a swift exit. When the train shuddered to a halt, he unlocked the toilet door, slipped out and stepped off. He walked to the opposite platform and stood against a wall, making sure nobody had seen him, before figuring out which platform the next London train was going from, then went to wait at the far end of it, behind a pillar. *The next train to arrive – on – platform – three…*

He got on last, beelined for another toilet and took possession, felt himself breathe again. He sat on the loo, propped his arms on the edge of the sink unit and cradled his heavy forehead, allowing it to roll gently from side to side.

It was a strange moment when Bin Man Joe drove off, leaving him outside the station alone. He'd felt naked and vulnerable and, for the first time, black. Literally everyone walking past him was white, luminously pale – a procession of ghosts. He became conscious that he was wearing his dirty overalls still, while the men all wore smart jeans or branded trainers, Nike, Adidas, Reebok… And the girls! Yonas hadn't seen a female human being for months. He watched a couple of slick-haired teenage girls go by arm in arm, cheeping with giggles, their jeans clinging so tightly that they showed every curve, and he imagined Sarama outshining all of them in her baggy camouflage.

Bang b-bang bang. Bang bang.

Yonas jerked awake. More knocks, louder. He rubbed his eyes.

Bang bang bang bang.

This person was persistent. Yonas flushed. He needed to pee now, after sitting on the toilet for hours without lifting the lid. He decided he would try. This was the purpose of a toilet, after all.

Bang bang bang bang bang.

'Just a minute.' His bladder was bursting but nothing would come out – he was too panicked. He zipped up, cleared his throat and unlocked the door.

'Ticket, please, sir.' An official-looking man was standing in the corridor with a small machine in his hands, and a blonde woman with a child were behind him, staring.

Yonas swallowed. 'But, I already…'

'You've been in here for a while now, sir.'

Yonas's kneecaps turned to goo. 'I just came in,' he said.

'No you didn't!' the woman shrilled. 'We've been waiting ages! My little girl here needs a wee. Come on, Evie.' She shoved her child ahead of her, past Yonas, followed her into the toilet and locked the door to his sanctuary.

Yonas gulped. 'I have a stomach problem,' he improvised, then grimaced and clutched his belly, leaning over as if in agony, thinking of his ballooning bladder. He did feel pretty ill right now – though that was probably the terror.

'I still need your ticket, sir,' the conductor said flatly.

Yonas straightened up, trying to think fast. Behind the conductor, he noticed a smart man in a suit, with blond hair and glasses, who seemed to be watching disapprovingly. He felt inside his empty pockets, as if he were about to find a crisp orange train ticket in there, and squeezed his little wooden rooster so hard the beak almost pierced his skin. Then he looked up at the conductor again, into those pale hazel eyes, trying to connect, to convey wordlessly how badly he needed his help. 'Sir, I do not know where the ticket has gone,' he said quietly. 'I must have dropped it. I am sorry – I am not myself today. I have just heard that… my brother and my parents have been killed.'

The conductor's face warped into an expression that was both sceptical and slightly aghast. Yonas imagined his own face in it, like a mirror, the moment when he first heard that news. It was so vivid still, that day, back in the revolutionary school – he was preparing to put on his first play, setting up the tarpaulin stage under an acacia tree, with Gebre's set painted onto old sheets, hardly able to contain his excitement about the moment when the actors stepped in front of the audience… when they were interrupted. *Yonas and Melat. Come with me.* The commander. What had they done wrong? *I have bad news for you. There was a surprise attack today, by enemy MiGs. Your parents and brothers were hit…* The assault of those words, their cold, factual finality. . .

A hand was patting his back. 'I'm really sorry to hear that, mate,' the conductor said, his voice softer than before. 'But I do still need to check your ticket. You sure you've lost it?'

Yonas jabbed his fingers in his pockets once more. But the conductor squeezed his arm.

'All right,' he said. 'Look, just make sure you hold onto it next time, okay?'

Yonas looked up at him, astounded, but just nodded mutely.

And then he heard a series of clicks, camera-like. Behind the conductor, that blond man was holding something in the air. Yonas tensed. Who was he? Why would he be taking pictures? Was he plainclothes police? Immigration? There was nowhere to run…

Sure enough, the man approached the conductor and asked if this passenger was travelling with a valid ticket. Yonas bit the insides of his cheeks. But then, bizarrely, the conductor told the man to back off and mind his own business. This seemed to anger the blond man who then claimed he was a politician. As the two men locked horns, Yonas saw his chance to slip away.

Down in the furthest carriage, the toilet was occupied, so he slouched down into a seat, so the top of his head couldn't be seen from behind. He realized he was rubbing his scarred fingertips together: a tic he'd developed since they were burned, as if he could magic the sensitivity back. Across the aisle an elderly lady was looking at him sideways, but when she saw him turn to her, she immediately pretended to return to reading her newspaper. She was wearing pristine pointed leather shoes and her hair was set in immaculate ringlets, like a wig, so white it was almost purple. Maybe it *was* actually a very pale purple. The headline on her newspaper read:

SMUGGLING GANGS WANT TO SNEAK CALAIS MIGRANTS INTO BRITAIN TO COMMIT CRIMES HERE

Yonas turned to look out of the window. Unseeing, he clasped his hands, felt the sharpness of his nails digging into his knuckles. He wondered how many smuggled migrants like him there were in the UK right now. And where were they all? How many of them had claimed asylum? He supposed he'd meet some more when he got to London. He wished he didn't have to find his way all on his own. He already missed Gebre like a limb.

At King's Cross Station, announcements boomed from the tannoy like a robotic priest's pronouncements across the hundreds, perhaps thousands, of people on the concourse. Yonas weaved slowly through them, thinking how strange it was to be surrounded by so much energetic life. White faces might even be a minority here, he was pleased to note. There were lots of other black and African faces around, and also Chinese faces, Indian faces, Hispanic faces and faces with features he couldn't place, so he didn't feel like he stood out too much. But he did seem to be the only person in the entire station who wasn't attempting to rush for a train, or staring with an anxious frown up at the departure board.

He leaned against a pillar in front of a coffee shop, closed his eyes to inhale the scent, and was right back in the Asmara house, walking down the stairs and towards the intoxicating aroma of roasting coffee beans emanating from the kitchen, mingled with incense and song. His mother, by the stove, her voice filling the room, wearing her favourite outfit, the burnt-orange wrap skirt and blouse resplendent with palm leaf patterns.

He looked inside, and watched the baristas standing at sleek chrome machines, bashing coffee grounds out of a filter gadget, refilling, locking the gadget into the machine and putting blue paper cups underneath to catch ebony streams of espresso. A perfect-looking concoction in seconds. He thought of how long it took his mother and Melat to make coffee, the traditional way: how they would measure out the bright green beans, pour them into a *menkeshkesh*, roast them until they were dark brown, grind them with a pestle and mortar, pour them into a *jebena*, heat and fan it on the stove, boil the liquid several times, filter it through date fibres... Melat loathed the ritual, but their mother insisted on it whenever guests were invited over. The rest of the time they all used a metal Italian espresso maker that his grandfather had acquired when it was left behind by the colonizers. Yonas and Melat both liked the coffee that came out of that just as well: sacrilege, according to their mother and grandmother. It was so long now since he'd had any kind of coffee. He watched the customers process out of the shop, blue paper cups of deliciousness carried unthinkingly in their hands.

A couple of sleek-haired ladies in high heels clip-clopped past, and the blonde one glanced at Yonas and wrinkled her nose. A targeted wrinkle. A clear message. He looked down at his overalls and tilted his head down to sniff his armpit discreetly. Bad. Of course it was bad. It was just hard to tell quite how repellent you were to others when you had got used to your own smell. Not just body odour – he probably reeked of fish guts as well. The thought prompted him to scan around for Aziz or Blackjack... but why would they be here? They were just small-time con artists. They'd never actually come after him, just as he'd told Gebre.

Outside the station, a road heaved with revving cars and grand, grumbling red buses, black taxis as glossy as aubergines and intent cyclists with helmets on, zipping through tiny gaps. It was all so loud, so intense... Yonas felt the sharp edge between pleasurable anonymity and terrifying loneliness. But he had to focus on the task at hand: to source some coins and call Auntie. He wondered whether she lived far from here, what she would look like, what she would be like, whether she would be as smiling and maternal as he imagined, whether she would be able to offer him a floor to sleep on, even just for a few nights. Surely she would be generous enough for that – she'd known his mother well, according to Melat. But even Melat had never actually met this Auntie. She had just read out her number to him over that crackly line. He'd written it onto the back of his hand, repeated it aloud over and over, and then he and Gebre had spent the next few evenings testing each other on it.

He went up to a couple of people, asking them if they had a coin for him to make a local phone call, but they just shook their heads and said 'sorry', as if the thing they were really sorry about was that their walk had been interrupted. He gave up, and walked slowly around, scanning the ground for dropped change, wondering if he would have to ask somebody to borrow their mobile phone or sit down and cup his hands, until, behind a kiosk selling newspapers and sweets, he spotted a silver glint. He squatted down. It was a small, angular, silver coin – twenty pence! He brushed off the dirt, examined the image of the Queen, who looked surprisingly pretty and young, and then looked around for a phone box.

When he found one, he was so anxious to get the coin in the slot that it sprang out and bounced on the floor, nearly rolling out of the booth. He rescued it, put it in with more care, and dialled the number. *Auntie, it is me, Yonas! I am here! How do I find you?* A quiet stuttering on the line, as he waited for the ring, but instead there sounded three notes rising in pitch, then again, then again. 'This number is not recognized,' a curt woman's voice informed him. He must have mistyped. He tried again, more carefully, concentrating on every button. The same three notes. 'This number is not recognized...' He let it repeat a few times, then dropped the receiver so it hung from its cable, groaned low and long, and sank down to his knees on the grubby floor. He closed his eyes for a few seconds, then opened them, and fixated on the abandoned Coke can and globs of old chewing gum stuck in the corner. Had he memorized Auntie's number wrongly? Surely not – he'd checked, and repeated it, so many times. Had he written it down wrong? Again, impossible – the line was crackly, but he'd had Melat repeat it twice. So had she been given the wrong number? Or had Auntie left the place where she was living? He would have to ask Melat when he had enough money for a long-distance call. If only he had an address for Auntie. What was he supposed to do now?

He stood up, pocketed the coin, and looked out at all the people passing by, each intent on a mission to get from A to B, to meet friends, family, to do business. If only he had someone to seek out in London, just one face that would light up in recognition and welcome and congratulate him for making it. But he had to deal with the situation he was in. The sensible thing would be to focus on finding some random Eritreans who could help him find a foothold. He'd heard that a couple of old army friends from back home were in the UK, but he had no idea where, and he wasn't sure he wanted to see them anyway. Amanuel, that distant cousin he'd met once, was supposed to be in Scotland…

Scanning the crowds for an approachable face, he spotted a woman who looked like she just might be Eritrean, with a curly cloud of black hair tied up. He remembered Melat styling hers just like that once.

'Excuse me,' he said, 'can I ask where you are from?'

'Er, London,' the woman said, looking faintly disgusted.

'Oh right. I thought—'

'Sorry, I'm running late.'

Yonas leaned against a wall. If he did spot an Eritrean who had time to talk to him, would he actually want to join an Eritrean diaspora community? He would inevitably be drawn into ferocious debates about the President and the current situation, and he'd be expected to go to church, and they'd quiz him on his past and he'd have to churn up experiences he didn't want to share, not yet, maybe not ever, if he was going to keep going and stay positive. What he really wanted was a fresh start in this city, to make new friends here, British friends, generous people like Bin Man Joe who liked singing along to Bob Dylan, who didn't have a clue about Eritrea and didn't even want to know what side he was on, who could help him reinvent himself and show him the best way to live well in the UK and feel like a native. But what would his strategy be for doing that, and for finding work and a place to sleep? He couldn't just linger here. He decided to walk while he thought, absorb the scenery, and keep an eye open for opportunities. Something would occur to him.

He picked up his bag, then strode out along the street. Caught up in the flow of people, like a leaf coasting along the surface of a river, he felt a surge of excitement. He was finally here, in *London* – and he was free! Freer than he'd ever been, without any commitments, tasks or other people to be responsible for – except Melat and the family back home, of course. His feet were pressing on *London's* pavements, his eyes feasting on *London's* oversized office blocks and *London's* shiny shops, his ears were filling with the vibrations of *London's* traffic, his mouth and lungs saturated by *London's* bitter air, and he was now one of the masses of *London* people, who were all so different, not just racially, but in how they dressed: he had expected reams of smart suits, but there was a woman with a purple coat and a rucksack covered in spikes, and there was an Asian girl with a red streak in her hair and a tattoo sprawling down her neck, and there was a man with a thick, black, rectangular beard and skintight jeans that made him look top-heavy.

He noticed that there seemed to be an unwritten agreement to avoid smiles, or any kind of eye contact with other pedestrians except when absolutely necessary. Was it just his stinky self? But no – even when people stepped aside to let others pass, he noticed, they never seemed to look at each other either. Probably because they were all in such a rush, which made sense in somewhere as busy as London; but he wondered if there was any street in this city comparable to Asmara's tree-lined Independence Avenue, where people would just wander along slowly, hand in hand with friends, sit outside espresso bars, watch the world go by, exchange greetings.

He stopped short in front of large metal sign outside an office block that read:

theguardian
The Observer

Was this really the headquarters of the famous newspaper? How fortuitous that he'd just happened to walk past it! Was it a sign? He paused, and imagined himself dressed in a pristine suit with a crisp shirt, briefcase in hand, getting ready to walk into the building. *I'm here for an interview,* he'd tell the receptionist assuredly. *Yes, for the columnist job.* A woman came out of the building, wearing jeans and a T-shirt, pulling her mobile phone out of her pocket, making a call as she passed him. Did she work in there, dressed like that? Was that normal here? What did he know? What would he ever know about the world of journalists in this city? Another woman came out, and gave him a long look – which prompted him to carry on walking. He couldn't be caught loitering outside somewhere important like that. Realistically, he would probably never get to walk inside such an office except to clean it.

Cleaning toilets for small change donations in a run-down shopping mall or something: that was the kind of ambition he knew he should content himself with, at least at the beginning. But how would he even land a job like that, with no connections? Should he find a run-down shopping centre, wait nearby in a discreet spot until it closed and cleaners arrived, then dash over and enquire about work? But there didn't seem to be any shopping centres around here, or anything particularly run-down. Perhaps he'd be better off away from the city centre and its elite workplaces, where police would no doubt be hyper-alert to scruffy, reeking black men…

The name Canning Town popped into his head. Bin Man Joe had said his brother lived there, that it was in the east of London. It was a bit random, but why not? The brother had moved there not long ago and found work, so why shouldn't he? He looked around for someone to ask directions. A black lady with a wide smile was leaning against a wall, chatting on her phone, and cackling every so often with an infectious wheeze. He waited until she'd hung up, then approached her. 'Excuse me. I'm trying to find Canning Town.'

She frowned. 'Canning Town? What's that on – Jubilee, I think.' Yonas wondered whether the meaning of this should be obvious. 'Take the un-der-ground train,' she said, splitting the syllables as if he were deaf. 'Farringdon's just over there. Good luck!' She walked off briskly, as if she didn't want to be seen with him for another second.

Inside this station entrance, Yonas came up against a row of waist-high electronic gates. He looked up to see CCTV cameras perched like hawks. He would have to walk. Not the end of the world; he could tell from the sun which way was east.

Shortly, the afternoon dimmed, dusk intensified, doubt and hunger set in. Having strayed from the main roads, Yonas found himself wandering a network of residential streets. The houses around him were tall and elegant and forbidding, and long windows wore neat flower boxes underneath like military moustaches. A glow from a basement drew him over. Peering down, he saw a cream-coloured kitchen, spacious and clean, with wide counters. On one of them sat a fruit bowl, piled with apples, bananas and oranges and – yes – a mango. Yonas was tempted to force open the window, leap down, grab it and bite right into it. He could just make out the smell of something deliciously savoury. Curved lamps in corners cast a warm glow. When he crouched, he could see a candlelit table at the back, around which two parents and three children were eating spaghetti and laughing. He pictured his mother staggering to the table with a huge, steaming pot for her rambunctious brood and it struck him anew that he would not only never see her again, he would probably never see any of them again, and he would be lucky if he ended up with any kind of family of his own. Even with a table of his own.

He continued along more residential streets, past some apartment blocks and up some dead-end roads, until he was so tired his bones ached. He spotted a wide doorstep, big enough for a curled-up body. Nobody was around. He sat down, hooked his feet up beside him, eased down into a foetal position, and nestled his head in the crook of his arm, feeling like he had just climbed into a cold stone coffin. He pulled his wooden rooster out of his pocket. *Just me and you, little friend,* he whispered, stroking it with the top of his fingertip – the few millimetres between the nail and the scarring. He thought about what would happen if he died here. Nobody would have a funeral for him. What did the UK authorities do with random African bodies found on the streets? Burn them? He imagined being stuffed in a bin bag, then deposited on a pile of other vagrants, and tossed into a vast, bright, smoky fire, crackling and fizzling with amber, gold, orange, red, his trousers catching, the flames licking eagerly up his legs, but it didn't feel hot, oddly, it somehow felt cold, numbing, stiffening...

He sat up, panicking, then rubbed his eyes. Daylight! He must have been asleep for hours. He was chilly, but intact. And alone. Utterly alone. No Gebre to consult with about what to do next. He watched the scattered white clouds drift for a minute or two across a faintly blue sky, imagining them floating gently over the ocean towards Eritrea. Then he got up jerkily, and staggered towards the sound of traffic.

Back on a main road, car horns blared like a tin pan band. His mouth was sour – all he wanted right now was a drink of water and a pee. He managed to blag some tap water from a small café, and the girl behind the counter reluctantly allowed him to use their toilet. The warm water from the tap on his hands and face felt delightful, the hand drier even better. Could he get away with a full body wash? Someone would inevitably knock on the door again. He wiped his armpits cursorily, and slipped back out.

By midday he found himself amid a glass forest. Here were the smart suits he'd been expecting to see everywhere in this city, the immaculate hair-dos, and each person he passed was talking on a phone, texting or listening to something through headphones. He passed a particularly well-tailored suit, whose owner's face was so glum that Yonas was tempted to stop him and ask: What could possibly be so bad in *your* life? Do you want to swap? He imagined the man walking through his front door back home, no doubt in a splendid Victorian house, hanging up that fine jacket as if it were an invisibility cloak, then hearing his children rush down the stairs shouting *Daddy! Daddy!* Would he finally crack a smile then?

A trio walked past eating what looked like lumps of rice wrapped in black paper out of cardboard trays. One of the women was whining: 'He didn't even offer to pay. I was like, hello, I'm a feminist and stuff but, like, I still want my first date paid for.' The other woman cooed sympathetically, and one chucked her box in the bin with at least half the contents left in it. Yonas walked over to the bin, eager, mouth watering for whatever the food was – but he couldn't bring himself to dig in. Not yet. And not here. It was too conspicuous.

He decided to carry on, but regretted that decision as his hunger deepened. Crowded though the pavement was, he noticed people were staring at him, and giving him as wide a berth as possible. He was tempted to walk into one of the shops displaying geometrically ironed shirts and trousers, take a few sets into a changing room to try on, leave his rancid overalls on the floor and walk out again.

His energy was plummeting now. He passed the open door of a corner shop, lined with brightly wrapped chocolate bars, and paused, salivating. Could he slip one in his pocket without being noticed? But the shop owner, an Indian man, gave him a hard stare, and he retreated. He was just turning another corner and summoning up the will to dig in a bin after all, when he spotted a man serving hot food from a cart to a queue of people. Several were already standing around eating it off paper plates… it looked like rice and curry. And then he noticed what seemed too good to be true: people were accepting it without giving the server any money! He sidled up to a man who'd just started tucking into his plateful to ask if he really just took it without paying.

'Mate, you'd better believe it.' He laughed, spraying out a couple of bits of rice. 'Those Hare Krishna dudes.'

'Krishna?'

'Yeah, it's a kind of religion where you have to give food away for free. Some people call them crazy bastards but hey, I'm not about to sniff at a complimentary lunch. Even if it is veggie.'

'You have to be a believer?'

'Na, mate, anyone can just take the nosh and those dudes are happy.'

As Yonas queued, saliva now exploding inside his cheeks at such a rate it was hard to swallow, he imagined the clamour there would be if a free food cart were to materialize at home. People would probably stay away, thinking it was a government trap. Finally his own plate was piled up, and he started shovelling food into his mouth. It was *so* good to eat! His tongue was immediately scalded, but he gobbled on regardless, almost ecstatic at the spices, the vegetables! Maybe this was the turning point. If he could pick up free meals as tasty as this on the street, life in the UK would be a breeze.

After a second helping, he headed eastwards again, re-energized. The city around him became multidimensional and multi-layered as he started connecting everything he saw with sparks of memory, films, BBC news clips, old magazines, his father's books. He noticed how many of the shiny shopfronts at ground-floor level were sitting at the feet of grand historic buildings, and how they were interspersed haphazardly among modern, linear blocks, and how all of them were in such good condition, none of them crumbling or dripping with telephone wires, and how every so often there would be little grassy parks and trees spreading nature through the city like a sprinkling of herbs on a salad. Passing one of these parks, he paused to watch a guy with a paunch being egged on by someone who looked like a personal trainer as he skipped furiously and kept tripping over his rope. A short distance away there was a wheelchair and a woman with a prosthetic leg next to it, doing press-ups. If only Sheshy could get a prosthetic in that league; it looked futuristic compared to the ones the martyrs got back home.

He was about to cross at a junction when he saw a van pull up with a huge black advert plastered on its side:

In the UK illegally?
GO HOME OR FACE ARREST
Text HOME to 78080

And in a square box in the top corner of the van, like an official passport stamp, it said:

106
ARRESTS
LAST WEEK
IN YOUR AREA

His stomach clenched, and he stopped dead still. He couldn't see in the windows, couldn't tell whether or not the driver had clocked him. He glanced down at his scruffy clothes, his shabby shoes, touched his matted hair, and nearly laughed at himself for not being more conscious of how obviously illegal he looked. He might as well be waving a flag saying *Arrest me!* What should he do? Was there someone in that van poised to jump out and make the 107th arrest? He couldn't cross the road right in front of it. Not now. But then if he turned and ran it would look suspicious… He crouched and pretended to do up his shoelace, making himself as small as possible. Time crawled, except for the demonic pounding of his heart. But after what can only have been a few seconds, the lights changed and the van pulled off.

Slowly, creakily, Yonas got up, and carried on walking, feeling as stilted as an old man. He was an idiot to think it might be easy just to wander around and make a life in London, like moulding a new version of himself out of a fresh piece of clay. How could he avoid getting arrested just for *looking* like this, never mind find work and somewhere to live? Maybe Gebre was right about waiting longer at the factory for fake papers… But he was here now. He had to keep going, and find somewhere to have a wash and get fresh clothes. But then he halted again, as he saw, walking towards him, a broad-shouldered white man dressed all in black wearing sunglasses… Oh God, it *was*… no, it wasn't, was it? Of course it wasn't. Yonas sighed shakily, and walked on.

Finally, he came upon a sign for Canning Town. From the name he had expected a small suburb full of pretty houses lined up neatly like tin cans in a supermarket, and he'd half-convinced himself he'd bump into a man who would look like the double of Bin Man Joe, just strolling along with his family, shielding his eyes with one hand as he looked around for his new Eritrean nephew. Instead, Yonas found himself on a highway under a huge concrete road underpass, roaring with cars, and after that, in the middle of an industrial estate. It didn't seem as if anybody lived here at all. There was just factory building after factory building. What a stupid decision to come here just because of Bin Man Joe, when he could have gone somewhere like Arsenal, or Chelsea, or, more practically, sought out an Eritrean church… But then he spotted a human being. A man, youngish, maybe about his age, wearing overalls. Yonas was just wondering whether to approach him, when the man saw him, and crossed the road towards him, walking fast. Yonas's heart raced – why was he being approached? Was he about to get arrested? Mugged? If so, his total lack of valuable belongings would either leave him unscathed or infuriate his attacker…

They were now standing face to face on the pavement. There was nobody else around. 'Hi,' the man said, not exactly threateningly. If this was a mugging, it was a strange way to go about it. The man had messy black hair and creases around his eyes. 'You are looking for work?'

Yonas laughed involuntarily. 'How did you guess?'

'Smells like you need somewhere for sleep too,' the man said, and smiled back, revealing a gap between his front teeth.

Yonas nodded. 'You know somewhere?'

'I do. I am happy I found you. You stay, then I get commission, okay?'

'Maybe, but I do not know yet what you are offering me.'

'Good point. I take you to see Uncle. Follow me.'

Uncle? Friendly or sinister? Maybe it was fate: lose an auntie, gain an uncle. Yonas followed the man through a gate into the potholed forecourt of a large building, along a narrow gap between the left wall and the fence.

The man turned as he walked. 'What is your name?'

'My name?' Yonas thought frantically, then remembered the bin man. 'My name is… Joe.'

'Joe, yeah?' the man said. 'And where you come from?'

'Eritrea. And you?'

'Emil. From Romania.' Emil pulled out a key and unlocked a side door, then led Yonas down a dimly lit corridor and up some concrete stairs to another door, on which he knocked three times. The words 'come in' floated out.

Inside, a grey-haired man with knitted eyebrows was sitting behind a computer, with three stooping table lamps poised around him like water birds. He didn't look up. Emil cleared his throat. 'Uncle, this is new guy. He say his name Joe. Eritrean. Been sleeping rough.'

Uncle appeared to ignore them and continued typing with two fingers. Was this going to be another Aziz? He could hardly look more different: gaunt, with a crooked nose, pointed shoulders and spindly fingers that looked as if they might snap at the next tap. After a little while he looked up, and his eyes were two spikes. 'So. Joe. You are new to the UK?'

'Yes.'

'You know nobody here.'

'No. I mean, I thought I did, but they… No, I know nobody.'

'You are willing to work hard?'

'Yes.'

'Okay. *If* I let you stay here, there are rules to follow.' Uncle pushed his chair back, stood up and walked around to the front of the desk on which he perched and leaned forward, his dark eyes locking in. 'How are you at following rules?'

'Good.'

'Well, my rules are simple enough. One' – Uncle stuck up his forefinger – 'I arrange the work. Two' – middle finger – 'you do as much work as I tell you to do, and you don't work for anyone else. Three' – ring finger – 'you never – ever – tell anyone outside about how you got the work or anything about this place. Got it?'

Yonas nodded.

'You haven't seen the film, have you?'

Yonas shook his head.

'Fine. Anyway, if you've got the rest, the correct answer would be *yes*.'

'Yes,' Yonas echoed.

'Because if you talk we are all going to get into trouble. Do you know the meaning of the word trouble?'

'I do.'

'Good. If you imagine to yourself the worst possible kinds of trouble, then you're on the right track.' *I don't need to imagine*, Yonas thought. 'So, blend in. Don't get yourself noticed. Keep yourself to yourself. Understood?'

'Understood.'

Uncle got off the desk and began to pace around the room. 'Good. You can stay for a trial week. You will do a mixture of work. Construction, cleaning and such like. You will get forty quid a week cash in hand from me, for working however many hours I tell you to work, normally around eight hours a day, for six days per week. In return you get to live here and sleep here for free and I give you work clothes to wear – which it looks like you need right now. If you want to leave I need two weeks' notice. Agreed?'

'Agreed,' Yonas said immediately. He fought with the corners of his mouth to stop them from smiling.

'Right. Here's a tenner to tide you over.' Yonas took the note and held it gently between his fingers as if it were pressed from gold. He imagined telling Gebre: *Only day three, and I'm already in the money, with a real job, and a place to live!* Was Gebre wishing he'd followed after all? Or was he still cursing Yonas for abandoning him and Osman?

'Any questions?' Uncle asked.

Yonas thought for a second. 'What's the film?' he found himself asking.

'The film! Oh. Well, I'm not giving it away that easily. You can ask the others. There's a TV in the living area, so if it's coming on I may let you know. Now, scarper. I suggest you prioritize a shower.'

Chapter 7: Emil

I will take one espresso macchiato, and two spoon sugar. Okay three, just today.

So, you wanna talk about Professor Jojo! Haha, yeah, that's how I call him, but when I first met him in street, Professor was like opposite word I would think of, okay, I had to even hold my breath, like he smell of shit mix with rotten fish and mouldy cheese in big bag of rubbish when you leave too long before taking outside. You got my point. But when I am looking closer I am thinking: Wait. Nice smile, tall, cheekbones, huuuuge fro all matted and disgusting like rats living inside – but with a proper wash it's gonna look good! I am even getting a little fantasy…

I can talk about it now, with you, no problem. But back when I meet the Prof, no way. I am *so* much hoping for another gay to come to live in warehouse, you cannot believe, but I can't say nothing. I mean, I came to UK because everyone said London scene is awesome and people easy-going compare to rest of Europe – Romania anyway – so I think, okay, maybe there I can be me. But when I arrive I cannot even get work to pay rent, not even think about going out, clubbing, all that. I mean, London is so expensive, so, so, so, SO expensive, it's not even true.

Even room size of small cupboard in shittest area is too much money. So after some time I was living with a load of straight, immigrant guys in warehouse. I mean, not even proper house – this big, old place where they used to repair cars, with one big room out back full of mattresses. Some guys living there even more gay haters than back home. Russians especially. So I try to keep secret, and in case they guess, I am always try to be comedian, so they will like me for being that guy who is making everybody laugh. Problem is, then they start to really *like* me and wanna hang out, and they like going to pull women, so I have to make excuse. Once I even went out and pulled three women just to make point and get them off my back. Ugh. It's like I just snog my sisters.

So anyway, Uncle tell Professor Jojo he can stay, and I show him spare sleeping spot – I mean, it is only mattress, okay, but he look right into my eyes and say *thank you*… like it is *biggest* favour anybody done him ever in his life, and he lie down, hands behind head, with biggest smile you've ever seen. He start saying something about leaving jungle, with like fox and snake kissing dove or something crazy like that, ending up in city with bed to sleep on… I have like no clue what he is talking about, but he tell me it was just a poem he remember, so I applause him and tell him that has got to be first poem anyone ever said in this place, but maybe if he want to fit in with guys here he better rein it in, and also, if he want to be friends even with me, he got to shower, like right now.

He jump up and ask if shower was with hot water, like that would be *impossible*, and when I said yeah of course, his face lit up like he just got papers from Home Office. I say I can lend him razor and I show him bathroom. He go to look at himself in mirror, then turn to me and his face is *angry*. I'm thinking, What did I do? He ask if I have scissors, and I'm like, Uhhh, is he gonna stab me or what? But I get them from kitchen. He take and say thanks, then start to chop at his hair like weeds! Just *chop chop chop* and throwing big lumps down toilet, I mean – I was still imagining it all brushed out ready for dance floor, so I'm like, 'Wait, please, my friend, keep some!' But too late. He smile little bit and tell me, 'My hair needs new start, like me.' I tell

60

him, 'Okay, fine, but you can't leave it all messed up like that. I can cut properly for you. I am cutting everybody's hair in warehouse – I do yours for free first time. But I am not even touching your head until it's had, like, three shampoos, okay?!'

When he came out of shower, he smell normal, and his face look so different with no beard, fresh and kind of fragile. But his body super-skinny, like bamboo stick. And his hair! There were tufts sticking out like clown, and now it's been washed, I can see it's not fro exactly, like looser curls, soft for touch.

So, I make him coffee in red Malteser mug and tell him to sit so I can start trimming, and we talk. Actually, it is me doing most talking at first. I try to ask him what he's been doing, where he's from, stuff like that, but he's not saying much, just asking me more questions back. And I like talking, you know, so I keep going, but after some time I say to him, 'Hey, it's your turn now!' But he just laugh and say oh, long story, he's just happy he made it here, then ask more about me. And I get that. I mean, lot of guys in warehouse have shit lives before and not like to talk about past too much, especially if they don't know you yet. So I just tell him about other guys and about work for Uncle and living in London. And for some reason I am already feeling easy with him, like, you know, he *listens*, and not everyone does that, right? And he's sounding interested, he's making jokes even… and then it just slips out. That I like guys.

I stop. I'm like, oh shit, shit shit shit, I kept that secret for so long, and now I just told to some new guy I don't even know, who probably hates gays, or is gonna tell. I feel super-nervous, and my hands start shaking, I'm thinking I'm gonna accidentally stick scissors in his scalp. I mean, you know, he seem nice enough, but most straight African guys in warehouse don't like gays from what I hear – but I am still hoping he will say, like, 'Oh my God, I'm gay as well!!!!' Haha. Actually he just say 'okay', you know, just 'okay!', like it's just one small thing about me, like my favourite colour, like he is totally cool with it. So that was big, big relief.

I ask him, look, can you do me a favour – don't say nothing? He say no problem, he can keep secrets. Then, still looking away from me, cos

I'm cutting his hair, he say his best friend from back home is like me, and he keep that secret too, because back home you can get put in prison. He tell me how that friend, Gebre, is closer to him than his own brother, how his parents basically adopted him as kid, after his father got disappeared. I'm like: 'Disappeared?' He explain how before independence Ethiopians would just come and take Eritreans from where they working, or living, no warning, then they never see again, no explain, nothing. He is telling me he feeling guilty now, meeting me, because he never tried to talk to his friend about it. I'm like, 'You mean you could not talk about his father?' And he say no – that is bad memory, but occasionally they talk about that – no, he mean he never talk to his friend about him being gay. Then he sort of burst out how he wish he could change that now, and also introduce his friend to me. I'm like, 'Sure! Bring him right over! And I hope he looks like you!' (I not really say that last bit.)

Then I ask him, 'How about you, you married?' And he shake his head, say no, but not look at me, just start talking about something different. He never ever talk to me about any wife or girlfriend, after that, even when we good friends – always keep private about that stuff. But also he don't say nothing to other guys in warehouse about me, not whole time we living there. He is solid guy, Professor Jojo.

At first, other guys try testing him. Make him do bins and tell him he's got to shower last in queue, all that. I'm thinking, How is he gonna deal with that, cos he's quiet kind of guy, and mostly guys at top of pile are alpha guys, you know – maybe they push him around. But no, he stay cool, he don't get intimidated. He even make people start to like him, just from small things, like buying pack of cookies, offering around.

So, Uncle tell me I gonna be Professor's mentor, you know, like, person who's gonna show him around for work and stuff. I remember first day we get on bus together, and he's like, *amazed* that seats are so nice! Stroking his like he got new puppy! I'm like, okay, so today we go to bank where all guys working there sniff coke in toilets, then later we go to gym where guys pump truckloads of iron and grunt like pigs, then tomorrow we have solicitor's company where they work all hours in clock, and PR company with *brainstorming* area like pre-school art room for kids who need to roll on beanbags and draw with crayons. He think I'm just being funny. Later he realize it's all totally true.

So, I show him main sights as bus goes into City, like tower that's named after a cucumber but looks like massive dildo, and Bank of England that looks like palace. We have fun, pointing out people wearing weird clothes, and just chatting. And he's good to work with too. Doesn't mess about, like me, but picks everything up fast, like I only ever have to explain one time, then he got it.

So one morning, after one week or two maybe, I remember one guy left newspaper on his seat on bus and Professor pick it up. Headline is something like 'Rapist asylum seeker caught with pants down taking a shit on a solid gold toilet studded with diamonds that he bought for his fifty-bedroom castle in Chelsea after selling cocaine to hardworking British businessman who believed they were just buying expensive cornflour', and he rips it out and puts in his pocket, then carries on reading. I'm like: 'Wait, what are you doing?!'

He goes: 'Collecting.'

I'm like: 'Why?'

He goes: 'This newspaper is always talking about immigrants and how dangerous they are. Like we are about to take over.'

I'm like: 'You're twisted, reading that.'

He just grins. He goes: 'I just want to know how British people think of people like us. Some of them, anyway. Lots, actually. I think this is the biggest selling paper.'

I'm like: 'So, you wanna walk around thinking how everyone hates you? I still don't get it.'

He goes: 'Look, some people collect stamps, I collect newspapers, okay? It's normal!' He's a geek, okay, but I still not realize how much, until we find out about library.

Oh yeah, so that's how he got name, Professor. He start bringing library books back to read. Of course, guys start laughing at him. I remember Alfonso ask him one time: 'How come you get library pass anyway if you're illegal?' And he just say he has ways. We know he must be nicking books and we tell him: 'Hey, if you wanna steal shit, why not get us drugs or alcohol or something useful? DVDs at least! Do you think you gonna win Nobel Prize from reading all these books?' He says it's not stealing, he's bringing books back to library after, and he likes to read, he studied literature at *university*. University! Turns out he wrote big essay on newspapers in his country. Boris was first one to start calling him Professor, and it stuck – then I added Jojo, so he wouldn't sound too smart. He used to read so much different stuff, like history books, story books, even dictionary – like, not just to learn English better, but reading meanings of words for *fun*. For fun! Who does that?

Oh, other thing about Professor I got to tell you is cooking. Haha, especially one meal! Okay, so normally in that warehouse, nobody cooks. Not properly. If we got enough money, we eat McDonald's cos it's easy and tastes good and you feel nice and full after. If we got less money, or wanna be more healthy, we eat like soup, or spaghetti hoops, or pasta and sauce or eggs on toast, that kind of shit. Basically, nobody cooks cos we're guys, and we're too tired from work, and all we got to cook in that place is microwave and two hotplates anyway. But when it came near to Christmas… okay, from like October – you know how in UK shop windows get stuffed way early with gifts, flashing lights, snowflakes, discount signs, and everybody is walking around with big fat shopping bags, cos all British people have credit cards – Professor read in one newspaper that average British person spend £200 on presents! What was I saying? Oh, yeah, so when it came near to Christmas, Professor ask me what we do in warehouse. Like, for celebrations. Especially for eating.

I tell him I guess we'll do like year before: put up tinsel and some pound shop lights, then on Christmas Day get drunk and eat chips and cheese and watch TV. And then on 27th when there is discount everywhere, last year I buy frozen UK Christmas food like mince pies and turkey and eat later. But basically there's no big meal or anything, we all eat our own stuff like normal.

But Professor say to me: 'How about we have Christmas feast all together?'

I'm like: 'Well, if you get the food and cook then maybe the guys will go for it!'

He goes: 'Okay, I can try if people chip in some money.' He tell me back in his country, only women cook, but he thinking it cannot be that hard – he seen male chefs cooking on TV and he want to learn himself now he is here. And also he say Christmas in his country is not even in December, so he wants to try British one.

I'm like: 'What? Christmas not in December? Are you serious?'

He goes: 'It's Orthodox Christmas.' Always happens on seven of January. And for dinner they eat roasted goat, and panettone, you know? – it's like Italian bread thing that is all light and soft and taste of lemons – and bowls of popcorn, and super-strong coffee, beans roasted fresh that day.

I'm like: 'Mmm, sounds nice! Wanna make it for me?'

And he say okay, he will try to make one of each kind of dinner, one for British Christmas and one for Eritrea Christmas, if he can get others to chip in money. I'm thinking the guys will just laugh at him, but they pretty much all up for it! They each give him, like, four quid or something.

So, on Christmas Day we all get up to eat toast for breakfast, then sit around on cushions and mattresses and get drunk, smoke, start to watch stuff on morning TV, like *It's a Wonderful Life*, and some film about snowman. Professor is sitting at table, chopping parsnips and potatoes – he got extra paper plates and cutlery so we can all eat at same time, and they are towered up on table next to him, all ready, and he's got stuffing and cranberry sauce, and we're all thinking, Yeahhhh, feast time soon, and getting hungry, you know...

And then there's this BANG! Like proper explosion. Like bomb. And everyone's like, What the fuck? Is this terrorist attack? Some guys scream, and we all look around, and Professor Jojo has fallen on floor on his back, and there's flames coming out of microwave, like, big flames! Oh my God, such a stink, of like burning plastic, and raw meat splattered everywhere like some crazy baby thrown its purée around... I grab fire blanket, and we throw on water and put out fire, then we asking if Professor is okay, and what happen? He gets up slowly and says he's okay, but he look shocked.

So I say to him again, like: 'What happen?'

And he goes: 'I don't know, I just put chicken in to cook...'

And then Histoire is like: 'Ow long for?'

And he goes: 'Just one hour!'

And Histoire's like: 'Fucking idiot, look what you 'av done,' – all angry. But I'm thinking, oh my God – putting chicken in microwave for *one hour*!!! Like, of course it's gonna explode, and maybe blow up whole building, and this guy probably never even used microwave before in his whole life, and it is kind of amazing all of us not covered in chicken guts and on fire ourselves, this is like most hilarious thing ever happen in warehouse, maybe even in my whole life, and I start laughing and laughing, like I'm crying, and other guys all start laughing too, even Histoire, and even Professor Jojo. We tell him don't worry, we don't need no microwave, we can live on McDonald's for a while! And Uncle will probably buy us new one anyway if we say it broke. Plus we can still eat rest of Christmas food, like stuffing and potatoes – by some miracle most of it is not covered in raw chicken. And actually it taste not bad. We give Professor big round of applause, then eat in front of Queen doing her boring speech, then fill up on mince pies, and life seems pretty good. For a day.

So, when Eritrea Christmas come around, Professor is still gonna go ahead with cooking special meal like they have back there, but he refuse to take money from guys this time round, even though we try to give to him – I think he's feeling bad about explosion even though it was just mistake. He fry up sausages for us, and make popcorn in a pan and strong coffee, and he keep on saying sorry it is instant coffee, but we don't care. He stew up apples with cinnamon to serve with sausages, and we all sit together again to eat – this is second time in two weeks, and I mean, most of guys in warehouse are bastards so far as I'm concern, and I never thought I'd be sitting to eat with them – but it did feel kind of nice, almost like family, just for couple of hours. Everyone does a big 'cheers' with drinks for chef.

But after, when Professor is washing up, I go to help him out, and he's kind of quiet. I ask what's wrong, and he says nothing, just thinking about family, what they're doing, if they've had Christmas meal already. I can tell he's homesick. All of us are, even if we hate our homeland, even if we never ever wanna go back. It's still home, you know? So anyway, I just got phone as present from sisters (Uncle banned phones in there but I had mine hidden), so I offer Professor to call home on it if he wants, so he not have to go out to phone box to speak to his sister like usual. He's super-grateful.

So he takes it to corridor, and when I go to take rubbish out, I hear him talking. It's not like I expected, a *Happy Christmas everyone!* type of conversation – he saying he'll send money soon. After, I ask if everything's okay. He tell me things are hard for his sister, cos she could get arrested any time, because of him. I'm like, *woah*, you like gangsta or something? And he's like, no, it's just he wrote article saying everyone shouldn't all have to do military service their whole life, and because of that, they put him in jail, and when he escaped, they came to his house and threaten his sister and took all his shit. I'm like, oh. That is bad. And then he say his sister got a little daughter and no husband, and she's got to look after their brother who got his legs blown off, and grandmother who can't remember what she did ten minutes ago, and they all rely on him for money cos their parents are dead, and now government is after them for *extra* tax money, just cos he *left*! He got all worked up talking about it, then suddenly he stop and ask if we can talk about something else. So we did. But I remember it, and I had proper respect for Professor after that. Like, my life was lush compared to his, but he never complain like me, he just tell me about it that one time, and then just cos I ask about it. I reckon if I was him, with all that going on, I would be in some kind of big black depression, you know, drinking vodka with Russian guys every night and crying like baby.

So anyway, yeah, few months in, we good friends, and one day I look at Professor Jojo coming out of shower, and remember day one when he's stick thin and stinking, and I'm thinking, Wow, you got muscles now! I don't say nothing, but I'm like: I *knew* you would be hot. And one night soon after that, Alfonso (who thinks he's Leonardo DiCaprio), he take Professor out to pull women. But Professor never come back after and go on about how he got laid, even though I know the girls went mad for him, cos Udaze said. He just said it was okay, but he can't believe how one drink in pub cost more than ten cans from supermarket, and he not get how people expect you to buy rounds for everybody, so that was last time he doing that. I told him he don't need to meet no girls in pub anyway, right, he's already married – to books!

Actually, one day I feel bored and I start looking into one of his books, and thinking, hmm, like maybe I need to make more effort with education, all that shit. But a few pages of English and my head hurt! So I put it down, switch on TV. I'm more, like, people kind of guy. For me life is for living.

And then I'm like: wait, but if life is for *living*, how am I still here in this *warehouse* after six months? I tell myself, okay Emil, you gonna focus now. You need get out of here and live in proper apartment or house or something, so you can come out to people you living with, like this whole London thing *supposed* to be about. No way you can save enough money or meet new people with this shit pay.

So, that night I take all my savings and I'm like, right this is it, I don't have any family to support like Professor, so I'm gonna take risk: I'm gonna go to G.A.Y. – you know, like biggest gay club in town – and I'm gonna party like it's last night on earth and meet people who got better places to live and can help make my life different, somehow. I mean, it's big gamble, I know. But I'm like, fuck it, I'm gonna do this one big night, for me, just how I want it, this one time, and it's gonna be amazing. So I go there, and oh my God. SO much fun. I dance like crazy, I pull a couple of guys and I go back with one of them to his flat and, wow, I'm like, life is *good* right now, even if it's shit again tomorrow.

But it actually works out! So, not too long after, one of my new friends tell me he play in this band and that's how I got to join... actually, I probably would not even be doing that if Professor Jojo hadn't come along. Let me explain.

Back in Romania I used to play violin. Like all time when I was kid, and then I play in wedding band and earn my living for some time – it's not much money, but I loved it. So I brought violin to UK, but I never play it. But then one day in warehouse when everyone's out and it's just me and Professor Jojo, he finds violin at back of big cupboard, and ask about it. I told him it's mine but I not play any more. He ask me please to play for him, and I say no, no, but he keep pressing. And I'm like, okay, fine, so I pick it up, thinking I can just scratch some tune and put it back. But then I play this song my grandmother teach me, and it is first time touching violin since I left my country, and since I saw her – and oh my God, this *feeling* just hit me. I'm not expecting it, you know? And fat stupid tears just start falling out of my eyes, like river, so fast I cannot even play, and I'm like, what is wrong with me! I put violin away, and I cannot believe I'm crying in front of another guy, but Professor tell me wait, don't stop, play more, and I tell him no, but I end up admit to him about my grandmother and how she disowned me when I came out to her, and how she die a year later, and how I feel so bad about letting her down. *So bad*, like maybe it was me breaking her heart and killing her, and how that was when I decide to get out of my country and come to UK.

Professor just listen. Then he tell me his mother used to sing, and he and his sister played an instrument called *car* or something like that, and he really miss music from home. He say, if I have violin here and I can play, I should do it, and keep my culture alive inside of me. He say my grandmother would want me to. But I tell him no no no – you know, I'm not into it any more.

But when I find out one of my new friends has got band that's like Eastern European folk but with urban twist, it sounded cool, and I remember what Professor said, so I ask if I can try out, just jamming with them one time, and now I play with them regularly! It's, like, music you go crazy for, and we perform wearing wigs and traditional dresses. It's hilarious. I love it.

So, anyway it was one of my friends from the band who offer me place to live in house after the warehouse got raided – like, proper house in Brixton that look on outside like kind of house with normal family living there, except inside there's six gays squatting. And then through another friend from that group I get proper job wrapping sandwiches for supermarket. Pay every week, better money – everything coming together. Best of all, I can stop pretending to be alpha guy – so I shave my hair at bottom and up one side, bleach the ends and get some piercing, and finally I can walk out on street and feel like me. Like the me I was supposed to be.

So anyway, I hope Professor's not gonna get deported. How his chances looking like? And how about one more coffee? We had late gig last night.

Chapter 8: Yonas

'Brother! Is it really you?'

The sound of Melat's voice for the first time, after so long, made Yonas's throat swell so that he couldn't reply straight away, and he had to lean back against the phone box wall. Part of him had been convinced that he wouldn't get through, that something terrible would have happened, that the police would have come, she'd have been beaten, worse...

'Hey, are you still there?' she asked.

'Yes, yes!' Yonas laughed, imagining her face in the contour of his reflection in the scratched Perspex window. 'Sorry – I was just... Never mind. So, I made it to London! How are you all? I have been so worried – they haven't come to intimidate you again, have they?'

'Not the police, thank God, but the tax men came, demanding their two per cent. I fended them off this time, and obviously I am still here, but they kept asking me again where you were, kept telling me I must know, I must be getting money from you... they searched your room again and took everything they didn't take last time. Of course I told them I didn't know anything, I insisted I wasn't getting anything from you, and said I feared you were dead, which was true – I even showed them what we had in our kitchen cupboards, just flour for *injera* and lentils, but they didn't care, and if it wasn't for Sheshy in his wheelchair, I think they'd have arrested me. But anyway, we're okay. Now you – where have you been all this time? Are you with Auntie?'

'No – I was about to say. That number you gave me did not work.'

'What?'

'I know. Every time I tried it said number is not in use. Can you ask if she has changed phone?'

'Oh. I don't know – the person who gave it to me moved away. I can ask around to see if somebody else knows but…'

'Okay, thank you but do not worry yourself too much. I have found a place to live for now. And I can send you some money soon.'

'Thank you, brother! We are really struggling. So how was the journey?'

'After Libya? Long story. The boat was bad but the main thing is it didn't sink. I had to pick vegetables in Italy for a while, and then I had to pretend to *be* a cabbage to get to France, and we got arrested there but—'

'Arrested? Oh no – did you go to prison again? Are they looking for you?'

'No no, do not worry, they did not keep us for long – some guys helped us to escape – it was easy,' he lied. 'When they got us to UK we had to work for them for some time to pay them back, so that's why I haven't called. But everything is fine now.' As a little boy, when he used to sit with Melat under the mango tree in the garden doing homework and sharing secrets, he had assumed she would always be there to confide in, to dispense big-sisterly advice. Now it felt like he was the one who had to keep things from her, to protect her.

'Oh brother, I am so glad,' she said.

'Why did I have to call you at Uncle Solomon's?' he asked. 'Is your phone broken?'

'Our line is cut off – we cannot pay our bills, even though I am braiding women's hair at our house every spare hour God sends, and mending clothes and sewing for people. And getting hardly any sleep trying to keep the house clean and cooking, caring for Sheshy and Grandmother; even with Lemlem helping me, it is hard, I am always tired… Things are really difficult here, Yonas. It is not just the tax and bills, we have no money for meat or vegetables, and I don't know how I am going to pay for Lemlem's school fees next term, never mind the new shoes she needs – the old ones are hurting her feet and have holes in. She knows not to complain, but she keeps asking when you can fly us all over.'

Yonas laughed bitterly. 'I would love, more than anything, to bring all of you here, but you need to tell the little one not to get her hopes up…'

'I know, I know,' Melat said. The sound cut off for a minute, but then her voice returned in a whisper. 'Listen, I'm scared, Yonas. If the tax men come again, they won't let me off so lightly. They kept telling me *you know where he is, come on, admit it, you know where he is.* They had guns and they kept putting their hands on them.'

Yonas could hear her voice wavering, and he winced. He knew what could happen to deserters' families… but orphaned families? Children whose parents had fought for liberation, who were national heroes? Whose brothers were maimed fighting in the border war? All that might as well have been for nothing now. To the authorities he was a traitor and a deserter and, thanks to him, Melat was tarred with the same brush.

'What else did they say?' he asked. He felt like punching the window and shattering it. 'Did they threaten you with prison?'

'They had guns for a reason.'

'What did you tell them?'

'Like I told you – I knew nothing. I made them come and see Sheshy, told them I was caring for a martyr.'

Yonas sighed. It could so easily have been him in a wheelchair. 'How is he?'

'Miserable. Only thing that makes him smile is playing chess with this friend of his who lost an arm. They play every week.'

Even after all these years it was still hard to imagine Sheshy twinless, having to make friends on his own who would accept him in a wheelchair. Instinctively, Yonas still thought of Sheshy and Tekle as a duo, a pair of cute but irritating toddlers, always together, always scheming and giggling, who pushed over his wooden block towers and tried to copy everything he did, but whom he'd have done anything to defend, even though they would always love each other more than him. 'Can I speak to him?' he asked.

'He's asleep.'

'Oh. Well, when he wakes up, tell him… he is brave. Braver than his big brother.'

'Right.' Melat's voice sounded tart, cynical, as if she were thinking: *Yes, well, it's true.*

'Now I am working, we can save up for his prosthetics, Yonas added.'

'Okay.'

There was a long pause. 'And how is Grandmother?'

'Worse.' Melat puffed out a long breath. 'She's gone downhill. I mean, she can barely remember who came to visit five minutes ago and she's got so cranky and frail…'

Grandmother had been fine before Yonas left, asking him to find her glasses and forgetting what she'd just been about to do, and complaining of the odd ache and pain, that was all. She used to be a strong woman, with a steely voice, hard to deal with sometimes, but she would do anything for the family, and adored Melat. Many older women would have disowned a pregnant unmarried granddaughter, but Grandmother had lied gallantly to the whole community, making out that Melat had a fiancé who was killed in battle. And it was Grandmother who had stepped in to help when Melat went through that crazy phase, leaving her tiny baby screeching in one room, and hitting herself on the forehead in another, swearing, saying that she couldn't look at her any more, that all she saw was *him*, that her life was ruined, that she wanted to throw the baby out of the window. Yonas had panicked, and tried to shout some sense into his sister, but Grandmother had kept cool, just told Melat calmly to rest, to sleep, and to let her tend to Lemlem for a while, even in the night-time. Gradually the darkness in Melat's eyes had faded, and she even started to take delight in Lemlem's smiles, her kamikaze crawling.

'I wish I could help you more,' Yonas said. 'At least some money will come soon. Right now I'm staying with some guys and we are doing things like cleaning mostly, and the money we are earning does not get me far – you would not believe what things cost here! But I will find a better job and place to live soon, and then I can send more...' He tried to assert this confidently, but heard his voice falter and changed the subject. 'And what about Lemlem?'

Melat laughed finally, and it was like music. 'Well, she's the ray of light. Her schooling is terrible, you know, education here has dive-bombed and most of her classmates can barely read, but at least thanks to Father I know enough to teach her at home. We're lucky to have his books. She is reading English now, all by herself, she can sit for hours...'

'Amazing! I wish I could see her.'

'She misses you. Oh Yonas, I can't bear the thought of my baby getting conscripted...'

'Melat, don't even think about that yet – it's more than a decade until Lemlem turns seventeen. Things will change.'

'Mmm. I hope so. Now, tell me about Gebre,' Melat said. 'How is he?'

'Oh, he made it to the UK with me... he's doing all right, I think.'

'You think?'

'He isn't with me just now – he will be joining soon.'

'How come? From where?'

He could hear the accusation in Melat's voice as well as surprise. He couldn't remember his childhood before Gebre was in it, and Melat probably couldn't either. 'He... found different work outside London. He wanted to stay and do that for a bit longer. Look, I'm about to run out of credit, but can I just say hello to Lemlem?' There was a pause, but he heard Melat call her name, then a fast, drumming sound.

'Uncle Yonas!' cried a tiny voice. 'I can read English now so Mama says I can come and stay with you and go to school in London!'

After hanging up, Yonas stood still for a moment, imagining them all at home, how they'd be chewing over the conversation later. Would he ever get to see them again? How would he forgive himself if the tax men came and beat Melat, or sent her to prison, all because of him?

The graffiti around the phone box walls read:

Emma n Ben 4ever
Live 4 the moment
Get Out this is my urinal

He pulled out Bin Man Joe's number and typed into the keypad. The ring trilled over and over, like a robotic bird. Just like Auntie, he was never going to answer – perhaps it was a fake number – but then:

'Hello?'

'Oh, hello!' Yonas replied. 'This is… You took me to the station.'

'Oh, *you*! Well, I never…'

'I just want to say thank you. I thought you would like to know that I found a place to live and a job.'

'Right! Well, that's fantastic – good on you.'

'Also I am calling because… I need to ask you for help one more time. Not for me, but for my friend. He might find you in the same place. I want him to know that he can come to join me.'

Silence.

'I don't have a phone yet, but there is a shopkeeper near where I'm living, he knows how to find me, so if you can pass the address to my friend – his name is Gebre – he can find me that way. I can give it to you now, if you have a pen…'

More silence. But Yonas could still hear breathing.

'It is only one more person', he added, 'and Gebre – he is a good guy. A really good guy. He is like my brother. I will be so happy if he can join me in London, and I can help him to get on his feet.'

'All right then,' Bin Man Joe said eventually, sounding unconvinced. 'I'll grab a pen. But I can't guarantee nowt, all right? Haven't seen any sign of any other chums of yours or nowt like that at all, so…'

From the scratchy sound over the line, he did seem to be writing down the address, but his goodbye after that was swift and gruff. Yonas couldn't help wondering if he'd only agreed to write down the address in order to get him off the phone, and had no intention of passing on any message, or giving any more random lifts to stinking, scared, illegal men. But at least he'd tried.

He walked home, hands in his pockets, staring at the tessellating pavement slabs. Would Gebre ever leave the factory? Would Osman ever be well enough? He should report Aziz to the police, now, today, for their own good... But then, Gebre was right: there was no obvious way to do that anonymously and not get arrested. And even if he managed it, Gebre had chosen to stay there, of his own free will, so what gave Yonas the right to expose him?

As he got settled in the warehouse, and came to know the others living there, he concluded he'd been incredibly lucky that it was Emil he'd bumped into and got as his mentor. The Russian guys were grumpy alcoholics who never washed their sheets, the Ivorian and Nigerian guys boasted and bickered, the Indian guys sneered and kept to themselves. Emil loathed the warehouse as much as any of them, but he was always on the lookout for something to laugh about, like the woman in a legal office who kept a vibrator in her desk drawer tucked under a book about the morality of law, and the overweight guy leaving the gym as they were starting their clean and wolfing two chocolate bars in the space of thirty seconds, then phoning his girlfriend and saying he was just going to grab a salad after his workout and then he'd be home, and the bus driver who kept overtaking other buses as if he were a bitter Formula One reject.

Yonas was glad, though, that Emil's joker mask had slipped on that first day, when he divulged his secret. Although he wanted it kept quiet in the warehouse, Emil genuinely seemed to anticipate a future in which he would live here openly as a gay man. And why not, if it was legal? Yonas had responded with assiduous nonchalance, as if people he'd just met came out to him all the time, while silently marvelling and wishing he could introduce Emil to Gebre straight away – but, he hoped, it wouldn't be long until his friend arrived.

The novelty of riding on a comfortable bus soon wore off, and the freedom to choose meals became less miraculous when all Yonas could afford or be bothered with was cheap pasta interspersed with greasy McDonald's, and when his days were defined by endless bottles of bleach and sprays and mops and dirty coffee cups and toilets and loo roll holders.

He didn't mind the tediousness of the work particularly – it beat the factory, and at least it was paid – but he minded how short a distance the money could stretch. The amount he had left over at the end of a week to wire home to Melat was pitiful, and the prospect of saving enough to pay for a place to live, with a bedroom to himself, a kitchen with more than one hotplate and a bathroom between twenty guys, and clothes that suited him better than the two clown-like outfits he'd got from the charity shop, never mind obtaining a visa, all seemed as remote as a trip to the moon. He couldn't risk part-time work, but he kept looking out for other full-time options, asking people in small cafés or restaurants about jobs. He got mildly excited about the prospect of teaching English in the dodgy language school above a corner shop, where they didn't seem bothered about visas, but even the few employers like that who offered him something there couldn't pay enough for him to rent a room, eat and send any money home.

Months passed, a biting cold set in, and there was no word from Bin Man Joe or Gebre. One day, when Yonas was walking home from work, a thin drizzle intensified into icy rain that needled his face and, looking around for a doorway to shelter in, he spotted a sign saying 'Public Library' above an old red-brick building. He walked up the steps and into a warm, brightly lit room.

Moving slowly among the rows of multicoloured spines, exuding words and ideas in such a calm, quiet space, felt exciting, but also unexpectedly emotional, wondrous, spiritual almost – the way Yonas remembered feeling as a little boy in the Orthodox church at Christmas, when the singing died down and there was a sense of people together, reflecting, being quiet. He spotted the fiction section, went over to A, and pulled out *Arrow of God*. He'd first read Achebe's first book, *Things Fall Apart* when he was about fifteen, under instructions from his father who had handed it to him while giving him a lecture about colonization, and he'd never read this one. Keeping hold of it in his left hand, he ran his right finger along shelves, pulling out books at random, just to flick through, to smell the sweet, musty paper and skim-read each back cover, remembering the library in the university back home, the hours he'd spent there in the fond belief that the political tensions would work themselves out, that his degree would lead him to an interesting career as a writer, maybe a professor down the line, that he'd be able to go home peacefully after work each night and choose some bedtime stories to read aloud to his children... He thought back to all the books he had got excited about as a student, the reading group he'd set up, the debates about realism and modernism, and how to get past the socialist, realist, moralist diet of the older generation, and how he'd got the group to read Orwell's *1984* and Kafka's *The Trial* way before they became a reality. He felt like reading them again now, in retrospect, and started to move towards O... but then stopped. It would feel too close to home. And he didn't want to look back, not now, not yet. He wanted to read some new things, books that would somehow point him to the future.

He browsed through non-fiction, history, cooking, travel and something called self-help. He pulled out a book called *Fat and Fed-Up? How to lose weight and charm people*, and imagined showing it to Gebre: *This is perfect for you! Haha...* Then he saw a law section, spotted *Asylum and Refugee Law Handbook*, and pulled it out eagerly. He lugged his pile to a table and sat down.

He opened the asylum book first, keen to read more about whether you could make a claim so late after an illegal arrival. But the writing was nearly impenetrable... and then the flyleaf revealed that it was nine years out of date anyway.

'The library is closing in fifteen minutes,' an announcement sounded.

Yonas turned around to see the librarian's desk. It looked as if people just presented a small card to her, and she scanned their books with a machine before they took them. No payments, apparently. He mustered the confidence to go up and ask if he could get a card, but a wispy-haired woman got to the desk first.

'I'd like to request that the library stocks *my* book please,' she said. 'Yes, the book I authored. I can give you the details, I've written them down here. But you'd have to buy it from me, not a bookshop, or a publisher or anything – it's self-published? It's kind of a self-help memoir? It's about the way I came to terms with not being in a relationship by bonding better with my dog – he's a Schnauzer, you know? – and all the techniques I invented like nurture grooming, and my own dog food treat recipes? So it's just in paper form now, like, A4 printouts, but I thought maybe you'd have a machine to bind it so it would look like a real book, and I'm sure you'd want to cultivate local writers…'

Yonas was starting to wonder whether libraries in the UK really were publishers too, and could commission local people to write crazy books on a whim, when the librarian gently started to persuade the woman that this was not possible. He was sure the conversation was concluding, when an elderly lady shuffled up at high speed, panting, and took the next turn, ahead of him.

'Hello, love,' she said to the librarian, 'now, here, let me get these out of my bag, I must remember to return them before I go, or I'll take them home again and be fined, when I brought them in specially… Excuse me? I just borrowed these? These ones? You're sure? Goodness, really? How do you know? My son stopped me returning them? Well, I think you're mistaken, I mean, they're my books, and I'm sure I don't know…'

An overweight man with greasy black hair joined her. 'Mum, you literally just got these out,' he said. 'I returned your old books when we first arrived, don't you remember?'

'What are you talking about, Roger? I don't recall you doing anything of the sort. I'm sure I've read these…'

Yonas wondered how Grandmother was doing, and whether she would even recognize him, in the unlikely event she got to see him again. Finally, the man manoeuvred his mother off, and it was his turn.

'Oh yes, getting a library card is very straightforward,' the librarian told him, with a smiling voice like warm caramel. 'All you need to do is bring in proof of your address, like a utility or council tax bill, and ID. A passport or driving licence is fine. And then you'll be all set! Meanwhile, feel free to browse – but we are about to close for today.'

Yonas nodded and smiled back – until he'd turned away. *Straightforward.* So much for borrowing books. Walking despondently towards his table, he noticed a cluster of computers in the corner of the room, with a FREE INTERNET sign behind them. Free internet! At least he could look up jobs here next time, or classes, or what was happening back home, or in the diaspora… A wave of new possibilities seemed to rise up in front of him, as if he could leap on and coast them with a surfboard. He went over to a computer, and his fingers jumped on the keys. But the screen instructed him to enter his library pass number.

Back at his pile of books, he sat down again and glanced around. 'The library is now closing,' the announcement sounded. 'Please make your way to the exit.' People were gathering their things. Nobody was looking his way. He rested his bag on his lap, then slipped four books inside. Checked right and left. The librarian was immersed in typing something. He got up and walked towards the door, reaching it at the same time as two teenage girls. All three were passing through when an alarm screeched. Yonas kept on walking, not varying his pace, heart racing.

He appeared to be the first person anyone at the warehouse had ever met who'd entered a public library in the UK or read a book in English, and these facts alone earned him the nickname Professor, which he knew Gebre would find hilarious when he arrived. He began returning to the library every week, more often if he had the time, and soon mastered the art of passing a book around the barrier to avoid the alarm. It wasn't as if it were stealing: he'd bring them back just like everyone who happened to be eligible for a card. The library came to seem to him like a beacon, like a symbol of all the different ways people could feel, live and think about the world, how everybody could be welcomed for free into a space, whoever they were, whatever they were interested in, however educated they were – just how the UK was supposed to be. And besides, it was good just to have a warm place to sit that wasn't the warehouse, where he could eat his own food.

The library was closed over Christmas and into the New Year. Several of the guys saved up and spent New Year's Eve out in the local pub or with friends, but most of them stayed in to watch the fireworks on TV. After Yonas had tried to cook an English Christmas dinner and almost blown the place up in the process he'd expected to be an outcast, but somehow a new camaraderie had emerged instead, and it was nice to sit down together to watch the old year roll out as the new one rolled in.

There was a big concert on the bank of the Thames opposite the Houses of Parliament, with thousands of excited people jammed on the riverbank to watch, and the display was spectacular, the fireworks shooting out of the London Eye, which was itself changing colour from blue to pink to gold. Yonas couldn't believe the opulence, the scale, how many formations and colours lit up the black sky: flamingo cascades, white carnations, fizzing sparklers, rising green rockets like giant reeds, fans of gold raining down and transforming the sky into an extravaganza of dancing light… But the sound of the explosions, the bangs, crackles, spits, whistles, even through the tinny speakers, gave him the shivers. He could almost smell the gunpowder, feel the blasts shaking the ground beneath him, ricocheting around him, and he found himself rubbing his scarred fingers together hard and chewing on his knuckles and had to focus determinedly on the screen so he remembered where he was, that it was just for fun, that this was the UK… And then the finale, the most intense bombardment of all, like a fleet of bombers overhead spewing out their entire arsenal, seeming to set the whole river ablaze… followed by a final flash of ice-blue light, and dark copper sputterings.

When they turned off the TV to go to bed, the warehouse felt suddenly more eerie, more silent, and less homely than it had done an hour earlier, when it hadn't been so obvious how many Londoners had so much more to shout about, or that for most of them the sounds of explosions and the smell of gunpowder signified only celebration.

On New Year's morning, Yonas went for a walk by himself. He meant to think about what he should do for the year ahead, what his goals should be, and how he could get himself out of this rut. But he felt drained of energy and inspiration. He was disconsolately focusing on his feet and the pavement when something cold brushed his face. He stopped and looked up. The air was swimming with white flecks. He stretched out his hand, and a crystalline shape landed on his palm and dissolved. It was the most strange, otherworldly thing, like a host of tiny spirits silently drifting in the air. He waited for the ground to turn white like it did in the pictures, but the flakes just seemed to vanish as they landed. Was

Gebre experiencing the same thing back at the factory, standing out in the yard perhaps, watching the slow, magical swirl, and making his own resolution to leave as soon as possible?

Back at the warehouse, Yonas changed out of his damp clothes, put the kettle on and pulled out yesterday's paper.

**Stowaway shambles: asylum seeker who keeps
trying to return to Morocco sues Britain for STOPPING him**

He tore it out. This was the first one he'd come across where an asylum seeker was attempting to leave and being *stopped*. That seemed crazy. He took his cup of tea to his mattress, pulled out the bag containing his collection, and laid all his articles out on the sheet. He'd amassed quite a lot now. On a rough tally, about 80 per cent were complaints about asylum seekers who were criminals or liars or money-grabbers living in fancy houses courtesy of the taxpayer, but most of the time it seemed the asylum seekers being complained about were still allowed to stay. He wondered how much truth there was in all this, and how unusual these scenarios were. Was he wrong to assume it was too late for him to claim asylum? If he risked it, could he get himself a house, even a flat with more than one room, could he bring Melat and Lemlem and Sheshy over to live with him, and even Grandmother if she could handle the journey, and put up Gebre and Osman when they made it to London? Almost inconceivable. But if he didn't try, he could well still be stuck here in the warehouse in a year's time, without any of them.

A burnt toast smell was wafting through from the kitchen. Yonas went in to find Histoire slathering two slices with peanut butter and jam, and Michel cracking open a bottle of cola. Both of them were from the Ivory Coast – surely they must have stories.

'Hi, guys,' Yonas said. ' Any chance of a slice?'

'Only for you, Professor,' Histoire said.

'So, I wanted to ask, did either of you claim asylum here?' He spoke as casually as he could.

'What you want to know?' Histoire asked guardedly.

'Anything you can tell me. Like, when did you claim, how you did it, what happened…'

'I wish I *never* did it,' Histoire declared, suddenly vehement. 'Thee 'ole thing, it is 'orrible. I claim at airport, when I get 'ere, like I was advise, and am told I am *lying*. But still they make me tell my story so many times more, and if I am saying *one thing* differently they say to me: Ha! This *prove* you are lying. Even after they say I was *lying* from start. And after that I am kept waiting, I cannot work, and I no get any decision for six years after. By that time I 'ad a kid with a woman living 'ere, but she 'ad leave to remain, and then I finally got the refusal. I 'ad a lawyer but they didn't give a *shit* about my kid. I start drink too much, from stress. And then she went and threw me out. And now I never see Alain at all and 'ee is five years old. Every day I am thinking about 'im. My life is gone to *merde*.'

'Sorry,' Yonas said, starting to wish he hadn't asked.

'*Et moi*, I 'ad to wait four years for them to say no,' Michel said. 'Now since five years I am 'ere illegally. My 'ole family was torture, but no one is believing me. The Home Office interview was worst experience I can imagine. I am telling you, the worst. *A fairy tale you just made up*, they said, after I say what happen to me. A *fairy tale*! I mean, what kind of person is want to make up a fairy tale like *that*? *C'est ridicule!* And now I am probably 'ave to live 'ere like animal for my 'ole life.' He gestured around at the chipped surfaces, the patched-together table, the brown-blotched concrete wall, patterned with rusty drip marks along the ceiling.

'And you?' Histoire asked Yonas. ''Ave you been refuse *aussi*?'

'I haven't claimed,' Yonas sighed. 'I think I am too late. But—'

'Do – not – bother,' Michel interrupted. 'That is my advice. Not waste your money and your effort to get treated like *sheet* and then refuse, in one letter which is like copy and paste from all the other letters from all the other fuckers who try to live their life 'ere.'

Just then Udaze, the chunky Nigerian, strode in, sniffing the air like a dog. 'Toast? Give me a slice.'

'Non,' Michel said firmly. 'You always take our stuff and never get nothing yourself.'

'Go oooon.'

'One slice, one pound.'

'What? That is extortion. We are supposed to be friends.' Noting the silent raised eyebrows, Udaze sighed heavily and fished a 50p from his pocket. 'Okay, give me two slices for this, you stingy bastards,' he said.

'Udaze,' Yonas broke in, 'have you claimed asylum?'

'Me? Of course. I got refused two years ago. But I will get there – I am just working on a new plan...' Udaze glanced at his watch. 'Okay, so today I am late – I am always late actually – but every week I go to church. One day I will choose a nice woman from there – who has British citizenship and a curvy ass – and then I will marry her and have kids. At least six kids. I am getting good vibes from one woman there at the moment. Two or three, in fact. Any one of them I might choose. And as soon as we get married, she will get pregnant, then I will just wait and watch my kids grow up to become doctors, accountants, lawyers, and then I will make a claim again. I know one guy who did that and the judge said he had family life. That is what I am going for.'

'So – your best advice is to go to church to find a woman and have six kids,' Yonas said.

'Exactly. The religious ones are more faithful, you know, not prostitutes.'

'But you 'ave been going to that Nigeria church since two years, Udaze, and you are still not married,' Michel said, smirking.

'Hmm, why could that be I wonder?' Histoire sniggered.

'I am waiting for the *right woman*,' Udaze said huffily, straightening his bulk. 'I am not going to rush into such a big thing as marriage with just any woman. I am talking about the mother to my *six kids*, you dumb asses.'

'Ahh, *that* is the reason,' Michel chuckled.

'You will be lucky to get a one-hundred-year-old virgin to marry you, Udaze,' Histoire said. 'If she see your yellow toenail and smell your breath...'

'Ehh shut up, you are just jealous. With your ugly Ivorian faces you could never satisfy a woman like a *Nigerian* man,' Udaze said, slapping an extra large lump of peanut butter on his toast and strutting out of the kitchen.

'Maybe you should go to Refugee Council anyway,' Histoire said to Yonas. 'They do English classes, and they can give you advice if you want.'

'But what if they find out I'm working illegally?' Yonas asked.

'You mean, will they reporting you? *Non!* Nice people. You can *try* there, no problem – just you can expect to go through a lot of *shit* and end up with *nothing*. But good luck to you, my friend.'

Chapter 9: Jude

'NO, I am NOT having a bath. UH.' Alec's eyebrows are downward diagonals. 'I WANT to PLAY with my TRAINS.'

You squat by the door of his bedroom, observing the apocalypse of toys with a strange detachment. It occurs to you that your son might in fact be inherently evil, that as he grows up and his voice breaks you might become physically scared of him, you might have to stand by and watch as he commits horrible crimes and injects himself with heroin and gets sent to prison… *I'm so tired,* you want to groan. *Don't you know how much effort I've made to make this evening nice for you, when I'm totally exhausted and need to work on my case? Don't you know how lucky you have it compared to thousands of asylum-seeker children?* 'Your bath is all warm and ready,' you chime instead, smiling. 'Come on now, Alec, you always love the bath once you're in it, and when you're done we can read your library books. How about the one about the hippo's bottom?'

'NO. I don't WANT to.'

You close your eyes for a moment, and remember his little face beaming with utter delight only an hour or earlier, when he'd heard your voice at the nursery door, run up to you and given you the biggest bear hug you could wish for. *Mummy!* he'd cried, his voice replete with uncomplicated love, and your heart sang. This is what toddlers do, after all. Enact insanely melodramatic mood changes just to test out their power, infuriate you with the lows, and charm you with the highs. You open your eyes.

'If you don't get in the bath right now, I'll have to take a sticker off your chart,' you tell him, gently.

'NO. Don't take a STICKER off. UH,' he shouts, picks up one of his train carriages and throws it across the room, where it slides to a clattering standstill under his play kitchen.

You stifle a laugh, and bite your cheeks. You wonder what kind of toys YK's niece, Lemlem, has back in Eritrea, and how much she would appreciate a play kitchen like Alec's. Or a train carriage. Or an Etch A Sketch. 'Well, I didn't want to, but now I'll have to take two stickers off because you threw your train,' you say, hearing your voice sound faintly petulant. 'You know we don't throw things when we're angry.'

'NO!' Alec yells at you, then starts to cry noisily.

Are toddlers actually the same everywhere? you wonder, or have you and Max managed to spoil Alec, despite your best efforts? Is it your fault he's turned into such an angry monster child? Are you the epitome of a terrible, uncommitted, pandering, weak Western mum? 'Then come here, give Mummy a cuddle, and say sorry.'

'No,' he whimpers, but he's cracking.

'If you don't, I might have to blow a raspberry on your tummy,' you add slyly.

'Don't blow a raspberry on me!' he orders, delighted, and runs over for a hug. You cling to him, regretting every cross thought, and then make the rudest imaginable sound on his belly, before carrying him in fits of laughter to the bathroom.

Where is Max? He was supposed to get back home an hour ago, and now his mother is due round any minute. He'd asked her to babysit so the two of you could have a date night, for the first time in six months. The subtext: *someone needs to take action to save this relationship*. He'd left it to you to decide what to do, and, of course, you still haven't made any sort of plan for if you eventually do make it out of the flat. You'll probably end up in the pub round the corner, talking about Alec for an hour or so, then finding some trivial thing to bicker about, and it will all end in Max saying, 'You've made no effort with this date and you're obsessed with work and don't pull your weight with Alec and the chores,' and you saying, 'Well, somebody needs to earn enough for us to pay the mortgage and provide for our son.' And you happen to be helping others more needy in the process, so you frankly don't see why Max can't be more supportive of your career.

'Broom broom, look at my BIG motorboat, it's going really FAST!' Alec crows. 'Mummy, can I have my submarine? No, don't splash me!'

Is a daily bath a luxury in Eritrea too? you wonder, allowing yourself to get splashed back. Is YK living somewhere in London with a bath? Who does he have to share a bathroom with? What's he doing right now, what's he thinking? Is he worrying about his appeal? Is he counting down the days – just five now – until a person he has never met will stand up in a tribunal to tell his story and try to convince a judge that it's true? Does he dream of having a family here? Is he missing anyone back home that he hasn't mentioned in his statement – a lover, children? Does he keep in touch with them by phone or email?

Email! It occurs to you that there is an obvious missing piece of evidence you could still get... but had your solicitor gone down that avenue already and failed? You'd better check.

'Mummy, don't wash my haaaaair.'

'It needs washing today, sweetheart. But you can keep it dry in the bath tomorrow, okay? Now, tip your head back...' After rinsing, you leave Alec to play with his boats for a minute, sit on the toilet seat, pop to the hall where your rucksack is and pull out your laptop to look up the organization YK emailed—

'Mummy, come! The motorboat is broken down!'

Your son is right. You shouldn't be working now anyway. And when you've got him to bed, you need to look up somewhere for you and Max to go tonight, a last-minute table somewhere that's nice enough but not too pricey. It's been so long since you've had a date night, you can't think of a single place. Then you remember that internet search you did back in chambers: *Eritrean restaurant London*. You repeat it. Yes, there's one near Oval. That's doable. You give them a call. Max doesn't need to know it's tangentially work-related, does he?

Chapter 10: Molly

**ASYLUM SEEKER WHO PARALYSED A
PENSIONER IN CAR CRASH ESCAPES JAIL**

Ooh, well now, let me see... I think I'll have a cappuccino please. Lovely, thank you. Oh no thanks, no sugar, thank you. Thank you so much, my dear.

To be quite honest with you I still find it hard to think of him as Yonas! He was Joe to me for so long, you know. Just like I believed he was a refugee for so long. I trusted him, instinctively I suppose. Invited him to my house the day I met him! Silly old woman, you're probably thinking, just like my daughter did. But he seemed so keen to learn, and I was curious. And of course I hoped I would do a little bit of good by taking a vulnerable person under my wing, you know. I never imagined where it would go...

It all started with my retirement. I'd told everyone how much I was looking forward to it, you know, time to re-read the complete works of Joyce and Woolf and Flaubert, a free bus pass... But I wasn't ready. I'll be honest, I was terrified! You know, of getting creaky and isolated and sorry for myself... But I'd always prided myself on being positive and pragmatic, so I tried to put on a brave face. And for a month or two after I went to every exhibition I fancied the look of, and concerts and theatre,

I visited old friends – I was living the high life, you know! But I'd always come back to my house alone, and wake up alone, and I started to feel like I was just flitting about, like a moth in the dusk, mildly irritating people, and generally fading into the background. Which got me a little melancholy. I mean, I'd already been on my own for twenty years – my husband died young, and I had a baby boy who died too, but I thought I'd healed from those wounds as much as I was going to. I never expected my retirement to knock the scabs off.

I still had Nina, of course – but things between us were always a little difficult. She was her father's daughter, really. The two of them used to go off and paint together and share secret jokes. And when George died, it was like Nina changed personality overnight. In twenty-four hours she went from being this vivacious girl into a withdrawn willow, just fretting all the time, and so thin. Ate like a kitten. I tried to be supportive, I reminded her that her father would have wanted her to go out and grasp her life with both hands, but she wouldn't listen. For my part, I threw myself into my work. I taught English in a secondary school which kept me on my toes, and helped me to feel connected again, even if it was to a bunch of mouthy teenagers, most of them totally disinterested in books – but when I did get them excited about a text, oh that never failed to give me a kick! And I hoped I could demonstrate to Nina that it was possible to carry on engaging with life you know?

But the decades just raced past, and all of a sudden work was over! And it left a big gap, a chasm, really. So, one afternoon I found myself twiddling my thumbs and gazing out at the garden, and I realized how much I missed the buzz of the classroom and just that sense of being *needed*, and it was then I told myself to pull it together and find something new to do, which is how volunteering came about. A friend from my book group suggested it, actually.

Now, between you and me, it did occur to me that it might also be a neat way of making a point to my son-in-law. I'm not a vindictive sort of person, but I do disagree with his politics. I remember when Nina first introduced us – it was in her final year at Oxford, and we all went for supper. She had told me beforehand she thought her new boyfriend might be *the one*, that he was *so* intelligent and good-looking and played the piano. Well, naturally I was thrilled, especially if he was someone who could manage her anxiety. And Quentin turned up all smart and smiling and held the door open and so on; but then during the meal he kept going on and on about his debating at the Union, even slipped in that he'd been tipped to be a future Prime Minister! Honestly. I remember I glanced over at Nina, to see if this peacock display was making her uncomfortable, but she was just moon-eyed.

Afterwards I said to her gently: 'He seems very *ambitious*, dear.' I didn't want to push it – perhaps he only talked like that because he was nervous. But after meeting him a few more times, I realized that he's just somebody who enjoys the sound of his own voice. Which I have no objection to at all – unless I'm the one obliged to listen to it.

So, Quentin was a barrister for a while, but then he was picked as a candidate for the Conservative Party. I have to say I never expected to have a Tory MP in the family – it was bad enough being married to a British man in the first place! Now that's a joke, but still, it did make me feel even more distant from my daughter. It just seemed so odd to me, that *this* was the man she would choose as her mate. I mean, Nina did grow up hearing a lot of political talk from her father, but George was political in the polar opposite direction – he was a socialist! Intelligent enough to do anything he wanted, but he was always adamant that there was no shame in doing physical work for a decent wage, and he liked the fresh air and the satisfaction of making things, which is why he stayed in construction. George was the kind who'd rather have dinner in a wasps' nest than with an Etonian Tory! It's only after you've lived in the UK for a while that you realize how British people use schools to judge each other – more layers of hierarchy than a metamorphic rock. So anyway, George and I had tried to bring up Nina to think that a good society supports its less fortunate through a good state education for all and so on. And listening to Quentin go on about privatization and curbing immigration and 'benefit culture', I wanted to say: hold on a minute, look at *me*! I'm an immigrant too, even if it's only from Ireland, and I happen never to have claimed a single benefit; but I'm also a state school teacher and I knew a lot of my students were from British working-class families who *depended* on benefits, and I wouldn't have wanted those children to be without any support! But I didn't say a word, for fear of upsetting Nina. I just kept mulling quietly over a way to make my point.

And so anyway, I found myself at the Refugee Council. Upstairs there's this big open area with tables, chairs and sofas where all the clients can sit and talk, and on my first day I met this beautiful young Malian woman with an enormous, welcoming smile, who introduced herself as Fanta, and was wearing a gorgeous orange and yellow dress, true to her name and her bubbly personality, and she made me a cup of tea and introduced me to some of the staff and volunteers – and it was already just lovely to feel part of something again. I was due to be sitting in on a class, to get a sense of how it worked, but at the last minute the teacher phoned in sick, so I said I'd be happy to give it a try myself. And as it turned out, she never came back.

Now Joe – Yonas, sorry – wasn't in my class to begin with. It was a mixed adult group. The standard was supposed to be intermediate, but that proved to mean pretty weak: most of them needed very basic help with speaking English and couldn't begin to write it. I think I had a couple of Eritrean women and one other Eritrean man, and then there was an Algerian, a Gambian, a Colombian and two Zimbabwean men, a Pakistani woman and an Indian woman. Quite a mix! So I asked them to introduce themselves and tell me one thing about their life that nobody else would know. And a few of them rolled their eyes, and the first two shook their heads and point-blank refused, and I thought, *oh dear.* But then Pablo told me how he had run away and sneaked on board a ship when he was just fifteen, and Padma said she used to be a professional singer, and Chido said he tried out for the national football team but didn't get in – I mean, *fascinating* things started coming out!

Once they'd relaxed a bit, I tried to improvise a comprehension class, but only Padma and Millicent engaged before Bandele put up his hand and said, apropos of nothing, that he'd bought some furniture from a company on credit which had broken and he wanted to return it but they wouldn't let him and they were charging interest, and could I help? He pulled out a huge bundle of letters from his bag, held together with an elastic band, and I said, well, of course I'd like to help him if I could but that I couldn't really do it in class time. But then Padma said could I help her understand a letter she'd got from her son's school? And Rabah piped up – could I help explain his solicitor's letter? And so on. I didn't have the heart to refuse. So my class ended up involving a vocab lesson for the first half-hour, and then a problem-sharing session for the second half-hour, followed by about three hours after class helping people individually with some issue or other.

So anyway, one day Joe – Yonas, sorry – turned up, and he stood out by miles. He's a striking young man – skin like milky coffee, and tall with lovely big eyes and lashes like we used to stick on our lids back in the sixties (and lose most of our natural ones, ripping them off again). He looked bored stiff for the lesson, but afterwards he came up to me and confided in very good English that he had hoped it would be a *literature* class, and did I know of anywhere he could study that! Well, I said of course I'd be happy to look into it, and when I mentioned I used to be a literature teacher myself, his eyes lit up.

The first time he came over he looked rather in awe, and it was a bit embarrassing – you know, realizing the home you've always thought of as a very ordinary house on an ordinary street seems unutterably grand through someone else's eyes. He beelined for my bookshelves, then he inspected my ornaments and photographs, and asked where my paintings were from… and that did make me feel momentarily anxious. But I decided he was just curious.

He accepted a cup of tea, so I made a pot of Barry's. I put out a little bowl of sugar, and he took four heaped spoonfuls, nearly finishing the lot, and drained his cup in seconds! I poured him another and put out some biscuits, and he ate the whole dish. I offered him some fruit, an apple and a banana, and he devoured both. I remember I asked if they had apples and bananas in Eritrea, which was clearly a silly question because he laughed and said 'yes'. But then when I asked him tentatively if he still had family living there, he went serious again and just said 'some'.

So I went ahead with the lesson, and fortunately as soon as he started talking about books he became much more animated. 'Now, Joe,' I said, 'tell me, I'd love to know – what's your favourite book? What single book would you take with you to a desert island if you had to...' And then I trailed off. I mean, how silly of me – of course, for him, that's effectively where he'd ended up, in a sense, and he probably hadn't even been able to bring one single book with him from home! He said it was hard to choose, but for an English-language book, he would probably take *To Kill A Mockingbird*, because his father liked it; his father was a playwright, apparently, but as a young man he'd studied law in America, and he always told his son how this novel by a white woman who lived in a small town in Alabama somehow still managed to say a lot about the kinds of human values that a free Eritrea should be all about. Then Joe – sorry, Yonas – went quiet again. I asked if he was okay. He said that even though Eritrea got the independence his father fought for, they had ended up with a flag only, not real freedom. I told him I was sure he wasn't the only young Eritrean who wanted his country to get better, and surely things would improve in time. And he gave me this polite, acknowledging kind of look, which I could tell was masking him thinking: *you don't know what you're talking about.*

So I told him I'd love to learn a bit about Eritrean literature, and was there a writer he'd recommend me to start with? Well, he said that not that much was translated, and a lot was poor quality, but that there was a strong oral literary culture. And then he modestly mentioned his *university* dissertation on – now, what was it – yes, how a British colonial newspaper had sowed the seeds for their national printed literature and how quickly it had developed a life of its own. Nowadays, most Eritrean novels were quite didactic, he said, but there was one brilliant writer he'd love to translate some day, who did interesting things with form as well as ideas, and he'd actually wanted to write his dissertation about this writer but wasn't allowed – too controversial, apparently. What was the name now? It's on the tip of my tongue. . . Anyway, I started to wonder if I should encourage Joe – sorry, Yonas – to apply for a scholarship to do a Master's here in the UK, but time was getting on, so I invited him to pick something from my shelf to read before we met again.

He had a gander, then pulled out *Pride and Prejudice*. 'I've heard of this,' he said. Funnily enough, as I told him, that book made a real impact on me as a young girl stuck in the Irish peat bogs, for the very reason that the society in it seemed as foreign to me as Eritrea, almost, but even so, Lizzie felt to me as if she *were* me, just transplanted back in time. Which surprised Joe – sorry, Yonas – he'd assumed I was English! Hadn't picked up on my accent. 'When did you arrive?' he asked.

'Well,' I said, 'I actually came for the first time to protest, after Bloody Sunday – that was a terrible day during the Troubles in Ireland, when the British army slaughtered a lot of defenceless people who were peacefully protesting about internment – but then I stayed a bit longer, and found myself falling in love with a British man, despite myself. Ironic, really!'

He was so surprised to hear that people had been interred by a British government so close by. And he asked me more about what it was like for me, back then, being in London for the first time. I told him a bit about it, and that seemed a good way in to ask him gently how he ended up over here. He said it was a kind of protest for him too. He was so angry about the regime and its censorship that he sneaked into internet cafés to write articles about the situation to send to foreign countries, and they threw him in prison!

My jaw dropped, then, literally. It just felt unbelievable, to be sitting there in my cosy kitchen in London talking about writing with a man who'd risked so much to write. I found it so hard to imagine this quiet, polite student, who wanted to read *Pride and Prejudice*, languishing in prison in a place like that. My skin crawled to think what he must have gone through.

Now, I hadn't told Quentin anything yet about J – Yonas. But I thought perhaps if he actually *met* somebody like *this*, he might reconsider some of his assumptions about asylum seekers. But then I thought how... Yonas (I'll get there in the end!) must come across to people like Quentin. And to prospective employers. Scruffy, would probably be the first thing. I offered to give him some money for new shoes, and even a set of clothes, but he refused. Said he didn't need charity. But I did persuade him to do some jobs for me. He turned out to be a whizz at carpentry and he built me shelves and things using George's old toolbox. And then I let slip about him to Nina.

She immediately started nagging me to check his ID – she said I *had* to if he was working for me, and issued all these dark warnings that he could be dangerous and could take advantage of me and steal things. And she foresaw *catastrophe* with Quentin's election campaign because he was so focused on immigration, and if it came out that I'd employed an illegal immigrant he'd look like a hypocrite and be pummelled by the media and so on. 'Look, darling,' I said, 'I appreciate your concern, but Joe is a very talented and intelligent refugee writer, and he's had a terrible time of it, so books are a solace for him, and I'm certainly not going to deny a student like that with a hunger to learn.' And she said her point was that I shouldn't be *paying* him. And I said, 'Well, I've used *my* judgement here, and I'm afraid you're being over-anxious and fretting unnecessarily, as usual.' But I put my foot in it with that, and she hung up on me. Of course, that was before she'd met Yonas herself – but I expect she'll tell you all about that when you meet her, won't she?

Chapter 11: Yonas

Yonas shifted from foot to foot at the bus stop. The charcoal sky was tinted orange from the city's lights, and he felt a sudden craving for real darkness. Darkness was the worst and the best thing about the desert flight after their prison break: it had made them stumble blindly over rocks and into acacia thorns that shredded their skin, but it had also revealed the breathtaking splendour of that bejewelled panoply of stars, spread across the velvety blackness above their heads. Here, every last star was smothered by luminous smog. *Come on, bus.*

It had been a long day of cleaning, and he had been up most of the previous night too, moving the contents of an office block from Borough to Mudchute – loading a van with printers as heavy as cars, shelves of files and personal bits and pieces. On one desk, Yonas had found a long chain of silver-framed family photographs, a cluster of blond children framed by ski slopes and swimming pools and restaurant tables, their faces bronzed, beaming, oozing delight, and couldn't help sitting down for a few moments to gaze at them. Now his muscles were shivering with fatigue, and he sat down on the bus stop bench, but it was too thin and slippery to lean back on comfortably.

At least he had a lesson with Molly to look forward to in a few days.

Being welcomed into her house with its polished wooden floors, soft carpets and an unlimited supply of tea was surreally pleasurable. It felt so good to be in a proper home. The kitchen, with its shiny pots and pans arranged in neat rows, reminded him of his family's back in Asmara, complete with his grandfather's shelving unit with hooks for the pots and pans, his scalloped dresser for crockery, and the best thing of all, the huge walnut kitchen table, twice as big as Molly's, with its half-moon feet, at which Yonas had spent so many hours eating, drinking, doing homework, reading, singing, drawing, helping to feed the twins, bickering with Melat… After their parents were gone, that kitchen table seemed to retain a residue of all those times.

'Do you have children?' he'd asked Molly one day, and she'd said yes – one still alive. Her first had died when he was a tiny baby, but her daughter was all grown up now and had a daughter of her own. There was a sadness in her voice as she told him this. He'd guessed they didn't see each other much. Perhaps that was why Molly was helping him, he thought: she was just lonely.

The red, reassuring face of the bus finally trundled around the corner. Yonas climbed on, fell heavily on the back seat and lolled his head against the back cushion. He wished he could lie across the seats for a nap, but it would draw unnecessary attention. A bunch of teenage boys got on at the next stop, wearing hoodies and blaring tinny music from their mobile phones, and a drunken couple began making out on the seat in front. He closed his eyes.

He awoke to the driver shaking his shoulder, and a crick in his neck. 'Final stop, mate.'

When he finally made it back to the cut-through passage to the ware-house, craving his pillow, he stopped at the sound of running footsteps. Pressed himself against the fence. But as the footsteps got nearer he recognized Emil with Udaze.

'Hi!' he called out, relieved, but Emil stopped, peering about in panic. 'Hey, it's just me, Joe – what's going on?'

'Police,' Emil hissed.

'Let's go,' Udaze said, and carried on running.

'What? Where?' Yonas asked Emil.

'Raid – warehouse – any fucking minute now.'

'What? How do you know? Where are you going? Can you wait? I've got all my things there.'

'Everyone has gone already, got to get out, I'm heading south.'

Yonas's mind raced. 'But my things…' He sounded like Gebre that day. At least he had his rooster in his pocket. And his other *things* didn't add up to much – his diary and workbook, his spare clothes and towel and blanket. But he couldn't afford new clothes, his workbook represented all the progress he had made, and the diary was definitely not for the eyes of anybody else. Especially not the police. It was full of clues. They would use it track him down, and Molly too… 'No, I've got to go back,' he said.

'Seriously,' Emil said, 'what stuff can you have that's so important? Oh yeah, your precious library books! I'm sure police will return them for you and pay your fines. Anyway look, I gotta go. I'm staying with a friend – I can write phone number down for you, if you want, but you might as well come. Sure? You're crazy. Gimme your hand.' He pulled out a ballpoint pen and scrawled. 'Good luck, Professor, okay?' He ran off along the alleyway.

Yonas carried on nervously, and turned onto the warehouse road, wondering if he was being foolish, but there were no police cars there yet – or not that he could see. He went up to the entrance, stood behind the gatepost and looked through. All was dark. Was there really going to be a raid? But why else would Emil and Udaze have left like that? His heart thumped as he remembered the internet café doors being kicked open, the stocky policeman grabbing his arms and pulling them behind his back.

He decided to enter the warehouse by the side window, just in case, and trod softly along the edge of the yard. A clatter made him jump, but it was just a discarded Coke can. He stopped. Nothing moved. He carried on to the window, pushed it open and clambered in. As he swung his legs down inside he caught his shin on the corner of the darkened table and smothered a yelp. He limped along the corridor and up the stairs to the sleeping room. He could see in the gritty half-light that most of the guys had taken their stuff already: sleeping mats, bags – even those M&S lingerie posters that Boris had taped to the wall. Only rubbish was left: an old McDonald's box, a ripped plastic bag, an empty cigarette packet. He grabbed his cloth bag, shoved his other bits and pieces inside, and put his blanket, towel and clothes in a bin bag. He'd have to leave the books behind.

He was about to leave the way he'd come in when he heard a car approaching. It was a dark colour... did it have a light on top? He u-turned, shoved the stiff back door with all his weight which made a horrible scraping noise as it opened, lobbed the bags over the back fence, then scrambled up, rattling and jingling like a tambourine. The wire spokes at the top stabbed into his sweaty hands, and he lost his grip, falling to the ground on the other side, winding himself. He recovered his breath, staggered to his feet, and sprinted through the industrial estate.

Out on the other side, he slowed down, panting, then found a phone box and called the number Emil had written on his arm. No answer. He hung up the receiver and retrieved his coin. So, here he was, alone again. Homeless again. It felt like he'd just struggled up a muddy slope, only to slide right back to the bottom. Except he did have Molly's house to go to now... but it was too late to knock on her door unannounced. On the other hand, she was kind, and he was so tired at this point, his bone marrow seemed to be dissolving. He would try it, he decided, and headed for a bus stop.

It didn't take long for a bus to arrive, and the cosy, bright interior was mildly comforting. Drops began to patter against the windows, making slanted patterns. After he got off at Molly's stop, one of two women walking ahead of him popped open an umbrella festooned with flamingos, and they linked arms underneath. Yonas felt a pang for Gebre that made him wish momentarily that he hadn't left the factory. But he reminded himself what it was really like there. And that there was no point in regrets.

When he got to Molly's driveway, the lights in her house were off. Typical. He walked slowly up to her doorstep and the porch lights flicked on, making him start. He sat down. The rain was slowing now, and the tiny droplets danced in the air. After a while it ceased, inky cloud blotches separated and drifted into fragments, and a fingernail moon floated above the rooftops. Lights were on in other houses, illuminating couples curling up together in front of the TV, drinking wine, eating dinner, washing up. A fox slunk across the front corner of Molly's garden. Yonas wasn't sure whether or not those things were dangerous, but he'd often seen them prowling around with light feet and dipped shoulders as if their very existence were illicit too. He pulled his wooden rooster out of his pocket and looked into its beaky face. *I'm right to have come, aren't I?* And then her car crackled into the drive.

He sat up. *Had she got a new car?* The door opened, and the slim silhouette of a woman in tight trousers got out. He froze. *Not Molly.*

She was peering into her handbag, fumbling for something. Had she got the wrong house? Had he? He opened and closed his mouth like a gasping fish. There was no way he could get out of here without the woman noticing, screaming for help, calling the police… As she reached the steps, she finally lifted her head. Stuck for other options, he just grinned inanely.

'What the…? Who are you?' She sounded as shocked as he'd predicted, but her voice had a wavery quality, as if she'd been crying. A mess of burnt orange hair framed a peaky face. She was short – barely up to his shoulder.

Yonas recognized her now, from Molly's photos. 'Oh! You are Nina, right? I just came to see your mother. I am her student.' As he spoke, he steeled himself; from a phone conversation he'd overheard, he was pretty sure Nina didn't think her mother should be having him around, student or not. And her husband certainly wouldn't think so; Molly had told him all about her son-in-law's political campaign in a less than approving tone.

Nina took a step back, as if he still might be preparing to lunge at her with a knife, and Yonas found himself leaning back too, in an attempt to demonstrate that he was unthreatening. He smiled. 'I just arrived,' he said, trying to sound chatty. 'I thought Molly would return soon.' A birdcall shrilled from a tree, even though it was dark. The strange ways that nature got twisted by this sleepless city.

Nina was still staring at him, wide-eyed, and he could hear her breathing, fast and shallow.

'I do not want to concern you,' he said. 'I can leave now, if you like...'

'It's okay,' Nina said cautiously. 'She's told me about you. I just wasn't expecting... how come you're here this late?'

'I am sorry about that. I have never come to your mother's house before without an invitation, but I just needed her advice. I have a kind of emergency.'

'What kind?'

'I have been. . . evicted.'

'Oh no. Why?'

'Because – because police found out that some people living in my place were working illegally.'

'Right. Including you?'

He didn't answer. Should he be honest? He suspected Molly assumed he was a refugee or a registered asylum seeker, but she had never asked.

'Look,' Nina said, 'I'm sorry to hear about your situation, but were you hoping you could stay *here* or something? I mean, my mum lives on her own so I don't think... and she's not even in.' Her voice cracked a little.

'No, no,' he said. 'I was just hoping for some advice from your mother on where I could go – she is very kind to me and she works at the Refugee Council so I thought...'

'Oh, sure, I see. They don't have an out-of-hours advice line?'

'Not that I know about.'

'Hmm. I would let you in and check for myself but I went and forgot the spare keys.' Her voice cracked again. She cleared her throat. 'Let me just check one more time.' She rooted around in her handbag for a few more seconds. Yonas waited. 'Oh,' Nina groaned, giving up and clutching her hair with one hand. 'I can't believe she's not here! I could do with her advice too, as it happens.'

'Are you okay?' he asked.

'Yeah, I'm fine, I'm just... well, no, not really...' Her voice dissolved into a sob, and she sat down on the doorstep and covered her face with her palms. Her hair tumbled around her hands. He wondered what it felt like to touch such shiny hair, imagined the fiery colour of it translating into heat, burning his skin. Her back was shaking a little. She was so skinny, he could see her ribs protruding. He hesitated, then sat down next to her.

'What happened?' he asked, after a bit.

'Oh, nothing, I'm just having a bad...' She wiped her face, then looked up at him briefly, and forced a quick smile. A smear of mascara ran down from her left eye. Her eyes were the colour of the moss that grew around the factory fence. She looked up at the night sky, and sighed jerkily. 'I just found out that... my husband is having an affair. God, that's the first time I've said it out loud! Makes it feel real. And trite, almost. I mean, how many women must this happen to, all the time? I shouldn't have assumed it wouldn't happen to me, that I was special. But I just – we've got a child, you know, a little girl, and I can't... I don't know how I could bring her up on my own, and I can't imagine having to take her away from her father, but... Oh, I haven't even confronted him about it yet, so I'm probably getting ahead of myself. But I just can't see a way to... get past this.'

'I'm sorry,' Yonas said.

'Oh gosh, thanks, I appreciate it – but I don't know why I just splurged all that on you! You've got enough on your plate, it sounds like.'

'You just found this out?'

'Yeah. Texts from her on his phone – so many of them, and so blatant. I can't believe he didn't even bother to delete them. It's almost as if he wanted me to find them. He doesn't know I know yet. I don't know how to tell him and not go to pieces. '

'It must be a difficult conversation. Especially with your daughter in the house.'

'I know. Oh, poor Clara! She doesn't deserve a broken home. Or bitter, bickering parents.'

'I am sure you did not deserve for your husband to cheat on you.'

'No! Well no, I didn't. Thank you for saying that. Oh dear. Look at us both, sitting here like lost waifs!' She laughed, and he followed suit. Her laugh was high-pitched and light, like clinking china, but oddly the same pace as his deeper one, so it sounded as if they were deliberately in sync.

Yonas stopped laughing abruptly, cleared his throat, and instinctively reached out and plucked a narrow leaf off one of Molly's potted plants. It smelled soothing, but now that he was holding it, he realized Nina was probably wondering why on earth he'd just damaged her mother's garden, and how much else he'd boldly steal from her house in plain sight.

But instead Nina said, 'Ooh, would you pick a sprig for me too, actually? Lavender is supposed to be calming, isn't it? I could do with that right now!'

A sprig… Yonas wasn't sure what that word meant. He placed his fingers at the bottom of one long stem and looked at Nina enquiringly.

'Oh, just the top part of that,' she said. 'Yes – perfect.' She took it from his fingers, brushing them with her own for a millisecond, and sniffed deeply, slowly. 'Mmm. So, since we're here, maybe you could tell me more about yourself? Mum told me you're from… Eritrea, isn't it?'

'Yes,' he said.

'That's on the east coast, right?' Then she grabbed his arm and whispered, 'Oh look, a fox!' He spotted it, sloping along by the fence, almost certainly the same one he'd seen before she turned up. 'I love foxes,' she confided. 'How they lead these secret lives right in the middle of the city, defying its order. How determinedly wild they are. Cousins of wolves. Quentin hates them though. Thinks they're vermin. Anyway, sorry, we were talking about Eritrea. How did you come to leave? I mean, if you are comfortable telling me…'

He thought about how to answer.

'Sorry,' she said. 'You don't have to.'

'It is okay, I was just going to tell you a story. A very short one.'

'Oh! Okay. Go ahead.'

'Well, God was surveying the world one day,' he said, 'and he was looking over all the mountains, valleys and seas, when he stopped and exclaimed: look at Eritrea! Why is it so green? I deliberately made that country dry and yellow. So the Angel Gabriel leaned over and whispered to him: my Lord, those are army uniforms.'

Nina laughed. 'Right. So I guess there's a war there, then? Sorry, I'm so ignorant.'

'Actually, there is no war there now. But there is no peace either. No-war-no-peace. That is what they like to call it.'

'What does that mean?'

'Good question. It basically means that every person in our country, men and women, from their last year at school until they are old and grey or until they fall down dead, has to do military service, or national service.'

'Wow. So you did too, then, I guess?'

'I was conscripted for the border war.'

'Border war with... Ethiopia?'

'Right. And after that I had to do national service.'

'And that can go on indefinitely? How's that justified?'

'*No-war-no-peace.* That justifies everything. It started after the war – the border line was actually never completely settled, so the President said that there was still a threat of invasion. That turned into a reason to abandon our constitution and our free press and militarize the whole society.'

'Wow. How long has that been going on then?'

'More than a decade.'

'Gosh. I can see why coming to the UK is tempting.'

'In the UK, if you have two cows, you sell one and buy a bull, then your herd of cows gets bigger, the economy grows, and in a few years' time you sell all your cows and you can retire in comfort on the money you have earned. Assuming that you are lucky enough to be a British citizen...'

'Indeed! Well, that's the ideal, I guess. It definitely worked like that for the baby boomers.'

'Baby boomers?'

'Post-war babies. Second World War, I mean. Not quite so easy for people in my generation, but we definitely have it easy compared to you.'

'In my country, if you have two cows the government takes both of them and puts you into the army, and if you refuse or speak out, puts you in prison or kills you.'

'Mmm. Not much incentive to be a farmer then. Sounds like one of the worst regimes in Africa, is it?'

'I think so. But different countries have different problems. If you have two cows in Somalia either you sell your milk to your neighbour at a fair price, or your neighbour will kill you and take your cows.'

'Right – dictatorship versus anarchy…'

'Exactly. Compared to China, where if you have two cows you are made to take care of them, but the government takes all the milk.'

Nina laughed. 'Yes! Communism in a nutshell.'

'As for the Italians, who used to rule my country, if a man in Italy has two cows he drinks an espresso, then looks around' – Yonas paused for effect, looking in both directions with his hand shielding his eyes – 'and he realizes he doesn't know where his cows have gone. So he decides to take a break for lunch.'

'That's hilarious! And in India, I guess, if you have two cows you worship them.'

'Right. But in Russia, if you have two cows you count them again and find you have five cows. Then you count them again and find you have forty cows. Then you count again and find you have ten cows. You decide to stop counting and have another bottle of vodka.'

Nina threw her head back and laughed. 'That's a more acute global political analysis than I've heard in a long time, and I've got a politician for a husband. Have you thought about a career in stand-up?'

'Stand-up?' Yonas got to his feet, then sat down again. 'You are telling me I can make money here by doing that?'

She giggled. 'You know, I feel better already! No wonder Mum is such a fan. Laughing is the best therapy, isn't it? I wish there was a laughter drug I could get prescribed. I saw a short doc the other day about laughter clubs which sound nuts, in a way – a huge group of people get together in a park just to laugh, which is infectious of course, and then there are laughter competitions, like who can do the best belly laugh – but maybe they're a stroke of genius. I mean, it's fair enough to feel upset when you find out your husband's had an affair. But I can't help feeling like it's my fault. I mean, I get so knotted up with anxiety sometimes I can barely leave the house, and being a mum – well, sometimes it makes me feel full to bursting with love, but other times, like today, I get in a total panic that my life is a failure and I've ruined my career and I'm a bad mother and I was never cut out for parenthood and I married the wrong man and it's no wonder my husband is fed up with me and I'm like a spider being slowly wrapped up and suffocated in its own web. But, compared to you, obviously, I still have several possible roofs over my head, and a bank account, and a family and an art studio, whereas you've just been evicted and don't even have a country to call your own. And yet you still manage to crack some jokes to make me feel better! So – thanks, I guess is what I'm trying to say, through all that ramble.' She smiled.

Yonas grinned back. 'There is no need to thank me.'

'So, the place you've been evicted from,' she said, 'had you been living there long?'

'A few months.'

'You don't have any family over here?'

He shook his head. 'I did have the phone number for an auntie, who was a friend of my mother's, but it did not work.'

'Oh, that's rubbish. So is your family back home then? Do you have kids? Or…'

'No, no – I am not married. I was going to get married, actually, but my girlfriend was killed in the border war—' He broke off abruptly. It was the first time he'd told anyone except Gebre about Sarama, and he wasn't sure why he was sharing it now, almost offhandedly, and with Nina, of all people. He imagined Sarama looking down on them now, listening in to their conversation, and swallowed. He did feel a little lighter, actually, just for having said her name aloud. Their relationship was just a fact, after all. A historical event from long ago.

'Oh no,' Nina said softly. 'How terrible. I'm so sorry.'

'It is okay.' He cleared his throat. 'My sister lives in Asmara – she looks after her daughter and our grandmother and brother. My brother lost his legs when his twin and our parents were killed. That was in the liberation war.'

'God, how awful!' Nina said. 'To lose half your family that way… and I guess your sister couldn't come with you, here? If she has to care for the others…'

He smiled bitterly. 'No, you are right, she is stuck. They are all stuck. I did not even get to say goodbye to them, because I left after I escaped from prison…'

'Wait, you were in prison? Why?'

'They caught me emailing reports out of the country, trying to tell people the truth about what was happening.'

'Oh wow, so, are you a journalist?'

'Not exactly. I am a writer. I studied literature and I even wrote plays, like my father, for my first job – but then when they brought in national service I had to do the opposite.'

'The opposite? What's the opposite of writing?'

'Stopping other people writing. They made me become a censor. And I got so angry about being made to do that, and about all the propaganda and the lies being covered up, I had to do something.'

'Brave to risk writing stuff like that. In the circumstances…'

'Brave, or stupid. But I would not do differently if I had my chance again. Maybe I would just have been more careful.'

'So – how long were you in prison?'

'About four months.'

'And how did you escape?'

'I escaped with my friend, Gebre. We could talk to each other over our cell walls. We waited to target this night-time guard, a guy who would always drink too much whisky, and we managed to trick him. When we got out, we had to run through the desert for a long distance, keeping as far away as possible from the army, from all the soldiers they would have sent to hunt us down. And then in the daytime, in the heat of the sun, we had to keep going, with no water, no food, thorns shredding our skin… It is very, very difficult to make that border crossing alive. Even if you are a man who is healthy and young like me. Many people die along the way.'

'I bet. I would have… I wouldn't even have dared to challenge the status quo in the first place, probably. It's amazing you made it – the journey after that must have been pretty risky too.'

Yonas nodded. He wondered if she had any idea. He closed his eyes and remembered that lorry journey, the sensation of being buried alive in a grave on wheels, the fetid stench poisoning all his organs, the heat melting his eyeballs in their sockets.

'So, your friend,' Nina said, 'did he make it with you all the way to the UK?'

'Yes, he…' Yonas took in a long breath of neutral air, picturing Gebre, still sitting in the factory, then huffed it out. 'He is not in London yet though. He got tied up, doing a job. I hope he will come soon. In the meantime, I need to find a place we can stay.'

'Of course. There must be a solution – I'll try to help. So, are you officially a refugee or asylum seeker, or…'

He paused. 'Not officially,' he admitted, finally. 'I hope… I mean, I did not tell Molly that I was registered, but I think she might have assumed—'

'But why not?' she interrupted.

'I know, I should have told her—'

'No no! I mean, why haven't you claimed asylum? Or is it that you've been refused already?'

'I have not been refused – I have not claimed.'

'But if you were imprisoned for writing the truth, then surely you deserve…'

He shrugged. 'Maybe, but I am too late. You are supposed to claim when you arrive, but I worked illegally. For smugglers at first, but even after that… And I know people who have been refused. I do not want to risk being deported. As soon as arrived back home I would be killed, or put in prison again. And I need to stay so I can send money home to my sister.'

He expected Nina to bristle at his mention of illegal working, perhaps to quote her husband. But she just said, 'You should definitely speak to a good lawyer at least – find out your chances. I'll research it, when we finally get inside – as well as the accommodation, which is obviously more urgent. If you like? I mean, I don't want to intrude. But… would that help?'

'Okay, sure. Thank you!' he said, surprised at her apparent change of heart – not only to sympathize, but to proactively offer to help. What would her husband think? Nina smiled at him, looking relieved, and the smile transformed her angular, elfin face. Unexpectedly, he wanted to hug her, and to be held in return. He felt the heat of her thin body radiating out, so close to him on the cold stone step. There was an awkward pause, as they looked at each other for a long moment, then both looked down, and away. Yonas was starting to get cramp in his leg, but felt he couldn't move an inch, or it would ruin a moment of… he didn't know what. And then another car drew up.

'Mum's back,' Nina said, and they both stood up.

Molly stepped out of her car, noticed them and gasped. Her keys dropped onto the gravel. Yonas dashed forward to pick them up.

'Good evening, Molly,' he said, holding them out. 'I am sorry to—'

'No no, Joe, I just didn't expect – and Nina! Have you two been introduced, then?'

'We have now. Can we come in?' Nina asked.

The next morning Yonas woke disoriented, and stared fixedly at the image of a sailing boat painted roughly in watercolour for some moments, before remembering. Yes: he'd put that picture up for Molly in the spare room, a month or so ago, and had longed for a quick lie down on this bed, but didn't think it was appropriate. Now he had slept all night in it, and it was undoubtedly the most comfortable he'd ever been in. He closed his eyes and snuggled his cheek back down into the soft pillow, its smooth pillowcase scented with fresh leaves. He must have drifted off again, because when he opened his eyes the sun was blasting through the window. He sat bolt upright, and swung his legs out of bed. Birdsong trickled in from the garden. Fresh pink towels were neatly folded on a chair. He peeked out of the bedroom door to see the bathroom door open, grabbed a towel and slipped in.

The shower was a huge walk-in space, with a shower head the size of a dinner plate that distributed the steaming water perfectly, strongly and evenly, unlike the sputtering stream of the warehouse shower which ran onto the bathroom floor and sprayed all over the toilet. There was a shower gel called Eden's Delight that contained botanical extracts like rosehip and white berry. He smothered himself in it, until every inch of his skin bubbled, and made himself get out after what felt like an acceptable ten minutes. He felt renewed, refreshed, alive – and ravenous.

Once he'd dressed, he walked down to the kitchen, hoping it wasn't rude to ask for something for breakfast. He was pleased to see that Nina was still there, her hair wet and tied up in a knot, laying out cutlery. Molly was chopping fruit.

'Good morning!' Molly sang out. 'Did you sleep well?'

They all sat down to eat together: muesli packed with nuts and raisins with fresh chopped banana and honey on top, and toast with butter and marmalade with real bits of orange, hot, sweet tea and fruit salad with berries and grapes, which they ate to peaceful waves of classical music on the radio. Yonas tried to savour every bite, knowing it was quite possible he would never enjoy any meal so much again for the rest of his life.

Nina handed him a piece of notepaper with phone numbers written on it; she said she'd already tracked down the names of a couple of places, including somewhere called the Refugee Legal Centre. 'They assured me you can get free asylum advice without being tied to anything,' she said. 'Obviously it's completely up to you if you'd like to pursue it, but Mum and I would be happy to support you if you do.'

He glanced at Molly, but she didn't show any signs of vexation. Had she suspected him of being illegal all along?

'The landline in the hall is all yours, Joe,' Molly said, as she cleared the table. 'Do try those numbers, and if nothing works out, we'll find you somewhere else, okay?'

He tried Emil's number first, and this time he got through. 'Professor!' Emil said, sounding as if he were reclining in a hammock wearing sunglasses and took calls from Yonas all the time. He said he had stayed the night at his friend Adil's place in Wandsworth, but that his friend Jean had just moved into an empty house in Brixton with five other guys, so he was moving in there later. 'I can ask if you can join if you want?'

'Yes!' Yonas said. 'Please. That sounds amazing. But… I am not sure if I understand. What happens when the owners come back?'

'Maybe they never come! Jean says house has been empty for more than six month, so that means anybody has right to live there. Until they get evicted, but that could be long time. Finder is keeper. You know what, I actually love those police for raiding warehouse, or I would not even know about this place! Only thing each person have to pay will be fifty pounds per month for bills and costs like cleaning stuff, shared food, TV. Can you believe?'

'Not really. When will you find out if I can join?'

'I will go there in a couple hours. Then I call you.'

Yonas nearly bounded back into the kitchen. 'Great news – I think I have got a place to live with a friend!' he announced. 'I might not even need to call those hostels.' Still, he was relieved when Molly insisted he stay on at her house until he was absolutely sure he'd got a bed. 'Is it okay if I make one more call?' he asked.

Back in the hall, he dialled Bin Man Joe's number. *Please pick up*, he whispered into the receiver. It rang, and rang, and rang, and rang. Then went dead. Yonas stared at Molly's leaf-patterned wallpaper. What if Gebre had decided to leave finally, had met Bin Man Joe, got the directions, followed them, and turned up at the warehouse today, to find it swarming with police? Should he go there, now, just in case? But then he'd risk getting caught, and the chance of Gebre getting there in the near future seemed minuscule. He went back into the kitchen.

'Want to help me dry?' Nina called over from the sink, where she was washing up. She handed him the dishtowel and smiled. 'Hey, I was thinking, do you need a phone?' she asked. 'I've got an old mobile in a drawer back home – basic as they come, but it works fine I think, and I never use it any more. You're welcome to it. It's pay-as-you-go.'

'Are you sure?' he asked, nearly dropping one of Molly's willow-patterned bowls. A mobile phone had seemed like a totally unobtainable luxury until now.

'Of course! I'll go back home later and dig it out for you. Look, I've got a while until I need to get Clara from nursery today, and I thought

I might go into town to an exhibition – Portrait Gallery, maybe. Mum's busy, but if you fancied joining me, you'd be welcome?'

Inside the tall, white, pristine space, moving silently behind Nina from one blown-up photograph to the next, Yonas felt like a pilgrim gazing at icons. One depicted a young woman with turquoise eyes in an emerald-green headscarf, standing by a faded mosque door, who seemed to be watching him, secretly amused, her lips pursed in a slight smile. She looked white. She must be, with those eyes. He supposed there were some white Muslims. Had this woman met a Muslim man and converted? What would that have been like? Would her parents have disowned her? He noticed she had a miniature dimple on one cheek, just like Sarama, and he remembered gently running his finger over that indentation. He bit his lip and moved on.

The next image showed a clique of Vietnamese girls in identical blue and white uniforms, one of them concentrating on typing something into a pink phone. Would Nina really give him one soon? If he could only get the number to Gebre, he could call any time. Next, a graceful old lady, with soft waves of ivory hair held back with a comb as she looked downwards at something in her lap: maybe a book or a photograph? A gang of Cossack girls at cadet school wearing camouflage and steel-capped army boots, wielding AK-47s. Two little boys on horseback at an Irish country fair, oozing excitement. About twenty child prisoners locked in a single cell in Burundi, waiting, waiting, under a dim, yellow light. He wondered how many of them were still there, still alive. It was hard to believe he and Gebre could have been in prison, still, if they hadn't broken out. So many multicoloured lives on these walls, he thought – and yet every single person was at some point just a naked, crying baby, a blank page of experience ready to be written on.

Yonas walked around the exhibition again, more quickly, taking in the contrasts, and imagining what would happen if the people in the photographs all suddenly came to life and stepped out of the frames. He glanced over at Nina, but she seemed absorbed; she obviously didn't expect to talk about it with him, at least until afterwards. He wondered what she and the other Londoners in the gallery were thinking as they processed silently around. Were they just feeling smug that their lives were so much easier than those of the people in most of the images? And how many other asylum seekers got taken around art galleries like this? If it wasn't for Nina, he would just have assumed a place like this was prohibitively expensive for someone like him. It was hard to believe that most of the gallery was totally free. If only he could tell Gebre.

'I'm so glad we did this – thanks for coming with me,' Nina said, after they'd finished, and stood on the gallery escalator, moving up past paintings of severe-looking monarchs with what looked like huge white lace frills around their necks. She followed his gaze. 'Ruffs have got to come back into fashion sometime soon,' she said. 'Scarves are so dated.'

'Those white neck things, you mean?' he asked. 'They would look good on you. You could wear them with jeans, for a more modern look.'

'Well, there's no way I'd try to bring corsets and hoop skirts back, that's for sure!' she said. 'Ruffs, though, they've got potential. But then this is London – even if I took myself to a fancy dress shop to hire one, I doubt anyone would give me a second glance! So, which photos did you like best? My favourite was that old Haitian woman totally rocking that scarlet dress with its puff sleeves and purple belt – defying the poverty around her.'

Yonas agreed that was a striking image, though he didn't see why it should be unusual for women of any age to dress vibrantly in the midst of poverty. But he supposed Molly always wore subtle grey and blue colours. Maybe all older women in the UK were expected to dress as if they were fading away into foggy air. He glanced at Nina slyly. 'I expect you looked at that picture of the teacher in the Malawian school and thought of me.'

'No, I didn't! I mean, you're from the same continent I guess, but…'

'Actually, our revolutionary school was even more basic,' he said. 'The picture of that girl with the red hair riding on a horse, you know the one I mean? She reminded me of you.'

'Oh that one! Yes, that was lovely. I wish my childhood had been all free and magical like that, riding in dappled woods. The only time I tried pony trekking it rained and I got the evil horse who bit the other horses' bums until it got to the front and then tried to throw me! Still, it was a happy enough childhood... until Dad died.'

'I am sorry,' Yonas said.

'No, no – you of all people know what that's like.'

When they got to the café at the top, Yonas glimpsed the view: a spectacular cityscape looking right across at the Houses of Parliament.

'Hang on a sec,' Nina said, 'I'm just going to pop to the loo.'

Yonas waited, transfixed by the sight of Big Ben, almost within his reach, like a toy clock. 'Can I *help* you?' a waitress said sharply, casting her eyes down to his ripped jeans and scuffed shoes. The tone with which she inflected the word *help* meant that he obviously wasn't the kind of person who deserved any from such quarters.

'I'm waiting for someone,' he said, and retreated further into the corridor until Nina returned. Following her in, he couldn't help smiling at the waitress's perplexed stare as she processed the fact that they were together.

Nina sat at a table by the window. 'I'll have a cappuccino – what about you?'

'Same, please.' Yonas gazed through the glass, trying not to seem overly excited about the imminent prospect of drinking a real coffee again. He wondered whether Quentin would get his chance to represent people in that Parliament building. It must be an amazing place to go into work every morning. He wondered if Eritrea would ever have a democracy whereby elected representatives from different political parties got to sit down and debate issues with each other. Nina couldn't be seriously considering leaving a man who worked there and befriending a broke, black, illegal, now homeless guy from a country that barely anybody here had even heard of. Pretty much the only experience they seemed to share was the death of a parent. Nina would have more in common with Gebre – at least they were both artists.

'Do you do photography, as well as painting?' he asked.

'No – well, not proper photography. Everyone is an amateur now, aren't they? Which reminds me, I'll definitely dig out my old phone for you.'

'Thank you,' he said, embarrassed, as if he'd just reminded her that he was the kind of person who had never even owned a camera, never mind a phone with a camera, if that was what she was suggesting. 'I really like your painting that is hanging in Molly's living room,' he said. 'She showed it to me the first time I went there.'

'Oh, did she? It's from my art school days. I don't really paint like that any more, but I can't persuade her to take it down! I'm glad you like it though.'

The two cappuccinos arrived, sprinkled with cocoa heart shapes. Yonas sipped his. It was hot and bitter, and almost as delicious as he'd hoped, and it reminded him sharply of his mother. He closed his eyes, to concentrate on the sensation, then opened them, fearing he would look odd. 'My friend Gebre, the one who came to the UK with me, he is an artist as well,' he said.

'Oh really? What kind?'

'A painter, also. He used to do portraits, sometimes – he would love to see this gallery. Hopefully he will come to London soon and I can show him.'

'I'm sure he will,' Nina said reassuringly, though she could have no idea.

They emerged out of the gallery into a mild, bright afternoon, with little white clouds gambolling across the sky like lambs. 'How about we ditch the Tube and walk?' Nina asked. They weaved through the masses in Covent Garden, past theatres with children lined up outside, through the hubbub of the cobbled market. An entirely gold man, skin glistening, stood stock-still while people chucked coins in a hat by his feet. A scruffy busker crooned effortlessly and strummed a guitar. A man on stilts juggled a rainbow array of balls. They wended their way through the narrow streets of Soho where Emil and his mates loved to go out, past porn shops and fancy restaurants and jazz bars, past rickshaws and clusters of early afternoon drinkers lingering outside pubs sipping beers. They crossed over Oxford Street, seething with shoppers, then strolled through some wider, grander streets, and up through Regent's Park, detouring through a rose garden and along verdant promenades. Today, Yonas decided, London was undoubtedly the most beautiful, exciting and vibrant tapestry of a city in the world.

Chapter 12: Meg

Double macchiato, please. No sugar. Actually, one sweetener.

So, I still haven't really met Yonas Kelati. I did write a piece about him, but that was before I even knew his name. Yes, that piece. I had nothing against him personally – like I said, I didn't even know him. I was just doing what I thought was the right thing. But, oh my fricking God, I don't think I've ever wished harder that a handful of words could be burned and eviscerated from the internet. Even if they made my career.

Here's how it happened. Nina, that's my best friend from school, was having a really tough time with her marriage, which I never saw coming. I thought she'd got it all sorted. I'm not married myself – never even managed a relationship for longer than six months – and, to be honest, I was pretty jealous of Nina for ages, before I realized what it was like for her.

Quentin, her husband, is super-clever, not bad looking in a clean-cut kind of way, and he's always had that sort of effervescent public schoolboy confidence and banter that's irritatingly attractive. I first met him when I came to visit Nina at Oxford, just after they'd got together. Obviously I took the mick out of his deck shoes, but secretly I thought he was a catch. He was only Nina's second boyfriend – neither of us had had much luck with boys before uni. We were called Laurel and Hardy at school – I was overweight and popping out of my school shirts, while she was so skinny her tights would go all wrinkly. We weren't exactly popular. Then when Nina's dad died, she got even more introverted, became borderline anorexic, and wanted to avoid the other kids completely, so we used to hang out together in the art room at lunchtimes, even though I had zero artistic talent (never, ever, pick me for Pictionary). But back to Quentin coming on the scene. So, he was really into politics, just like I was – I even studied it at King's – but Nina had zero interest in it. So I felt like he had more in common with me – but when Nina told me how supportive he was in helping her deal with her issues, I figured I should just get over myself and be glad for her.

Anyway, after uni finished, we both found ourselves in jobs we hated. I applied for the BBC but didn't get in and ended up doing accountancy. (It was just supposed to be a summer job, but for some reason they asked me to stay on – I've never been so well-paid or so bored in all my life!) Nina's degree was maths and philosophy; she'd always said she'd do an art foundation course after that, but instead she totally sold out and went into management consultancy. I mean, all Oxford students get swamped by bribery dinners and drinks from blue-chip firms – but it wasn't just that for Nina, it was Quentin, who told her that being an artist was a *'pipe dream'*, and convinced her she'd be happier just doing it for fun and getting a *'real job'*. And she waltzed into one of the top firms, thanks to her maths brain. Out of everyone I know, only Nina could rattle off an answer on the spot to a ridiculous question like *How many postboxes are there in London?* and draw a perfect postbox with the street scene around it at the same time. (Not that she did that, as far as I know, but she definitely could have done.) Of course, she despised the job as soon as she started it.

So a few years later they got engaged, and Nina and I went out for a drink to celebrate. She said she didn't want a big wedding and asked whether I thought she should put her foot down. I told her not to be ridiculous, just to go with the flow and enjoy the attention. We talked about the rites of passage, and where our old ambitions had gone, and drifted into the usual moaning zone about our jobs. Then she said, 'Look, if you hate accountancy so much, why not just quit? You always wanted to be a political journalist. Get an internship, or just write some freelance stuff and pitch it – give it a go before it's too late!'

And I thought, *She's right. She's bloody right!* But then I said to her, 'Well, why don't you do the same? Do that art foundation course – follow *your* dream?' I didn't think she actually would. But she did – we both did.

And Nina loved every minute of that course. I remember visiting her there, and she was all smiles, saying how she was happier than she'd been in years. She looked amazing too – she'd filled out a bit, dressed creatively and styled her hair. I wish people from school could have seen her. The ugly duckling personified. Not that she was ever ugly to me.

She did an MA the following year at the Royal Academy, and at their end-of-year show, her stuff was noticed by this big-shot collector who bought a piece of hers for way more than she'd priced it, and on the back of that she was offered a solo show – everything was going in the right direction. I remember her telling me she had no idea why she ever imagined that making companies fire people might be a better career choice than making art. The only problem was, once she was out of the cocoon of the MA, she started feeling anxious about the scrutiny that came with all the attention she was getting. Especially since her tutors had told her she had to put out this narrative about her work that characterized it as a kind of therapy for her 'severe' anxiety. Like, I remember her telling me how they expressly told her to edit her blurb to include the word 'severe'. I mean, it was the truth, in a way, but she felt like selling her work under that label diminished its value, even if it made her more money. Which I thought was rubbish; I mean, most art now is talked about as conceptual and autobiographical, right, so if you've got a distinctive personal issue to make you stand out, why not embrace it? I did get how it would make her feel self-conscious. But then she started getting really paranoid that people were watching her all the time for signs of weirdness, and I got a bit impatient with her – I mean, she was doing so well compared to her peers; that's what they were really thinking, I was sure of it.

In the meantime, I was objectively struggling. I was barely getting any commissions, and living in this tiny, shitty room in a shared house with a bunch of people I didn't like. I felt like a failure compared to Nina. But I didn't want to bring her down by talking about it. Plus I was sure I'd get my break soon enough and it would all take off for me too.

And then Nina had Clara. The birth itself didn't sound bad, relatively speaking, but after that her anxieties mushroomed. She couldn't seem to get out of the house, couldn't deal with all the shitty laundry, couldn't cope with how her own routines were all screwed up because of the baby. I mean, I'm sure it's hard for all new mums, but for someone with Nina's personality I could see it was a nightmare. She seemed to retreat completely – at least, I barely ever saw her any more. She'd had a couple of shows lined up but pulled out of them. I kept asking how she was doing, but she'd hardly ever reply, or would just send a two-word text weeks later, and there never seemed to be a good time for me to go and visit.

Obviously Quentin should have been there to support her more. But he was always working, and she didn't get much support from her mum either – they never got on all that well. When I texted Quentin to say I was worried about her, he texted back saying something like, 'your concern is noted but we're fine'. Feck off, basically. I felt really low, then: I was still going nowhere with my job, I was tutoring most evenings to make enough to pay the rent, but I couldn't bring myself to go back to accountancy just yet, so *I* really needed a friend, but my bestie had been swallowed up in a whirlpool of nappies and was being shielded by a snarky husband.

Luckily Nina got better, by the time Clara turned one, but she stayed way too thin – I had to go round and force-feed her wine and chocolate, and endure her going on about sleep routines and competitive parenting (not that she called it that), and barely ever asking how my work was going. Not that there was ever much to tell. I remember one evening like that, when Quentin's campaign was getting going, when she finally asked, and I gabbled something along the lines of 'Oh, all right, but it's so hard to get commissions, and just to be in the right place at the right time…'

When *she* said, 'So, I'm really worried. I'm pretty sure Mum is *employing* this *illegal immigrant man*, and having him round at her house when she's on her own, and not listening to reason, and Quentin's furious, because if it came out in the press his career would be shot to pieces, but she won't listen…'

'Don't stress about Quentin!' I told her. 'I mean, realistically, what journalist is going to find out?'

It wasn't long after when Nina called me and asked if I was free for a drink, which I wasn't, as I was just heading out to tutoring. I was about to hang up, when I heard a break in her voice and asked what was wrong. And she blew her nose like a trumpet down the phone and said, 'He's had an affair!' And then she cried through what sounded like rivers of snot, and I knew before she'd even told me that it was his fecking campaign manager. Alice, her name was. Pretty. And young. I'd seen her with him, giggling at every other comment he made, and nodding seriously at the next, like he was Woody Allen crossed with Socrates. In hindsight, it seemed obvious. Inevitable. Like, of *course* Quentin was just the type of egotist to abandon his wife-in-need while she was struggling to care for their child so that he could scramble after his political ambitions and have himself a bit of fun on the side.

Nina was distraught – understandably. I told her that if he didn't even have the guts to own up and apologize and promise it was over, she should just leave him, but she said she couldn't – she'd ruin Clara's life. I reminded her that my parents broke up; it happens, and what about her self-respect? But she'd got too upset to really talk. So I said I'd cancel tutoring and come and see her straight away, but she told me not to, said she would be okay – she didn't want to mess up my work – so we made a plan to meet later in the week.

So the next morning, while I was getting dressed in my pokey room, trying to drown out my housemate's morning techno rave with John Humphrys and thinking about Nina, I had a brainwave: *I* could be the one to make it come out, that story she had come up with, the one that she'd foreseen would bring Quentin down before he'd cheated on her! Now that she *wanted* his campaign to implode, it was the perfect hypocrisy scoop.

Conservative parliamentary candidate Quentin Lambourne, who has been calling for a clampdown on illegal immigration, has chosen not to mention that his mother-in-law is employing an illegal immigrant...

I could see the text in my head, as clearly as if it had already been printed! And then it was. Now look, I do know Nina's mum really well, from spending half my childhood at their house, and I never wanted to get *her* in trouble. I mean, I was never going to name her directly. But still, in hindsight it was inevitably going to be easy to identify her, so I do feel bad about that. Having said that, she shouldn't have been employing the guy illegally, right?

I can see you still think I'm a bitch. But have you tried getting into freelance journalism? It's tough, especially when you're struggling to pay the rent and you're single in your mid-thirties so you're totally priced out of the property market, and all your best friends are married with kids and houses they own and lives that revolve around a 6 p.m. dinner at home and weekends at the playground, and you try to make your single life sound way more exciting but in reality you spend all your time scouring dating sites or watching TV alone, or panicking about the biological clock, or wondering whether or not just to settle for a guy you just met and felt queasy kissing, simply because he has sperm and can probably put an Ikea flat pack together better than you... Your mummy friends tell you you're so *lucky* that you have time to focus on your career, which means your career starts to look even more crucial. And *that* means any opportunity that comes your way needs to be seized. You see what I mean? And in this case, there was public interest to think about too. But... all that aside, I *never* meant to get Molly investigated or risk my friendship with Nina. She was my best. . . God, that 'was' makes me want to cry. I honestly thought I was helping her.

So, she called me when the story came out, and she was livid. Nearly spat down the phone that I was the most selfish, duplicitous person she'd ever met and if she'd known this was how I saw our 'so-called' friendship, she would have ended it years ago. She'd never, ever, spoken to me like that before.

'I'm so, so sorry,' I told her, genuinely contrite. I should have asked her permission first. I had started drafting her an email, actually, but failed to send it. 'I thought you'd be pleased,' I said. 'You remember what you said to me about Quentin's campaign, and you said you were leaving him, so…'

'I hadn't decided whether to leave, and I didn't mean you could just go ahead and expose him, and my *mum*!' she said. But weirdly, she seemed most upset about the bloody *immigrant* guy. 'He was just trying to learn, and survive in this city,' she said. 'Mum was giving him a chance, and she was thriving on his company, then you went and blew it for both of them. How could you be so cruel?'

I mean – *what*? She didn't know the guy any more than I did, to my knowledge! And last time I heard, she'd been actively trying to persuade her mum to get rid of him. Plus, Nina had never told me she disagreed with Quentin's basic campaign message that illegal immigration was the plague of modern society. And the police almost certainly wouldn't trace the immigrant guy on the back of my article anyway, without a name or any other evidence in there. So I could *not* understand why she was so caught up on him! And then she cut me off. I couldn't believe it. I was utterly gutted.

Career-wise, it was brilliant: the paper headlined the story, and I suddenly got loads of commissions, including a spin-off piece about Quentin's rumoured affair, to which I thought: why not? It might help salvage our friendship and persuade Nina I was on her side in all this. (Risky, I know. It didn't work.) And my editor was so happy, he offered me a regular column! Of course, as soon as I'd got that, all I wanted to do was crack open a bottle of fizz with Nina.

And Quentin responded in the worst way: he published a reply in the paper accusing me of having a personal vendetta against him and his wife, who he described as a 'former' friend of mine, and pronounced everything I'd ever written to be unprofessional rubbish. He flatly denied he knew of any 'employment relationship' between his mother-in-law and the immigrant, whom he'd clearly understood was a student she'd been teaching voluntarily. He added that if he *had* known she was employing an illegal immigrant then he would have been the first to report her. (Nice, right?) And, predictably, he denied the affair as well, which he described as a 'baseless and offensive accusation', and said that the spin-off article was a prime example of 'irresponsible and reprehensible' journalism. But who wasn't going to believe he hadn't cheated on his wife with that Alice? (Who, I've got to admit, is hot.)

It wasn't long until I could afford to rent my own place, and was engrossed in my dream job (or near enough). I didn't regret shafting Quentin to get there. In fact, I felt vindicated watching him getting quizzed over it – though, surprisingly, his campaign didn't crash and burn over it like I'd imagined. All publicity is good publicity, I guess, and clearly some of his constituents liked the fact that he came out even *more* strongly against immigration in his defensive mode.

The only thing I really regretted about it all was hurting Nina. I would wake up every morning with a physical ache at losing her. I posted her and Molly cards and flowers, apologizing again, and explaining. But neither of them replied. And I didn't see or hear from Nina for months – until I spotted her, in the street, and couldn't believe my eyes.

Chapter 13: Yonas

'I WAS POSSESSED BY ANCESTRAL AFRICAN SPIRIT': ASYLUM SEEKER'S ASTONISHING DEFENCE OVER NOISE COMPLAINTS

Yonas sat on the bucket chairs of the waiting room in the Refugee Legal Centre, rubbing his fingertips together, then twisting his hands, then stilling them so as not to look nervous, then twisting them again, then rubbing his fingertips together. Was he right to have come? And to have given the receptionist his real name? It was Nina who had assured him that he wouldn't be at risk by talking to this lawyer, that his meeting would be confidential – but then she had lied to him, and exposed him in the papers, so why should he trust her? As soon as the lawyer called him in, he would ask for confirmation that the interview couldn't be used against him before going ahead. But what if the police were still trying to track him down on the back of that article – what if they asked the lawyer for information for their investigation?

Nina was a conundrum. How could she have transformed from being so prickly when they first met, to being so warm and helpful to the point of researching accommodation and lawyers for him, taking him out to a gallery, and giving him a phone, with *credit* on – only to go and inform on him to a journalist? And putting her own mother in the spotlight too… Was she unhinged? Sadist one minute, altruistic saviour the next, then back again?

He pulled the phone out of his pocket and turned it around in circles between his fingers. NOKIA. The screen was cracked, but it worked fine. He had been so incredulously grateful to receive it at the time, but now Nina's past ownership of it taunted him. The last time he saw her was back at Molly's house, when he went round to do some weeding and have a lesson. Perhaps it was the last time ever. She wasn't there when he arrived, which had irrationally disappointed him, but turned up in the afternoon with her daughter Clara in tow, a scowling little blonde girl with bright blue eyes, who refused to say hello to him and hid behind Nina's legs instead. After making a bit of small talk, Nina had pulled the phone out of her bag and handed it to him like it was a spare set of nail clippers or something – not worth even talking about, no big deal. He'd half-heartedly tried to refuse, but she'd insisted she never used it, and said she thought it might still have a pre-paid SIM card inside…

She had been interrupted by Clara yanking at her top and whining that she wanted to watch TV. Nina asked her gently to play with toys instead, to which Clara said NO. And then Molly offered to read Clara a story, to which Clara said NO, even more loudly, and instead started whacking Nina's leg, whining, 'But I WANT to watch TV!' Aren't you going to discipline her? Yonas thought, but Nina just tried yet again, quietly, and completely ineffectually, to persuade her to desist, before backing down, taking her to the living room, and switching on the TV. He tried to imagine Lemlem behaving like that, and what Melat would do in response, but he couldn't. No Eritrean child he knew would even try.

Yonas had stayed in Molly's kitchen, staring at the phone in his hand. All he had to do now was get through to Bin Man Joe and give him the number, and Gebre could contact him directly, any time. When Nina came back to the kitchen, she handed him a slip of paper with a number on that she said he could call for free whenever he needed to check how much credit there was left on the phone.

As soon as he'd said goodbye to them that day, and headed back towards the squat, he'd dialled the number to see. *You have… twenty pounds… credit remaining*, the automated woman informed him. He'd wanted to jump in the air – twenty pounds! – and then was embarrassed at himself, as it occurred to him that such a round, high number probably meant that Nina had topped it up for him deliberately. Which felt demeaning. He had never accepted money from Molly before unless he'd worked for it. But credit seemed different if it was already inside the device, and anyway, some proverb about gifts and horses was on the tip of his tongue, so he went ahead and called Melat. With all that money, he could afford to get past a functional catch-up for once, and he spent at least ten minutes telling Lemlem a story, swallowing up £7. He'd wondered if Nina had any idea how much he appreciated this, or, if not, what he could do to thank her. He tried Bin Man Joe next, but didn't get through.

Nina had been the first one to call him, a few evenings later when he was covering a cleaning job for Jean. 'Hi! How's it going?' she'd said cheerily. 'I just wondered whether you'd like to go to another exhibition with me tomorrow. It's at the Tate Modern. Quentin's taking Clara out for the day…'

He'd agreed, as casually as he could, as if he knew the place well, as if gallery trips were just what he did now. But after the call ended, as he was spraying and scrubbing the disabled toilet, he'd felt so ebullient he couldn't resist singing out loud.

Te'akeba emache weAlla
Sergaya welbasa wetgedela…

He'd got up from his knees to grab the bleach, and as he swivelled back to squirt it he couldn't stop twirling around once again, twice, three times. He strummed on an imaginary *krar*, and heard the *kebero* keeping the beat… He hadn't danced for so long, his limbs were aching for it.

Te Ande Qa wenaberit abshla
gasha biye shaym wogebayla

He increased the volume, and bobbed up and down on one leg, then the other, spinning around the cubicle, dodging the flush… He was back in his grandmother's village, it was evening, and he was watching a wide circle of dancers, each taking turns to go forward into the centre, the women crouching down low in front of the men and then rising up again, swinging their hair from side to side, and his mother – his mother standing back, then being pulled by the hand to join in, and there was a huge wave of clapping and hooting as she shook her hips and joined in line with the other women, their bodies bending together as they circled around, making spiral shapes in the dust… He imagined Nina dancing in a group of women like that, her hair flickering like a firefly. He could teach her – she would probably start off like a robot with jerky stiff hips like most white people, and maybe she would have no rhythm, but he would take her hips in his hands—

A knock on the door had interrupted him. *Excuse me. I need to use this toilet.* Yonas had scooped up his bucket and materials and walked out, avoiding the woman's gaze and trying to invert his grin. Out of the corner of his eye he could see stiff brown curls and machete eyes.

Back at the squat, he'd told Emil about Nina's text, who'd wolf-whistled and said that the Tate Modern was an awesome converted power station by the river, and that if his date wanted to go there, she must be really into him. Yonas was still grinning when he got on the bus the next morning to go and meet Nina… until he picked up a newspaper from the seat behind. He was about to tear out the headline:

PARLIAMENTARY CANDIDATE CLAIMING TO BE TOUGH ON IMMIGRATION IS HAPPY FOR FAMILY TO EMPLOY ILLEGAL HOUSEKEEPER

When his eyes flicked down to the text beneath:

Conservative parliamentary candidate Quentin Lambourne, who has been calling for a clampdown on illegal immigration, has chosen not to mention that his mother-in-law is employing an illegal immigrant…

He bit his lip, and re-read the entire article three times until he was certain it was real and undeniably about him. But, housekeeper? Had one of Molly's neighbours seen him going in, got the wrong idea and told the press? There was only about £1 worth of credit left on the phone by that point, but he decided to use it to call Nina. There was no way she could know about this, he thought, but he had to check before seeing her. He dialled, and kept his voice low, so the people in the seats around him wouldn't hear.

'Hello?' Nina answered. She had such a sweet, clear voice.

'Nina, I need to tell you urgently, I have just found a newspaper—' he began.

'Oh, I'm so, so sorry about that,' she jumped in. 'I was going to tell you when I saw you at the Tate. Shall we discuss it when we get there? I know the journalist, she's a friend of mine, but I—'

He pressed the red button to cut her off, hurt and panic surging in his belly, and pressed the bell to get off the bus at the next stop.

She knew! he said to himself, incredulous, stamping down onto the pavement and pacing furiously back in the direction he'd just come from – a totally wasted bus fare. She must have told her friend about him working for Molly. Who else could be behind it? But why on earth would Nina have sucked him into her life, only to spit him out like that? Because he meant nothing to her, that was why. He was just a distraction from her cheating husband, and now a convenient way to get back at him.

A text came through from Nina: *Please let me explain.* He switched his phone off.

'Veata will be ready for you shortly,' the receptionist told him. 'Can I get you some water?'

He shook his head. 'No thank you.' He was starting to feel nervous about the substance of this conversation now, as much as its potential consequences. The lawyer would be intimidatingly brusque, like all lawyers were. He'd be expected to talk in detail to a total stranger about the very worst things that had happened to him, to lay out on the table all the memories he'd been determinedly suppressing for so long, the blackest, festering memories that rotted in a place deep inside him, and threatened to infect his whole mind and body like gangrene if he let them out. And what if the lawyer didn't even believe him? He should never have come here. He should have disappeared as soon as he saw that article, away from the police trail, and started afresh with a job somewhere else, a new city, somewhere among a group of friendly Eritreans...

But no. He had to think further ahead. This was his best chance for a visa. For a future where he could work here legally. For Lemlem's future. And coming to see a lawyer, announcing that he wanted to make a claim and starting on the track to being legal – even just saying his real name out loud again after he'd got used to being *Joe* or *Professor* for so long – had felt surprisingly good. On the other hand, by coming here he could have just pulled the trigger to start his own race towards deportation. And, perhaps, a descent into madness. He'd tried so hard to keep everything – his past, his parents, Melat, Sarama – locked away, so he could keep focused on the future, on survival. No one he'd met so far in the UK knew anything like his whole story. Was he really ready to bare his soul to a random British lawyer now? He wished Gebre were here to talk it all through. But if this meeting went well, he could make the whole process much easier for his friend once he did arrive.

The strip lights on the ceiling glared, making the woman sitting in the opposite corner look haggard, emphasizing the pitted pallor of her cheeks. She wore a black headscarf, and she might be Iranian, Yonas thought, but he wasn't sure. He wondered what had caused her to leave her country.

He ran his palm over the tiny, hard bump of the little wooden rooster in his pocket, and remembered all those hours spent in his grandfather's workshop in Asmara as a little boy, especially once his parents began to be out more often, at secret meetings, when bad things were escalating around them that he didn't fully understand yet. That workshop was a haven. He had felt soothed by its sweet, woody smell, the peace of it, and the way lumps of wood could transform into smooth-edged stools, chairs, tables and shelves. Objects that were so solid, and had such an integral function once in use, it seemed as if they had always been there, in that form. His grandfather had tried to get him into carpentry too, but he didn't have the talent or motivation – he preferred to watch, or read on a chair in the corner or work on his scribbles. Grandfather kept up that workshop all through the war, even when Yonas's father took the family off to join the fighters. He *must* have been intimidated by the Ethiopians, but he wasn't a talker at the best of times, so kept it to himself. Nobody made better furniture, and Yonas supposed it was that skill that had saved his grandfather; even the Ethiopians needed chairs.

It wasn't long after independence when a fever confined his grandfather to bed for three weeks. He had tried to return to the workshop, but his knobbly fingers trembled like long grass, and he didn't have the strength to finish the cupboard he'd been working on. Sheshy and Tekle were always supposed to take over the carpentry business eventually, but now of course there was only one of them, and, stuck in his wheelchair, Sheshy flatly refused even to go inside the workshop. Yonas saw the pain in his grandfather's eyes, as he tried and failed to persuade his youngest grandson that it would help him to occupy his hands, that he could always get people in to help with the more physical work – but Sheshy just shook his head, stubborn. Yonas knew it was because he couldn't bear to be there without Tekle. He considered offering to do it himself, and even attempted to complete the commissioned cupboard under Grandfather's direction, sitting up with a file and sandpaper all night working on it – but under the bright morning sunlight the scalloped edging looked uneven and lumpen, like a toddler's handiwork. After Grandfather passed away in his sleep, Grandmother silently posted a FOR SALE sign up, and the workshop was promptly sold, together with all the tools and pieces inside.

'Hello there!'

Yonas looked up, shocked for a second to find himself back in a legal office, in the UK.

'Mr Kelati, isn't it? Lovely to meet you! My name is Veata. I'm your caseworker.'

He got up, and she shook his hand. She was petite with Asian features – not how he'd imagined a British lawyer to look – and she seemed friendly. Not at all intimidating.

'Would you like to follow me?'

They walked along a corridor, and Yonas's heart started to thump as he tried to predict what questions she would ask and how he would answer, tried to practise hurriedly in his head, to work out which words would be best for describing military service, or trekking through the desert, or prison… This made him feel dizzy, so that when they arrived at an office and she showed him the table at which he was to sit, he almost fell into the chair.

'Are you okay there, Mr Kelati?'

'Yes, sorry, I just…'

'Let me get you a drink of water.' She went out again and returned quickly, with a glass of water in hand, which he sipped gratefully as she opened her laptop. 'Ah!' she said. 'My computer is out of battery. Sorry, but I'd like to take notes on it while we speak. Would you mind bearing with me again please, while I go and get a cable?'

She went back down the corridor. Alone once more, he worried: had he done the right thing, giving the receptionist not only his name but the squat address, when they weren't really supposed to be there?

Jean, who was the one who'd originally found the squat, insisted it was totally legal. 'It's the law,' he said confidently; he didn't seem to know which law, but Yonas didn't press him. From the outside the house looked quite smart – old, brick-built, Victorian maybe, with curlicue carvings under the roofs, until you came closer and saw that several roof tiles were broken and the window sills were all rotting. Inside, the place had been stripped bare, exposed plank floors were covered with bits of sheet or patchy cracked lino, the only furniture was rescued from skips and wires stuck out of damp walls like patchy stubble, but it was still a house intended for human habitation, on a respectful residential street. And it was Yonas's real address now. If he was going to go down this legal track, he wanted to do it honestly, from start to finish. There was no alternative anyway; he couldn't very well give them Molly's address, not now. Molly wouldn't even want to talk to him again, never mind allow post to be sent to her. She was probably furious with herself for allowing Yonas – or Joe, as she still believed his name was – ever to cross her threshold. Probably regretted ever volunteering to teach people like him. He was sure that she, like Quentin, was now pretending that article was a complete fabrication. He hoped so. He would hate for Molly to get fined on his account.

Veata returned, plugged in her laptop, and settled in her seat, smiling. 'So, to begin with—'

Yonas interjected. 'I want to just check – is this interview confidential? If I decide not to claim, or…'

'Of course,' she said. 'I can guarantee that. You are completely safe talking to me.'

'Okay. Because I want to say that I have been working without a visa, first in a factory, then doing cleaning, and now I'm holding up a sign on the street pointing people to a Chicken Cottage – high-prestige jobs…' She laughed in surprise, apparently taken aback that he had cracked a joke – which was probably not appropriate, he reflected. 'So I would just like to know, if I claim asylum now and they find out I have been working, can I be punished?'

'No, no, don't worry about that,' she said. 'It won't exactly help your claim, but it won't invalidate it either. You're certainly not the first. But once you do proceed, you won't be able to continue working for money – are you aware of that?'

'No work at all? Okay. So, how long will the claim take? I heard it can be years.'

'It can take some time, I'm afraid. You would be unlucky if it took years, but it's possible.'

He nodded. 'And what about if you were forced to work? Does that help?'

'If you were trafficked, you mean?'

Yonas paused. Wasn't trafficking something to do with sex workers?

'For some time I was forced to work in a factory because they said we had to repay them for our journey…'

'Ah, that does sound like trafficking,' the lawyer said, 'so yes, it's definitely relevant.'

'And can I also ask you,' he said, 'if the police find out about that factory, will they punish the workers who are still there?' He thought of Gebre, sitting there, patiently shelling shrimps – how terrible it would be if he got thrown into a prison here because of his friend's big mouth.

'You think that operation is still going on?' the lawyer asked. 'Well, it's very unlikely they'll be punished, as such, if it's an abusive situation as you say.'

Yonas nodded slowly. Abusive, she'd termed it, and she didn't even know the half of it. He pictured Osman's red, devil eyes… Should he tell her about Gebre?

But Veata was talking. 'Sorry?' he asked.

'I was just saying, could you perhaps start by telling me a bit about growing up? Like, where you were born, and what your childhood was like?'

That sounded easy. But then, when Yonas thought back to his child-hood, he seemed to float on his back into a calm lake surrounded by images like leaves on the surface: the house with its high ceilings and green tiled floors; the kitchen exuding delicious smells; the paintings and masks and books; the mango tree out the back where he used to sit for hours to read in the shade while the hens clucked; the brash splashes of pink and purple bougainvillea over the side wall; the iridescent sunlight pouring through the bedroom window onto Tekle and Sheshy's identical sleeping faces; his father's happy cackle from his wicker armchair; Melat practising her dancing up and down the hallway… And then the way the knowledge crept in. The conversations overheard. The gun-toting police in the street shouting abusive words at women that he didn't even understand. The way they were forced to speak Amharic at school. That evening his father came back with a purple welt on his face and an anger burning in his eyes. That awareness that nothing was safe, even inside the apparent sanctity of their home, because they were Eritreans, and Ethiopian forces were in control.

'Everything okay?' the lawyer asked.

'Sorry,' he said. 'I was just thinking what to begin with…'

'Take your time, don't worry,' she said. 'But do try just to tell me even a few basic things if you can, like where you lived, and your family. Do you have any brothers and sisters?'

Yonas opened his mouth. He could do this. He had already talked quite a lot, in snippets to Emil, Molly and Nina, about his writing, his parents, his siblings; but now that he had to tell a lawyer everything, in detail, for the record, he couldn't help visualizing Tekle's carcass decaying under the ground, revealing his small, child's bones, or Sheshy, now a twinless man, sitting in his wheelchair next to an empty chessboard, or Melat, bathing their arthritic, grumbling grandmother, fearing another knock at the door… He took a deep breath. 'I have two siblings who are living,' he said. 'One brother was killed with my parents in the war. Our family left Asmara to fight with the EPLF – I'm not sure how much you know…'

'Yes, I've represented a few Eritreans, so I'm familiar with the basic history,' she said. 'I'm sorry to hear about your loss.'

Yonas's throat swelled, but he had to keep his emotions in check.

'So, how did they die?' the lawyer asked softly.

Yonas opened his mouth to answer. Could he compress their death into a sentence? How much of their story did this lawyer actually need for his asylum claim anyway? What did she want from him?

'Please take your time,' the lawyer said.

'Okay. So…' He took a deep breath. 'They were killed towards the end of the war – the liberation struggle. Their group was shot at by MiGs when they were travelling back from a show; my father led the Cultural Troupe. My mother sang.'

Her singing voice was probably Yonas's earliest memory, and it was the soundtrack to waking up in the Asmara house; he would come downstairs yawning, listening to it expand like a flower opening until he got into the kitchen and saw her standing by the stove making breakfast and coffee, swaying to her own rhythm.

'And where were you?'

'I was at the revolutionary school. Behind the front line.'

He remembered arriving there, at dawn, after the family had journeyed through the night from Asmara, leaving their grandparents behind, how his father had kept them buoyant by telling them story after story about brave Eritrean soldiers and glorious victories. Even when they discovered how basic the tents were, and that there was no building as such for the revolutionary school his father had raved about, no running water, and hardly any books, Yonas still felt excited – this was what being a freedom fighter for real was all about! Gebre, who'd come with them, didn't agree. He didn't complain, but went very quiet, and spent his spare time mooching around, drawing on rocks with pebbles or charcoal. Still suffering from the shock of his father's disappearance, Yonas knew, the last place he wanted to be now was in a war zone, even though the whole point of the war was to avenge people like his father.

All the children were kept busy, though. Most of their days were spent sitting cross-legged in front of the blackboard, doing lessons, and reciting revolutionary poems and songs. In the afternoons, when the heat was less fierce, they would do military exercises, and Yonas couldn't help a tingle of excitement at the feeling of holding a gun, that power between his fingers. Melat took to it too, and was soon the belle of the school. She used to accompany their songs on their mother's *krar*, and had a knack for writing songs of her own. Sheshy and Tekle kept to themselves, even more than they used to, and developed a secret language of their own that acted like an invisible wall fending off the world.

But once the novelty wore off, Yonas soon missed all the books he had at home, and grew bored with the usual teacher. Many of the other children couldn't even write. One slow afternoon he came up with a brainwave: like his father, he could put on a show himself about the Eritrean cause! Once he got the go-ahead, he ran straight to find Gebre, who was glumly drawing stick men flying out of explosions. *Good news! You can be a set designer!*

'So, what did you do when your parents and brother died?'

Yonas felt an echo in his body of the memory of hearing that news: a shudder down through his spine, a loosening of his bowels and a heaviness that came with the new understanding of what mortality really meant: that his parents and Tekle were nothing but fragile animals, just like he, Melat, Gebre and Sheshy were, and that any one of them could be extinguished for ever at any moment.

But he was supposed to be telling the lawyer about what happened. He had to focus on the facts. *What did you do?* she'd asked.

'I stayed with the fighters – with my sister and Gebre,' he said. 'My little brother, Sheshy, was taken to the underground hospital, and they thought he would die but he came through okay, just without his legs. So then they sent him back to Asmara, to be with my grandparents.' They had all wanted to go with Sheshy, but had been told firmly that their parents would have wanted them to stay. 'Around that time, the fighting got more intense,' Yonas said. 'I was sure we would all die also, very soon.'

He remembered the commander announcing one night that Eritrean People's Liberation Front companies were going to have to start retreating. 'This is it,' Gebre had said darkly. 'This is the point when we find out we are about to lose the war.' But, miraculously, a few weeks later they were informed that the EPLF were advancing again; the tide was turning.

It was the morning after that when Melat came to him, sobbing, and told him what the commander had done. Yonas looked up at the lawyer, who was making notes on her laptop. 'Then my sister…' he began, but as he tried to make the words come, he knew they were going to break. He had to hold it together. It had worked out okay, in the end, after all – for the time being, anyway. And if it hadn't been for that terrible day, Melat wouldn't have Lemlem. But was this relevant to his claim? Did he have to say it here, out loud?

'Yes?' the lawyer said.

'I'm sorry,' he said. 'I was just… we were close to winning the war, but then my sister was abused. I mean, she was raped. But it was a commander who did it, so we could not report it. She became pregnant, and there was a part of the hospital where fighter women had their babies, so she said she would just go there and then give the baby away… But then – we won.'

'You won? You mean, the war?'

Yonas smiled a little. 'Yes. Finally. I never really believed it would happen. The odds were so stacked against our little Eritrea. And that war had been going on my whole life. But we really won, and so we were able to go back home to Asmara, to our grandparents. I was sixteen years old.' Somehow, from being embroiled in an infinite hell, it had all happened oddly quickly. Everything his father had dreamed of for their country appeared to have come true, to be right there in front of them, as bright and light as a cascade of balloons, ready for them all to grasp at with their bare hands like excited toddlers.

'It was an amazing moment,' he told the lawyer. 'Euphoric. We were all still grieving, and Melat was still recovering, but we knew what independence would have meant to our parents. All our suffering was for that purpose. They would have wanted us to celebrate.'

And it was impossible not to. The atmosphere was infectious. Independence had come to seem like a mythic word, yet now it was here, and everyone around them exploded like a bottle of fizz that had been shaken, and shaken, and shaken; they bubbled out onto the streets, heady, incredulous, for the celebration of all celebrations. *The war is finally over! The future is bright and safe and happy for all free Eritreans!* He remembered rolling ceremonially into Asmara on the back of a tank packed with children and young fighters, part of a slow procession into a wild cacophony of ululating and screaming and dancing and laughing and singing. Every resident, old and new, rich and poor, and from every religion, was out on the streets, jubilantly welcoming the victorious troops, as the tanks honked their horns and flaunted the Eritrean flag from their cannon barrels. Hot, sultry air, vibrating with people's favourite revolutionary tunes, songs of freedom, clapping rhythms and drum beats. People waving palm leaves, flags or whatever they could get their hands on. Children and adults alike leaping, hugging, weeping with joy. Villagers from miles away descending upon the city on foot, some piling onto the tanks with the fighters.

They approached their neighbourhood, and when they finally saw their grandparents wheeling Sheshy along amid a group of other maimed martyrs, they clambered down and ran towards them, arms outstretched. As he embraced his family, Yonas felt his heart was going to fly out of his chest, a bird released from a cage.

'So, after independence, you were able to live back in Asmara for a while?' the lawyer asked.

Yonas nodded. There had been a slow let-down as normality sank in, like the balloons were gradually seeping air, as they registered the gaping absence around the kitchen table of their parents and Tekle. 'We were together again – what was left of us. We tried to get used to being a half-size family but it wasn't easy. Especially for my brother. He was trying to get used to having no twin, and no legs.'

Sheshy had been the quickest of them all to retreat into gloom. *It wasn't worth it*, he pronounced one morning. *I don't care how much better things are going to be for some people. Look at me.* And Melat, whose bump was now pronounced, began to panic about how she would look after a child on her own, with no husband or mother to help.

Yonas tried hard to keep them all positive, to remain buoyed by the new energy in the city, the fizzing plans for the future, for the new government, the new society. It wasn't hard; out on the streets, most people were still walking around with wide smiles, talking excitedly and obsessively in coffee shops and street corners about visions and possibilities and freedoms.

'Eventually my sister had her baby,' he told the lawyer. Even Sheshy had cracked a laugh at the little bright-eyed bundle with her miniature fingers and tufty mohawk. They all passed Lemlem around and gazed at her adorably crumpled face, her bright, trusting, inquisitive eyes. 'I finished school, and went to university.' He had been so eager to study, to get good grades, to prove that the revolutionary school hadn't held him back, that he could still excel and then he could go on to work as part of the new government, which was revving up, getting in gear for change, for building the future out of solid planks of law and policy, cemented by hope. The horizon glittered.

'What did you study?'

'Eritrean literature and languages,' he said. 'I graduated top of my class.'

'Great. And what did you do next?'

'I got a job working in the Department of Cultural Affairs. It was a good job, the job that I wanted – I was happy. But then after a short time I got conscripted for the border war.'

The day they announced that conscription was beginning again, Yonas had left work early and gone over to see Gebre, who by then had his own art studio. He found Gebre in the middle of a painting, and persuaded him to take a break and come for a walk. They found their way to Independence Avenue as the sun dipped behind the palm fronds and the buildings glowed pink. Everything still looked serene, but it felt now as if the air were laced with an invisible pollution they had no choice but to breathe. As they talked, Gebre began to panic. 'I can't do it,' he said. 'Not again.'

'You probably won't get called up,' Yonas had lied. 'And this should be over soon – we've all had more than our fair share of war.' He was thinking guiltily, as he said it, that his job was more likely to protect him from conscription than Gebre's. But, almost as if they had been overheard, the next day they were both served with conscription papers, to different places.

'I was posted to Badme – you know, the town at the heart of the border dispute,' Yonas told the lawyer. Barely a green shoot grew there, and Yonas wondered why either side would want to claim such an uninspiring backwater. And to be back in a war zone, now fully exposed on the front line, and without Melat or Gebre around, felt even more forbidding than he had expected. Every day he stepped out of the barracks with a dry mouth, physically shaking. Life descended into a cocktail of terror, boredom and exhaustion, which he got through by mindlessly following orders... until, to his surprise, he was promoted.

'After six months, they made me head of a platoon, and I got re-posted to Senafe. And I met a girl.' He found he was smiling now, remembering that moment he first saw Sarama. How he felt his legs walk him over to her before his mind had worked out what to say, so he ended up standing right in front of her, speechless. She had a long neck like a swan, supporting a three-inch-thick fro, and perfect crescent-moon eyebrows framing improbably huge almond eyes that bored into him.

'Hello! You are new here, right? I – thought I could – maybe show you around. I am head of a platoon here,' he'd said, managing to sound both desperate and pompous at the same time.

She'd laughed dismissively. 'I am fine, thanks,' she'd told him, and started to walk off.

But he'd kept on walking next to her. 'So, where are you from?' Now he felt like one of those street kids trying to sell a car driver some plastic object they knew was useless.

'Dekemhare,' she'd said brusquely.

'I have never been there...' Yonas found himself stuck for questions, but was desperate to keep the conversation going. 'My father is Abraham Kelati,' he said, a fact that was completely disconnected from their conversation so far, but might just impress her if she knew a bit about culture. 'I am a writer as well,' he added.

Then she did look at him, but only momentarily, before rolling those eyes up to the sky and then returning them to the path ahead. 'I am a poet,' she said. 'But my father is a farmer and none of my family are educated, so I guess my poetry has to be good enough to stand on its own.'

He told her he was sure it was, and pressed her to tell him more, and gradually she began to loosen up. It turned out she had gone to the University of Asmara as well, two years after Yonas, and had landed a plum job with an NGO after graduating, moving quickly from admin to management, until she was called up. It was during outside work, she told him, that she used to recite poetry – a tradition among all the women in her family – and she did it regularly at a bar he knew in Asmara. They both agreed it was strange that they had never crossed paths before.

In the days that followed, Yonas kept on looking out for Sarama, and finding excuses to snatch snippets of conversation with her, and one evening he spied one of her girlfriends watching him stare at her, then tapping her on the shoulder, pointing at him, giggling and whispering something behind her hand. He walked off; it was risky to cultivate rumours that you were interested in someone when all relationships on the front line were forbidden. But the next time he caught Sarama alone, filling up a cup of water in the canteen, he grabbed an empty cup and went over to stand next to her. 'As an officer here, I think it would be a good idea for me to understand the diversity of skills in our division.' She'd looked at him quizzically, but flirtatiously. 'You mentioned you are a poet,' he said. 'I would like to hear some of your poetry, in private.' She giggled and asked him how this would contribute to military tactics, and he said that was the brilliant thing about poetry: it could have so many meanings that even the poet might not expect, and that sometimes going on a walk was the best way to understand those meanings. She asked what he had in mind.

They met the next evening, after dinner, and walked up the track behind the barracks at dusk, and found a quiet spot to sit. 'So. You really want to hear a poem?' she asked, and looked at him, and in that moment of silence his whole body seemed to turn from flesh into electricity. And then she began. And her words seemed to contain such music that even though they were just sitting by themselves in the dust, in their dirty uniforms, he felt lifted up, transported – and he could easily imagine her captivating crowds.

When she'd finished, he told her he was impressed, which seemed inadequate, so he offered to recite something in return. 'Go ahead,' she said. At the last minute, he decided against the romantic poem he had been thinking of, and found himself reciting a Siegfried Sassoon poem, in English, that he'd been slightly obsessed with at university because of how it seemed to cut to the quick about what happened to Sheshy and the attempts of so-called patriots to suppress the brutal effects of war on soldiers, which resonated with him even more now that he was back in the fray. But as he finished, he felt embarrassed about his choice, and hoped Sarama wouldn't disdain him for showing off, or picking something colonial, or conclude that he wasn't romantic enough. But she wasn't unimpressed enough to stop him kissing her afterwards. And from then on, life in the barracks was transformed.

Nobody could know about them, of course – but somehow the risk to them both if it were discovered made each secret touch, each hidden moment, more significant, more precious. For a couple of months Yonas injected a new vigour into military exercises, feeling almost deliriously happy. 'Isn't it crazy,' he said to Sarama one evening, 'that I can be in the place and doing the work I *hate* most in the whole world, but with the person I *love* most in the world, and that makes it all okay, even if I die tomorrow?'

It was around three months later that she told him she had something important to say. She said it so solemnly, her big eyes glittering, that he immediately thought of Melat, that terrible day, and started to panic. She waited until they were out of earshot, then pulled him to look at her, and held both his hands. 'Yonas, I'm pregnant.' She was staring into his eyes, wanting him to respond.

'Who – did someone…?'

'What do you mean, did someone! You did, you idiot!'

'But I thought… that's incredible!' He laughed, giddy with relief. 'I mean, you can get discharged, so you'll be safe, and we can get married, as soon as we next get leave, and you can finally meet my family…'

In weeks that followed, hostilities heated up, but the warm glow of the new knowledge somehow warded off Yonas's fear. One day, though, that warmth seemed to morph into a strange heat and wooziness, and during a training session Yonas collapsed at the front of the line, and was almost trampled on as the men around him tripped over each other to avoid him, falling around like dominos.

Malaria, the doctor pronounced. Yonas's fever was at its height when a vicious battle kicked off. As he lay, shivering, he was unsure how much of the agonizing racket pounding in his skull was gunfire and how much was his over-heated brain. Time distorted and he had no idea how long he had been lying there, when the voice of Eyob, a guy from his unit, swam into clarity as it told him that sixteen soldiers from the company had just been killed in a blast. Through his fuzzy brain Yonas managed to articulate her name, to raise the pitch of his voice into a question.

'I'm sorry,' came his reply, as if into muffled darkness. 'I wanted to be the one to tell you, before you found out another way...'

Yonas remembered where he was, realized that the lawyer was looking at him, concerned. 'But she... my girlfriend... she got killed,' Yonas managed to utter, before shoving his chair back and running down the corridor all the way to the end, where he pushed his palms hard against the wall, and leaned his forehead against the cold, hard paint.

In his fevered state, Yonas had thought perhaps he was just in an extension of the dream he used to have about the day his parents died, where he'd seen the planes roaring across the horizon towards them, and had somehow managed to focus his eyes into a fierce heat of concentration that slowed the flight of all the ammunition down to a crawling pace, and he had redirected the fatal bullets back up in long, curving lines to the sky, where they collided back into the planes which exploded in the air like fireworks. Wet and shivering, he kept on finding himself calling out Sarama's name and thinking she might be sitting there next to him, before remembering. He had already imagined their wedding in Asmara, surrounded by Melat, his brothers, his parents and his grandmother, all laughing, clapping, dancing, and he couldn't make the scene go away; but then he was on the back of a truck, bumping and shuddering, and then he seemed to be in a bright, white room. Gebre materialized every so often to sponge his forehead with cold water, but wasn't Gebre fighting? Was he a ghost, too?

Slowly the fever passed. The doctors informed Yonas he'd had a particularly virulent strain but he was on the mend now. 'You were lucky,' they said. *Lucky.*

He returned to the lawyer's room after a few minutes, and took his seat, determined to carry on. 'I was discharged from the army soon after that,' he told her slowly. 'I had been very sick with malaria, so they let me go home to Asmara.' And that was that. The story of Sarama, and the end of his military service, compressed and handed over for the legal record. He still couldn't bring himself to expose the secret of the unborn baby that he had kept swaddled in his chest all this time. He doubted now that he ever would.

Chapter 14: Veata

I will have a mocha, please, with extra chocolate. Thank you.

I have had so many clients that some of them blur together after a while. But there was something about Yonas Kelati that was memorable: he had a strong presence, but it could disappear into a haunting absence, like a star getting sucked into a black hole. What I mean is, he would be talking to me in a really compelling way one moment, but the next he would just go off somewhere, in the middle of a conversation, staring at empty space. There was a lot more going on in his head than he was saying – that much was clear.

I've learned that one of the most important ways to help my clients is just to be a good listener. I know from experience that it hurts so much, finally to arrive in an unfamiliar place where you believe that, if you can just tell your story, you'll at least be safe – but the person you are speaking to is not interested. Still worse, if they accuse you of lying. If you are properly listened to, it makes a difference. Still, they are not always easy to help, our clients. A lot of them are traumatized or depressed so it is hard for them to communicate their stories. And that affects us too – hearing about such terrible suffering is hard to shake from your mind after you leave work. Even so, I wouldn't change my job for anything.

Before we started our interview, Yonas Kelati was very concerned to get my assurance that I would not report him if he decided not claim asylum. 'Absolutely not,' I said, and reassured him that it was all confidential. He looked so relieved. It is a big responsibility, being an asylum caseworker for people who are so vulnerable here, so fearful all the time that they will be deported or punished for the smallest thing. Sometimes if my children's school friends' parents find out I am a lawyer, they say wow! Like it's glamorous. But this kind of lawyer is not the glamorous kind. Your clients are scared. They are desperate. And the government is cutting and cutting legal aid so it has got really hard to do a decent job for them. Our office building is old with no air conditioning, no kitchen and a miniature staff room, and I don't get paid much, especially as I work evenings and weekends. I had never had a holiday in this country until my girls were old enough to do paper rounds and shop work, and then we all went to the Isle of Wight to stay in a caravan for a week and it rained. But that is the UK! At least it is safe here. We did drawings and played games and found ways to have a nice time, and when the girls complained, I just reminded them: 'You are lucky to be alive and to have a holiday at all. Our freedom is what we make it.' But they don't get that. They don't remember what came before. Every day I walk into work from my flat in Stepney Green and I tell myself: I made us free, and today I could help to make somebody else free too.

So, my clients and my kids, they are what keeps me going – but it is not easy. I am never going to feel truly settled in the UK. For my girls, it is home. They speak just like British girls. Chanthy doesn't remember anything at all about what happened in Cambodia, and Devi's memory is hazy, and I am glad about that, although I wish they had more memories of their father. But even my memories of him are fading now. It is hard to work out what is real and what is not. So imagine how hard it is for my clients who are expected to remember everything perfectly over and over again!

So, Yonas Kelati told me about his childhood. It was hard for him from early on, as it is with most of my Eritrean clients. His family were part of the liberation struggle, and when he was sixteen his parents and a younger brother were all killed, and his other brother and sister were badly harmed. Terrible things for a young boy to experience. But he spoke about it fluently in English, and calmly, most of the time. Somebody who has not spent so much time as I have engaged in conversations like that might have witnessed the interview and thought it was not very emotional for him to recount such events. But he was just working hard to keep it together. He almost gave way at one point, when he was talking about his sister's rape, and a few minutes later, telling me that his girlfriend got killed in the border war seemed to be too much for him, and he walked out. I didn't go after him. Usually, clients just need a bit of time on their own, to collect themselves, to process their emotions in private.

I remember well my own first attempt to talk about what happened to me. It all came out in a jumble, and what my mouth was emitting didn't reflect my real feelings and thoughts at all, and I started to cry and cry. It felt like I was trying to pass my caseworker a black and white photograph that was vital evidence for my case, but I was spilling water all over it, blurring the image, and just as he was trying to take hold of it, it was falling apart into soggy lumps of papier mâché.

It is not just the stress and pressure of talking to a lawyer when there is so much at stake – it is memory. The way memory can be hidden inside you, it can change and transform into a beast and then come out to bite you. For me, I remember, the worst times were so frightening to confront in words that for a long time I could not articulate them at all, but still they started to dominate my thoughts. All I wanted to do was shove them down in a box and close the lid, and to remember the happy times instead, but I couldn't do that either. So even though I was quite educated, I just could not tell my story in the logical, chronological way that I knew the lawyers needed. I did my best. But I remember being given a copy of the witness statement that had been written up and edited for me – like this was supposed to be the definitive version of my story, made up of the right words, and the right facts, in the right order – but it *wasn't* mine, it didn't *feel* like mine. But it was what it was. And I read it over so many times, that after a while it threatened to *become* my memory, and I had to work hard to fill in the gaps.

I mean, my statement said that we were chased from our home in the city when I was pregnant, because I had an administration job and Kamol was a lawyer – but it didn't say how they told me, sneering, *you've had it too easy*. My statement said that they put me to work in the countryside in fields for hours every day – but it didn't explain that I had never done that kind of labouring work before and that I was vomiting daily from pregnancy and that, even one week before Chanthy was due to arrive, I was still out there, picking and cutting, feeling like I would die. My statement said that we had to drink water that other workers had used to wash the filth off themselves – but it didn't say that Kamol used to feed me his own meals so that the baby and I could survive. My statement said my husband died from the exertion and hunger – but it didn't say this happened just two weeks after Chanthy was born, or how I shook him, pumped his chest, or how I was so very sad, not just because I lost him, but because I felt like it was my fault.

My statement said that I fled when the bombs fell on my village – but it didn't describe properly how the bombs were spraying around us, everywhere, as far as we could see, killing all the fish in the river, or how we used to grab the fish with our hands to feast on even while the river was filling up with human bodies. My statement said that my small children and I were ambushed and chased by Khmer bandits when we tried to leave – but it didn't mention the piles of corpses we had to walk past, cooking in the sun, letting out a terrible smell, flies clustering over them and swarming around my girls' eyes.

Now, so many years later, in this cool, comfortable and strange world of London, there is no longer any pressure on me to make anybody believe my story. But I have given myself the responsibility of making other people's stories believed, and that responsibility weighs on me. I have strategies. When I wake each morning, I always start off by thinking at least one positive thought. I read about this in a self-help book I found in the library. *Be Happy!* I think it was called… Usually my positive thought is about how my girls are doing. Devi is doing her A levels this year and Chanthy is doing GCSEs, and they are bright, conscientious girls, so I feel hopeful that they will be successful and happy. But Devi wants to be a vet, so she really needs good grades and she will be disappointed if she doesn't get them, and that makes me anxious. And sometimes it is hard not to think about my own lost dreams for my future with Kamol and get sucked underwater... but then there is always work to focus on. Unlike me, my clients are still stuck in the middle of that terrible uncertainty over whether they are allowed to put down roots here, so I can't get too sad about my own problems.

Ah, I remember when I first got leave to remain – I was so happy! I thought my life would finally be easy. But it was harder than I expected to find a job. After a few months all I could get was packing meat in a supermarket. But I worked hard at my English every night when the girls were in bed. I thought, maybe, if I really try, I can get to be a lawyer like my Kamol. So I stuck to that ambition like a snail to the ground. And then I got a scholarship for university, and after eight more years I did it. I know Kamol would be proud. But nowadays, he would also tell me to slow down. I take on too many cases. Partly it is pressure from the management. But partly I cannot say no. Every client could be me, and I think of all of them like my family.

Which is tough, when many of them get so sad that they want to end their lives. It happens a lot. I have to be a counsellor then, like the Samaritans. I always try to be calm and caring, but often the clients tell me angrily that I cannot understand their pain. I remind them that I was once an asylum seeker too, which does usually get through to them on some level, and they start to trust me more. But I still fear for them, because I know what they are likely to have in store.

I was happy that Yonas Kelati reappeared in my office to continue our conversation – I was beginning to worry he might have left the centre. He said he was sorry for walking out, but I told him: 'Don't worry at all, you were doing really well.'

I asked him some easier questions, so he could get back into talking, then led gradually into his military service, the articles he wrote and his imprisonment. When I asked how he was treated in prison, I knew it would be grim, because all Eritrean prisons are torture houses if my clients are anything to go by… But after he told me a few of the things that went on, he turned, slowly lifted up his shirt, and showed me a shiny mesh of scars the size of a tea tray across his entire back, most from whipping, but also these huge splodgy scars like paint, which he said he got from being tied up and left in the sun with sugar and oil on his back. 'The helicopter, they call it. I have seen similar wounds many times, but they can still make me shiver, and this scarring was especially bad. I told him gently that I was sure his scars would assist him as evidence. He said he had scars on his fingertips too, and showed me. Again, that is common among my clients who are smuggled: their agents tell them they have to burn off their prints if they don't want their identity registered before they make it to their destination country.

Yonas Kelati told me how he had to do forced labour in a factory for a while, before he came to London. That was good. For his claim, I mean. The fact that he worked illegally after that isn't so good. But at the end of the day, I felt he'd be a convincing witness: he was obviously intelligent, and he spoke clearly – in between the pauses – but I certainly believed him.

After the interview about the merits of his claim, I asked if he needed emergency accommodation while waiting for his asylum support decision. He said he was okay for the moment, which was a relief. Because the situation was getting really bad for emergency accommodation. I'd literally just found out that one of my clients, a pregnant woman, had been put in a hotel in Crystal Palace, which sounded nice enough on its website, but turned out to be housing 350 asylum seekers in forty-five filthy rooms, and my client had to share a room with nine other women, with just one en-suite toilet and no shower, and they all had to share the one bathroom on the floor with three other jam-packed rooms-worth of people, men and women, which meant my client had to resort a few times to vomiting her morning sickness directly out of the bedroom window. And there were mice running around, and the place was so dirty that she was getting palpitations of anxiety about the health of her unborn baby… But I didn't mention any of that to Yonas Kelati. 'So,' I told him, 'I can apply for weekly asylum support on your behalf, which would be £35 a week in vouchers – no cash.'

'No cash at all?'

'I'm afraid not.'

'But can I exchange a voucher for cash?'

'Not legally, no.'

'I cannot work to get any cash at all?'

'Absolutely not, I'm afraid. No asylum seekers are allowed to work for money, whether you're deemed eligible for support or not.'

He raised his eyebrows. 'But £35 per week is even less than I earned in that warehouse. And how can I help to support my sister if I only have vouchers?'

'I am afraid you'll just have to wait until you get leave to remain,' I said.

'Right.' He sounded calm enough, but one of those long pauses followed, and I could tell he was working hard not to express his frustration at me, which I appreciated. 'Can I use the vouchers in all shops?' he asked.

'Only in certain big supermarkets,' I told him. 'You will be given a list of places in the area around where you're accommodated.'

'And where would I be accommodated?' he asked.

'Well, I'm afraid you'd have no choice about that,' I said. 'You'd have to take whatever accommodation you're allocated. You would have to share with others, and it might well mean being dispersed to somewhere outside London, maybe even to Scotland.' His face fell at this. 'However,' I added, 'I should warn you anyway that you might not be deemed eligible for support in any case, because the authorities could take the view that you didn't claim as soon as reasonably practicable when you arrived.'

I watched him work this out, then smile wryly. 'Okay,' he said. 'So they could tell me: you cannot work for money, but even so we will not give you any support, and also we cannot even say how long we will take to process your claim.'

'It's possible.'

He laughed then, a bitter little laugh, and looked straight into my eyes. 'I want to know one thing from you, honestly, please,' he said. 'What are my chances? Not just of getting the support, but of my claim? Of getting ILR?'

'Well…' I took a deep breath. I didn't have the heart to tell him that about 90 per cent of applicants were refused after their first Home Office interview, and the majority who go on to appeal were refused again. 'The basic test is that the person has a "well-founded fear" that they will be persecuted if they go back home,' I explained. 'So, you've clearly been tortured, you say as a political prisoner, which you've clearly explained, and you had to flee the country. So long as the Home Office accepts this and finds that you'd be considered a traitor or a deserter on return, they should grant you leave to remain. But nothing is guaranteed. As I said, they won't like the fact that you claimed late, once you were free to go to the police, and they might also draw inferences from the fact that you still haven't reported the factory.'

'But why does it even matter if I have worked here illegally, if, like you said, the decision is supposed to be about what happened to me in Eritrea?'

'Good question. It's about credibility. To prove someone has a well-founded fear of persecution, they test all aspects of that person's story. They can use pretty much anything to do that.'

'But how do they tell what is credible?' he asked. 'I mean, I have no evidence for most things I've told you.'

'You have your scars, and you have your words,' I told him. But he was right. The evidence deficit is why credibility is such a nightmare in these cases. They turn on the believability of the person's testimony, but like I said, so many of my clients have difficulty expressing themselves well, and talking about their experiences. And of course translation makes all that worse. But you know, some are so traumatized they find it hard to talk at all, or they get memory blanks, or they just get things mixed up in their heads, and many are not educated or even literate in their own languages, and some are just so scared of being sent back that they start improvising extra facts when they don't really need to and get themselves into an unnecessary tangle. Of course there must be some who lie about their whole claim deliberately. But I've never had a client whom I've suspected of that. Perhaps I'm soft-hearted. But I don't think I'm naïve. 'They will look for inconsistencies—' I told him, but he interrupted.

'So, do you think I have a good chance, or not?' he asked again.

'I would say you have a reasonable chance, compared to most,' I told him, and I saw his face relax a little. 'Provided you stick to the rules,' I added. 'But I strongly recommend you go to the police about the trafficking, because if they find evidence of the factory to back up what you're saying, that will really help. Also you still need to tell the Home Office your story, remember, and they are a very different kettle of fish to me.'

He nodded, and thanked me for my help, then left.

I really hoped he would get a reasonable immigration officer. I liked him, and could tell how much it had taken for him to talk to me. As soon as he left, I got down to transcribing the recording and making notes of our conversation; if he didn't get the kind of respect he deserved from the Home Office, he could at least get it from me.

Fortunately, he was granted asylum support, within two weeks, and he didn't get dispersed far – only to Enfield. He asked me how he was expected to get there from Brixton once he'd got the keys, as it was a long way to walk, and he pointed out that he couldn't easily carry his stuff all that way or afford to take the bus. So I offered to meet him at the office to sign the forms, then go with him on the Tube and train to the new flat and pay his fares. But it turned out to be a good twenty-five-minute walk even from the station, and I was exhausted when we arrived.

The flat was down a narrow, quiet residential street, on the top floor of a house. We opened the door to a whiff of damp. I called out, 'Hello!' and heard murmurings. We went through to a low-ceilinged kitchen, where two Iraqi men and three Afghani men were sitting around a small table, listening to Arabic radio. They didn't appear to speak any English, beyond smiling 'hellos', and 'welcomes'. While they were polite enough to stand up, shake our hands, and point to the bedroom that Yonas Kelati would be sleeping in, they immediately returned to their listening. There appeared to be two other bedrooms there, and no living room.

Yonas's bedroom was very long and narrow, like a small train carriage, with a brown, thin carpet, frayed at the edges, and mustard-yellow walls. The only furniture inside was a child-size bunk bed, a metal clothes rail on wheels with several trousers and shirts hanging from it, and two plastic bucket chairs under the window. The lower bunk must have belonged to one of the other guys, and was already made up with leopard-skin bedding, and the upper bunk was empty, with no linen or duvets except a *Postman Pat* duvet cover folded on one of the chairs. 'Well, your new flatmates seem friendly, and I've seen worse places,' I told Yonas brightly. 'The area seems really nice and quiet, doesn't it? Hardly any traffic noise in here! And at least you'll still have friends in the same city…' Though of course, it occurred to me, it was about a five-hour walk for him to get back to where he'd been living down in Brixton, and I didn't even know whether the people he'd been living with were good friends or not.

'Thank you,' he said simply, and waved me off, standing there alone by the little bunk bed, his head almost touching the ceiling, his arm span probably as wide as the room.

Chapter 15: Yonas

After Veata left, Yonas hovered at the kitchen door, but his new flatmates were still sitting there in silence, drinking tea and listening to Arabic radio around the table. They didn't look up at him or acknowledge his presence. It was as if they were posing for a portrait photograph, and had deliberately etched the brown stains onto the swirly yellow wallpaper backdrop. If only he had a camera, he thought, he could snap the scene and show Nina – ask her if she reckoned he could submit it for that annual exhibition they went to . . . But he would have to stop thinking about Nina. He wondered if he should ask to join the guys, but there were no more chairs in the kitchen, and it was so small he doubted he could squeeze another in – even a stool. He wondered which of these men he was going to be sharing a room with. He fancied a cup of tea, but didn't want to ask for some from their pot if they weren't going to offer it. Feeling a wave of claustrophobia, he decided he would go straight out to find the nearest big supermarket on the list where he could trade in a portion of his first voucher, buy some nice food, and come back to cook all six of them a meal. That would surely break the ice.

He set off with a welcome sense that he finally had a purpose to be outdoors again. How much of the voucher should he spend in one go?

Perhaps £25, he thought, leaving £10 spare. He'd buy something celebratory: a pack of beer cans maybe – unless his new flatmates were teetotal. They were Muslim, after all. But then, he could always drink it himself. If only Gebre were here to share it though! Soon he would come, surely. But was he right not to mention to Veata that Gebre was still trapped in the factory? He was pretty sure he was wrong, actually – she'd said he was unlikely to be punished, and if he was still there, it was surely in his best interests to be found. Osman was almost certainly still there, needing help. He resolved to call Veata and tell her, and then maybe she could take on Gebre's case as well, and Gebre could move in with him in different accommodation – Osman too if the kid was well enough – and they could finally make the best of this rubbish asylum support situation together while they waited for a decision.

He went up and down the supermarket aisles, carefully picking things out, calculating their value and making substitutions, until he was satisfied he'd made the best possible use of £25. He queued at the till and unloaded his items onto the conveyer belt. For dinner he'd gone for two frozen lasagnes and a bag of fresh salad, with two mangoes and a tub of ice cream for pudding, and beers to wash it down. His mouth was already watering, and he wanted to rip open the chocolate bar he'd slipped in and wolf it down, but waited impatiently until the spotty teenager at the till had scanned them all through. He packed them neatly into plastic bags, then presented his voucher.

The spotty teenager took it. Looked at it, then examined it more closely, apparently puzzled, then sceptical. He looked up at Yonas, frowning. 'What's this?' Yonas had to explain that he was an asylum seeker, while the queue behind him listened, tutted, muttered. The spotty teenager frowned even more, then called the manager to come to till number 3. In the meantime, Yonas waited for several other people to be served.

The manager finally turned up, a beige-skinned man with a horizontal, lipless mouth. 'Oh yeah, it's just one of them vouchers – it's legit,' he said to the spotty teenager, without giving Yonas so much as a glance, then muttered something, pulled a sheet of paper out of a cupboard, handed it over and sauntered off.

'Okay, he says we can take it,' the spotty teenager said. 'But you'll have to put your items through again. Also, some of your stuff isn't valid, according to this list. Like this.' He pulled Yonas's bottle of conditioner out of the bag and put it aside, even though it was a two for one offer when you bought shampoo, so the bottle should have been free. He pointed to the sheet of paper from the manager. 'Shampoo you're allowed – that's it. Oh, and beer's not allowed either. No alcohol. And no ready meals – you can't have that lasagne. No exotic fruits so the mango will have to go.'

It seemed absurd, but not worth contesting, so Yonas kept quiet. Finally, his bags were re-packed, six items down, and the spotty teenager processed his voucher. He waited for his £20 or so change, but the spotty teenager just called the next customer.

'Excuse me, I need some money back,' Yonas reminded him. 'I would have had £10 back, but you took those things out...'

'Nah, sorry, you used the voucher up. Don't get no change.'

'But... I only spent about £15 out of £35 after you took out–'

'That's how it works, sorry. You have to use it all up at once.'

'Why? I did not know. Okay, wait, I will go and pick some more items...'

'Transaction's processed now, it's too late for that.'

'But then I've lost...'

'Sorry, not my rules – guess you'll know for next time. All right? I need to serve the next customer now, if you could move out of the way?'

Yonas took a step back, silenced. Not only had he wasted his precious money – or money's *worth* – but if he always had to spend his whole voucher at once like this, there was no chance of saving up for anything that would cost more than the weekly amount. Like a new jumper, after his only warm one had shrunk to Lemlem–size in the wash.

Walking back to the flat, fuming, he remembered the stories his grandfather used to tell about the Italians, how they'd marched in and stopped Eritreans from using the same shops, bars, schools, and then forced them to give up their currency.

He let himself back in, with his one pathetic shopping bag, and hovered again by the kitchen door. His new flatmates were all still occupying exactly the same positions around the radio, and still didn't acknowledge him – they could have been engaged in some kind of sonic séance. 'Hi, everyone,' he said, walking through the kitchen to the fridge to unload his meagre spoils. 'I just went to get some food for dinner. I thought I would cook for you all tonight. To celebrate… our meeting. But they wouldn't let me spend my voucher money on what I wanted, so all I can make is beans and rice. I tried to buy beer as well, but it was not allowed.'

For a few moments, nobody responded, the radio voice jabbered on, and Yonas wondered if he were being deliberately ignored. But finally, he got a tight smile, and a nod of acknowledgement from one of them – Ali, was it? 'Thank you,' he said. 'But no alcohol.' He returned to his fixed gaze at his tea.

'Right.' Yonas waited, unsure whether they'd understood what he'd just said about dinner. 'Anybody want more tea?' he asked, switching the kettle on. He noticed mould growing around the little window, grease all over the hob, the plastic edging of the kitchen units hanging off at one end.

A couple of them shook their heads.

He wondered whether to say any more, or whether he would just annoy them with further interruptions, and how much they would understand anyway. He tried to work out what they were listening to, summoning up his smattering of childhood Arabic. It sounded political… something to do with education… but he was too rusty. The broadcasters spoke at an insane speed, as if someone had pressed fast forward, or as if they were sprinting along towards a seemingly vital rhetorical goal.

'Have any of you had any problems with the vouchers?' he asked. 'Is it right that you have to spend one voucher all in one go or lose it?'

A couple of them looked up at him, as if confused.

'Vouchers?' said the one he thought was called Hassan. 'Total shit.' He promptly descended into a tirade in Arabic, to which the others chipped in for a few minutes, before they all reverted to their silent radio worship. Fortunately a song came on then, and the singer had a beautiful, soothing voice. Almost in unison, the five guys sat back in their seats, teacups in hand. Yonas poured his own cup of tea, picturing those beers that he'd basically paid for now being stacked back onto the supermarket shelf.

He went back to his room, laid the ridiculous children's postman duvet cover on the yellow-splodged mattress, then sat in his plastic bucket chair to drink his tea. He stared at the frayed, football-sized hole in the brown carpet, and wondered who or what had caused it. He got out his mobile phone and tried calling Bin Man Joe for what must be the fiftieth time now, but again he got a recorded message: 'This caller is not currently accepting calls.' At least he'd left his mobile number now with Bilal the shopkeeper in case Gebre ever made it to town. He reached into his bag for his library book, The Wizard of the Crow. He should have returned this before coming all the way up to Enfield, but he had wanted to finish it too much. He read a couple of paragraphs... But this was the world's most uncomfortable reading chair – hard, bent like a spoon, with no lower back support – and the letters seemed to be swimming together. He closed it, and climbed up onto his bed, which was so short that his feet hung over the end. A couple of mattress springs poked into his back, and he shifted position slightly.

He was already nostalgic for the squat, with its threadbare sofa in the chaotic living room where he could sit and read or chat with Emil or Joachim or whoever was around. He even missed the squat kitchen, in which it was normal practice to spread butter over toast without bothering with a plate, flick jam around like flecks of blood on the floor, tip baked beans straight onto a plate and leave the remains sitting on the sideboard like gloopy rabbit droppings, and allow a pan thickly lined with lumpy porridge to congeal on the hob. But at least there were people there who would ask how he was doing, and make some sort of conversation in English, or just give him space to read.

They had been kind to let him stay without making any contribution to bills while he was waiting for his asylum support decision. He'd offered to be their resident cleaner in return. He remembered how restless he'd been, then, to get his letter so that he could leave and move into his own place; how he'd imagined his new asylum accommodation being a tiny but light and airy studio flat, above a friendly local grocer's shop nearby, where he could live as peacefully as he wanted, and drop in on the squat to say hello to the guys every so often. So much for that. Of course the squat had its problems: now he remembered being back in the bathroom, scrubbing at an array of dried urine spots on the toilet floor, complaining how it might as well have been one of the pissing areas in the bushes out in the Eritrean hills that you could wander into and make line drawings in the dust, and how someone – he suspected Joachim – apparently had continual squits and yet could never recall the purpose of the fluorescent orange toilet brush sitting right there… Still. He missed Emil calling him Professor Jojo. He missed having a living room. And he missed the Brixton buzz and markets and geography that he'd only just started to get to know.

Why should he have been forced to move up here, to the other side of the river, five hours' walk away, with these Middle Eastern guys he'd never met who barely spoke English and hogged the only living space, just so he could qualify for those stupid vouchers? Why shouldn't he be allowed to work for cash and pay his way and live where he chose like any normal human being? He was perfectly healthy, capable and willing! And it wasn't as if he wanted to enrich himself – he just wanted to be able to shop for basics and send money home to Melat. If there was work to be done, how was it not good for the British that people like him were around and keen to do it for them cheaply, at least until a decision was made?

He hadn't called Melat yet to tell her why the money had dried up since he'd made his claim. He felt too ashamed and guilty, especially since he'd sort of led her to believe he was already on track for a permanent visa and was working legitimately. He couldn't help hoping Veata might call with a decision soon so that he'd be able to phone Melat and say: 'Sister! I have news you might actually want to hear…'

He flipped over onto his stomach, but another spring dug into his rib, so he shifted again, then pillowed his head on his arms. The mattress smelled of mildew and dust. He sneezed. If only Gebre would arrive. He felt a sudden hunger to see an Eritrean face again, to hear a friendly Tigrinya word. He knew nobody at all up here in north London, except

Molly and Nina of course – but they were history in his life now, and lived nowhere near Enfield anyway. But then he thought of something.

He climbed down from the bed and rooted through his bag for the slip of paper he was sure should still be there; it had been thrust into his hand by one of the Eritrean women ages ago, that day he'd gone along to Molly's class at the Refugee Council. 'You should come and join us one Sunday,' the woman said as she left the classroom, and he'd thanked her, thinking he probably never would, but kept her piece of paper just in case. And yes, here it was: *Eritrean Church. Sunday service 10.30–1.*

When Sunday came, he set off down to Wood Green early, on foot, with Molly's old *A–Z* in hand. He found the street without much difficulty, but it appeared to be residential; he couldn't see any building that looked like a church. But he walked along it anyway, and sure enough, there, at the end, was a peeling white sign, with Tigrinya script under the English font. The script alone was reassuring – the mere shapes of the lettering seemed beautiful in a way they never had before. He turned down a little alleyway piled each side with crates, and saw a white door in a wall ahead. A couple of women were about to go in, ahead of him, and as they opened the door, out floated the sound of ululating, clapping, Amens and the slow cascade of a voice leading a prayer in Tigrinya. Pentecostal, it must be, he thought – churches like this were banned now back home.

He made his way inside, and was greeted by a pretty woman wearing a satin sash with 'USHER' printed on it, whose wide smile was full of friendly curiosity. Her almond eyes reminded him with a jolt of Sarama's – oh, if only she were Sarama, alive after all – and this in turn made him think of Udaze's strategy of finding a woman in church and having multiple children with her, before reapplying for asylum, and he felt embarrassed at the thought, as if he'd come to this church with that agenda himself. He nodded and smiled awkwardly back at the pretty usher, but gestured that he would be fine seating himself, and slipped into an empty row near the back.

Pictures of galaxies were projected on screens at the front, above a stage where the prayer leader was walking up and down, proclaiming the grace of the Lord into a microphone. The seats were about half full so far, and most of the congregation were already on their feet, raising their hands, swaying, murmuring to a her stream of speech. Yonas had heard so little Tigrinya lately, not having spoken to Melat in a while, that the waves of familiar vowels and throat sounds felt soothing and mesmeric. Gradually, the hall filled up completely, and then, seamlessly, as the prayer leader went to take her seat, the choir filed up onto the stage – about twenty Eritreans dressed in red and blue robes – and singing began to swell around him. The sensation of being physically surrounded by so many fervent, joyful voices joining together in song, in his own language, so many Eritrean faces, so many passions uniting in this one yearning melody, this longing moment, growing their collective sound in spirals, in tunes familiar to him from years ago, singing on and on in a perpetual, glorious torrent, many of them closing their eyes and turning their faces to heaven, enraptured, wet-cheeked and smiling, adding claps, ululation, swaying hips, moving feet, raising arms, throwing their whole beings into the sound, into the place – it was overwhelming. Yonas soon found his own eyes stinging, his imagination flooded with memories. 'Ade,' he mouthed silently. 'Abo.' He found himself searching the faces of the choir on the stage for traces of his parents' faces, for Melat and the twins' faces, for his grandparents' faces, for Gebre's face, as if a strong enough force of will and faith could morph one of these familiar strangers into one of them.

Adeln, Adeln, Adeln kabaka
Zelalemawi qewami rstey
Zeyteffe zeytebers
Menberey...

Whatever you have in life, you can never be satisfied unless you have God... But no. No, no, no. Yonas just couldn't believe that. No God could satisfy him as much as having any one of his family back, even for a week, a day, an hour. But then, this music...

It shifted a gear, to a happier, more upbeat tune, which got everyone around him properly dancing, moving their feet and their arms, their heads and their hips. Yonas wished he could join in, throw himself into the thrill of their expressive, exuberant release – but he couldn't. He felt tied down to his seat in the corner. He was a hypocrite by being here. Everyone else seemed to be passionately religious. On the other hand, just the look and sound of all these Eritreans was so comforting, so familiar and so tempting to slot into. He could be part of a community again here, part of the diaspora, part of a new, extended family. Maybe here he could make peace with losing Sarama, and find himself another girlfriend, a wife, create a real family of his own... But before that could happen he would be questioned, interrogated, judged. He would have to introduce himself, talk about his past, yet again, and step back into the wasps' nest of Eritrean politics. He would have to pretend he still had faith...

The singing was over, and the minister was speaking. 'Any newcomers here today? Please put up your hand and introduce yourselves, so you can be welcomed!' He was looking directly at Yonas now. His face was so kind and smiling, his voice so warm and inviting. This minister seemed like a genuine, kind man, someone with a twinkle in his eyes, someone who might be good to chat to in Tigrinya, someone who would probably deliver a sermon with character and depth. There was a collective pause, as everybody waited for the chance to hear who this newcomer was, and to put their metaphorical arms around him in a loving embrace, as if welcoming a prodigal son. It would be so easy to surrender, to accept, to join. But Yonas found himself grabbing his coat, and pushing along the row of puzzled people. He saw the almond-eyed usher gaping at him as he rushed out of the door, and ran blindly back down the alleyway and the street.

Chapter 16: Jude

ONE-LEGGED ALBANIAN KILLER WHO PRETENDED
TO BE A KOSOVAN ASYLUM SEEKER TO GAIN
UK CITIZENSHIP WILL FINALLY BE DEPORTED
AFTER 14 YEARS OF LIVING ON HANDOUTS?

Alec is running like a lunatic in circles around the submarine in the Imperial War Museum, until another child leaves the captain's seat, when he immediately beelines for it and clambers in. 'Daddy, look, I'm driving the eNORmous submarine!'

'Pure euphoria!' Max says, looking on and radiating pride. 'Why haven't we brought him here before? Apart from the fact that you're always working.'

'Bit disturbing though, isn't it?' you say, ignoring the passive-aggressive aside. 'Boys and their warmongering toys.' Had it been up to you, you wouldn't have chosen this museum, but you'll have to work tomorrow with YK's appeal coming up, and three other hearings this week, and so, in a fit of guilt about how little you've been around, you'd told Max he should choose a venue for a family outing.

'Yeahhh,' Max says tolerantly, 'but he doesn't get all that yet – it's just a collection of fantastic moving machines to him. And when he's old enough, there are loads of exhibits here describing the fallout of war. Hey, Captain Alec, where are you taking us in your submarine under the sea? Shall we go find a killer whale's underwater cave?' He goes over to squat down next to your son, who's attacking the steering wheel like he's in Formula One.

You smile at the backs of your boys' matching mousy-brown heads of shaggy hair, and wander away from the submarine and around the cavernous museum. Such huge bombers and such compact Spitfires – unthinkable that grown men could fit into those cabins and sit in there for hours – all of them sleek and streamlined, like blown-up versions of Alec's wooden planes, and yet each one a massive murder weapon.

Walking around a gigantic tank, like a green alien-mobile that could squash you into a bloody pancake if it were to rev up its engine, you remember that picture you found online of a tank graveyard in Asmara – a vast area on the edge of the city, crammed with the rusted beasts, like a zoo full of decaying elephant carcasses, that was originally intended as both a dumping ground and a memorial to their fight for liberation. Now, apparently, those tanks were being recycled by the government.

'Can I climb on it, Daddy?' you hear a little girl ask. You picture YK, as a boy, in the army with his brothers and sisters, hiding out in that implausible-sounding revolutionary school, with tanks like this one thundering by and explosions shaking the clouds, and hope you never have to see a tank in action. But you shouldn't take that for granted. After all, the First World War erupted out of a tiny incident, one crazed assassination. What will start the Third World War? Will it even involve tanks, or will it be a nuclear Armageddon? Will North Korea finally flip? Will America and Russia descend into another Cold War? Or will it start somewhere else, like in the Middle East? And what will the asylum-seeker situation here look like after that? Especially as the seas rise and climate change drives populations away from their homes. Will the popular media ever be sympathetic to people fleeing from violence and disaster? Or will politics just swing further and further to the right?

You head out to the front steps, and ponder the phallic cannons sticking out of the front of the grandiose building. And why, with all we've discovered about science, all we've learned through history, all we've expressed in art, why do human beings – men, in particular – go this far to be brutal to each other. You sit on the top step and look beyond the cannons at the green lawns. Grass, flowers, unthreatening vegetation – all that will ultimately survive, even if humans bomb each other to extinction. The tiny green blades will push on up towards the sun, through the rusting relics of tanks and planes. Weeds will wind themselves around the rubble of once-lived-in apartment blocks. The world will become wild again. Maybe dinosaurs will return. Alec would love that idea.

Back inside, after another half-hour or so of wandering around climbable exhibits, your son has a hangry meltdown and you tell him firmly that it must be time for lunch, even though it's only just 11.30, and suggest a picnic outside on the grass.

Naturally the sun has just gone in, and you forgot to bring the picnic blanket, but the three of you line up on a bench. 'Mummy,' Alec says with a mouthful of sandwich, 'when I'm big, I'm going to fly a big aeroplane and shoot guns.'

You glance across at Max. 'No,' you say shortly. 'You won't want to. It's not fun at all, you know, the real thing.'

'It *is* fun. Kill kill kill!'

Alec had come back from nursery saying that for the first time the other week, making you wish momentarily that you'd had a girl, before wondering whether little girls came home saying that too. 'Alec, *never* say that again please,' you tell him. 'It's not funny. I mean it.'

'It *is* funny.'

You find anger bubbling up and turn him to face you. 'In some countries in the world,' you snap, 'where there is war going on, right now, mummies and daddies get killed, or taken away from their children for ever, and the children are left all on their own. Sometimes children get killed too. Is that the kind of world you want?'

'Jude,' Max remonstrates.

'I want ice cream,' Alec says, his voice small but petulant. 'Can we have ice cream? Chocolate ice cream?'

'If you finish your sandwiches, and say please, then we can see if they have ice cream,' you tell him, regretting your temper, and throw an apologetic look Max's way. Even so, you hope that on some level your son was listening.

Chapter 17: Gavin

**MIGRATION OFFICER SANG UM BONGO SONG
TO AN ASYLUM SEEKER FROM CONGO**

No coffee for me – I'll take a tea. Make it strong, and three sugars. Cheers.

Yonas Kelati. Oh yeah – that was the one who came in saying his solicitor had sent a statement and he wanted to '*check I'd read it*'. Cocky bugger. Well, there was no statement on my file, and no time to hunt around either, so I told him we'd just go ahead without. It's a double-edged sword, a statement. If they've learned it off pat they sound like parrots, and it sounds fake but there's no legit way of saying that in our report; but on the other hand, you can use the statements to point out inconsistencies. Anyway. That day I was already in a fucking bad mood, so when he asked if I was '*sure*' the statement wasn't there, and could I look for it, I got even more pissed off. 'I told you: I don't have one,' I said. And then, when we got in the room, he had the gumption to say his solicitor had advised him to check the interview was *taped*! We don't tape any interview unless a sol requests, and he didn't have a letter proving any such request. And anyway our recorder was broken. So I said I'd take a note, and that he'd be well advised not waste any more of my time.

I was already behind on my targets for that day, so I was hoping he'd tell me a flimsy story and I could move on. All the management fucking care about are targets – basically deporting as many people as possible as fast as possible. When I applied, they made the job sound really good. I mean, the title, 'Higher Executive Officer, Case Owner and Presenting Officer', sounds like you'd have some authority and control over your life, right? And they said it'd be all about interpersonal communication and relationship building. Whatever! Our line managers treat us like shit. They're never interested in what we have to say, they just spend their whole time telling us what targets we've missed and what we're doing wrong. And they're just a buffer between us and senior management, who we never get to talk to! It's obvious they don't give a fuck about the people. We constantly get told by our line managers there's time pressure, time pressure, time pressure, but we're already working as fast as we can all hours, so what more are we supposed to do?

It's not just the interviews – and they can take ages – we have to write the letters too. And on top of that we're supposed to correspond with sols and help out with claims in other ways. But where's the time for all that? We're massively under strain as it is. Plus we get sent to court for the appeal hearings to nail the deportations, but we don't get any legal training. All we get is a bit of *e-learning*. E-learning is bollocks as far as I'm concerned. It doesn't prepare you for the real thing, and we can get humiliated if there's a good barrister on the other side. Management don't give a toss. All we want is to be appreciated and get the chance to do our job properly, right? Not be treated like rubbish the whole time.

Oh, and the money's crap too. My pay cheque's just big enough so I can be a member of a five-a-side team, and if I didn't have that pitch to vent on three times a week – there's nothing like kicking a football and sprinting around to get your anger out – I genuinely don't know how I'd hack it. My marriage has fallen apart over this job and I hardly ever get to see my kids. I've applied for other jobs, but no luck. I guess it's not really like anything else. Anyway, there's not enough free time around this fucking job to write applications to get yourself out of it.

Anyway. So, yeah, my mood could have been better when I spoke to your Eritrean guy. I'm pretty sure I remember him right… Black but not that black. Not that old either. Thirties, I think. Tall. Big hair. Seemed pretty calm when you looked at his face, but he was twisting his fingers so I could tell he was nervous. You're not actually allowed to take body language into account when you decide on people, which is another fucking annoying thing about this job, because a lot of the time you can tell from that straight away if people are lying. Straight away. And it goes against real human communication not to factor that in, you know? There are so many things you can't put into a formal letter! Like if someone starts wailing and crying at a difficult question, it seems so much more fake than if they'd dropped a single tear. But that's just what we have to live with.

Anyway, I asked your Eritrean the usual kinds of questions. I've looked over my notes so I can remember pretty much how it went…

So, we tend to start off with the big ones, like why are you claiming asylum? And I remember, when I asked him that, he went: 'I cannot go back. I was tortured. I have a real fear of persecution.'

I just laughed out loud. He'd so obviously been coached! I said, 'Okay then, tell me about your *real fear of persecution* and we'll see if there's any truth in it.' He leaned forward like he was about to say something bolshy, but then sat back again. 'Come on,' I pressed him, 'or can't you even tell me where you're from now?'

'As you know, I come from Eritrea,' he said, all smug.

'And where were you born?'

'In Addis,' he said.

'Addis, Ethiopia?!' Brilliant, I thought – he wasn't even born in the fucking country he said he was from. I could already see the next paragraph of my letter…

But then he added, 'In 1975 they were not separate countries. But both my parents are Eritrean and I lived in Asmara from when I was one year old.'

So, he was a mouthy bastard too. 'So tell me why you say you have this *real fear of persecution* then,' I said. So, he started telling me he was a political prisoner and he was tortured, all that, and I thought, yeah yeah, you've been told which boxes we need to tick, so I jumped in and asked him what he was a 'political prisoner' for.

'My writing,' he said. 'After they made me work for the censorship board—'

And I was like: 'So, hang on, you were a censor then? But now you're asking for protection so you can stay here because of your writing. Hmm, okay.' I've got to admit, I do get satisfaction from picking up on an inconsistency and watching them squirm.

'I was trying to explain, I was a writer, and then had to accept that posting against my will—' he said.

'So they forced you to take a government job? As a writer? Isn't that a kind of desirable job?' I would take a job as a writer over this shit any day, I was thinking. I mean, I do have to do some writing, but not the kind I want to be doing.

'You have to take the posting you are given,' he said. 'But I could not keep going and accept the situation, so I wrote secret articles—'

'Oh, *secret* articles, is it?' I said. 'So where's the evidence for that, then?'

'Evidence?' he parroted, like it hadn't occurred to him.

'Yes, *evidence*. Copies. Any documents that prove you wrote *secret articles* and the like. Or all we've got is your word that they were secret. Which seems a bit pointless anyway if you ask me. I mean, most people write things to be read, don't they?'

'I did want them to be read, but I had to write them secretly and send them—'

'Listen,' I interrupted, 'to the question I asked you. Have you got copies of the articles you say you wrote or not?'

'I could not print copies, it was too risky, even to keep on a memory stick – so I just typed them in internet cafés…'

'What about links online?'

'Yes, yes,' he said, 'you can find two of them that were published by human rights organizations, with my pen name—'

'Your pen name? What was that then?'

'Massawa Tekle,' he said.

'Right. But your name is Yonas Kelati, according to your forms, anyway, which is totally different. So I'm supposed to believe that a couple of pieces on human rights websites, attributed to a writer with a totally different name, are actually by you. That you didn't just come across these pieces and decide to claim them as your own.'

'I sent the articles out by email,' he said, 'and I still have the email address I used, but I had to delete the messages—'

'Convenient. No proof of authorship, and no proof of messages.'

'You can check with the people I sent the articles to.'

'Have you met these people, in person?' I asked.

'No,' he said.

'And of course you have no papers either. Or ID.'

'No, but like my statement says, I had to escape prison to get here so I couldn't get papers, they do not grant passports to travel abroad any more unless you are a diplomat or football player.'

He was vexing me by that point – all the answering back. I get enough shit from my line managers. All of a sudden I got one of those sharp stabs of hate for this job that I get sometimes, and I felt so fucking claustrophobic, locked in that windowless box of a room we have to sit in, even though I work in there every fucking day. I had to take a moment and chill a bit.

'So, what books have you published then, if you're a real *writer*?' I asked. I've got a book in me as it happens, a fantasy novel, this whole world with vampire bats and werewolves – it's all there in my head already – just never have the time in this job to write the bloody thing.

'No books,' he said, 'not yet, but in my language I have published the texts of five plays and many articles…'

'No books yet, says the famous writer!' I couldn't help chuckling.

'I did not claim to be famous,' he said. 'But I did write plays and many other communications when I was working in the Department of Cultural Affairs.'

'You wrote *plays* for a job in *government*?' That was a properly ridiculous thing to claim. There's embellishing a story, and then there's farce.

'The department organizes national events…', he said, still pursuing it.

'So, let me get this straight. The government paid you to write *plays*, then gave you the chance to *censor other people's* plays, then you repaid them by writing secret articles *against* them. Even if that's possible – and it sounds like a bloody play itself to me – why would you risk losing that kind of job? Sounds cushy, compared to what some people have to do in the army.' Compared to what I have to do now, I was thinking.

'I wrote the articles after they took away my job and posted me to the censorship board.'

'Okay,' I said. 'So have you written any *plays* or *articles* since you got here?'

'I have been too busy surviving,' he said.

'Or too busy making up fairy stories for interviews,' I said. 'I can see you're *all* about making things up.'

He shook his head, and muttered something that sounded like *that's what they said*, but I wasn't sure.

'You've been here a while now, haven't you?' I said.

'Yes.'

'Over a year,' I said.

'Almost a year.'

'And it just didn't *occur* to you to claim asylum before now.'

'I was scared,' he said quietly.

'Scared? Okay, so what changed? Was it just that you heard how good the benefits would be if you got asylum support when you wouldn't even have to lift a finger?'

He stood up then, suddenly, and I saw his fists clench, clocked how tall he was, taller than I'd thought, and reached for the panic button. But he just turned his back and walked towards the door.

It felt good, for a moment, like a victory. But then I felt a little burn of doubt I sometimes get in my belly. Lots of them claim they're traumatized when the questions get tough. *Oh, that's why I suddenly couldn't speak or went off on one.* Of course, I get that if most of them actually *had* been through the experiences they *claim* to have gone through, then they *would* be traumatized. And I'm *obviously* not unsympathetic to people who've been *genuinely* traumatized. Occasionally I do get those people. But most of them haven't, or they exaggerate to improve their chances. I mean, sometimes it is hard to tell what's true and what's lies. Fucking hard, actually and the management don't fucking care. Anyway, fuck it,

I thought: fuck off with your plays and your fucking human rights – at least this'll help me catch up on my targets. Refusal: tick… well, I was about to tick the box, when he turned around and came to sit back down in his chair again.

'I just needed a moment. I want to continue with the interview,' he said, firmly.

I rolled my eyes. 'This is your last chance,' I told him.

Chapter 18: Yonas

A glossy crow hopped along the construction yard fence, then stopped and cocked its head at Yonas, as if to say: *You've claimed now. You even got asylum support. You're really going to risk doing this?* Then it cawed, loudly and repeatedly, the sarcastic laugh of a bitter old woman, before hopping on. Yonas thought of that red-faced, snub-nosed Home Office interviewer, talking down to him as if he were a recalcitrant child.

He had felt quite confident beforehand, after talking through everything with Veata. He just hadn't expected the interviewer to be so aggressive, to have been *trying* to trip him up – just like Histoire and Michel had warned. Yonas had got so agitated that he'd started burbling. He knew he wasn't explaining himself clearly enough, and it didn't help that the interviewer kept interrupting and accusing him of lying, and exploiting his background as a writer to keep insisting he must be making everything up.

The crow took off. Yonas watched it flap over to the opposite side of the fence, perch and survey the construction site, as if deriding all the people who had to work in it, who couldn't just fly around at will without having to worry about pesky things like visas. *You're not allowed to work for money. Under any circumstances.* 'They don't want people like me to get a chance to prove their worth, do they?' he had asked Veata, and she hadn't contradicted him. Anyway, he'd given up his asylum support now, so he had no choice.

Yonas walked into the yard to join the other workers, who were still milling around, waiting. Half a shell of a building was standing, and the rest of the site was a scramble of rubble and concrete stumps.

'Hey, man. *Selam!*' Another man had tapped him on the shoulder, and was smiling. He looked Eritrean. Like Yonas he was tall and lean, but his skin was slightly darker and he had a match-thin moustache. 'Remember me? I was in that English class. At the Refugee Council.'

'Oh, yes!' It was true that Yonas recognized the man now, but he couldn't remember his name. They had barely spoken.

'Tesfay,' the guy said, extending his hand. He had a slight squint, and his smile seemed to stretch his moustache so it looked ready to ping off. Yonas felt a familiar glow in his belly at hearing Tigrinya spoken again. When Tesfay heard that Yonas wasn't really connected with any other Eritreans in London, he literally threw up his hands in mock horror and said they would have to hang out some time.

But then the boss turned up, cutting off the chit-chat. He introduced himself as Kev and began barking instructions. He was one of those butch, white, stubbly British types Yonas had come to be familiar with, doing this kind of work. Their task, he said, was to demolish the remainder of the building, clear the area and set it up for new foundations. 'And what do I expect?' he asked, rhetorically. 'I expect each and every one of you to work your *effing arses* off until you've done a full seven hours of hard graft, that's what I expect. And that means when *I* decide you've done seven hours, no one else.' At this, Kev beat his chest like Tarzan.

Yonas started shifting rubble into skips. It felt good to be working again, for money. Even if it was doing this. No, he didn't regret walking out of his free flat and ditching those useless vouchers and that *Postman Pat* linen. He smiled as he remembered getting his stuff together, then standing at the kitchen door, where his flatmates were still all assembled, listening to Arabic radio, in exactly the same configuration. 'I'm leaving!' he'd said with a cheery smile. 'Good luck!' Ali had lifted his hand in a surprised wave, as Yonas closed the squeaky front door for the last time.

Veata was perplexed when he told her. She warned him, again, that if he chose to work for money while his claim was pending and was found out, he'd put his future on the ropes – but he told her he had good friends who would put him up for free, and that he'd be fine. Which was true, in a way: the squat was cheap, and if he had anyone left whom he could call a friend now, it was Emil, who'd welcomed him back by calling out 'Professor Jojo!', bounding down the stairs and giving him a smacking kiss on each cheek.

He was walking back for his sixth load of rubble when his phone shrilled from his pocket. He pulled it out, and Nina's name flashed up. He couldn't suppress a surge of pleasure, but then remembered what she'd done. Couldn't she just get the message and stop contacting him? He pressed cancel, and switched the phone onto silent. But he couldn't resist checking again a few minutes later. Sure enough, there was a message.

Hi Joe. Hope you're okay. I just wanted to let you know that the police did come to question Mum, but she said it was all a mistake, that you were just a student of hers from the Refugee Council, and they apologized for wasting her time! So there's nothing to worry about there. I still understand that you were angry about the article. But I promise I was just as angry. I would really like be friends again. Let me buy you a coffee? Nina x

'Oi, you,' Kev's voice barked. 'Get off your phone.'

Yonas shoved the phone back in his pocket and walked over to the next load. He could make this work by himself – he didn't need Nina. Maybe he should start charging for teaching English to other, richer, immigrants. That would be more enjoyable than working for guys like Kev. He would use his brand-new library card and do some research on the computer...

A loud crunching sound came from behind him, where a couple of guys had started demolishing the remains of the standing wall. 'Wooaaah!' someone shouted. Yonas looked up, and glimpsed a lump of concrete hurtling towards him from his upper left like an asteroid rushing towards earth… his mind told him to move, but his body wasn't fast enough… Then, a sickening crack.

A searing pain.

Blackness.

He came to slumped in the front seat of a moving van. His left elbow was on fire. He looked down. It was wrapped in a filthy dustsheet and soaked in blood. His jaw throbbed. He turned to see who was driving.

'Thank fuck you're awake,' Kev grunted. 'What the fuck were you doing standing right under the fucking demolition ball not keeping a lookout? Fucking eejit! You've got to learn to listen to basic instructions if you want work in this country! Sometimes it doesn't collapse the way it's meant to.'

Yonas said nothing. The world was still hazy. The right side of his face felt odd. He put his right hand up to touch it lightly, and it felt like one giant blister.

'Anyway,' Kev said, 'I don't know where you live but I'm just gonna drop you off here. Homerton Hospital's just round the corner. Go on, off you go.' He might as well have been shooing off a stray dog.

Yonas gave him a long, hard look, then opened the van door with his good arm and got out, hoping he'd be able to walk. He was about to slam it shut again, but a wave of blood rushed to his head, and he couldn't stop himself leaning in, looking Kev right in the eye, and saying, 'Fuck you, you heartless piece of shit.'

After a beat, the van tyres squealed and Kev drove away, with the door hanging open.

Yonas stood still, watching the vehicle disappear. His little outburst was probably the only retribution Kev would get. At least it was something. His legs felt hollow and wobbly. It occurred to him that he hadn't even been paid for the job yet, and there was no chance of that now. And could he actually go into this hospital, and expect to be treated, with no papers? Veata had told him he was eligible to get emergency treatment on the NHS now that he'd claimed asylum, but he didn't have any documents – they were back at the squat, under his pillow. Plus, he would have to come up with a lie to explain to the doctors how the accident had happened, in case they were connected to other authorities who could use this to prove he was working illegally. Yonas felt dizzy, and bent over. His elbow was excruciating now. He straightened up, and tried to move it. He couldn't. No, he definitely couldn't. He really needed a drink of water and ideally something sugary. He had better risk going into the hospital, if he could make it all the way.

A woman behind the Accident and Emergency reception asked for his name and gave him a form to fill in. Fortunately it was his right hand that still worked, but his injured left hand could barely hold the paper still enough to write legibly. The form asked for his address, phone number and details of his GP. 'And do you have any documentation to prove your eligibility for NHS services?' the receptionist asked. 'A passport or driver's licence?'

'My documents are at home.'

'Hmm. All right. I'll see if the doctors will see to you. Take a seat.'

Some newspapers lay on the table. Yonas picked one up and turned the page with his good hand. Election fever: polling day was just a week away. He thought about Nina's husband Quentin, who was probably giving a speech right now about how illegal immigrants should be kicked out, maybe denying in an aside that any foreign person had ever stepped over the threshold of any home belonging to any member of his family for the entirety of British history. The latest polls said Labour looked likely to win, but it was a close call. It occurred to Yonas that he hadn't eaten anything since a piece of toast at 7 a.m. His head felt woozy, and his elbow throbbed like a drum.

He asked the reception lady if they had anything he could eat or drink. 'Sure, there's a machine in the corridor,' she said. He went to look, and had to lean against it for strength. Rainbow rows of sweets, chocolate bars, crisps. A tube of fruit pastilles cost him his last cash. Back at his seat, the wrapping was hard to get into with one hand, but once he'd peeled off the paper, Yonas chewed through them – orange, lemon, blackcurrant, lime, raspberry – every last juicy, life-giving one.

Finally he was called into a small room. A black woman doctor introduced herself warmly, pulled a curtain across the cubicle and put on plastic gloves. 'Now then, Mr Kelati, do you mind if I take a look?' she asked. She had a gentle, singsong voice, and her accent wasn't African – he guessed Caribbean. She unwrapped the dustsheet tenderly, but it felt like she was ripping a plaster off his raw flesh, and he breathed in sharply. The dried blood had turned brown at the top, and was thickly speckled with dirt. Thick red oozed underneath.

'This looks nasty,' the doctor said. 'How did it happen?'

'I fell,' he said.

'You fell? Well, that must have been a serious fall. There's a deep scrape down your upper arm too. We'll have to put some stitches in, and clean up this grit, to start with. How's the pain?'

'Painful.'

'On a scale of one to ten, ten being unbearable?'

Yonas thought about the helicopter position, the bleeding, sizzling back, his face pressed into the stony dust. 'Six?' he offered.

'Okay!' She almost laughed in surprise. 'Well, I expect you've had a lot of painkillers – what have you taken so far?'

'Nothing.'

'Nothing! You're a brave one, then. Are you allergic to any medication?'

'I don't think so.'

She brought him some tablets and a glass of water. 'Have you had a tetanus vaccine before?'

Yonas shook his head, and she stuck a needle in his arm.

'Now, can you move your elbow for me?'

He tried and grimaced. She felt gently around it, and asked him to wiggle his fingers. He managed to lift one.

'Right, we'd better do an X-ray. So what was it you fell on?'

'Just… a hole. In the pavement.'

'I see.' She gave him a brief look, and Yonas could tell she didn't believe him. She dabbed his raw flesh with disinfectant, and the pain burned. The sweets had stopped him shivering for a while, but he started again now, in convulsive jerks.

'Are you cold, Mr Kelati? Do you think you might have a temperature?'

He shook his head.

'Have you been feeling unwell?'

'No.'

'Have you eaten today?'

'A piece of toast. Some sweets.'

'Right. Hang on.' She pulled some sachets out of a drawer, and ripped the top off one. 'Here, pop this in your mouth. It's glucose gel.'

'But I have no money…'

'Oh it's okay, my love – just suck it up!' *My love?* She fed him three sachets in a row and, mercifully, the shivering ceased. He wanted to hug her, this wonderful doctor, with her tightly combed hair and her warm brown eyes who called him *my love*, but she was making notes, and then had to go off to see another patient.

After some agonizing stitches, an X-ray and several hours of waiting and snoozing, Yonas was told he had fractured his elbow. He was fitted up with a splint and a sling, and instructed not to lift anything with his left arm for two weeks before coming back for a check-up.

'Next time,' the nurse told him, 'make sure you remember your documents, okay?'

As he walked out, his relief and gratitude for the NHS disintegrated into worry. How was he going to earn any money at all with a busted arm? How was he even going to do up his shoelaces?

Back at the squat, the guys were sympathetic. He offered to clean and cook for them all again while he couldn't earn money, but this time Emil said he shouldn't be an idiot, and told him to relax and get his arm better first. Though later on that evening, he heard Anders ask, when he thought Yonas couldn't hear from the bathroom, how long they were all expected to cover his bills while he stayed in all day, used up their hot water and watched their TV.

Or perhaps, it struck him, Anders had wanted him to hear.

Chapter 19: Tesfay

I will take a double espresso with one extra shot. Yes, okay, triple. And sugar. A lot of sugar.

When I first saw Yonas I was so happy to see another Eritrean guy who looked like he was the same age as me, coming to our class! But as soon as he started to speak, we could all hear that his English was much better than ours. I remember looking across the room at him and thinking: how are you speaking so well? You better not get ILR before me! But maybe we can be friends and you can help me practise my English. After the class finished, I planned to speak to him, but he was talking to our teacher, so I went away to get some coffee – and when I came back, he had disappeared. He never returned to the class, so I forgot about him. But then, months later, he turned up for the same job!

I was even gladder to see him that time. There were no other Eritreans on that construction site, or even any other Africans, and I was not happy about having to do that kind of work again. Before, I was doing security in a big office near Canary Wharf, in one of the tall skyscrapers, and I thought I was moving up in the world. Security is good work, you know – it can be boring, but you are not at risk of breaking your neck every day, and you have spare time for talking on the phone and relaxing.

But one day I got sacked. Just like that: boom. My boss, he just told me they were doing some ID checks and I had to make myself disappear. Actually, I think he just knew that I was more popular than him because those guys working in that office, they *loved* me! They were always working very late in the night, and usually, when they would come out of the building to go home, I would say to them, like 'Hello, my friend!!' and make a joke, and they would laugh and say hi and call me 'my friend' back and we would chat together. I had big hopes for promotion, after I got my papers. But then that job was pulled from under my feet. And the only work I could find was construction. So I went to the site that day thinking, I do *not* want to be here. But I needed the money – my wife Jamila was pregnant with our second baby. I had to provide. If I did not, she would have kicked me out and taken our daughter Freweini to live with her sister.

So, I was waiting there, just looking at all that rubble and thinking, I am *no good* for this work any more… and that is when I saw Yonas arrive. I went up to him and said '*Selam!*' and we started talking. He told me that he missed speaking in Tigrinya. And I said to him, 'But why are you not speaking your language?' He said that he did not know any Eritreans in London. I laughed at him. But he was serious! I said, 'What?! Not *any* Eritreans? That is *crazy*. I mean, there are *thousands* of us here.' I told him that there is a lot going on in our community, and I could introduce him to some people, and spend time together. He seemed happy about that. But then we had to start our work.

It was just before lunchtime, and I was getting hungry, looking forward to the rice Jamila had packed for me, when I heard this shouting, and a big crash like an avalanche. I ran over and saw Yonas, lying on the ground. This huge concrete lump fell down during the demolition and hit him, they were saying. My first thought was *thank God it was not me*, but then I felt so bad for him, and I thought, *probably he has not even got his papers yet!* He had just passed out on the floor, and I even got scared that he was dead. I tried to feel his pulse, and I said to the boss, 'What can I do, do you have a phone so that we can call an ambulance?' But he told me to get away from him – actually, he swore at me – and told me to get on with my work. I looked at him, and I thought, *Really? We Eritreans are worth that little to you?* He made a couple of other workers lift Yonas into his van, and drove off by himself.

I did not have a phone number for Yonas, and I did not know where he lived, or where the boss had taken him, and I did not know of any friends or family – nothing. And, when the boss came back alone, looking angry, I did not dare to ask. So, that was how Yonas disappeared, the second time.

But not so long after that, I received my own good news. . . I got ILR! I tell you, that was the biggest moment of relief in my entire life. The celebrations we had then – my brother and sister and all our friends around at our flat, eating and drinking and dancing!

It was a month or two after that when Yonas called me. I did not even know whose voice it was at first.

'Hey, good to hear from you!' I said. 'I did not know if you even survived that injury. What happened? It looked bad.'

'I just fractured my elbow,' he said. 'It is nearly better now.'

'I am glad,' I said. 'The NHS is the best thing about this country, right? They were so good when my Freweini was born – you know, her heartbeat actually stopped, but they got her out, and she is totally healthy now. And I want to tell you, I have some good news!'

'What?' he asked.

'I got ILR! Can you believe? I got ILR!!!!' I could not get enough of telling people, even then. I still could not believe it myself.

'*Leave to remain?*' he asked me, almost whispering the words, like it was a folk tale.

'I know! I mean, it took TIME. Six years,' I said. 'But I got it. I am sure you will too. So, are you coming to Martyrs' Day?' He said no, like he did not even know what was happening. I said, 'Are you serious?' I mean, Martyrs' Day is one of the most important events in the year, a time when we Eritreans respect all the people who gave their lives in the struggle for our country. 'There is going to be a big event in the park with hundreds of people and speeches and music.' Yonas said he would come along. 'And before you go, tell me, brother,' I said. 'Are you married?'

He laughed and said no, and I clapped my hands. 'Then you are in *luck*, my friend. There are some sexy Eritrean women just *waiting* for you to meet. Like my wife's cousin, Nigisti. She is *available*, and she is *sweeeeet* to look at, and she can *dance* – not that I am watching closely because obviously I am married, but you know what I mean.'

When he showed up outside Kennington Tube, we walked to the park together, talking. It was a perfect day: the sky was blue as blue, the sun was yellow as yellow, the trees were green as green, and our Eritrean flag was everywhere – even small flags on strings were decorating the trees, and one enormous flag was flying from a pole. Most importantly, we Eritreans were out in force. The children were playing on the grass, the women were dressed in bright colours; it was a shame that Jamila could not come that time, because Freweini was ill, but that is how it goes. Some of the children were carrying plates piled with Hembesha bread, offering it around. I watched the eyes of Yonas get big as he took a piece. I told him: 'There you go – no need to miss our national food any longer, my friend, you have arrived now!'

So, then the donation box for martyred families came around, and I put in money. Yonas said he did not have cash. I told him how I sponsor a family back home, and send money to them every month; they have got one son who was killed, and one daughter who lost an arm.

And he said, 'It is good to help people who are suffering. But how can you even afford it here – it is so expensive, and all my spare money, that I got when I could work, anyway, I had to send to my sister.' He told me how she was looking after her child, as well as his brother who lost his legs in the struggle, and his grandmother.

I told him, 'Do not worry. After a while you will get ILR, and you will be able to earn enough.' Not that I earn that much now, even, but you have to send home what you can. It is not a choice for us Eritreans – we have to defend our country, and support our martyrs, so we can carry on fighting to keep our freedom.

But I remember he said to me, 'Do you think it is still worth all the sacrifice?'

And I realized, then. I said, 'Wait – are you part of the opposition?'

He didn't answer directly. 'Our President started off with good intentions,' he said, 'but he got greedy for power and now he is ruining our country.' I sighed. I liked this guy, by instinct, you know, and I did not want to argue. 'I think a lot about what we fought for in the first place, what our parents fought for,' he went on. 'It was not just getting an independent Eritrea, right? It was about our freedom and democracy. But we still have no constitution, no rights, nothing. Of course we are all proud to be Eritrean, but how much does that mean when so many of our people, like my brothers, are maimed or killed, and our whole society is militarized, there is such terrible poverty, and we cannot even speak our minds?'

It was this big speech, and I could feel my eyes rolling. I wished he had told me this was his attitude before coming along to Martyrs' Day, of all days! The whole point is *respecting* the sacrifice of our people. 'Of course it is worth it,' I said. 'Unless you want to lose everything we have already fought for? Unless you want to forget all the thousands of our people who have died in the name of a free Eritrea and give everything back to those Ethiopian bastards? We have got to keep defending our country, until the end.'

'But when is the end?' he asked. 'My parents already died. My brother, my girlfriend… and *nothing* has changed for the better. Everything has got worse – does that not make you angry? Does there not come a point—'

'Hey hey, listen,' I said, putting my hand onto his shoulder. '*Melahaye*, it sounds like you have had a hard time. I get that. I am sorry about your family. My father died in the struggle as well. And your girlfriend as well – that is really bad luck. But you have to remember the bigger picture. We would not even have our *country* if it was not for our President. He has been protecting it, despite all the strongest countries in the world being set against us. We have to stay strong, stay together, stay united, because the Ethiopians want to take our country back and the rest of the world does not give a *shit*. *Nobody* is going to stick up for Eritrea except Eritreans. We have to keep fighting. As long as it takes.' There was a long silence, and I knew that he was not agreeing.

Eventually he said, 'It has been too long. People cannot live like this any more. We need to stop conscripting everyone, stop censoring everyone, let our people speak and vote freely, let them start businesses to grow our economy, and go online to connect with the world, and trade our goods, so that our people are not stuck in poverty and ignorance.'

He was starting to make me angry now. At the same time, I was thinking that I should not be too hard on him because I understood his suffering, and I knew he had been separated from his own people for so long, not even speaking his own language. I thought, maybe once he gets integrated into our community, he will see things differently.

But then he asked me, like he was still making his point, 'So why did you leave?'

I nearly punched him. Right? I mean, I had just taken him under my wing, and I did not *have* to help him out. I brought him here to Martyrs' Day, to introduce him to the community, I even offered to set him up with a woman, and now he was basically suggesting I was a hypocrite! I mean, sometimes I do feel guilty. I did leave because I did not want to do military service. But I came to the UK to study so that I could help Eritrea better; we need engineers to help build up our infrastructure and extend our railways and roads, so I thought if I study engineering in the UK, then when I come back I can make a real difference. It turned out I could not afford the fees to study engineering in the UK, and I could not get into a university because of my status, but at least I could earn enough to send money home. Also, now I have to look after my wife and my baby girl, so it does not make sense to go back, just to be conscripted. And the economy and education are still not good there, because the government has to focus on defence. But if Freweini goes to an English school, maybe she can become a doctor or something, and help Eritrea that way in the future. So I just told Yonas, 'I came to study, and then I got married, and my wife wants us to stay,' and then I put the question back onto him: 'What about you? Why did *you* come?'

He told me: 'I was put in prison for writing the truth.'

Well, I have heard that one before. But the thing is, people *can* write and publish in our country. There are newspapers and books and TV and radio, all supported by our government. Okay, so our government sometimes punishes people who want to broadcast things that could split the people apart and damage our national cause, but they have no choice! We are still fighting a *war*… Okay, no-war-no-peace, but if our people read articles criticizing our government at a time like this, they will start losing faith and fighting between themselves, and Eritrea will get weaker, and then we will lose. Simple. You can watch any Jackie Chan film: once the enemies start fighting between each other, they are done for. But some Westerners who claim to know all about human rights but who do not actually know or care about the Eritrean situation, they do not understand this. They go on and on about freedom of the press and all that, but it is okay for them to say, from here, when there is no country threatening to take *them* over. I was going to say that to Yonas, but then our ambassador got onto the podium and started to speak.

He talked about our fallen heroes, about how it is the duty of all Eritreans in the diaspora to support our martyrs and their families, and to be proud of them, every single day. 'We should all light candles and plant trees and think of them,' he said. I nodded, and the rest of the crowd nodded too, and murmured yes. I started to relax. I got that tingle you feel from standing in the middle of your people and thinking about why you all feel the same way, why you all look and sound the same way, why you all want to have a homeland where you can live together again some day in peace and harmony. I looked at Yonas, and I hoped that some of this was affecting him too.

After that speech, music started. A *krar* began to play, with a singer, and I clapped my hands… there is nothing better than music, especially Eritrean music, and especially Eritrean music played live, right in front of you! Yonas told me: 'My mother was a singer.' I felt sorry for him then. Even after all the shit he had been saying. I mean, music is like your soul, and it is hard for any man to lose his mother.

By the end of the song a few of my friends had spotted me and came over. I introduced them to Yonas and they all said, 'A new brother! Welcome!' But I wanted to tell them: wait, watch out, this guy is on the opposition side. I could have invited him to a party later on, but I knew that he probably would not fit in well, on a day like Martyrs' Day. So, after a couple more songs, Yonas gave me a wave and left. That was it. He never got to meet Nigisti. His loss, I thought.

Like I said, at that time I had recently got my ILR, so that was a high point for me. But I have to say, it did not take long before I realized that ILR did not solve all my problems. It was actually still difficult to find a job, the kind with payslips and stuff like that. I was still out of work after one month, and I was starting to panic about paying our rent and I could not afford nappies for Freweini, and our new baby was coming soon, and Jamila was getting stressed out. But then, I got a call from a friend of mine who had got dispersed to Newcastle.

He had a very bad time up there at first. There was nobody he knew, and hardly any Eritrean community, but then he got ILR as well. And because rent for property is cheaper there, he was able to set up a garage, for car washing and maintenance, and he called to tell me that he had a job going if I wanted it. I told Jamila, and she agreed we had to give it a try, so we packed up and headed north.

As we were preparing to leave, I texted everybody in London that I knew, and then I came to the name of Yonas in my contacts list. I nearly deleted it. But I was feeling good about the world because of my new job, and at the end of the day he was an Eritrean brother, so I decided I would just text him with my new address. I even said that, if he was ever coming up north, he should come knock on our door.

Chapter 20: Yonas

On election day, Yonas turned on the squat's new-old TV and watched the British people queuing outside local schools with POLLING STATION signs outside, chatting on their phones, and telling the newscasters how they were planning to vote, some as lackadaisically as if they'd only just considered the question while brushing their teeth that morning. One girl said she wasn't going to vote at all. 'What's the point – they're all the same, aren't they?', she asked, apparently without expecting a response.

That night, he was the only one interested enough to stay up watching as the results rolled in. After a string of blue rosettes, he started to feel a bit panicky, though he reminded himself that it really shouldn't bother him as both the main parties were pretty much as anti-immigration as each other and this election would likely make no difference to his claim and he'd probably never gain the right to vote himself here, or in any country, for his entire life. But when it came to Great Grimsby, he leaned forward despite himself, searching for Nina, dressed up all smart and willing on her husband... No, he couldn't see her.

There *he* was though, Quentin Lambourne, blond and confident, chatting easily to the people milling around him. A pretty girl stood off to his left, dressed smartly. Was that Alice? Did they, or didn't they?

Surely he would lose, after those newspaper articles. The candidates filed onto the stage and a man stepped up to a lectern to declare himself the returning officer and read out the scores: Marlow, Dave, United Kingdom Independence Party, 8,263; Ackroyd, Jim, Monster Raving Loony Party, 254; Jessop, Anna, Green Party, 6,689; Summers, Tim, Labour Party, 11,521; [loud applause] and finally, Lambourne, Quentin, Conservative Party, 11,561 [even louder applause]. A majority of just forty? He'd really won? Yonas's new favourite British saying came to mind: *by the skin of your teeth*.

He curled up on the sofa in a renewed gloom until the red line on the illustrative graph crept up. *Maybe not everybody in the country was thinking what you were thinking after all*, he thought, and sat up again. When the final result was declared, he got to his feet and clapped.

The next morning, he left before breakfast to hunt for some newspapers for the commentary. In twenty minutes he'd found three, one from the Tube station, one from a bus stop, and one from a recycling bin. Back in the kitchen, he read slowly, keeping an eye out for coverage of Great Grimsby. And there it was:

Great Grimsby was the site of a surprising victory for the Conservatives, after their candidate, Quentin Lambourne, managed to regain the lead after being the subject of controversy. It was alleged, several weeks ago, that Mr Lambourne, whose main campaign pledge was to fight illegal immigration, had been concealing the fact that an illegal immigrant was working for his family. It was later alleged that Lambourne had been having an affair with his campaign manager, Alice Teal, eight years his junior. The candidate strongly denied both allegations, and while they caused his popularity to dip initially, his resilient response apparently caused it to rise again, higher than before, resulting in a narrow majority of just 40 votes over his Labour rival, the incumbent, Gloria Jensen. Lambourne's wife was not with him while the results were announced, prompting renewed rumours over the alleged affair...

So, Yonas wasn't the only one to speculate over Nina's absence. But the article was probably just grasping at straws – she could well just have been looking after their daughter at home that night, or standing off-screen somewhere. In any case, now that he was an MP, and all that campaign stress was over, she would obviously stay with him.

A week or so later, he was attempting to wash up dinner plates in the kitchen, cursing his still useless left arm and the state of his life and the tedium of waiting and Gebre for taking so long to get to London and find him, when his phone beeped. Message from: Nina.

Hi Yonas. Hope you're well. I've been thinking of you. Knowing how closely you keep up with the news, I expect you heard the election results. Just wanted to let you know that Quentin and I have separated. I'm currently living at Mum's with Clara…

Would love to see you again. There's an exhibition I think you'd really like at the Serpentine. An artist of Nigerian descent – Chris Ofili. Would you go with me?
Nina x

Yonas read it three times, then put his phone back in his pocket. His gut told him to go, but his head warned otherwise. He had to get used to the idea that Nina was just a character from his past. She'd betrayed him. He did not need her to take him along to galleries now that he knew they were free. And yet nothing had ultimately come of that article her friend wrote. And she had consistently denied knowing about it. Also, she had really been persistent about apologizing and asking to see him, and for no discernible reason other than that she either felt guilty, or liked his company. Or both. He decided to sleep on it and reply in the morning.

When he awoke, there was a promising swathe of blue sky outside his window and a single, lonely cloud. Everyone else had already gone out. He made himself a cup of strong, sweet tea, and got out his phone to type a reply.

Thank you for letting me know.

Yes, I would like that. When shall we go?

One minute later, she texted back.

How about tomorrow? 12.30?

He looked up the Serpentine on his *A–Z*. It was in Hyde Park, and close to Buckingham Palace, which he thought was probably a place he should see.

The following morning, the sun was even brighter, so Yonas decided to leave his jacket behind as he stepped out of the squat, and felt almost glad that he couldn't afford to take public transport. It felt liberating to be walking somewhere with a purpose, to meet someone, to have a change of scene from the neighbourhood.

As he approached Buckingham Palace, hundreds of people crowding at metal barriers slowed his pace. He was just wondering whether the British were always so enthusiastic about their royal family, when he heard music, drumming, the sounds of a band, and then, over the top of a few heads, he saw a parade of soldiers marching along playing brass instruments, dressed in bright red jackets with huge black furry hats, three times the height of their skulls, fastened by straps that seemed to go across their lower lips, which looked like the most uncomfortable and ridiculous military attire imaginable. These must be actors, putting on a show for the tourists, mustn't they? But their marching was precise, and their faces solemn with responsibility. Yonas couldn't help remembering his own military training, and the strangeness of learning to march, like being taught a dance for the first time. It was disorientating to see the military here in action, even these absurd-looking characters, when he'd envisioned the UK as a peaceful, soldier-free landscape, only ever deploying troops abroad to dispatch rogue leaders of oil-rich states.

'Excuse me, do you know what occasion this is?' he asked a woman next to him.

'This? It's the Changing of the Guard!'

He decided not to ask what this meant. 'Are they real soldiers?'

'Yeah – with real bears on their heads and all!'

Yonas felt like he was part of a mass re-enactment of the British Empire. The hundreds of people watching seemed to be loving it – but he reckoned, from the smattering of languages he could hear, that most were tourists. He wondered if the Queen were sitting right now next to one of the many windows in the palace. Was she lapping up the glory, or was she thoroughly bored of the spectacle by now, and wishing they would all just leave her alone? Would the British people ever rise up and knock their monarchy off this pedestal? In a way, it didn't really matter, as long as they still had a parliament and a legal system, Yonas thought. As long as nobody was being *forced* to dress up in military garb and march. The bears probably didn't have much choice though.

He headed away, and walked through Green Park, a pretty space that lived up to its name, before crossing over a busy junction and passing through a set of tall gates to enter Hyde Park.

Pausing by a lake, he watched people pedalling around in bright blue plastic boats that looked like oversized bath toys. Near the bank, a party of people were already eating a picnic they'd set up with full foldable furniture including a wicker hamper and real wine glasses. Not far off, two guys lounging under a tree were shooting up, apparently for all to see, although nobody else seemed to be watching. Yonas wandered up and down some paths, lost his way a little, and found himself gravitating towards a small crowd, standing around a man in a tracksuit bellowing into a loudspeaker. 'THIS CREEPING CAPITALISM IS A CATASTROPHE WAITING TO DECIMATE OUR SOCIETY – PRIVATIZATION IS STRANGLING OUR NHS, IT'S PUT UP OUR RAIL PRICES AND OUR HEATING BILLS, IT'S RUINING OUR EDUCATION SYSTEM, IT'S POLLUTING OUR ENVIRONMENT, IT'S DISTORTING OUR MEDIA, AND IF WE DON'T ACT NOW, IF WE DON'T GET TOGETHER AND PROTEST, IF WE DON'T STAND UP AND DEMAND RADICAL CHANGE FROM OUR GOVERNMENT, IF WE DON'T

RAISE OUR VOICES LOUDLY, IF WE DON'T DO THIS RIGHT NOW, TODAY, IT'S GOING TO BE TOO LATE! WE NEED A REVOLUTION!

A few children were giggling, some people were taking photos as if the man were another tourist attraction, and a few observers were listening intently. Who was this person? Yonas wondered. Why was he here? Who did he represent? Was this an organized event? Was this man really free to say all that through a loudspeaker to whoever wanted to listen, almost within hearing distance of Westminster and the Palace? He lingered, transfixed, until he realized the time, and had to jog to get to the gallery on time.

It was Victorian-looking, built from brick, with white columns at the front and a triangular roof with a birdcage-like tower on top. Leaning against the wall, holding a paperback, was Nina. She looked up and glanced around left and right, her forehead creased down the middle, and started biting the insides of her fingers. Obviously hadn't seen him yet. He'd forgotten how slight she was, how small and pale and pointy, like she could be folded up and slipped into a letterbox. His residual crossness with her was already fading.

He walked towards her, and when he was a few metres away, she noticed him. 'Joe! I'm so glad you came,' she exclaimed. He smiled back, but felt himself flush at her use of the name 'Joe'. Veata knew his real name now, and the authorities knew it, so if he and Nina were going to start again – if she was really going to be a friend – shouldn't he tell her? He halted when he reached her, unsure of the appropriate gesture for a greeting, but she leaned forward and kissed him awkwardly on the cheek, her lips barely meeting his skin, like a bird pecking tentatively at a tiny berry, and then seemed to change her mind and hugged him, tightly but briefly. He couldn't stop himself from an audible in-breath at the twinge as her body pressed against his bad arm.

'Oh God, I'm sorry, Joe… What happened to your arm?'

'I just fell,' he said lightly. 'On the stairs. It is fine now – it was just a small fracture.'

'Must be so hard to manage with a sling,' she said. 'I remember breaking my arm playing netball. It was so hard, just doing up buttons and silly things like that, things you don't even think about normally.'

'Putting make-up on is the hardest for me,' he said, which made her laugh.

'Well, your face looks immaculate,' she said. 'So, shall we go in?'

As they queued for tickets, Yonas skim-read the leaflet. The artist had won a major prize, made portraits of black people and pop culture, and liked splattering elephant dung on his paintings. Yonas bet he'd be yet another example of an African conforming to an infantilizing, exoticizing stereotype, and prepared to be cynical. But when they stepped inside, the paintings were so bright and vigorous, so confident, soulful and funny, that he felt immediately uplifted, and wished he could show Gebre. This was an artist having fun parodying perceptions of black culture, not submitting to them, and it felt thrilling to be admiring the work of a black African artist in a place like this, with the Palace and that grandiose parade a stone's throw away. He laughed out loud just at the title of one picture – *The Naked Soul of Captain Shit and the Legend of the Black Stars* – before he'd even looked properly at the painting itself, but then heard the sudden, jarring sound around a faintly shocked space and cleared his throat, embarrassed. He glanced over at Nina, but she was silently engrossed, just like she had been at the Portrait Gallery. Drawn though he was to the paintings, after a while he found himself surreptitiously spending more time watching Nina look at them, observing her concentration, the set of her lips. He wondered what she was thinking, and whether she saw what he saw. Was she getting creative ideas from this for her own painting? he wondered. What was she working on?

'Right! Are we done?' Nina asked, and they started walking out. 'Shall we go to the café in the Pavilion outside?' she suggested. 'It's a temporary structure, designed by a different architect every year.'

'Sounds great,' he said. 'So, what did you think of the exhibition?'

'Fantastic, wasn't it?' she gushed. 'So carnivalesque! I'm not convinced by the dung, to be honest, but hey, why not throw a bit of shit at the establishment?' He laughed. 'How about you?' she asked. 'What was your favourite piece?'

'I liked *The Holy Virgin Mary*,' he said, instinctively. This was the picture the leaflet said had caused a big stir in the art world – not only was the Mary figure black, with a wide, flared nose, but she was surrounded by porn magazine cuttings and had an elephant dung breast. He suddenly worried that Nina would think him lewd for choosing a picture with an exposed breast. An exposed breast made of shit, no less, and multiple naked bottoms…

'Good choice – definitely sensational in both senses of the word,' she said. 'And I love the idea of a hip hop old master.'

The Pavilion was built of wood, with a dome-shaped roof and slanted sides, planks criss-crossed into hundreds of small square shapes, and windows open to the elements. 'I like how different this is to the gallery building,' Yonas said, crossing the threshold. 'Who is the architect?'

'Let's see…' Nina pulled the leaflet out of her jeans pocket, and read aloud as they queued for drinks. 'A Portuguese duo, who wanted it to have a dialogue with the neoclassical house…' She looked around. 'The wooden beams are supposed to refer to the trees outside.'

Yonas looked out at the leaves fluttering in the breeze. It was delightful to be sitting in this light, wooden space in the middle of a park, like a giant tree house. The geometric patterns of the wood contrasted with the curvature of the ceiling. 'It reminds me of Asmara,' he said. 'Did you know that our capital city was a playground for Italian futurist architects?'

'Seriously?' Nina asked, as they joined the queue for the counter.

'Of course. We have many buildings from that period. A huge petrol station, a building that used to be a prison but is now a bank, three cinemas… Some people call it La Piccola Roma.' Yonas's stomach rumbled, and he wasn't sure whether Nina would offer to pay, and whether it would just be for a coffee or for food, and whether he should immediately accept or demur…

But then she made it easy. 'Tell me more, but shall we decide what to order? I'm starving.' 'I'm going to get one of these salad boxes, I think. And a coffee. On me obviously. What are you having?'

Yonas picked out the biggest sandwich on offer, and said he'd love a coffee too, trying not to feel emasculated. There was just no point in him offering anything. He couldn't even afford the bus, and she probably knew it. He should focus on what he could offer her. 'Asmara also has one of the ugliest sculptures in the world,' he said, as they took the coffees over to a table by the window and sat down.

'Oh? Of what?'

'A huge pair of plastic sandals. As big as a house.'

'Sandals?' Nina laughed. 'Why?'

'The liberation fighters wore them, to beat off the Ethiopians in their big army boots. So the sculpture is very symbolic. It means a lot to many people. Which does not make it beautiful. But it is unique. Asmara is a nice city – the cleanest in Africa, probably. There are wide streets, palm trees, coffee shops… You should go there, one day. When things get better. Fifty years from now, maybe! I will show you around. You would like it – there are lots of espresso bars and tree-lined avenues, and the city is up on a high plateau so the temperature is always nice.' He remembered talking to Sarama about walking arm in arm around Asmara together once the war ended, going to the cinema, being a normal couple, their relationship out in the open. 'Maybe we will both need sticks by then and have grey hair,' he added – but immediately felt he'd stepped over the intimacy line. It was overwhelmingly unlikely that he and Nina would be in touch as old people. Unlikely that he would even make it to old age, if he got deported.

'Oh yes, I would love to go!' Nina said. 'I really hope the situation there does improve soon, so you get to go back and see your family. Although – it's great having you here too, Joe. I'd be sad if you left.'

He smiled across the table, concealing a wince at the name, then looked down at the dregs of his cappuccino. It felt good to be with Nina again. So unexpectedly easy to spend time in her company. He couldn't let her carry on calling him Joe. He opened his mouth… but wouldn't she be angry to learn that he'd deceived her about something this fundamental? Wouldn't her trust in him disappear in a puff of smoke? 'Have you travelled anywhere in Africa before?' he asked instead.

'Oh, only to Morocco. I went there on a package holiday for a week with my ex, years ago, at university. Who was also called Joe, bizarrely.'

'Oh,' he said. 'Really.'

'Yep. But he cheated on me too, later that same summer, as it happens.' Yonas clenched his teeth. 'Don't worry, he didn't tarnish the name Joe for me for life,' Nina added, sensing his discomfort. 'I got over it soon enough.'

'Right,' he said, took his last sip of coffee, then choked on it. 'Sorry. I was actually just going to say that, talking of names... I would like to tell you mine.'

'Yours?'

'It is not Joe.'

'Oh. Okay. What is it then?'

'Yonas.' There was a pause. He scrunched his toes under the table.

'Yonas,' she parroted back musingly. He liked how it sounded when she said it.

'I did not want to deceive you or Molly,' he added, 'it is just that, before I claimed asylum, I wanted to hide my identity, you know, in case the smugglers or anybody came looking. . .'

'Yonas is a much nicer name,' she said.

'Oh, you think so?' She didn't look cross at all. He suddenly felt much lighter inside.

'Definitely. Anyway, it's you I've been getting to know. A name is just a label.'

'I suppose.' They smiled at each other, and Yonas looked down at his empty cup, embarrassed.

'Having said that,' Nina added, 'I wish I'd kept my maiden name. Lambourne sounded like a lovely surname to me at the time Quentin proposed – romantic, even. And he was insistent I should take it so that we'd eventually have the same surname as our kids. But if I could turn back time, I'd stick with Muldoon. You know that's Mum's surname? It was actually her maiden name too. She kept it and insisted Dad changed his name to hers if he wanted to have the same surname as his child – and he agreed! Which is super-unusual in the UK. Even now. We're supposed

203

to have equality here, but women and children almost always take the man's name still, as I went and did. That said, Dad's surname was Smith, which is about as dull an English name as you can get, so he stepped up in the world with Muldoon. Gave himself an Irish flourish. His friends took the mick, but he didn't care.'

'Muldoon. It is a good name, especially for an artist like you. It sounds poetic. Could you change back?' Yonas asked.

'I could,' Nina said. 'I think I will.'

Chapter 21: Nina

Hi. Skinny latte, please. No sugar, but just a tiny drop of that hazelnut syrup. Just for the flavour. Is that okay? Thanks so much.

So when I first met Yonas – or Joe, as he had us believe back then – I was petrified. I was sure he was about to mug me! He just appeared out of the shadows, this terrifyingly tall silhouette, right on my mum's doorstep. Thankfully I'd gone round there for help as well, and I was too upset to scream. If I had, we'd probably never even have managed a conversation.

Before that night, all I knew about him was that he was a student in my mum's English class at the Refugee Council who had somehow talked her into having him round for private lessons – which was okay (but I did wonder a bit about her safety) – and had then started working for her. So obviously at that point I'd asked Mum some basic questions, like what proof she had of his immigration status, but she went all vague on me. 'You've got to check his papers at least,' I told her, but she made some excuse and told me I was being over-anxious 'as usual'. I was like: 'Mum! Apart from anything else, you know Quentin's *campaigning* on illegal immigration! Have you even thought about what'd happen if this came out, for him, and more to the point, for you? You could be fined. A lot of money. It's a criminal offence. And you'd better hope this guy doesn't steal all your jewellery first and dump you in the compost.'

But within minutes of actually meeting Yonas, I knew she was right about him. I don't know how I knew, apart from a gut instinct – a feeling that I could confide in him about anything, from foxes to political philosophy to parenting. I mean, it really is quite strange, in retrospect, how natural it felt to sit there on the step and talk to him like that, when I usually take a while to open up to people, and minutes earlier I'd thought he was an axe murderer. I mean, rationally I had still been right that Mum should have checked his status, but still, once I'd talked to him myself, I regretted the assumptions I'd made that'd sent my tone all Bertha Rochester. On the other hand, Mum didn't need to rub it in by calling me 'over-anxious' – she knows anxiety is a real struggle for me, and she has never dealt well with it. It all goes back to Dad dying: her way of grieving was to get out there and do things for others 'as he would have wanted', whereas I found it really hard to recover, which she saw as a failure, and has constantly felt the need to remind me to stop worrying and embrace life ever since. Which I do, as best I can. Making art helps a lot. But Mum always manages to hit the old nerve!

Still, I wish I'd listened to her years ago when she was sceptical about Quentin and I was determinedly telling her that *she* was the one being over-anxious, for once – it's galling to think that, there I was, having a go at her about Yonas, partly to defend Quentin, while he was busy betraying me – I just didn't know it yet.

I just never expected he'd cheat. We'd been together since our last year of university. We've always been very different, but he was just so absurdly confident, he made me feel safe, I guess. Actually, my first impression of him was of cockiness. I couldn't help noticing him in lectures (philosophy – that was our overlap subject), because he was always the first one to ask a question. You know, the kind of question that's more about showing off your knowledge than finding an answer? I didn't speak to him until we found ourselves at the same orchestra rehearsal, when he turned up to play a Mozart piano concerto. He played so sensitively – it was calming, just listening to him from the middle of the cellos. Watching his fingers ripple around the keys reminded me of my dad a bit – he used to play piano too, although Quentin is way better, technically, and also loathes jazz when all Dad ever played were standards. But anyway, as I watched Quentin at the piano, I thought: maybe I was wrong to judge him. And that would have been that, but I was just packing up when he tapped me on the shoulder, said he recognized me, and ended up asking me out.

He whisked me off to classic films – like *The Godfather* which I'd never seen before – concerts and union debates. He soon picked up on my anxiety, but he took it in his stride. It was even he who suggested I get back into making art, as a way to deal with it. I'd mentioned to him how I used to love painting with Dad as a child, and he knew I'd done art for A level, so one day he said he'd heard there was an art room in Christ Church, and I should try it out. I obediently went along, expecting to be uninspired and rusty. But actually, it was a lovely, peaceful space, and there were a couple of artists making beautiful prints there and several friendly students, and I experienced this sudden yearning to create, just to make expressive marks on paper, and as soon as I did, it felt like a miraculous release. So I got back into watercolours, and being able to retreat to that room most days, splash colour around, then scrunch up the paper or leave it behind, got me through the rest of university, for sure.

And, I mean, when it comes on, my anxiety is physical. I get insomnia, and it feels like there's this tight fist lodged in my chest, where my ribs join, and it seems to get more and more compressed, and my heart starts fluttering and my breathing gets shallow… Quentin got really sharp at anticipating my episodes, and basically ordering me to go off and make art. Which made me think he was the only person who understood me.

So when we got married and got our own place, and I quit my soulless consulting job and started an art foundation course, I was super-happy! I poured everything into it, working all hours, loving every minute – barely saw Quentin, actually – and went on to do an MA in Fine Art at the RA. Honestly, those two years were just the best fun – I started experimenting with fashion, wearing eccentric shirts and doing up dresses in kooky ways, I went to tons of exhibitions and lectures – and most of all I just so enjoyed the licence it gave to make art all the time, without having to think about selling it. Most of the other students were younger than me, but that was okay – they accepted me, and I felt so lucky that I'd had enough life experience to really appreciate the opportunity I had. And then I was lucky enough to get noticed at our end of year show – some well-known collectors bought a couple of pieces... But then I had just got pregnant.

Even during pregnancy my anxiety levels rocketed again. I started obsessing about which toiletries and cleaning products were safest as well as nutrition, worrying that every element I touched or ingested could harm her development, and then when Clara arrived I obsessed about her routines, to the point that I'd panic if I was one minute late with her bottle, and when I weaned her I was convinced she was going to choke or would be poisoned by any purée that hadn't been made by me that morning with organic ingredients less than an hour before she ingested it, and I made everyone use sterilizing hand gel before touching her or her things – I secretly hated letting strangers hold her... And yet I was constantly worrying I was parenting badly, and wanted Quentin's reassurance. It was just my bizarre take on postnatal depression, looking back. But it coincided with Quentin launching himself into politics, which meant he was around even less, and I ended up more or less abandoning my own career, just as it was taking off.

Quentin started to get outwardly impatient with me, to the point where I got too nervous to talk to him about anything much. He never encouraged me any more to go off to make more art like he used to, or to have time away from Clara, probably because he was too busy to look after her himself, when that was what I really needed, but I couldn't admit to it because I felt like that would make me an even worse mother. And when Quentin *was* home, all he wanted to tell me about was his campaign, and in this lecturing way as if I were a dim constituent who needed to be educated. And hearing him orate on all these different issues made me realize, subconsciously at first, that it made me uncomfortable – that I actually didn't agree with him on most things. I used to describe myself half-jokingly as apolitical. But now I started to realize that Dad's socialism must have sunk in deeper than I'd thought. Before long, I dreaded even being in the same room as my husband, so one day I snapped – I told him I just couldn't talk about his campaign, or politics, any more, until the election was over, which infuriated him, as I knew it would. But I stuck to it. At the same time I craved his support.

Looking back, I realize Quentin had never actually been all that great at listening to me. A bit like Mum, his attitude was always that I should pull myself together – and making art, to him, was just a solution that didn't have to involve him. It sometimes felt like I was a machine he'd paid a lot for, but was prone to malfunction, so he'd demand I be serviced promptly, but didn't really care how, or even why I wasn't working properly, as long as I came back fixed. And then he found himself a new machine anyway.

When I found those blatant texts from Alice, I was devastated. He'd left his phone in the kitchen one morning while he had a shower, and one came through. My initial response was to panic inside, but act normal outside – I just put the phone back, watched him hunt for it, find it, and slip it nonchalantly in his pocket, and said goodbye to him as normal, then dropped Clara off at nursery. It was only once I got home again that I started to lose it. I thought about all the consequences for our daughter if we broke up, and how I could possibly manage on my own, and that fist inside me tightened, and my breathing went all shallow – I thought I was going to hyperventilate, or faint, or both…

I called my 'best friend' Meg, but she was busy. I didn't feel like calling any of my other friends yet, or Mum – especially since she and I had just had this big row over her employing *the immigrant*. So after a while of wandering around the house wailing at nobody, I texted Quentin to say he would have to pick up Clara that evening, as I was going to the studio for a long session; but I wasn't really in a state to work, and instead I found myself heading for the Heath. Once I got there I just walked and walked, all afternoon, looping all the trails, barely noticing where I was going but just processing what had just happened and somehow absorbing the surroundings. That place always calms me down and makes me feel better – the wildness, the greenery, being above it all… but when the sun started setting, I realized I hadn't eaten anything since breakfast. And I couldn't bring myself to go home yet. Meg's phone was off, and the only place I could think of to go was Mum's.

And then she was out! Instead, there was this stranger. After I'd got over being scared, I was really spiky with him, but he didn't react angrily, like he could have done – he just asked me if I was okay, and we started chatting, and soon we were sitting next to each other on the doorstep and I was telling him about my marriage and the affair – things I'd never even told Mum, or anyone! He turned out to be such a good listener. And he cracked a few jokes along the way too, which helped put me at ease. But also, somehow, I sensed that he really wanted to know how I felt, that he genuinely cared, even though he'd only just met me – and even though, in comparison to him, my problems were the tiniest molehill next to Everest. I mean, he'd been forced to leave his accommodation with no notice, had nowhere else to stay, no job, no family, no way of going back to his country without being tortured and imprisoned, *again*… And once I made the effort to listen in return, I was almost dumbfounded by how he'd been through all that, and yet still had the headspace – and the heartspace – to listen to me. It was like realizing I'd been looking at my own little world through a microscope for years, and I'd only just stepped away from the lens.

So, even when he admitted that he wasn't a refugee and he had been working in the UK illegally – which I'd blown up to being such a big issue in my head – I was surprised to find I didn't care. Especially when he started to tell me about why he'd left Eritrea, being a dissident writer, and what had happened to him. He talked so evenly about these extraordinary experiences that I, bizarrely, felt almost comforted, at the same time as feeling I should offer comfort of some sort and not knowing how. He's got a lovely, mellow tone of voice, too, I hadn't heard an accent quite like his before, and he's so striking to look at, from a *purely* artistic point of view, of course, that I found I was completely captivated by him – my own problems seemed to vanish, and I could have listened to him all night.

Anyway, then Mum finally arrived back home from her book group, and we both ended up staying over. In different rooms, of course! After he'd gone to bed, I apologized to Mum, and then told her about the affair. I tried to sound together, but I couldn't stop the tears erupting, and then I could see her start to panic as she foresaw yet another anxiety phase, and how she would now going to be expected to pick up the pieces around me, when she thought her son-in-law had finally taken over that mantle. I mean, her immediate response was: 'Oh, how *could* he, I never liked him – but don't rush into anything, single parenting is *hard*, Nina, believe me; how would *you cope?*' Honestly, she managed to convey in one sentence that she'd always disapproved of my choice of mate, and yet she also thought I was so pathetic because of my anxiety that I would fall apart without him, *and* implied I would therefore be causing irrevocable harm to her granddaughter! So I told her I didn't want to talk about it any more, and went to bed.

It was great having Yonas there the next morning, actually, because Mum and I were forced to be nice to one another while we all ate breakfast, and everything from the night before was defused. I gave Yonas the phone numbers I'd looked up, and then I knew I should get ready to leave and head home for the inevitable confrontation, but that would mean I'd have to decide what to do, and also I really wanted to see more of him… So I made an impromptu suggestion that he come with me to the Portrait Gallery.

It felt like such a treat to introduce it to someone who'd never been – not just there but to any gallery in the UK! Made me remember what riches we have on our doorstep, especially in London. Conversation flowed about the pictures and other things – he has a good friend who's an artist – and we walked all the way back to Mum's afterwards. I'd been having such a nice time that, again, I'd almost forgotten about my own little apocalypse.

But I had to deal with it in the end. So I drove back home, picked up Clara, smiled and asked the normal questions about how her day was, gave her supper, and put her to bed… and then the panic started sweeping through me again.

It was hours later that Quentin finally walked in. He wasn't due to be back so late, and I bet I knew where he'd been. He didn't seem to think it odd that I was just sitting there in the kitchen in the dark, or even ask how I was, or why I'd stayed over at Mum's. Instead he switched the light on, started preparing himself a snack and telling me about all the meetings he'd had that day. So, for once, I told him to shut up.

'Excuse me?' he said.

I felt a little glow, then. I wished I'd had the guts to say that to him before. 'I know,' I said.

'Know what?' he said.

'You know what.'

'I don't know what.'

'You really want me to spell *what* out?' Apparently he really did. 'Okay,' I said, 'I *know* about you and Alice: that's what.' I expected him to break down and apologize, maybe even kneel at my feet and plead – but he denied it! I made him get his phone out to prove it. And then, he accepted the texts were there, and looked embarrassed, at least, but insisted it was all one-sided on Alice's part and claimed he never sent flirty texts back and demanded I look at his sent message folder. And I said, well I have looked at it and you might have been careful enough of your own career not to be *obvious* about it, but you hardly made efforts to put her *off*, did you? He claimed he *had* in fact asked her to behave more professionally a few times but he didn't want to 'dent her enthusiasm' as she put in a lot of hours and was doing a great job for the campaign and they had a good 'working relationship'.

'Don't give me that!' I said. 'You must at least have led her on for her to send repeated texts to her *boss* full of kisses and gushing about what an "amazing time" she's had with you, sent as late as midnight on days when you'd put in our calendar that you were working late, like a clutch of teenage love letters that you *chose to preserve*. You cannot expect me to believe that nothing's happened after reading all that. Just admit it!' But he still wouldn't – claimed that if he'd had anything to hide, he'd have deleted it. So we had a massive row, and of course poor Clara woke up.

So then there was a stand-off in the house for a few days, where I refused to speak to Quentin or argue in front of our child again until he admitted it. Which he still refused to do. I told Meg and asked her for advice, and she sounded suitably affronted on my part, but just said

I should leave him immediately, as if it were obvious. She had no real empathy with the quandary of being a mother in that situation. And, do you know, I think the only way I stayed strong was the memory of my secret encounter with Yonas – that new feeling it had given me that I wasn't alone, that somebody would listen to me and not judge. And also that I wasn't the most unlucky person in the world, by any stretch! If he could stay balanced in his situation, so could I in mine.

But then Meg, knowing how upset I was, went and gave me another wonderful surprise by publishing an article in the paper saying that Mum was employing an illegal immigrant, and accusing Quentin of being a hypocrite! So, while I'd been reaching out to her for help, she'd been planning to expose my family behind my back. Quentin accused me of masterminding it to get back at him for the affair that he still said was non-existent. He lost the plot, and started shouting in my face, saying he couldn't believe I'd deliberately sabotaged his campaign, called me a 'psycho', said my anxiety had 'spun out of control' and he'd 'had it up to here' and he should just 'take me to get psychiatric help'. It got really nasty. I was still reeling, after he'd finally left for work, when I remembered I was supposed to meet Yonas again that day. But before I could work out how to explain Meg's article to *him*, Yonas called *me* to say he'd already found it in the paper. And then hung up. Didn't respond to my messages. Just disappeared off the map.

So, my biggest worry at that point was obviously Clara. But I also found, to my surprise, that I cared more about Yonas believing that I'd exploited him and cutting me off than I did about the likely collapse of Quentin's election campaign. And even our relationship. I was worried for Mum too, of course, in case the police got onto her, and I was livid with Meg. I mean, we'd been friends for twenty years, and to her that apparently meant nothing, if she could just use me for blatant career gain like that. So I phoned her and told her our friendship was over, and then sobbed – I'd never imagined having that conversation with her, of all people.

I had to tell Mum about the article, then. Poor Mum – she was so confused and hurt. She said that Meg had spoken to her, but never mentioned she intended to publish anything. She also pointed out that *I* must have told Meg about her employing Joe in the first place, because nobody else knew, and said she would 'just have to hope the police didn't follow up', just as I'd 'threatened', and while she was 'sorry my marriage was going awry', this was 'no way to deal with it'.

I hung up. I really didn't know what to do. I felt utterly alone. Even though I was furious with Quentin, I couldn't help feeling guilty that it was me who'd unintentionally caused this hand grenade to hit his campaign by talking to Meg, and generally by being over-anxious, and I couldn't bring myself to walk out of our marriage yet, which would mean taking Clara away from her father. So I decided to stay on at home, and maintain an external illusion of a normal family life until the election was over, on the condition that we slept in separate rooms. Then I'd decide.

So for a few weeks I concentrated on looking after Clara, getting through the daily routine, never speaking to my friends, or Mum, never taking calls or checking my email, not letting on to anyone else what had happened. Unbelievably, Meg wrote a second article about Quentin, this time publicizing his affair, and had the gall to email me, suggesting I should be grateful. I didn't reply. I ignored the reporters loitering outside our house, and pretended they weren't there, until I absolutely had to leave to take Clara out; then I'd open the door feeling so shaky and tight-chested I could hardly breathe. 'Mrs Lambourne, tell us your side,' they'd shout at me, and I wouldn't look at them, and insisted Clara didn't either. I told her they were just some nasty people who wanted to make her daddy's life difficult and it was all part of a nasty political game run by boys and they would go away soon. And they did. They got bored, and drifted away like flies from a dried-up apple core.

I got used to going to bed before Quentin got home – which was invariably late in the final days of the campaign – and walking around him when we happened to coincide in the kitchen early in the morning as if he were a ghost. And I thought a lot about Yonas, hiding out somewhere too. How, in a different way, he must also be having to go out and face the world every day, concealing so much. (I didn't realize how much, then.) But I figured I would never see him again. I mean, if you're illegal and you think the police are onto you, you're likely to go on the run, and you're definitely going to cut off the person you think shopped you, right?

But the timing felt like such a shame, because I'd researched an immigration lawyer who sounded great and, after some initial caution, Yonas had agreed he would see her. Meg's article had probably spooked him into giving up on the idea. I sent him lots of texts trying to explain, and encouraging him to go, but he never replied.

I couldn't stop thinking about him though. I'd barely met him, really, and I told myself it must just be my imagination going into overdrive – you know, everything else in my life was a mess, and I was constructing Yonas into this unlikely saint who'd parachuted in and pulled me out of my despair, and appeared to be the absolute polar opposite to Quentin in so many ways, which somehow added to the justifications I needed to leave my marriage! I reminded myself I hardly knew him at all. But I just felt deep down as if I did.

So, one day, Mum called, and she told me that the police *had* come round to question her, but she'd told them in no uncertain terms that her student was just her student, and that she was frankly indignant at how she had been treated for doing charity work like a conscientious citizen. 'And can you believe,' she said, 'they actually apologized to me, and assured me they'd drop it?'

I almost laughed with relief! 'Well done, Mum,' I said, 'that's brilliant!' I apologized again for my unwitting leak, and this time she said it was *her* fault for employing Joe in the first place, that she should have listened to my advice after all. 'No, no,' I said, 'please don't blame yourself! I shouldn't have made such a big deal of it. And I guess neither of us should have trusted Meg.' Mum said she was sorry I'd lost a friend, but I said I was probably better off, only wishing I meant it – I was still missing Meg, despite what she'd done. And then I asked Mum if Clara and I could please move in with her if I decided to leave Quentin.

There was a long silence. Then she said she didn't think that was a good idea. I felt a bit sick. I had to plead with her, and tell her how Quentin had shouted at me and said awful things, and how I was worried about

Clara… until she finally conceded. Which didn't fill me with joy about moving back home, even for a short time. But it was still a relief to know that I could.

Quentin did get elected, of course. Despite the article. And I was glad, purely because he would get the job and status boost he wanted, and wouldn't then feel like he'd lost everything when I moved out with Clara. Because I'd finally made up my mind by then. Still, I didn't have the courage to tell him we were leaving – gutless, I know – I just waited until he was out at a celebration lunch the following day, then packed up a suitcase and left him a note.

The hardest part of it was picking up Clara from nursery, and telling her we weren't going home, that we were going to live with Ganna for a while. 'What about Daddy?' she asked, and I nearly broke down in front of her. I plied her with treats and kisses, I was so worried she'd be traumatized and would rightly blame me and I'd have unwittingly destroyed our future relationship and we'd get on even worse in later life than I did with my own mother, and she would probably move to another continent to get away from me and would only ever send me a Christmas card once a year and I would probably die old and alone… But she was surprisingly okay with it! So that took the pressure off a little.

But a few days later, once we'd settled in at Mum's, I got embroiled in flat-hunting and divorce lawyer communications and my anxiety started rocketing again – I couldn't sleep, and I could tell that me being so on edge was annoying Mum, and we kept bickering. So one morning she offered to look after Clara for an afternoon while I went out to a gallery to take my mind off things. I agreed – and then it occurred to me to text Joe to let him know what had happened. I didn't really expect a response, as he hadn't responded to any of my other messages, but to my surprise he got back to me, after all, and agreed to meet. So I suggested we go to the Serpentine. And as soon as I saw him there, it felt weirdly familiar, like I was reuniting with an old friend.

We both loved the exhibition – Chris Ofili – and had a great chat about it over lunch afterwards. There was an unspoken agreement that neither of us would mention the article, or the election, or my marriage – but he said he had gone ahead and met the lawyer I'd found, and made a claim after all, which was brilliant. The poor guy had broken his arm in a fall, and was living in this squat still with a bunch of guys, not allowed to work, and I could tell how hard that must be, especially when I knew he was expected to send money to his sister. But amazingly, to me, he hardly complained. He told me a bit about Asmara, about its architecture, culture, weather, things like that.

And it was then that he paused, looked really nervous, and then revealed to me that his name wasn't actually Joe. It was Yonas. He looked so worried when he said it, as if I'd be angry! But it made total sense that he would have used a pseudonym in his situation. And I was just glad he wanted to share his real name with me, and that he cared what I thought. So I found myself telling him I wanted to change my surname back to my maiden name, which was the strangest thing, because I hadn't even thought of doing it until that moment! But as soon as I'd said it, I knew I would follow through. I guess, subconsciously, it was also a way of telling him I was available – but he didn't give me any sign that he'd read it that way.

We got back to talking about the art, and he asked about my work, and so I said, spur of the moment, 'Well, you're welcome to come and see it, if you like? My studio's just over in Hackney.'

I still remember the look on his face when he took a few steps inside and stood, staring. It *is* a lovely space: airy, open-plan, with tall windows that let in lots of light, in a converted warehouse. I share it with three other artists, and we each have our own space in one corner, and cover the walls with our work. I hadn't been in there myself for months, and ever since Clara was born I'd been by far the most sporadic artist there, to the point where I hardly felt I deserved to have a space – which, incidentally, Quentin had been paying for.

Yonas gravitated towards Tim's corner first – Tim does woodturning, and displays his pieces on long white shelves. 'Feel free to pick them up,' I said. So he turned a wooden bowl slowly around in his hands, running his finger over the silky outer curve and then around the rugged rim…

and I couldn't help imagining it running down my cheek. But that was the first time I noticed that he wasn't touching the wood in the normal way, with his finger pads, but with the lower part of his finger, or the very top part of the fingertip, by the nail, and I looked closely and saw that his finger pads were all dark pink and ridged. I knew there was a story there, but I didn't feel I could ask, not just then. But again I became almost transfixed by his face, how composed his expression was but how much it concealed, and his incredible bone structure – I wished I was half decent at portraiture.

'Is this walnut?' he asked, holding out a dish, and I had no idea. It was a hard wood, fawn-coloured, with dark patterns scattered like water droplets. He sniffed it and smiled.

'I love that smell,' I said.

'It is my favourite too,' he said, and he picked up piece after piece, holding and replacing them so gently you couldn't hear a sound. 'This work reminds me of my grandfather,' he added. 'He was a carpenter.' I asked him what kinds of things his grandfather used to make. 'All kinds,' he said. 'But not like this – not art, exactly. More ordinary. Furniture, mostly. But he made us toys as children. Actually, one of those is the only thing I brought with me.'

'Really?' I said, super-curious. 'What is it?'

He smiled, quite sheepishly, and pulled something out from his pocket, but held his fingers over it at first. I went across to stand next to him, and looked at his closed fingers, and it struck me how long they were, and then he opened them up, exposing those scarred fingertips, and I peered down, and there in his palm was this little wooden rooster, all pert and comical and delightful. Its edges were worn smooth, and I imagined how much it had been handled, how many memories were stored in it for him. It made me think: what on earth would I take, if I had to leave the UK for ever?

I asked if I could hold it. It still felt warm from his body heat, and I examined it more closely, then wrapped my own fingers around it. 'He's just lovely!' I exclaimed. 'What a brilliant treasure to have kept. Actually, I have a bit of an obsession with rescued objects in my work. "Found objects", I normally call them…'

'Can I see?' he asked, so I led him over to my workspace, worried he'd think my stuff was garish in comparison to Tim's. The obsession I'd developed during my MA involved uniting found objects with new paintings – on canvas or other materials. I would go out to places and look for discarded things that you wouldn't expect to find there, then I'd photograph where I'd found them, and take the objects back to the studio, then make paintings of the places from the photos, and attach the objects in conjunction – often distorting the proportions, and abstracting the images – so defamiliarizing both. Which means the viewer has to construct their own story of the object and the scene and how the two connect. And I try to give each picture a title that alludes to either the object or the place in a way that could make the viewer associate them with something else entirely. So, for instance, I remember the picture Yonas started looking at intently that afternoon was called *Teeth*, where I'd attached a broken orange comb to a blurry charcoal image of a multi-storey car park...

Well, he didn't laugh at it, exactly. He was really interested, or pretended to be. And showing him the series reminded me how excited I'd felt when I first came up with the idea. I'd go off to these random places to get ideas and forage, picking up discarded things and thinking about where they'd come from and what they'd meant to their previous owners, and how I could locate them in not only the scene I found them in, but also bigger narratives about urban diversity and interconnectedness and disconnectedness and time and chance, and reflecting on the importance we place on objects and places and ownership and memory and what it all really means in the end...

And more practically, in terms of my anxiety, that series turned out to be a brilliant way of reconciling myself with randomness and uncertainty. You know? It was comforting to contain these little objects, to contextualize them, and give them a home in a piece of art. Quentin didn't say it, but I knew he thought it was stupid. Proper art, to him, was beautiful, and probably representational, but ultimately would look pretty on the wall of a living room. I mean, he always lied and *said* he liked my stuff, but I'm sure that was just because he knew how much the making of it reduced my anxiety.

So Yonas asked me where I got all the objects, and when I told him, he said, 'Ah, so you are a rubbish collector!'

I burst out laughing, and admitted that was basically it. 'But the idea is to transform rubbish into art, by making the viewer imagine how it came to be rubbish in the first place.'

He nodded at this, slowly, looking sceptical, I thought – but then he said, 'You rescue abandoned things and make new homes for them in painted stories.'

'Yes!' I said. 'That's a lovely way to describe it, actually. I'd better write that down…' And then we were staring into each other's eyes. 'I'll make some tea,' I said, a bit flustered. 'Do you want a cup?'

'Sure,' he said. 'With sugar, please.' And then he asked, 'What was the first object you rescued?'

I laughed. 'Good question – actually, weirdly, it was a disembodied Lego man's head. I found it in a park. I've still got the picture I made with it, over there.' Yonas walked over to it while I got mugs out. 'It reminded me of Dad,' I said. 'He was killed when he fell off scaffolding; and afterwards, I couldn't stop imagining his body split like a tomato, with his head rolling away across the floor… It gave me this terrible fear of heights, and other things… So anyway, I'd been looking for a way to express all this in my work, and commemorating him somehow. So when I got the idea of using the Lego head, and combining it with a painting – Dad and I used to paint together, you see – I felt like I was communicating with him, in a weird way. And that was how the series started.'

'I see,' he said. 'I like your work even more now.' He smiled, and told me how, when his father died, he was like me – he wanted to write plays because that's what his father did, and the process of writing made him feel closer to his father. He told me how Gebre, his friend who's an artist, lost his parents too, and how his painting helped him.

'It'd be so great to meet Gebre,' I said. 'And he'd be welcome to borrow my studio space once he comes to London.'

'Really?' Yonas said, and his face lit up.

'Sure. I'd love to see his work as well.'

'He does not use objects like you,' Yonas said. 'But I suppose his paintings are a bit like yours, because they are quite abstract, but you can still recognize some places or things. Most of them would contain one or more small figures, usually fighters, looking as if they were standing alone in a seething mass of paint.' He launched into telling me about Gebre's studio in Asmara, and how his paintings of wartime memories were a way to deal with the trauma. But also – and I found this really interesting – he told me how Gebre was spotted by a government official who exclaimed at how *patriotic* he thought his paintings were, by portraying the *heroism* of the fighters and martyrs. So the official bought three to display in his house, and that sparked Gebre's reputation, so he started selling lots more to people high up in government, when it wasn't really about that at all. And then Yonas started telling me about their childhood – his friendship with Gebre went way back. He told me how Gebre used to draw these cartoons of their teachers at school, and could capture their quirks in seconds. 'He wanted to be a cartoonist when he grew up, but you cannot do that in a country with state-controlled newspapers,' he said. I hadn't really thought of that, how dangerous a cartoon could be in that context.

It really made me think, hearing about Gebre and his artwork. I mean, I've always had access to materials, even if I haven't always had my lovely studio. But Yonas told me about the time he and Gebre were in prison; Gebre had no materials at all, but he managed to make a paste out of brick dust and water so he could draw on his cell walls. 'And what about you – how did *you* stay sane?' I asked, and Yonas said it was only by reciting poems and things he knew by heart out loud over and over, and writing his thoughts on the walls. He told me how Gebre never recovered from the terrible journey they had to get to the UK, and how he got very low. Then he paused, and added that Gebre was gay, which wasn't allowed in Eritrea, and that being here, in a country where that was okay, had made him wish he had talked about it more to Gebre, and been a better friend, but he was determined to rectify that when Gebre got to London. 'You sound like a great friend,' I said, thinking bitterly about Meg – about what can happen if you *do* talk to a friend. And then I realized my tea had got stone cold, and it was getting late.

'We should go,' I said. 'But I'm so glad you came – you've made me realize I've been taking this studio space for granted and not using it nearly enough. I just get so preoccupied with Clara and everything... But I'm going to get back into it now, and put work out there again. Put myself out there again.'

'You should,' he said.

'Yeah, it really shouldn't be so hard,' I said. 'Being a mother and an artist – millions of women do it – but you find yourself worrying about responsibility, and all these tiny dilemmas multiply until they dominate... But I just need to remember that making always helps. And also that I shouldn't need anyone else to motivate me to do it.'

'Clara must like having a mother who is an artist,' he said.

'Maybe,' I said, struck that I hadn't really thought about that.

So I guess that was the day we connected, Yonas and me, in a way that wasn't just accidental and instinctive. And then, what cemented how I felt – if you can use such a stolid word to describe feeling – was how good he turned out to be with Clara! He's a natural with children. Even though he doesn't have any of his own. He managed to defuse one of her tantrums when he'd only just met her. I'd told her it was dinner-time so we had to switch off *The Clangers* and that we were going to have fish, and she started screeching that she wanted to watch more and that she didn't like fish, even though she had happily eaten it the week before. I was about to tear my hair out, but Yonas asked Clara if she knew what penguins did when they knew they were going to get fish to eat. And she stopped, thought about it, and said no. So he said, 'Well, they normally waddle about like this' – and he did a ridiculous penguin impression with straight arms and turned-out feet – 'and then, when they hear there's fish for dinner, they do this' – and he made some squawking noises and pit-patted across the room at top speed, then challenged her to have a penguin race with him to get to the iceberg where the fish were waiting. And she smiled, giggled, and actually did it – I mean, I could never have got her to snap out of demon-child mode that fast! And they proceeded to spend the whole of dinner doing different animal impressions, while Mum and I looked on. Clara adored him from that moment onwards.

I was watching them play together a week or so later, when I realized that there was this unlikely match between our needs. Yonas was unable to work officially for money but really needed cash yet wouldn't accept a loan or a gift; and I really needed someone to help look after Clara on her non-nursery days while I dealt with my marriage fallout and tried to get back into making work, so that I could pay for my own studio space. And regain some self-belief! I had a new project about equations, chaos and beauty that I wanted to work on, harking back to my maths days. But Clara was only at nursery twice a week, there was a waiting list to increase it, and Mum couldn't step in with childcare to the extent I needed (she dotes on Clara, but she's a bit physically frail these days, and the idea of taking a small-bodied but strong-willed child to the playground and dealing with the possibility of her running off freaks her out; plus, she's the busiest person I know). So that was how Yonas started looking after my daughter.

I tried it out once, thinking it probably wasn't appropriate, and Quentin would freak if he knew, and Yonas had no childcare training, and it almost certainly wouldn't work out. But Clara didn't bat an eyelid when I left them together. I was almost offended! And she seemed as happy as Larry when I came back. So we tried it again. And, for a while, the three of us had this little secret quasi-family life going on together. I didn't tell any of my friends – and certainly not Quentin. But it somehow felt entirely natural.

The only person who can have had any idea about what was happening between Yonas and me was Mum, but we were never overt in front of her. She did stay in and babysit Clara while we went out for drinks a few times, and to the cinema – she encouraged that – but I think she just thought she was helping us to get our lives back on track. Which she was, in a way. She just didn't realize how much our life tracks were converging. You know, it's so funny how it's Yonas who – unintentionally – pushed Mum and me even further apart than we'd already been for decades, but then brought us much closer together.

Anyway, it was all going fine, but then there was this one moment when Yonas and I had taken Clara to the playground, and we'd stopped off at the supermarket to pick up some things, and I'd put my arm through his when we were laughing at something, and then, on the street outside, I saw Meg, just walking along, looking at her phone. I panicked, grabbed Clara and yanked them both into some random dry cleaner's shop, and started asking at the counter about prices – Clara kept complaining that I'd pulled her, and Yonas must have thought I'd lost the plot! Meg didn't come in, so I don't think she spotted us. But I guess that should have made me realize that the situation couldn't have gone on for ever: that I'd inevitably have to encounter Meg at some point, and tell Quentin about Yonas and the temporary childcare arrangement, and, actually, work out for myself what was going on between Yonas and me, and where I wanted it to lead. But it struck me that I'd been putting all that off because I was happy – happier than I'd been in a while, anyway – I was simply enjoying spending time with him, as was Clara, and I didn't want the pressure of having to define it publicly or fight about it with Quentin or make a big deal about it with anyone else. And so, once Meg was out of the way, I told the shopkeeper I'd get back to him about the fictional load of overly complex dry cleaning, and we stepped back out onto the street and carried on our way as if nothing had happened.

Chapter 22: Yonas

Yonas stood in Molly's kitchen, keeping an eye on the first *injera* of the evening as it started to sizzle and brown, releasing its soothingly sour scent. He seasoned and stirred a pot of *zigni* with his good arm, contemplating the fact that Molly was away, and Nina was lying in the bath upstairs, right now, naked, about to dress and come down to him. This was real. This was his life, right now – his life that could so easily have been ebbing away in that shellfish factory, or in prison. He took one of the gleaming porcelain plates from the rack and rotated it slowly, watching the slim gold rim catch the light. Sarama would be happy for him, wouldn't she? She would have expected him to move on, to find someone else. She wouldn't have wanted him to be alone. But how on earth was he here, now, standing in this house, with all this luxury around him, when poor Melat probably still couldn't even afford to buy meat, even after he'd sent her most of the money he'd earned looking after Clara?

Not that he was cooking real meat now. And he was pretty sure this fake stuff Nina had insisted upon was going to be disgusting, and would ruin the dish. He hadn't been able to bring himself to taste it yet. Apparently Nina had an ethical issue with eating animals – and he remembered his own horror at watching goats and chickens being slaughtered as a child, but they were adults now, and that was just life, wasn't it? Animals ate other animals, and humans needed meat for nutrition and strength. Nina argued that these days it was easy to get the equivalent nutrition from other things, like nuts and seeds and avocados and spinach. *Easy if you live in a country with supermarkets like this*, he'd thought, but didn't say so.

It was time to taste the *zigni*, and to force himself to try the Quorn lumps. He looked at the packet to check the ingredients. Fungi? As in the stuff that grew on damp tree-trunks? Cautiously, Yonas fished a piece out with a spoon, and bit off a corner. It was spongy. It tasted of nothing much but the sauce. But it wasn't hideous.

A tinge caught his nostrils... The *injera* was burning! In his haste to grab the spatula and scoop it out of the pan, Yonas knocked over the jar of paprika that had been perched on the edge of the counter, and it bounced in slow motion across the floor, spewing a rusty trail of powder over the tiles. Then his phone rang. He switched it to silent, and tried frantically to wipe up the mess. The screen flashed up: a voicemail. Unknown number. He would listen to it later.

He turned the heat down under the stew, put the singed *injera* into the oven to keep warm, and poured the next portion of batter into the pan, circling the jug in a thick spiral to create a circular shape with an even depth. Then he swirled the mixture around, the way he remembered his mother doing, until the edges started to sizzle and teeny holes began emerging in speckles across the surface. He wished he could package up this meal and fly a portion over to Asmara. He wondered if Melat was cooking right now, in the battered old vat...

'Ooh, something smells wonderful.' Nina! He hadn't heard her come in. She rubbed her hand up his shoulder. 'Your phone's flashing by the way.'

'Here – I want you to taste this and imagine you are in Eritrea,' Yonas said, and offered her a teaspoonful of sauce.

She sipped, and considered. 'Mmm! Lush.' Emboldened, he slid the spatula under the *injera* and flipped it deftly onto the waiting plate, while Nina took out a beer bottle from the fridge. 'Speckled Hen?' she asked.

'Wait, I thought you didn't eat hen,' Yonas said. 'But you drink it?'

Nina laughed, and poured out the beer. 'I'm a total hypocrite.'

They clinked glasses. 'Ooh, also I bought some music you might like,' she said, and went to the CD player.

Familiar rhythms flooded the room and Yonas turned around. 'Bereket Mengisteab!' – and it was as if his parents were just behind the door, ready to dance out and clap their hands to the beat.

'Yes! Do you like it?' Nina asked. 'I just asked the guy in the world music section…'

'Of course I do…' He didn't want to tell her about how Mengisteab had been co-opted by the regime after liberation. It would sound ungrateful, and it wasn't as if he no longer liked the music – it was just complicated. 'Do you?' he asked.

'Yeah… it's… really interesting.'

Yonas got the sense that *interesting* meant not much, and felt a jolt of disappointment. It felt so discombobulating to hear this music in this place. He closed his eyes for a second and was transported back to that night when Mengisteab came to play for the fighters, back when the family was still together, all alive. 'I saw him play once,' he told Nina.

'Really?!' she said, but just then there was a knock at the door. 'I wonder who that could be?' she said, with the kind of effervescent curiosity that a chat show host might use as she prepared to admit a film star onto the stage.

Yonas closed his eyes. Nina couldn't know what an unexpected door knock meant to someone like him, how it felt like a hammering on his skull shooting fear down his spine. The police. They had caught up with him after all. They'd found out about his illegal working, they were coming to arrest him, and the spiral of prison, detention and deportation had begun. He could almost feel the cold metal of the handcuffs about to encircle his wrists. More loud knocking followed, and he remembered the claustrophobic panic of that day in the train toilet.

'I'd better answer it,' Nina said.

She got up, and Yonas followed her to the kitchen doorway and looked through, ready to put his hands in the air.

But it wasn't the police. It was a white man with a receding blond hairline, glasses, a check shirt, deck shoes and high colour in his cheeks. 'Quentin!' Nina gasped. 'What are you doing here? Where's Clara? Is she all right? Why…'

Yonas drew back. In real life her husband looked even more familiar than he had done on the TV. Where had he seen him before?

'Nothing's happened to Clara,' Quentin said. 'I wanted to see you. Darling, I miss you so much. You've got to believe me – I never cheated on you. Not once. I swear. I've even got Alice to sign a letter to confirm nothing ever happened. Here, I've brought it…'

'Oh Quentin.' Nina's voice softened, like chocolate held over a flame. Yonas could tell she was relenting already. He might as well chuck the whole meal in the bin, climb over the back garden wall and run.

'Like I said, I should have nipped her messages in the bud earlier,' Quentin said. 'I should have been firmer. But it never ever went any further than that, and maybe some flirtatious body language, on her part, which I stupidly failed to quell. I wish I'd insisted. I never imagined you'd see the messages, never mind leave. Please…'

Yonas didn't want to hear this. Why was he stupid enough to have believed he was about to spend the night with this man's wife? He shouldn't be here. He was an interloper in every possible sense.

'Don't touch me. You shouldn't assume,' he heard Nina snap.

'Love, I know you're angry, and rightly so, but you've got it *wrong* about the affair, I promise. Look, all I want is for us to work things out.'

'It's always about what *you* want, isn't it.'

'That's unfair.'

'Expecting me to come home because you *want* it! You probably just want to salvage your reputation.'

Yonas couldn't help walking back towards the kitchen door to hear better.

'No, I want to salvage our marriage.'

'You should have thought of that before you cheated.'

'Look, you've got to believe me, I didn't. I swear. Darling, look at me.

Missing you is killing me. And Clara, the idea of living apart from both of you... I can't bear it.'

Yonas felt embarrassed to witness this, though he did feel bad for the guy now, despite himself. It must be awful to have your child taken away from you, whoever you were, whatever you'd done. And Quentin sounded pretty genuine in his regret, if not the denial. Or was he just a good actor?

Nina was silent. She must be poised to kiss and make up, Yonas thought. But he couldn't help poking his head around the door to see. They were holding hands... and then Quentin looked up and saw him. Looked him straight in the eyes. There was no point in him withdrawing now, it was too late... Then, he suddenly made the connection: the guy from the train! How had he not realized on polling night, from watching him on TV? He couldn't tell if there was any mutual recognition. But what was clear from Quentin's furious stare was that, if he could shoot Yonas in the head right now, he would.

'I see you have a guest,' Quentin said drily.

'Oh,' Nina said, turning round to Yonas and back again. 'I do, yes. This is Mum's student. He's just round for supper.'

'Where's Molly?'

'Out. And we're just about to eat,' Nina said. 'So it's not a good time for you to come round here unannounced. You should have called first. And where's our *daughter*, more importantly? You're supposed to be—'

'She's with Bernard.'

'With your brother! I thought *you* wanted to spend time with her, that's what—'

'Bernard *said* he saw you with a man the other day,' Quentin said. 'A man... of that description.'

'He must have made a mistake. But, Quentin, you need to accept that I have moved out, and we need to give each other space, so let's not get into conspiracy theories, or imaginary scenarios or spying on each other, okay?'

'Spying! I had no intention of spying, but Bernard told me – I assumed it was his imagination. And I wouldn't even have mentioned it if I hadn't seen *him* here, with you. The only reason I came was because I miss my *wife* – you're the one who's now made me feel like I *should* have been spying, to make sure you haven't completely lost your mind and started putting our child at risk by starting some kind of relationship with—'

'Don't you *dare* start harassing me and bringing my mental health into this – you know I'd put Clara's welfare above anything else.'

'I didn't even mention your mental health, though now you mention it, I'm pretty worried. Are you on medication? And what the hell is he doing here with you now, anyway?'

'As I said, he's her student. Anyway, who I have dinner with is none of your business any more. At least I have some company.'

'What's that supposed to mean?'

'All those late nights "working", coming back home and expecting a plate of food to be ready, missing Clara's bedtime…'

'I was running for election! And the hard work paid off, didn't it? But I might not have done it at all if I'd known you'd fuck off with an illegal immigrant.'

'That's rubbish. And insulting. To him and me.'

Yonas closed the kitchen door, as quietly as possible. But Quentin's voice penetrated. 'You'd better not be letting this guy, whoever he is, look after Clara. I don't want her anywhere near him…'

'You know full well my top priority is what's best for my daughter.'

Yonas turned the music up. He stared at *zigni* that was starting to look dull and unappetizing. At best, the mood of the night was ruined and he wouldn't get to sleep with Nina for a while, if ever. At worst, Quentin was about to report him to the police.

Footsteps stamped, the kitchen door opened, and Quentin was inside, adopting the sort of stance that immediately precedes a punch. Yonas stood back against the counter, wooden spoon in hand – the most pathetic of weapons. 'Excuse me for disturbing your intimate meal with *my wife*,' Quentin said vehemently. 'I don't know who the hell you think you are but you're obviously a manipulative little bastard. And I want to warn you right now that if you cause my wife or our daughter any upset whatsoever, I will…' He paused. He frowned. 'Have I seen you before?'

'I am Molly's student. I did not want to cause a problem.' Yonas spoke as softly and calmly as he could manage.

Quentin paused, his face going a dark shade of red, like ketchup, as if he were preparing to say something explosive – but then walked out. The front door slammed.

Nina slid into her seat at the dining table, her face wet, flushed and swollen. She smiled a little, and then let out a sob. 'I'm so sorry.'

Yonas walked around to her and rubbed her back gently. 'You will feel better for some food.'

'I'm not hungry any more,' she croaked. 'I've ruined Clara's life. I'm a terrible mother.'

'You are a very good mother, and you must be hungry,' Yonas said hopefully. He served her a large helping of *zigni* and showed her how to tear off sections of the *injera* with her hands and use it to scoop up the stew. Brown juice dripped down her chin as she ineffectually shoved it in her mouth, and several chunks of Quorn fell onto her plate. Yonas told her she looked especially pretty with her face covered in food. She giggled with her mouth full.

'Okay, this is amazing,' she said when she'd swallowed. 'How do you say delicious in Tigrinya?'

'*Ti'um.*'

'Tiyoom,' she echoed. Wiping her chin with her napkin, and her eyes with the back of her hand, she told Yonas that he should set up as a chef when he got his papers. By the end of dinner she seemed calm again, and she got up to put on another CD. 'I feel like some Nina Simone. My namesake, actually. Do you know her music?'

'Of course,' Yonas lied, and went to start the washing up. But actually he did recognize the voice that bloomed behind him. It sounded more like a man's voice than a woman's, but it was rich and warm and vibrated with feeling. Then he felt Nina's finger down his back, her palm resting at the bottom of his spine.

He swallowed, wiped his hands on the tea towel, turned around and let his lips sink into Nina's. He took her narrow waist gently in his hands, hoping she couldn't feel him trembling. She ran her hands down to his buttocks, and squeezed. *This is less than an hour after her husband left,* he thought. *This cannot be a good idea.* But she took one of his hands, and pulled lightly, and he followed her silently out of the kitchen and up the stairs.

When Nina went out to the bathroom afterwards, Yonas splayed his body out on the bed, heart slowing, fingers tingling, yellow light swimming around his body. Whatever happened after tonight, he thought, it was all worth it! There had seemed so many possibilities for his life in the UK, but not one within his remotest contemplation had involved falling for a British artist who happened to be a politician's wife and acting as a secret nanny for her child and finally sleeping with her, in her mother's house... And then he noticed his mobile phone on the floor where it had fallen out of his pocket, still flashing. It occurred to him that he'd never listened to the message that came earlier in the evening, and now there was another.

'You have – two – new messages. Message one. *Yonas. It is me, Gebre. I am in London! Where are you?* End of message.'

Yonas's whole body clenched. The relaxation of a second ago felt suddenly like treachery. Gebre. He'd come, finally. Gebre!

'Message two. *I am at a phone box by a supermarket, I am so hungry, I have no coins left after this, can you come find me?* End of message.'

Both calls were from blocked numbers. Why didn't Gebre think to say which road he was on? Yonas tried to put himself in his friend's panicky shoes. Where would he have gone, if he saw police at the warehouse, if he had to run but didn't know the area? He drew a mental map of the area around Canning Town, and all the supermarkets where Gebre might be. He remembered his own first sight of a supermarket, and a British shopping street, the bombardment of all the colours and signs, each bearing a different logo but somehow blending into each other... He had to go and search. Should he tell Nina? Now, in the middle of the night, when everything was still perfect? She would panic, and see Gebre's arrival as the lid coming off a can of maggots... He pulled on his clothes, too fast, he couldn't get his leg in his trousers...

Then Nina returned, dazzling him momentarily in the doorway. 'Yonas, what's going on?'

'I am sorry, I have to go out.'

'Oh. You have to go – right *now*?'

'I am really sorry.'

'What's happened?'

He didn't have time to make anything up. 'It is my best friend from Eritrea.'

'What, Gebre?'

'Yes, he's in London now, but he is hungry and lost – I have to help.'

'Do you know where he is?'

'I am not sure – I think he is at a supermarket near Canning Town.'

'I'll drive you!'

'Are you sure? It is late.'

'Just let me get some clothes on.' She pulled on a pair of jeans, flung on a jumper, grabbed her car keys, and they ran out together into the night.

Chapter 23: Gebre

SCANDAL OF THE 'GAY' ASYLUM SEEKER RAPIST

Coffee? The last time I drank coffee was back in Eritrea.

If I could see you I would draw a cartoon of you. I used to boast that if I met any person for one minute, I could draw a cartoon of them in another minute that would make them laugh and cry. But I was only a kid. Just bragging. I soon learned not to brag about cartoons.

You must think I am stupid to be caught stealing bread from a supermarket. But I made it all the way to the UK, then all the way to London, then all the way to the shop that Yonas told me to go to. I even found the place the shopkeeper said that Yonas would be, but then I was so tired and hungry, and I had only one silver coin left. I found a telephone box outside a supermarket and I tried to call Yonas but I could not get through, so I left a message. I sat down on the floor, and I had no strength left to move.

When I managed to get up and walk into that supermarket, there was so much food right there in front of me – bright tubs of sparkling pink watermelon, marigold mango pre-cut to the perfect size for your mouth, salads with goat's cheese, walnuts and aubergines, and next to them plastic forks with napkins in special packets, rows of baked goods like caramel cupcakes with chocolate patterns, clear tubs of blue-white prawns that I might have shelled myself with special lemongrass butter included for cooking, rainbow layers of different vegetables ready to steam in a microwave for just two minutes, and at least a hundred different pre-prepared sandwiches in triangular boxes, filled with egg, prawns, bacon, tuna… It was like one more kind of torture. Like I was a dog and they were dangling a juicy bone in front of my mouth, just beyond the length of my chain. They would not miss one loaf of bread, would they, amid these riches? A plain brown one, not even pre-sliced, and a pint of milk?

The detainees I told about this laughed at me. 'Supermarkets here throw so much good stuff away,' Banda said, 'you could've filled up from the skip – sushi, tortilla chips, chorizo sausage…' Things I had never even tasted. But as I was walking around the corner, ripping off a hunk of the bread, I was grabbed from behind. It was the security guy from the supermarket doorway, a black man, he looked African like me, and I looked hard into his eyes, I said *please*, but he dragged me back, called the police, and they came fast. They arrested me like I had just stolen a gold watch and a laptop computer, and when they tried to handcuff me I was so desperate, I just lashed out with my arms and legs, like a trapped animal, but that only made it worse.

When I got to the place they call an 'immigration removal centre', and saw the barbed wire, I knew it was a prison. My freedom was over before it had started. I tried to find the phone number for Yonas, but it must have got lost when the police searched me, and they told me they never saw it. They managed to lose my photo of my parents too – the only thing I managed to bring with me. And when I watched how, every day, another detainee would get sent back or choose to go back, and when I heard the staff call us animals, I knew how it was going to be. I knew that this was the end of the line.

It was not like prison back in Eritrea. I mean, you did not get tortured, and the food was okay, and you could drink as much water as you wanted – but it was still a prison. And so grey. Living there was like slowly drowning in greyness. Grey walls, grey sky outside, grey faces. At first I talked a bit to the other detainees, but then, after two weeks, one guy I quite liked got deported.

To the officers, I was nobody. I could just have been a donkey they had to keep an eye on so as to get paid. One nice lady worked in the library, and I used to go there, but reading English is too difficult for me. The letters get mixed up. Even when we were kids it would always take me five times as long as Yonas to read a book, even in Tigrinya – my father used to tell me I was lazy, but it was not true. I tried, but I could not concentrate, and I had no energy for exercise, so I just stayed in my cell. Which I was supposed to call a room.

Most of the staff could hardly wait to get away after their shift each day, so they could go to the pub or go home to watch TV. They pretended they cared when they told me to stop cutting myself. They even sent a psychiatric doctor to 'help' me. But really they just wanted him to stop me hurting myself to protect their jobs. A dead detainee would mean a lot of forms, and they were always filling in forms as it was, and complaining about having to fill in forms.

After a while I did not feel like eating the food we were given. I thought about not eating at all, just stopping, fading away, but I saw one other guy who did that, and they just took him to the hospital, fed him through his nose, and brought him back.

One good thing about that place was that I had pens and paper to draw with, as much as I liked. So I sat in my cell and I tried to draw, thinking maybe I would feel better. At first I drew cartoons of the other detainees, then faces of people like Yonas and Osman. But then I would think how I would never see these people again, and I began colouring over the faces, colouring over everything, until the whole sheet of white paper was black. I got through many pens, many sheets of paper, like that.

I kept replaying my Home Office interview in my head, the one they sent me to before locking me up. That man made me talk about things that I never admitted to anyone before. Even Yonas. When I said I had been tortured, he made me tell him all the details. So I told him, about the beatings, the hard labour, carrying those rocks in the sun, the helicopter position – and I mentioned to him how the guards did worse things to me. I thought he would guess what I meant, or that the other information I gave him would be enough. But he told me he wanted all the details. So

I told him how the prison guards mocked me. *You like men, don't you...*
You have had sex with men... and how I tried to tell them the truth so
they would leave me alone, so I admitted how a soldier abused me when
I was still a boy, and they said I was lying. They told me I would have to
take off my clothes to prove it. And then they did things to me.

I thought the Home Office interviewer would understand that. But
he said, 'So now you are *gay* as well?' And laughed.

I had heard one of the detainees say that in the UK being gay was a
reason to be protected, so I thought, maybe it is the time to be open.
'Yes,' I admitted.

'*And* you've been *sexually abused*? Sounds to me like a convenient, erotic
little story you have come up with for this interview! Right?'

I said I did not invent it.

'Oh, so let me get this straight, haha, *straight!*' he said. He laughed
again. I did not see why this was funny. 'So now you are saying you are
gay, and you had sex with adult soldiers when you were still a child, and
you then had sex with guards when you were in prison. Is that right?'

'I was forced to,' I said.

'Are you saying you have *never* had sex with a woman?' he asked.

I said that was true.

'And you are now thirty years old.'

I nodded.

'So what are their names, then, all these men you say *forced* you to
have sex with them?'

I took a breath. I had never said it since it happened. 'The first soldier
was called Adonay...'

'Oh your *first time!* Romantic. Okay, so where exactly did you and
Adonay have sex? Describe the place.'

'Outside. Behind some rocks,' I said.

'Outside! So you are an exhibitionist.'

I did not know what he meant.

'Did you put your penis in Adonay's backside?' he asked me. I stared
at him, aghast. 'It's a simple question. Yes or no?' he said.

'No.' I was wishing I had never mentioned any of this.

'But he put his in yours?'

I did not want to answer. But I could not contradict myself. I had to go through with it. I wanted to curl up like a beetle.

'And when he did that, did you have an erection?' he asked. I was not sure what the word was, but he demonstrated for me. 'Tell me the truth.'

I did not answer.

'And did Adonay ejaculate inside you? Did he come? You know what I'm asking you. Like this.' He mimed shooting a gun from his crotch.

I did not answer.

'Did you use a condom?'

I just stared at him.

'Answer me, come on, this is an interview, remember. Do you want asylum or not? You have to answer my questions if you want to stand a chance.'

'No,' I said finally.

'So tell me, what is it about men's backsides that attracts you? Come on. It's an easy question. Have you gone mute? *Surely* you *know* what turns you on?'

I did not answer.

'Well, this seems like a neat way to add a bonus human rights layer to your asylum claim. Did your lawyer tell you to say this?'

I said nothing. And he was not finished. 'Are you religious?' he asked.

'Yes,' I said, though I wasn't really any more. But I was relieved he'd changed the subject.

'What is your religion?'

'Christian.'

'What kind?'

'Orthodox. My parents were Orthodox…'

'So how can you justify being homosexual? The Bible says it is a sin, correct? Orthodox Christians are very strict about that kind of thing.'

'Yes,' I said. I knew he was laying a trap now.

'So how am I supposed to believe that you defied your entire culture and religion to have all this twisted gay sex you are now claiming you had?'

He had not even got onto asking why I left Eritrea yet.

As I sat in my cell in the detention centre – my room – this interview went around and around and around in my head. I wondered if Yonas had been questioned like that. I wished I had left the factory with him. I wished I had got on a train like him. But I was too much of a coward, I just walked, and that is why I ended up shovelling animal shit and sleeping on hay at a farm, and then sneaking into a pesticide delivery truck to get closer to London. I got off at a petrol station near a place called High Wycombe when the driver was paying, and walked along the side of the motorway until I arrived.

It is strange how two people's lives can be in parallel and then fork apart, so one ends up on the right path, and one on the wrong path. When Yonas and I were little boys I was the confident one! Yonas was shy, skinny, always reading books, and I used to protect him. I was faster at running, and my cartoons made people laugh, and made even the teachers respect me. But I had no brothers or sisters, my mother died when I was very young, so all I had was my father, and then he was 'disappeared'. If he was killed that would have been terrible, but at least I would have known for sure, but after he was 'disappeared' I both knew what had happened and didn't know. I could never make peace with it.

So then I was alone. My aunts did not want me. I was lucky that my father and Yonas's father were good friends, so his parents took me along with them to join the liberation struggle. But I was never part of Yonas's family. Not really. And near the front line, I was so scared. Yonas and some of the other kids were kind of excited, but I *hated* the war and everything to do with it, right from the start. I felt terrified just to open my eyes every single morning. And then, when Yonas's parents and brother were killed… I think it affected me almost worse than him. I could not sleep at night. I kept on thinking: *I am next.*

It was at that time that I just started following Yonas in everything. Even if what he was doing was risky. The only thing that was mine alone was my drawing; but of course when he asked me to make theatre sets for his plays, I said yes. When he had any new ideas, or when times were hard, I just did everything he suggested. I did not want to lose him, after my father. And I loved him. More than a brother. At one time, when there was a big battle close by and I thought it was our last moment, I nearly told him – but I stopped myself just in time. After our country's independence, when I started my art studio in Asmara, and people started to buy my work, finally I thought I would be able to stop being scared and I could start enjoying my life. Maybe I could even look for love elsewhere.

But then I was conscripted for the border war. And every day I was there in the army was a nightmare. Until one day I could not pick up my gun. I mean, physically, I could not. Everything froze, and I felt like I could not breathe, and the world became very small and far away, and I thought I was dying. I came to in the hospital ward. When I went back the next day, the same happened. I could not make my body pick up a gun one more time. It was a kind of panic attack, they said, and they could not stop me having them, even by beating me. So I was sent back to Asmara. And Yonas was sent back too, because he got malaria.

After that, I had to take a national service post in the transport office, which was as boring as anything I could imagine, and Yonas was made to take a post in the censorship board, which made him furious. So when he suggested we should send out messages to foreigners to tell them about the situation in our country, that he would write articles and I should draw cartoons to communicate to people more directly, I agreed. We were arrested together in an internet café – caught red-handed, as you would say.

When Yonas said he had a plan to escape from prison, of course I agreed. Anything was better than being in there. It was only after we finally got to the UK, after a journey I thought would never end, when the factory was horrible and cold, and our boss started torturing people just like prison back home, that I thought, I am done now. I cannot do this any more. I have no fight left. Yonas has fire still. I have to stop dragging him down. I have got to let him go. He will be better off without me. I will just stay here and look after Osman, and maybe find a way to kill myself once he is not there to stop me. And Yonas left. But in the end it was Osman, once he was getting stronger but still could not walk properly, who told me I had to leave too, and try to find Yonas. He said that he would see us in London one day.

So, I got on the rubbish truck, like Yonas did. And I thought the driver had not seen me, but then he stopped the truck on a quiet road just around the corner, and looked around, so I jumped off, ready to run, but he called out: 'Wait! Your friend has something for you.' And he gave me a piece of paper with an address of a shop in London. It was an amazing moment. I even started to feel hope again.

But then, after all my efforts to get to that address, I was arrested before I even found Yonas. As they put me in the police van, I was sure I would never see him again. I thought that if he did not get my phone message he would have no way to know I had left the factory, and even if he did get the message, he would never know where to find me. But he did find me. Actually, his lawyer, Veata, she found me. Yonas had told her to ask around at detention centres for an Eritrean named Gebre Merhawi, and when she found me, she offered to represent me, for free. It was kind of her. But I had already done my Home Office interview by then. She looked disappointed, like she would have been able to prepare me. I knew I had probably done it wrong. But anyway, it was too late.

Yonas tried to visit me but the first time he was turned away. One of the guards told me he had just left the reception to go home. It felt like I had just been offered a drink of water in the desert and then it was pulled from my lips. Even now, when they had taken my freedom, when they had taken my photo, they had everything, they would not even let me see the one person who wanted to visit me, the one person I could talk to in my own language, the one person who could maybe give me back some hope. I started cutting myself again, just to feel some pain that I could focus on, pain that I could manage, pain that made me feel alive, just to feel something. But as soon as that pain went away, I would feel even worse. So I had to cut again.

When Yonas was finally allowed to visit, I had been moved to isolation. I had been wanting to see his face again for so long, but by that point I was on so many drugs I was numb, in my body, in my mind. Even when Yonas was finally sitting there in front of me, he could easily just have been a life-size painting of himself on canvas. I heard the words he was saying – he was trying to cheer me up, to tell me things would get better, he was telling me about his life, what was going on – but I could not concentrate, all I wanted was to be left alone. When he left, he gave me a bar of chocolate, some phone credit to call him, and a copy of this book in Tigrinya, *The Strange Painter* – I still don't know how he managed to find that.

Back in my cell, I held the book for a long time, looking at the cover image, the font, feeling the shape of it, the weight of the pages. I finally opened it and tried to read, but I could not concentrate. To think of an artist character painting freely like the one in the book seemed so far away. Like it could never have been part of my life.

When I was lying on my bed, with no energy, no appetite, trying not to think about cutting, I would try to imagine my mother, to draw a detailed picture of her face in my mind. I could not remember much, because she died when I was very young, when she was giving birth to my sister – that was the end of them both – but I had her photo, for many years, and I remembered how she had these deep creases in both her cheeks and a laugh that was like bubbles coming up from deep, warm, blue water. Then I would try to draw my father's face in my mind. He was always more focused on his work than on me, but he was still my father. He was all the family I had. And they took him away before I could say goodbye.

I would try harder to remember the good things about my life, about my country, not just the bad. I tried to remember the light back home. In the UK, and especially inside the detention centre, I could barely imagine what sunlight was like any more. Proper sunlight, I mean, the kind that puts out heat as well as light, that warms your bones, that transforms the sky into a blanket of blue and palm trees into emerald butterflies, and makes skin glow like honey, makes women's clothes dance like flocks of parrots and bee-eaters in the urban jungle. I thought about *passagero* in Asmara after independence, walking with Yonas, the early evening air fragrant with meals being prepared in the restaurants, and feeling excited for the future, like we were finally going to be living in some kind of dreamland all our own, watching the sun fling persimmon ribbons around the sky.

I tried to remember what it was like when I had my studio in Asmara, how eager I was to rise before the sun just to go there and get to work. Sometimes I would paint dark pictures of the struggle, but other days I would paint joyful images of the city – of the trees and buildings and vases and markets and people walking, and I would add bright splashes of colour, make the shadows teal and violet instead of grey, make the clouds a soft mint green. But the important clients only wanted to buy the pictures of the struggle and to see all my work as a document of patriotic struggle that they could hang in their houses to prove themselves.

When I was not lying on my bed, I kept on drawing on white paper with black ink, then colouring in my drawings until the black was everywhere and all the white was gone. The greyness of the detention centre was colouring in my brain just like that. Smothering all the light. I just wanted to feel the pain of cutting. One day soon I will get something sharp, and I will be ready to make my last cut, I thought – right into the artery. But then, one day, Yonas paid me a surprise visit, and he told me I had to get on board with just one more of his plans – the most crazy, ridiculous, and maybe the most brilliant plan he had come up with yet.

Chapter 24: Yonas

From the moment Yonas woke up, he had a feeling something was going to happen. The envelope lying on the doormat said: *I told you so.*

He picked it up, went to the kitchen, looked at it. He put on his coat and went out, deciding as he turned left that he would walk down to the local park to open it. He sat on a bench there under a tree, and pulled out the envelope. Inside would be his ticket to join Gebre in the detention centre, almost certainly. But it could, just possibly, be a missive of good news – spectacular news. Maybe he should open it in a more significant place where he could feel truly celebratory, or a place that could at least remind him of his time being free in London… He got up, and decided impulsively to head to the South Bank.

For once, the air was gloriously crisp and the sky was blue, and it felt good to be going somewhere while he was still officially free to do so legally. Unlike Gebre. Why had he been so unlucky as to get caught for stealing something so small, to fill his starving belly? Did the police have no heart? Nobody more important to arrest?

As he paced past council estates, he imagined the buildings as rocky outcrops in the wilderness, as if he were back on one of those walks with Sarama on a mountain path, along the rim of a vast crevasse, the rocky screes around them dotted with scrawny thorn bushes and hardy *bau bau* trees sweeping steeply down to sun-baked planes; how liberating those walks were, despite the sick fear at the thought of all the Ethiopian eyes watching them across the impasse.

He got to Vauxhall Bridge and paused to take in the view. The Thames glinted as it churned, windows gleamed like scattered sequins, and London was a radiant postcard of itself. He continued along the river, weaving among jostling commuters. The chain of people crossing on the far side of the bridge was silhouetted by the sun, and the sight reminded him of a line he'd read: *life is but a procession of shadows.* He remembered underlining it but couldn't remember the book now, and wondered whether Nina and Molly would visit and bring him books if he ended up in a detention centre too. Would he be put in the same one as Gebre?

He paused again opposite Westminster, which hovered at the water's edge like an ancient wedding cake turned parchment – on the brink of crumbling and dissolving, like the empire during the last gasp of its historical power. He continued, past scampering dogs, joggers, cyclists, a homeless woman with a cardboard sign and a tin bowl, to Hungerford Bridge, with its diamond-lattice metalwork and huge metal fan shapes. This would have been Gebre's celebratory moonwalking spot, right here. It was too galling that Gebre was finally in the same city now, yet was more distant than ever.

Yonas's first visit to the detention centre, when he was finally let in after a failed attempt, had been worse than he'd imagined. Gebre had been cutting himself badly, and was barely able to make eye contact. Questions like *how are you doing, how are you feeling,* were met with almost imperceptible shrugs.

'Hey. Look at me,' Yonas had said, 'please, Gebre. I know this is hard, I can't believe the bastards arrested you, but the main thing is that you're here, I've found you, and you've got to try to stay positive – which means no more cutting, okay? Veata is working on your case, and she's a really good lawyer. She can set you free – if you keep believing it!' He sounded like one of those self-help books from the library.

'No,' Gebre said.

'Why?'

'Don't patronize me, Yonas. I am detained here "indefinitely" – that could mean for ever.'

'Okay, in theory, but it won't for you. We'll be together again before you know it. You can come and live in my house. And guess what – I have a British friend who is an artist. Did you hear me? An artist! She even has her own studio space. And she says you can use it, she can get you materials, you can make art again, Gebre – paint whatever you like. People will appreciate your talent more here, you will have freedom to paint or draw anything at all. You can even start doing cartoons again… Satirical cartoons are in all the papers here. No politician bats an eyelid.'

Gebre's face twitched, but it wasn't clear whether it was in acknowledgment or a tic.

'Look, I know you've had a nightmare time since we got to the UK,' Yonas continued. 'Way worse than me. And it does feel so far from home… but it's not so bad, there are good people around, British people, who are kind, some of them, but there's also an Eritrean community – I've met some already who are super-friendly. And you get used to the cold weather, it's just about getting the right clothes, and British people love nothing better than talking about it… ' He could hear the insincerity in his voice. And he might as well have been talking to himself anyway, for all the acknowledgement he was getting.

But then Gebre replied. 'Yonas, I am not even allowed outside here. I do not care about the weather. One of the guards said we were caged animals.'

'What?'

'And as for British people, that Home Office guy… Please do not ask me about that interview, not ever. All I can say is, after that, there is no way he is letting me stay. I do not have to get a refusal letter to know that. They will just make me do my time here and then they will send me home to die. And if I refuse to go, they will keep me here until I do.'

'They won't. My interview was terrible as well, so humiliating – but everybody's is. Everyone I've talked to who's done one. But did you… did you tell them…'

'I said, don't talk to me about it.'

'I hope you did tell them; it can help your case – and it's fine to be gay here. Most of the guys who live in my house are gay! One of them is a good friend of mine now, his name is Emil, he's from Romania and he's so funny – you'll like him. When you come out you can meet him!'

'I'm not going to get out.'

'You will. Veata is on your case. They can't send you back to die just because you needed a tiny bit of food.'

Gebre shook his head. 'I am a mosquito to the people who run this place. A criminal mosquito carrying malaria…'

'No – you're a talented artist, you're an excellent friend, you're a brilliant person.'

'These psychological doctors, officers, all of them, they understand nothing. I am tired. Tired of these people and tired of myself.'

'Gebre, of course you are feeling sad because you are stuck in here. But your time has come for better luck now. You deserve it. And I'm going to help you. So is Veata, and so can my British friends. I can introduce you to Nina, the artist I told you about. She is beautiful with red hair like copper and green eyes… When you meet her you will want to paint her.'

This at least provoked a cynical eyebrow raise.

'But you can't meet anyone or do anything if you make yourself too ill to leave this place. Are you hearing me?'

Gebre's eyes danced, and an upside-down smile contorted his lips. 'So now you have had these fragments of good luck, you think it will all be fine, you think you can just marry this red-haired woman and stay here and make children with her and everything will be happy ever after?'

'I didn't say that! She's already married. Look, Veata gets people asylum every week. She even represented this Eritrean guy who travelled here with a woman he met on the journey, and they had to hide under the chassis of this big lorry together to cross from Calais – he was hiding inside the spare tyre, and she was sitting inside the shell – and they were travelling really fast, at least seventy miles per hour, and the woman told him she had to let go because her back hurt so badly and she could not take it for one more minute, but he persuaded her to hold on, that she would die if she fell, and he wanted her to live, and so she held on – and they made it, and now they are married!'

'Okay, very nice story. Romantic story. Go ahead and write a play about it. But you saw one lucky guy, on the outside. I see all the rest of them, stuck inside this prison, alone.'

'TIME,' yelled the guard, louder than was necessary.

If this letter would only contain good news, Yonas thought, he could go back to the detention centre and tell Gebre: 'Look: there's still hope!' He picked out a bench, resolving to open the envelope finally, but after turning it around a few times he got up again. He needed to walk some more. He walked, faster now, along to Tower Bridge and all the way down to Greenwich before turning back and retracing his steps. A boatload of tourists passed him on the river, crammed in and craning out with their cameras, excited to visit this iconic place they could descend on, pick the best images to document for their families to prove their travel stories were true, and leave again freely. A hundred years ago, grand vessels used to sail this river, he thought, carrying merchants and seamen from far away, bearing commodities like sugar and coal and oil from his continent, from the empire. It didn't have the same importance now as the city's artery, but it still had as much physical power as ever, and he might as well be a speck of soil being carried along in its current – that was how momentary and insignificant his life was in comparison, and how little control he seemed to have to set his own direction.

Dusk began to smudge the sky. His legs felt stiff, and he could put it off no longer. He picked out a bench outside the huge Tate Modern building, where he had been supposed to go with Nina for that date and now maybe never would, and sat down. He took out the envelope and looked at it again, ran the side of his finger along the line of the seal on the back, started to loosen the glue with his nail, but stopped before it came apart. A lifeboat was zipping eastwards, a clipper was trundling west, and the cluster of grand, static shapes were lined up across the water like a theatre set in which he was supposed to be both the actor and the audience. He felt as present in this place, in this moment, as if he had just stepped on stage. The people down the towpath to his right, their faces still illuminated by the evening light, seemed to radiate positivity, whereas the people to his left, their faces submerged in shadow, seemed to exude grimness. The world was divided into two halves, two possibilities.

To stay, or not to stay.

To be in or to be out.

He tore, fast now, and roughly, along the top of the envelope and wrenched it open, nearly ripping the letter in his belated haste.

Dear Yonas Kelati,

This letter is written following your application for leave to remain on asylum and/or human rights grounds...

You claim to be an Eritrean national of thirty years old. However, you have not produced any identity or travel documents to confirm this. You claim to have arrived in the United Kingdom without such documents, and that you were under the control of traffickers and worked at a factory. However, when questioned you were unable to provide any meaningful information as to the identity of the traffickers or the precise location of the factory.

He scrunched up the paper in a silent fit of anger, and nearly tossed it into the water. It was obvious where this was going. He should have talked more in the interview about Aziz, about the torture... But perhaps he was being too hasty. The letter was long – maybe it would get better. He smoothed it out again.

You claim that you were involved in dissident writing... you claim you were imprisoned... you escaped and fled Eritrea. However, you have not provided any evidence of politically dissident writing attributed to your name...

But I told you, I couldn't even print articles... I had to go round different internet cafés and use a pen name...

Since you yourself worked for the country's censorship office, actively engaged in restricting the writing and speech of other Eritrean citizens, it does not appear credible that you would have in fact espoused values such as freedom of expression as strongly as you now claim to, or have produced dissident writing yourself...

Yonas's hands started to tremble. He rested the paper on his lap.

'I can't believe we've got this to ourselves! Great idea...' A girl's voice, coming from beyond the wall. Yonas craned forward, and saw a small beach down by the water's edge, where two teenage girls were standing by the water. One picked up a stone and skimmed it deftly, and it flew in three arcing leaps before sinking. He returned to his letter.

The Secretary of State notes that there are significant differences between your various accounts. This casts doubts on the credibility of your claim. For instance, in your SEF you stated that you were in prison for three or four months but in your asylum interview you stated that you were detained for more than three months.

That's what you pick up on and label a lie? It's not even a contradiction.

The Secretary of State notes the evidence you presented of marks on your body, which you claimed in your asylum interview were caused by severe beatings while in prison. However, you have not provided any medical evidence to confirm how the marks came to be there. Furthermore, you stated that you managed to escape from prison soon after, run for miles and spend two days without food or water. The Secretary of State is of the opinion that a person as injured as you claimed to be would not be able to achieve such physical feats. He considers that this casts doubt on the credibility of your claim.

'You haven't got a fag have you, mate?'

Someone else had come to sit on his bench, and a sour, unwashed scent hit Yonas's nostrils. He looked up: an old tramp with straggly hair. Yonas opened his mouth to reply, and found he was breathing in short, sharp jabs. Finally, he said, 'I don't smoke, sorry.'

The tramp pulled a can of cider out of his bag, and opened it with a hiss. He took a swig, and looked out at the river. A small trolley next to him was loaded with plastic bags, presumably bulging with all his possessions. Yonas looked back at his sheet of paper. Such a light and fragile thing. And nobody around him knew what he was reading, and what it meant, not the tramp, not anybody.

'Supermarkets,' the tramp said suddenly. 'Who called them super? Horrible places. *Super*. Ha. The name is the only *super* thing about them. Most godawful places on the planet!'

'I like them,' Yonas found himself saying, thinking of the long, colourful rows of perfectly formed fruit and vegetables… 'When I have money to spend.' He returned to the letter.

> The Secretary of State is of the opinion that if you had been of significant interest to the Eritrean authorities as you claimed, you would not have been able to escape from prison as you claimed because there would have been more stringent security in place.

But someone escaped from Belmarsh here in London! I read it in your papers…

> You claimed to have been invited to stay with an 'auntie', in the UK, but have not provided any evidence of the identity of this 'auntie', whom you claimed you could not find after you arrived.

'Want some?' The tramp was proffering the cider can.

Yonas nearly said no, but then thought: *Why not?* He took it, tipped his head back and glugged. Sweet and tinny, the alcohol spun around his veins. 'Thank you!' he said, handing it back.

'Welcome. Where you from then?' the tramp asked.

'Eritrea. Have you heard of it?'

'Oh yeah, love it there, had the time of my life on holidays the other week, helluva place,' the tramp said. 'Ha! Kidding! I ain't never even been to France,' and he descended into crackly laughter. Yonas smiled. *Helluva place.*

The Secretary of State considers your delay in applying for asylum to be unreasonable. He considers this further undermines the credibility of your claim. He must question why, if you believed yourself to be in genuine fear of your life and wanted to seek international protection, you would not have availed yourself or attempted to avail yourself of the protection of the United Kingdom by claiming asylum at the earliest opportunity at the arrival port.

Not sure how I was expected to break out of my container at the arrival port.

You mentioned other people whom you said had been trafficked to this country like you had. The Secretary of State has reason to believe that the credibility of your comments in relation to those people is flawed.

What was this about? Reason to believe? What reason? Surely not Gebre... Could Gebre have given a contradictory account? What could he have said? Yonas turned, slowly, to the last page.

It is considered that your submissions do not qualify for asylum or humanitarian protection. It is also considered that they do not qualify for limited leave to remain in accordance with the published Home Office Asylum Policy Instruction on Discretionary Leave.

You have no basis of stay in the United Kingdom and should make arrangements to leave the United Kingdom without delay.

In all the circumstances we prefer that those with no basis of stay in the United Kingdom leave voluntarily, but should you fail to do so then your removal may be enforced.

Yonas sank his head to his knees. Screwed up his eyes. Scrunched up the letter again and encased it in his fists.

'Bloodyell, would you look at that? Coupla lezzies down there on the beach! My eye!' the tramp said.

Yonas straightened up and glanced over. The two girls were embracing now, and as their lips briefly parted while they gazed at each other, the long hair of one tumbled around the face of the other in the breeze. 'I am glad someone is having a good time,' he said.

'Well, I'm having a ball,' the tramp retorted, 'especially now there's a free show on. Always regretted never having a threesome, but I reckon my time's passed.'

Yonas stared past the girls out to the river, as it churned on, and on, and on.

Veata had said that if he did get a refusal there was still a chance of a fresh claim, but only if the police got new evidence. So far there was no sign of that. The factory might already have closed. And even if it was raided, Aziz would probably deny Yonas had worked there just to spite him.

How could he break the news of this letter to Gebre? Or to Melat? Or Nina? How could he put a positive spin on things this time? He felt strangely compelled to jump down to that beach, swim out into the brown water, and let it wash him down to the open sea.

'Most people got no time for reflecting in this city, have they?' the tramp mused. 'Too busy, too caught up in their own business, their phones and whatnot.'

Behind them came the sound of a folk soundtrack and a scraping violin. Yonas turned to see where it was coming from, thinking of Emil and his late-night fiddle practice. But it was a fresh-faced boy in a tie-dye shirt with a stereo. He had his instrument case open in front of him and was sawing away, grinning eagerly at passersby.

The tramp winked at Yonas, reached down to one of his plastic bags, pulled out a tin whistle, and started playing a squeaky song of his own. It clashed with the folk tune. The violinist frowned, but carried on playing.

'Come on, sing along with me.' The tramp clapped and gestured to Yonas, wheezing with laughter. '*Oh when the saints.* You must know it.'

Yonas laughed a little and shook his head. 'Sorry. But maybe you and that violin player should start a band together,' he said as he got up and walked away.

That tramp probably had the right idea though, Yonas thought. If you don't have power, then mess about, playfully disrupt, find reasons to laugh. But when things really got tough, cracking a joke was easier said than done. It was all right for the tramp – whatever he had been through, he would never have to fear being deported out of this country with all its human rights lawyers and hostels for the homeless and buses with soft, furry seats. Yonas stuck his hand in his jeans pocket and felt his wooden rooster lying on its seam. He slowed his pace so he could fish it out for a second, looked at it, then replaced it. No: he wouldn't give up just yet. He must be able to come up with a new plan that would get him and Gebre through this. He'd always managed before.

Three skateboarders in a concrete cavern under the Southbank Centre made him stop in his tracks for a moment and watch – teenage boys with skinny legs in baggy jeans and scraggy hair, shooting up ramps, spinning off their peaks, turning in circles in the air and flying as free as birds, before clattering to the concrete floor.

Chapter 25: Clara

Babyccino! Can I have chocolate sprinkles? Can you make it so you can't see the foam because there's so much chocolate everywhere?

I wish Yonas would come back. The last time I saw him he came to babysit me so Mummy and Ganna could go out to a film but he was late so they were cross. I was even more cross because I wanted to play with him and not them, especially because they were cross. But then he came!

We played all the best games, the puppet game, the monster game, the copying game, hide and seek and the tickling game. Then he gave me dinner, and when I said I didn't want any more he fed me like an aeroplane, and we made up stories about the two sausages on my plate. They were best friends, and one was getting eaten up by a scary monster – that was me.

He's good at stories. He does all the voices. Daddy is good too but he reads faster, and the stories sound a bit the same. Once we met Yonas, we didn't live with Daddy any more.

That night I couldn't sleep. I crept downstairs. Yonas was writing something on a piece of paper in the kitchen. I said in my saddest, scaredest, smallest voice, 'Yonas, I had a nightmare, there were monsters.' (I didn't have a nightmare really!)

He did a sigh, but he said okay, he would read me one more story with no monsters in it.

We went upstairs, and I was trying to think what book I wanted Yonas to read, when he said he would tell me a story without a book.

He took the wooden lion off my ark and held it on his knee. Then he took something out of his pocket and held it on his other knee.

'What's that?' I asked him, sitting up.

'It's my rooster. Want to hold it? My grandfather made it for me when I was about your age.'

I took it. I liked it. It was made of wood as well, but it looked old – my lion was better. 'Cockadoodledooooo!' I said, and he said that was even better than a real rooster could do, and he should know, his family used to have one in their garden. Then he started telling me the story, holding my lion in one hand, and making it walk up and down my bed.

'There was once a beautiful lion who lived in a cave in the mountains. She was the most golden, smooth and shiny lion you could ever imagine. She had lovely green eyes like fresh grass. Even her paws were elegant. But hidden inside her paws she had sharp claws. One day the lion gave birth to a cub and became a lion mummy. She loved her cub more than anything. Inside the cave she built her cub a bed out of doves' feathers, and it was the softest bed in the world.

'The lion mummy had to move to a different cave because she wasn't happy living in the same cave as the cub's daddy. She used her sharp claws to fight off anyone who came past the cave who might put her cub in danger. She fought off giraffes, and hyenas, and even a giant rhino, as big as a bus. But she could not stay in the cave to look after the little cub all the time because she had to go out to get them both food.

'So one day, after she had hunted, she came back to her cave and was shocked to find a stranger inside. It was a rooster!'

'Like your rooster?' I asked.

'Yes, but this rooster had a bright red crown on his head and a flappy beard hanging from his beak. He had a golden chest and blue feathers in his tail the colour of the sea. He was saying… now, I need your help, what does a rooster say?'

'Cockadoodledoo!' I said.

'Exactly. And the lion mummy thought that the rooster was attacking her cub. She was filled with a terrible anger. She gave a snarl so loud that the walls of her cave shook. She crouched down low, and she was about to pounce. But just then, the cub jumped out of her bed. *Mummy, stop!* she said. *He was just playing.*

'The lion mummy put her head on one side. She was not sure if this could be true. What do you think the rooster said?'

'Cockadoodledoo!' I said again.

'Exactly. And the lion cub said, *Mummy, now rooster can look after me while you go to hunt for food!* The lion mummy didn't think the rooster would be much good at that. He couldn't even roar. But she agreed.

'And for a while they were all very happy. The lion mummy liked having somebody else to play with her cub, and she was even having fun playing with the rooster herself. Sometimes the rooster would pretend to be a lion and would crouch and squawk as much like a roar as he could. Sometimes the lion mummy would pretend to be a rhino and would walk around slowly on three paws with one paw sticking up above her head.

'But then, after a while, the other lions who lived in the same colony found out that the rooster was living there and that he'd been looking after the lion cub. *Roosters aren't allowed to live here!* they told the lion mummy. And one day they found the rooster when he was on his own, stood in a circle around him, and told him he would have to leave, today, or they would put him in a cage. The rooster didn't want to be in a cage or leave the lion mummy and the cub behind, but he thought maybe they would be better off without him anyway. And then – to his surprise – the rooster got a message from an old friend of his: another rooster! *I've come to the lion colony too*, he said, *but they put me in a cage and I'm scared. Can you come and rescue me, so we can go on an adventure?*

'The rooster knew he had to help his friend escape from the cage before he was put in one too. But he loved the cub and wanted to play with her one more time. He would make it the best play they had ever had, so that the cub would remember how much fun they'd had together, and then he would run away with his rooster friend, and the lion mummy and the cub could carry on just like they had been doing before.

'They had a brilliant playtime, and then the cub went to sleep. She was a bit sad when she woke up and realized that the rooster had gone. She missed their games. But soon she made lots of other lion cub friends. Sometimes she would remember the rooster with that crown on his head and that flappy beard hanging off his face and those big blue feathers in his tail and she would smile and laugh. It was her own secret story which she stored inside her heart all her life, even until she was an old lion with her own cubs. And when her own cubs started asking her for stories, can you guess the first story she told them?'

'The rooster story?'

'That's right.' Then Yonas picked up his wooden rooster and put it back in his pocket.

I grabbed his arm. 'What about the rooster? Where did he go?'

'Ah, that's another story.'

'Tell me that one!' I didn't want him to stop, but it was hard to keep my eyes open.

'It's time to sleep now.' Yonas kissed my head and walked out of the room.

The next day, Mummy and Ganna got really upset in the kitchen because they didn't know where he'd gone, and they were even crying, and that made me scared because I hate it when Mummy cries, and I've never seen Ganna cry – I thought she was too old. So I crept upstairs, and played with my ark quietly for a little bit, and thought about my new secret story.

Chapter 26: Yonas

ASYLUM SEEKER SEWS UP FACE

Yonas walked to the detention centre fast, purposefully, trying to generate positive energy through the movement of legs and arms, while his mind ground with the effort of finding the right words to break his news to Gebre, words that wouldn't send his friend over the edge. *By the way, I have an appeal date now, and it's coming up pretty soon actually... Oh, yes, didn't I tell you I got a refusal letter a few months ago? Sorry, I thought I'd mentioned it! It is no big deal though – most people get refused initially. Veata thinks I have a good chance!* But he suspected Gebre wouldn't buy a word of it. That said, he had been surprised by Melat's reaction when he belatedly told her on the phone about his appeal a few days earlier, having led her on to think he was on track for ILR any day. She said she wasn't worried for herself and the family so much as cross at him for keeping the truth from her. But then, she was always more resilient than Gebre.

Each time he'd been to visit the detention centre so far, Gebre had seemed more depressed, less communicative, harder to reach. Yonas knew he was the only person in the world who could keep his friend afloat now, but that wouldn't happen if he allowed himself to descend into panic at his own situation. And yet panic churned at the thought of an immigration judge telling him firmly that his time in the UK was up – that his life was up. He kept telling Nina he was feeling okay about his appeal, that Veata had done her best and what would be would be – but the truth was he hadn't been sleeping properly since he got the hearing notice. Nina could tell he was more worried than he was letting on, he knew. And by now he could quickly recognize the expression on her face when she was battling not to express her own worries to him.

When Yonas was led through to the visiting room, he saw the crown of Gebre's head, which was hanging down, as if the muscles in his neck had given up the ghost. 'How are you doing, my friend?' Yonas said. 'It's good to see you…' But he faltered as Gebre's face lifted, and he saw the deep black tunnel eyes, the freshly bandaged arms. Yonas persisted with small talk, but got no meaningful response. Just as he was about to toss in a light mention of his appeal hearing, Gebre said, 'I got refused.'

'Refused? You mean, a Home Office letter?' Yonas asked, feeling a wash of guilt that he hadn't mentioned his own earlier. Gebre would realize this as soon as he heard about the appeal date. He would be hurt, and doubly depressed. 'Oh, sorry to hear that,' Yonas said. 'I got one too, actually. But Veata is already working on the appeal…' Gebre didn't seem to be listening though. He'd let his head slide right down onto his bandaged arms on the table. 'Hey, don't get too down,' Yonas pleaded. 'We expected a refusal the first time round, right? It's normal.'

Gebre half looked up. 'You don't know what they wrote in my letter,' he said. 'They are never letting me out of here unless I agree to leave the country. Never.'

Yonas reached over and put his hand on Gebre's shoulder. 'It is just the initial letter, remember – and they are making themselves sound tough. We can't let them intimidate us; we've got to focus on our appeals. We will get there in the end –you'll be out of here, and we'll explore London together like we planned. There is so much I can show you…' He tried to lift Gebre's head so he could meet his eyes, but Gebre suddenly pushed his chair back.

'Get off me,' he said. 'Stop lying!' A few people looked round. 'You are trying to make me feel better, but I am not *stupid* – it is *not* fine, I *know* it is not fine, and nothing you say can make *it* fine, and nothing is going to get me out of this fucking *prison* except death.' Gebre's veins bulged out of his thin neck.

Yonas was scrabbling for the right words when the guard came over, told him the meeting was over, and led Gebre away.

That night, Yonas stayed up in the living room, waiting for Emil to get home. He wanted more than anything to talk, to finally confide in Emil about exactly how bad a state Gebre was in, to ask if he would please visit Gebre, to try to give him some hope, at least about living life in London as a gay immigrant man. Yonas also needed to talk to Emil about the consequences if his own appeal were rejected. Could he could stay on in the squat? Where else could he go – what would he do? But time ticked on. Emil was clearly out late, and would probably stay out all night, but Yonas made himself a cup of tea, just in case.

Back on the sofa, he was just finishing the dregs when he got a text from Nina, hoping the visit had gone well. He knew he should be talking more to her about all this. They were still acting like a secret couple, whenever they snatched moments alone, and he relished that time – he wanted it to be as pleasurable as possible, not bogged down by his plight, so he had largely kept his fears from her. He had felt himself getting drawn into her orbit, and he could see how comfortable she had become with him now too, trusting enough to let him look after Clara, whom he was growing fond of, and whose energy was infectious. Nina asked so often about his case, anyone listening to their conversations could be forgiven for thinking she cared about it more than him. She had become so exercised about the wider system he was caught up in that she'd started volunteering at the Refugee Council, like Molly, and was even planning to organize an art auction to raise money for them. But the more their mutual attachment deepened, the warier he became of it – it only made the prospect of getting deported after all more terrifying. His appeal date was now only a week away, and the deafening tick of the clock in his head made his time with Nina seem all the more implausible, impermanent, fleeting. What was the point in connecting with her any more deeply? What could she possibly understand about him, really?

He thought of Gebre sitting in his cell, colouring white paper in black, fuming over his refusal letter, probably scheming ways to procure breakable objects he could cut himself with, and started to feel more than ever like he related to his friend's despair, and how tempting it would be to succumb, to give up.

He went to bed, eventually, but couldn't sleep a wink. Even his breath felt shallow, constricted, like he was taking in air through a thin straw. He tried to get up and read a book, but couldn't concentrate, then found he was gnawing on his knuckles, and felt his remaining confidence slipping away, through the thin curtains and out into the night air. His life in the UK had peaked, and now was slipping down, irrevocably. At his appeal hearing he would be forced to humiliate himself yet again, to face yet more aggressive questioning about his story, now not just in a suffocating boxroom, but in a public tribunal with Nina and everybody watching, only to be spat out of the asylum machine for ever at the end of it, alone. Why should he let this system process him like this, as if he were a bit of food waste, like one of those hundreds of reject sandwiches from the supermarket, thrown out into a big skip at the end of the day because there were too many, even though they were still just as good as all the rest?

The next morning, feeling slightly crazed from lack of sleep, Yonas drank three strong cups of coffee, then set out to visit Gebre again, this time with a new mission. He was going to find a loophole for them to escape again, together this time. He had no idea what the loophole would look like, but he was sure he would spot it if he kept his eyes open. Just like he did in the prison that was actually called a prison. It would be harder to find here, but the risks were lower, and the stakes just as high.

As he submitted to the security checks, he made a mental list of every door, every key object he could see, numbers of staff, cameras. Nothing came to mind yet. But it would.

When he finally got through and sat down in the waiting room, he was surprised to be called up to reception, and led by a guard down a corridor into a private room. 'I'm afraid Gebre is unwell today,' the guard told him, her face impassive. 'You will have to come back another day.'

'What is wrong with him?'

'I am unable to give out that information. But he should be able to receive visitors again in a few days' time.' She was making it sound as if Gebre had a mild cold, only to be expected.

'He's been cutting himself again, hasn't he?' Yonas said, hardly able to control his voice. 'Why are you keeping him in here? He shouldn't be here! You have to let me see him.'

'Please calm down, sir. I can't let you see him, I'm afraid. But he is being well looked after, rest assured.'

'Then what is wrong with him?'

'I'm sure he'll be better soon, sir.'

Loophole, come on, Yonas muttered furiously to himself on his way out. There had to be a way.

He asked to stop off at the toilets in the corridor, just behind reception. As he was coming out, he noticed a cleaner pulling some purple material out of a cupboard in a room opposite, marked STAFF ONLY. The cleaners he'd seen all wore purple overalls. Yonas walked swiftly across the corridor and into the room as the cleaner went out, catching the door just before it closed. 'All right?', he said, a British greeting he'd now adopted and learned was rhetorical.

Sure enough, the cleaner just nodded at him, said 'all right' back, and walked off.

The cupboard had a laminated sign on it saying SPARES, and in it were several of the purple garments. Yonas pulled out two. Since he had no bag, he stuffed half of one down his trousers, and the other half up the T-shirt he wore underneath his shirt. There was a mirror on the other side of the room; he walked over and looked at himself. The overall bulged out from his back. He took off his shirt and T-shirt as hastily as possible, popping a button, then put both overalls on, before replacing his own garments on top, just as another staff member came in. He could tell she was staring at him, asking herself whether she'd seen him before. 'See you later,' he said amicably – another British saying he'd learned was standard, even if you weren't going to see the other person again that day, or that week, or perhaps ever – and strolled out.

He went back to the reception, sweltering and self-conscious with his extra padding, fearful that that woman would come out after him, point and tell the receptionist in urgent tones: *Hey, that guy was just in the staff room, call the police* – but she didn't reappear.

Back at the squat, Yonas selected his least conspicuous shirt and trousers, then tried one of the overalls on over them. He paced about in his room, thinking. His idea was nuts. But it had to be done, there was no choice, not with Gebre in a too bad state for a visit – it was probably a medical emergency that the real doctors were pretending didn't exist.

He phoned Veata. 'Hi. I just wanted to ask, when are you planning to see Gebre next? He is in a bad way. I saw him yesterday and told him about my letter, and he started shouting. He was very disturbed, even more than last time, and they are doing nothing still. And he has been cutting again... Today they wouldn't even let me see him and refused to explain.'

'I will make a call now, and go tomorrow morning first thing to check on him,' Veata said. 'I'll ask for the doctor to re-examine his condition as a matter of urgency, okay? I'll make the case for Article 35 again – I don't know why they're being so bullish about it.' He could hear in her voice that she suspected she'd fail.

The next morning, Yonas went to the detention centre wearing one of the overalls under his clothes. He waited behind a hedge until he saw Veata arrive, held off for a couple of minutes, then put on the second overall and followed her in. His blood seemed to be shooting around his body at three times the normal speed. Passing reception was the riskiest bit – but when he said he was sorry but he'd forgotten his pass, the security guy just grunted and handed him a temporary one.

He made his way through to the visiting area, and saw Gebre sitting opposite Veata at a table. So, he was okay! Okay enough to have a visitor now, anyway. Therefore okay enough to do this.

Another toilet was nearby, available to detainees and visitors. Yonas waited until the guard was looking the other way, then moved into Gebre's line of sight and waved wildly. He caught his friend's eye, put his finger over his lips, pointed to the toilet, and retreated into it. In a cubicle, he removed the inner overall and waited, heart racing. *Would Gebre do anything? Would he tell Veata? Was he too far gone to care?*

But after a few minutes, the door squeaked open. He opened his cubicle door, and it was Gebre!

'What the hell are you doing?' Gebre said, but he was unable to help grinning back at Yonas, as he took in the overalls.

'I'm getting you out, that's what! Prison break number two. And this is your disguise. I've got some extra bits too. You just need to put them on and follow me. Veata's waiting there so they won't suspect anything. And look at this!' Like a conjuror, he whisked Emil's wig out from his pants, relieved to rid himself of the itch. It was shiny, loosely curled, long, and a patchy shade of brown. (It had been platinum blonde, but some cheap dye from the pound shop had made it more subtle.)

'You are even crazier than me,' Gebre said, shaking his head wryly.

'I've never been more sane. We can do this!' Yonas said. But Gebre's face seemed to crumple. It made Yonas realize how much he was asking, by putting Gebre on the spot with no warning like this, when he was at his most fragile. He might say no. Maybe the most sensible thing would be for him to say no. But then, who was helping him in here? Who knew him? Who cared? Gebre would cut himself to death if he stayed any longer. Well, now Yonas was taking control, and at least he was giving Gebre a chance to do a joint escape again, to be together, free in the UK, even if they both had to be on the run from now on in.

'Okay, so what do I do?' Gebre said.

Yonas reached out impetuously and hugged his friend's skinny body. He felt Gebre stiffen in surprise. 'Right, we haven't got much time,' Yonas said, pulling back. 'So, first, we need to dress you in this.' He shoved the overalls over Gebre's head. 'Next, we need to beautify.'

He placed the wig on – thanking his stars that Gebre's hair had been cut short and his beard shaven. Gebre stood still, compliant, his mouth curled up at one side. Yonas stood back to inspect. 'Oh yes. Yes, yes, yes!' he said. 'But don't look in the mirror yet. Wait a second.' He reached into his pocket, and pulled out a pink lipstick he'd found in the pound shop where he got the dye that he thought looked suitably subtle. 'Here,' he said, reaching for Gebre's face. Placing his palm gently on his friend's cheek, he drew the lipstick slowly over the shapely lips, traversing the familiar deep bow on the lower one that disappeared when Gebre smiled, as he did now – even let out a laugh, from lips that were more mauve than pink in fact, but never mind. 'Gorgeous!' Yonas said, clapping softly. And it was true – womanhood suited Gebre unexpectedly well. 'Oh, except I brought you a scrunchie to tie the wig hair back so you look more like you're at work,' he said. 'Just turn round for me.' He swivelled Gebre to face away from him, then twisted the fake hair awkwardly into a knot above his neck and secured it with the scrunchie, remembering, as he did it, the sight of his mother spending hours plaiting Melat's hair, how glad that had made him not to have been born a girl.

He swivelled Gebre back around. 'Perfect!' he pronounced, wondering if he'd overdone the lipstick. He grabbed a tissue from the toilet. 'Just pad the lips a little, for some extra sophistication, a "natural look". NICE!' Gebre did as he was told, then pouted flirtatiously. 'You could charm any man you want, looking like that.' Gebre raised an eyebrow.

'Okay, so now it's simple,' Yonas said. 'We have to move fast, but look like everything's completely normal. So, you just walk out of here and towards reception, then I'll follow. When you get to security, if the guy there looks up, you just raise your hand and say *see you later* or something like that – sound happy, relaxed, low-key, okay? Then when you get into the car park, take off the purple overall and stuff it up your jumper. At the end of the car park, there's a driveway, and at the end of the driveway, you turn right up the road. You'll see a bus shelter on the left. There's a high wood fence next to it, and you can chuck the overall over that. I'll be close behind, and we'll catch the bus – they come every five minutes, and I've got you a ticket already – then we'll be out of here. We'll be free! Got it? It'll be great.'

Gebre looked at him, seriously now. Yonas began to worry he'd change his mind again, wondered if he should go through it once more, but then Gebre nodded, turned and left.

Yonas waited for an interminable three minutes before following. No alarms sounded yet. No shouts. Nobody running. All quiet, all normal, all oppressive and grey, just like any other detention centre day.

At reception, the guy at the desk was reading a book – didn't even look up. Yonas started jogging through the car park. As he turned the corner at the road, he saw Gebre walking ahead, towards the bus stop, slowly, as if he were out for a stroll. Miraculously, the bus was already coming. *We're going to make it!* Yonas thought. *I'm the new Houdini!* He sprinted to catch up, slapping Gebre on the back with delight. Even if the authorities got to them in the end, somehow, it didn't matter – they were doing this together, and for however long it lasted, they were going to be free here, just like they'd imagined.

But as the bus slowed to a standstill and its doors opened, Gebre stopped too, and started shaking his head.

'Come on. What's up?' Yonas asked.

But Gebre put his hands over his eyes. His head carried on shaking. 'I can't,' he said, into his fingers.

'What? No! We made it already, you've escaped! The bus is right here. We need to go. Come on! When we're on the bus I'll tell you the rest of the plan...' He pushed Gebre gently, but he resisted.

'I'm going back,' he said.

'You gettin' on or what?' the driver asked impatiently, as the doors stood open.

Yonas began to panic. Surely Gebre wasn't really pulling out, not now, not at this point, traumatized or not. 'Don't do this,' he said, as gently as he could. 'You can't go back in now anyway – they'll realize what you did and it'll be worse. Come on – we've done the hard bit!'

Gebre shook his head again, looking up at Yonas now, tears standing in his eyes. 'I can't. I can't hide any more. I can't run any more.'

'You can rest, soon...'

'No. I'm done. If I stay in prison, Veata can give my case a try, but if that fails I'm dead anyway, and I'm ready for that. I was ready a long time ago.'

The bus driver beeped his horn. 'Last chance, love birds. I'm closing the doors.'

Yonas stuck his foot in to stop the doors closing. He glanced down the road, certain the security guys would be running towards them, or that sirens would come wailing, but there was nobody yet. 'Trust me,' he said to Gebre, squeezing his friend's arm, pulling it, tugging it, wrenching it. 'Come on, don't do an Osman on me. Let's go!'

But Gebre snatched his arm back. 'You go. Quickly, get out of here before the bus goes.'

Yonas wanted to rage at him. 'I'm not leaving you again!' he pleaded.

The bus doors slammed onto his foot, and reopened automatically. 'All right, that's it. I'm driving off now, even if I take your leg with me,' the driver said.

'Thank you for trying,' Gebre said. 'I know you want the best for me. But if I come, it will bring both of us down. This was meant to work out for you. Not me.' And before Yonas could contradict him, he felt his friend's palms hard on his chest, and now he was being pushed backwards hard into the bus, with a strength he hardly imagined Gebre had any more; then his body slammed against the driver's cubicle window, and he fell to the floor.

The doors closed. The engine revved, and the bus moved off. 'You people,' Yonas heard the driver say wearily, as if he had to transport crazy folk like this all the time. Yonas grabbed the luggage rail to pull himself to his feet, regained his balance, pressed his face against the door, and watched Gebre's figure recede into the distance. His friend was waving, slowly, ceremonially, like a father sending his child off to school. Then he slid out of view.

Chapter 27: Martina

**GUARDS AT ASYLUM SEEKER CENTRE
UNMASKED AS BNP MEMBERS**

You've got flat white? New Zealand style? I'll have a small one.

That guy Yonas Kelati? I wish I could give him a piece of my mind. He got me *this* close to being sacked! If I hadn't been so soft, maybe the whole fiasco would never have happened. When he first turned up at the centre, I was on the front desk, and I turned him away – I had to.

'I am here to visit Gebre Merhawi,' I remember him announcing casually, as if I'd just say: *Great, come on in!*

I asked for his name on the visitor list, but there was no record of it. 'Have you given notice of your visit?' I asked. He shook his head. 'All visitors to any immigration removal centre in the UK need to give notice, twenty-four hours in advance of any visit,' I said.

'Oh. I did not know that.' He looked crestfallen, then asked me: 'Could you please make an exception this time? I know that Gebre really needs a visitor – he is like my brother, and he has no other family here, and he's had a very difficult—'

I had to cut in. 'It's not just the notice. You also need to provide ID and a utility bill for proof of address. And then you would have to be searched, have your fingerprints scanned and have a photo taken.' He had a large, battered rucksack on, I noticed. 'You can't take a bag in, either,'

269

I added. 'There is a lot of security, and it often annoys visitors, but it's important, or you could get anyone going in.'

'But I didn't know all that,' he said. 'Please, just let me have a very quick visit, just one minute even, so he can see my face and he knows I came. I can write down my address for you, you can check it,' and he started scribbling on a scrap of paper! When I repeated that he would need a utility bill to *prove* his address, he said, 'But I am staying with a friend. I don't pay bills there.'

'Well,' I said, 'you will need an official letter as proof of address if you come again. Council tax, for instance. And ID. We can consider other official letters, like bank statements, but they won't necessarily be accepted on their own. I can't let you in without those items. And don't forget the twenty-four hours' notice.'

'But I paid to travel all the way here to visit today,' he said. 'It's a lot of money for me.'

'There is nothing I can do for you now, I'm afraid,' I said, fed up with him by then. He looked at me angrily, but didn't shout or swear like some.

'Can you just pass a message to him that I came, then, please, and I will be back,' he said. 'Can I write something?'

'You can leave a note and I'll put it in the post tray,' I said. He thought a moment, wrote something down on a receipt, folded it, handed it to me, and left. I unfolded it, out of curiosity. Just some scrawls in a script I didn't understand.

A lot of the detainees and their family and friends think we staff want to make their lives difficult, but it's not true. We are just doing a job. The failed asylum seekers failed for a reason. We have to make sure they stay where they're supposed to, and we look after them while they're here. It's not like prison. Okay, they're locked up, but it's not that bad. For one thing, they can go back to their home countries if they want, any time. Another thing is that it costs ninety quid a day to look after them in the centre – that's like staying in a pricey B&B. And they get services to match. There are classes and things they can do, an area where they can exercise, and the food's okay – it's a bit like being in a holiday camp, almost. I mean, I've never been to a prison but I assume it's much worse.

You have to keep a distance though. I got close to a couple of the detainees when I first started – I really got on with this girl called Esme from Ivory Coast, she was funny and we both liked basketball – although I soon learned that was a bad idea. You know, the other detainees got jealous and the staff told me it was inappropriate, and then Esme got deported anyway and I knew I'd never see her again.

My boyfriend Ben hates what I do. He says that asylum seekers should all be allowed to work here and live freely and pay tax and we'd all be better off, as well as better, morally. But then where would it end? And he's never actually met a failed asylum seeker. Most of the detainees I see can't speak English well, or are too messed up in the head to do useful work here, even manual labour, and there are plenty of people from Eastern Europe who are happy to do that and can integrate better. Like me and my parents. I've been here since I was seven so I sound British, and I'm part of British culture. I mean, I support Arsenal like Ben does (okay, so most of the detainees support Premier League clubs so maybe that's a bad point). What I'm saying is, there have to be limits.

I know it isn't easy for the detainees. It's not like I don't get their point of view. It must be gutting to get locked up after making a long journey to a place they thought would make life easy. But it's a risk they took.

My parents took a risk when they arrived too, but theirs didn't involve breaking the law. My dad got work as a translator, and my mum worked super-hard so she could open up a small shop selling Polish food in our area. It was the first Polish deli in London, I think. My classmates used to say, *Eeeeew yuck, her family eats sour cucumber and tripe soup, don't ever go round there*, and I felt embarrassed, but then I made a couple of friends and they liked coming for dinner. Anyway, the point is that my parents came here legally, made a good contribution to the country paying taxes and everything, and so they deserved to stay – but that doesn't mean that everyone from everywhere does.

So, the following week Yonas Kelati came back, and told me he'd given twenty-four hours' notice and had his proof of identity with him. I checked, and he was on the visiting list. I was glad – I'd hoped he would come back. I'd heard talk that Gebre Merhawi had gone downhill fast, and was cutting himself. It also occurred to me I might have forgotten to put that note in the post tray – I might have just left it on the reception desk, and maybe the cleaners had thought it was rubbish. Anyway, there was talk about whether Gebre Merhawi was fit to be detained, and whether the doctor should have reported his condition under Article 35. But for now he was just being looked after at the centre, in the special wing. So, Yonas Kelati dug around in his inside pocket and produced a letter from the Home Office confirming that he was seeking asylum and that the address was his, and temporary ID. *I knew you were an asylum seeker too*, I thought. But the letter was all folded up and was a bit torn on the edges. 'I am afraid this is not sufficient as proof of address,' I said. 'As I said last time, we ask for a utility bill.'

'Oh come on!' he said. 'You told me I could bring other official documents – you didn't say I would need more than one.'

'I told you we couldn't *necessarily* accept other documents,' I said.

And then he burst out at me: 'You can't turn me away again! Do you even know my friend, Gebre? Have some compassion! Let me tell you what he has—'

'It's nothing to do with compassion,' I said. 'It is just the rules.'

'Okay. Look, I understand you are just doing your job. But please can you ask your manager, just in case he can accept these documents, this time?'

I hesitated. I knew Gebre Merhawi hadn't had any other visitors, I'd checked, and it did seem wrong that people with depression like him should be kept in here indefinitely. I mean, that situation could send anyone a bit crazy. So I relented, and said I'd call the manager, but that it was unlikely he'd make a different decision.

After I'd put the call through, I sat Yonas down. There was nobody else at reception, so I explained to him, out of goodwill, that Gebre had recently been moved into isolation for a while because he had been harming himself.

'How?' he asked sharply, leaning forward, almost as if he were accusing *me* of hurting the guy!

'I heard that he broke a canteen plate by stamping on it, and used the shard of plastic to cut into his wrists,' I explained. I knew I probably shouldn't be the one sharing this information, but I felt like Yonas Kelati should know as he might be able to help, and also I kind of owed him for failing to deliver the note, though I wasn't going to admit that. 'Does he have a history of doing this, do you know?' I asked. He didn't answer straight away but he frowned as if he were remembering something. 'Any information like that could help us to help him.'

He sighed. 'Gebre is traumatized,' he said. 'So much has happened to him, torture in prison, for one thing, but so much more: his father was disappeared when he was a kid, war, the journey. . . And from what you are saying about his condition, I know Gebre; he needs to be in a hospital, right now, or out of here, in a house with friends, people to support him. He should never have been put in here.'

'Okay, well thanks for sharing that,' I said. 'I'll pass on your comments. But you can rest reassured that the doctor here is monitoring him. Now, since we're still waiting for the manager, I'll take your photo and fingerprints.' I took his photo first. He was quite striking, actually, with prominent cheekbones – I mean, not my taste, but he could probably do modelling or something; they like darker skin these days, don't they? Then I showed him to the fingerprint scanner. He lifted his hands, and I noticed they were shaking.

'I don't think this part is going to work,' he said. Slowly, he turned his hands over, and I saw the bright, uneven scars on each of his finger pads, as if a child had persuaded him to do some finger painting with a pot of bright pink paint. I wondered if he had any sensation in them, and imagined the scene when they were first burned, probably by some smuggler in the wilderness near a border, with no painkillers. I swallowed.

'No, I'm afraid it won't,' I said. 'And I can't let you in without scanned fingerprints, so—'

'But please,' he said. 'They just burned off in a fire – it was not my fault. That could happen to any British person as well, right? You would not refuse a British person permission to visit family in here because they had been in an accident?'

But it wouldn't happen to them, I thought, *and they rarely do have family in here*. 'I'll ask the manager when he comes,' I said.

We waited in silence for a while, and I felt increasingly bad about Gebre Merhawi, who was about to lose his only chance to have a visitor, again. I got up and called through to my manager to see what the hold-up was. 'He's gone on lunch,' the secretary said.

'But he was supposed to be coming down to check an issue with a visitor's paperwork,' I said.

'Must've forgot,' she said.

I put the phone down and looked at Yonas Kelati. He looked back at me, pleading. 'Okay, fine, I will let you in this once,' I said. 'Just because your friend is unwell and he could do with a visitor, probably. But I am making a note that nobody was around to authorize your damaged fingerprints. And next time you'll need to bring additional documents, okay?' He nodded.

I led him through, and handed him over to the guy who was supervising visits. I went to the staff room to grab my sandwiches after that, and then I walked back via the interview area and looked in. The two of them were sitting at a table in a corner. I couldn't hear what they were saying, but it was probably in their language anyway. Gebre hadn't visibly cheered up at his friend's arrival. I watched Yonas reach out to touch the bandages on his arms, then hold Gebre's shoulder and ask him questions. Gebre just gave short answers, then Yonas got worked up, and then Gebre got even *more* worked up, and I thought Dan, the supervisor, would step in to calm it down, but then they quietened again. Gebre seemed to get upset again, his body shook, and Yonas tried to comfort him. I did feel sorry for them then. Both of them. Of course I did. But the fact was, Gebre was at the end of the road here, and this was the system, and there was nothing we or either of them could do about it.

The one other visitor Gebre had, at least the only recorded one, was his lawyer. Asian looking, quiet, a polite lady. But on her way out once, I asked if her meeting went okay, and she said, 'That man should not be detained here in his condition – it's a breach of his human rights, he's seriously ill,' and looked at me hard, the kind of look that said: *I am the good angel here and you are evil.* It really annoys me that people like her think they are so righteous, that they are 'saving the vulnerable', and that we're all on the dark side. I'm just doing my job! Same with my colleagues. We're a nice bunch, mostly, just ordinary people, working hard. And all the detention centre is doing is helping to make sure people don't break the law. Plus, the law is the way it is so the UK doesn't overflow with illegal immigrants, especially criminal ones. Anyone who commits a crime here has to take the consequences, and if you're an illegal immigrant like Gebre Merhawi then the consequence should be you don't get the right to stay, and if you won't leave, then you have to be detained. Simple. Look, I know, the lawyer was just doing her job too. And maybe she wasn't thinking that I was evil. Maybe I was reading that into it. But anyway, I don't trust all the human rights stuff that much. It sounds nice, but as far as I can see from what you read in the papers, it's mostly used by criminals to get away with stuff – like, *I know I'm a terrorist and murdered a bunch of children, but please don't deport me, I have a human right to see my own child once a week.*

But, whatever. I don't think I or anyone at the centre could have stopped what happened next. It wasn't as if we didn't have a doctor monitoring Gebre Merhawi. All the appropriate procedural steps had been followed.

The day the alarms went off, it was in the middle of a visiting session and I was supervising. I remember, me and the other guard were chatting about her hen night which was coming up that weekend, and everything was calm. Until suddenly the bells shrilled and there was this big commotion, and one of the other officers ran in and told us that there was a code red, and when we asked what happened, he whispered that Gebre Merhawi had escaped. Escaped! I couldn't believe it. He seemed such a passive, quiet guy, always depressed and sitting around, I just couldn't imagine him initiating anything major like that. Plus, the detention centre is super-secure – I mean, there's barbed wire and high walls and triple gates.

We had to get cracking, shepherding out visitors and getting detainees to their rooms. And as I was rushing around, doing the lockdown procedures, it struck me: I bet it was that friend, Yonas Kelati. He must be behind it. He *was* the type of guy who would try his luck: he'd tried it on with me, getting into the centre without the right documents – he'd even told me he thought Gebre shouldn't be detained. But when we checked the book later, he'd never signed in. Anyway, the staff were all mega-stressed, and the lockdown was extra tough because the detainees started getting agitated as the news went around. Everyone's rooms were searched, but there was no evidence of a break-in.

But then, Gebre Merhawi came back into the centre of his own accord and – get this – he was in drag! I mean, he had a long wig on, and purple lipstick, on top of his normal clothes. It would've been hilarious, if his face hadn't been so strange and sad. He just walked in the front door, all silent, and waited to be cuffed. Refused to say anything about what happened, how the fuck he escaped with that as a 'disguise', how he even got hold of the wig and lipstick, not to mention why he came back! Later, the police found one of the cleaner's uniforms. It had been thrown over a wall. He insisted he hadn't taken it, but he must have done. Clever bastard. I wonder how much he used his mental health originally to dupe us into thinking he wasn't capable of something like that. Of course, we had to punish him so the other detainees learned a lesson, and he was put in solitary. He went without a word of protest.

Eventually the others calmed down, and it was all over so fast that the centre managed to avoid a media storm – over the escape, anyway, and the kerfuffle after it among the other detainees. The staff just had to give our version of events for an internal investigation, and those of us on duty got formal warnings. Not that it was our fault, in any shape or form.

But what happened next… We have protocols to stop it happening and we followed them all, so there was nothing more we could have done. Gebre was watched all the time, so there was no way he could cut himself; all reasonable steps had been taken. But when one of my colleagues went for a pee, for like *one minute*, he took his shirt off and hanged himself from the light fitting.

Well, that sent the other detainees crazy: they started rioting and shouting and throwing stuff, and we had to handcuff some and isolate them, and police were called, so then they had to be told about the escape incident too. Just when it seemed like the whole thing would stay out of the media, we got a headline about a detainee suicide, accusations that the centre wasn't fit for purpose, and, sure enough, a whole new raft of forms and protocols followed.

On the day it happened, there was too much firefighting to do for me to really process it – but when I got home that night, I cried. Only time that ever happened to me after a day at work, except the day when Esme was deported. I kept thinking, What if I'd remembered to pass on that note, before he got into a really bad way? My boyfriend said it wasn't my fault, it was the fault of the system I work for. Still, every day I go into work now, I remember it. So I'm even more careful not to get attached to any of the individual detainees, because it'd just get me down too, you know?

Chapter 28: Yonas

Gebre is dead. Gebre is dead. Gebre is dead. Buildings, fields, trees, buildings, fields, trees, buildings, fields, trees, oblivious sun on smeary windows, oblivious cars on crowded roads, a village, a farm, a canary-yellow field, a river sparkling through emerald green, a picture book scene… It wasn't long ago that he and Gebre were back in a war zone, when a verdant, peaceful landscape like this was an impossible dream. But now that it was here, outside the train window, with only him to see it, it seemed like a skein of hyper-realistic painted wallpaper that he could reach out to, peel back, and reveal a grotesque cartoon of Gebre's body hanging in a darkened room.

He sat back, away from the train window. Contemplated the small sink. The tap dripped. Dead. Dead. Dead. Someone had left a handful of toilet paper in there which had swollen to a wet, white clump.

So, here he was again. Back in a train toilet. But heading in the other direction. Away from the city he and Gebre had aimed for. Away from the hopes they'd had. Away from Gebre's dead body. Dead. Gebre.

It was still impossible to believe they'd been so close to escaping, but that it hadn't happened. That the worst had happened instead.

After the bus drove away from the detention centre, Yonas had stayed on until the end of the route, in a daze, and only got off because the driver told him to. He'd walked for some time, aimlessly, trying to contain his fury and despair, trying to be practical. He couldn't go back to the squat now, could he? What if the police investigated the escape and found it was all down to him? What if Gebre had confessed and told them everything? Surely he wouldn't do that. But if he did they'd both be punished. They could find him easily. The detention centre had his address – he'd given it to them freely when he was finally allowed to visit – and he was undoubtedly Gebre's only visitor except Veata. Not only that, he'd even gone and told that officer woman that Gebre shouldn't be in there, and that he was Gebre's only friend, so of course they would suspect him right away! But would they pursue him, after Gebre went back in and gave himself up? They might. Just to teach people a lesson. Oh, why did Gebre change his mind again? *Why?*

Yonas had found a small park, and sat on a bench, hugging his knees, rocking, until it got dark. He lay down. Slept, on and off. He rose with the sun, and walked around the park a few times, listening to the birds, appreciating the thick, green leaves, the delicate scent of grass. If only he could have shared this moment with Gebre, he thought. He decided to go back to the squat. If the worst came to the worst and they identified him as an accomplice to the escape attempt, he'd end up in detention too, and maybe he and Gebre would be together again. And if he got away with it, he would just carry on and proceed with his appeal, and hope that the law here could save them both in the end. Trust in Veata. Though she would surely know what he'd done by now and be furious with him.

He'd left the park and headed south, as the streets gradually populated with commuters. At a bus stop coming up, he spotted a newspaper abandoned on the narrow seat. Worth a look, he thought – he might find a new headline for his collection. As he got closer, he was pretty sure he could see the words 'asylum seeker' on the front cover, but when he picked it up it was a story about 'ambulance chaser' law firms. He turned a few pages... and then... *Oh no. Oh no no no.* In a small article, at the bottom right-hand corner of page five, he read:

The words below blurred. No. He was imagining this. Hallucinating from stress. This article must be about a different person, a different centre…

But he'd read it again and again, then made himself read on, and it was the same place, it must be the same person, it said the man was Eritrean, a thirty-year-old… There was no doubting it. *NO!* He wanted to bellow into the sky, to grab the nearest person by the shoulders and shake them, to demand they explain how something like this could happen, or to tell him he was crazy, he was making up fairy stories again, it was all fine…

He'd walked, blindly, back to the park, to be alone, sat back on the bench and opened the paper again, and read the same words again. Black and irrevocable and endlessly re-readable. While he was sitting here yesterday, Gebre had been… It was unbearable! He wanted to yell at the birds in the trees. How dare they chorus on so cheerfully as if the world were the same? He put his hands over his ears and finally, after so long, he was sobbing like a child. Gebre, Gebre, Gebre.

After a while he'd looked up and wiped his face. He watched a jogger run past him wearing headphones, a flamingo-pink T-shirt and lime-green trainers, bouncing lightly along, immersed in her own world of colour and sound and movement, not a care in the world. He wondered what she was listening to. 'Billie Jean'? He pictured Gebre, as a kid, moonwalking to school…

He'd got up and started to walk, his feet hitting the concrete in a robotic rhythm, while his mind turned into a moving collage of Gebre and him, all the things they'd done together that nobody else had or could remember or share or understand: the first kick of their elastic band football, cartoons passed under school desks, singing while dragging heavy rocks in chains, dancing to Helen Meles, *injera* feasts, bowls of fish mud, the day when Gebre's *Thriller* T-shirt ripped, playing hide and seek among the thorn bushes, candles burning flesh, discovering that shepherd's water container in the desert, that miraculous oasis, the unbelievable feeling of letting the water run over their swollen tongues, gently applying that absurd mauve lipstick… Was it really all over?

He saw a sign for King's Cross, and then he was clinging onto it, as if it were a lifeline. Suddenly he was ravenously hungry. A tiny voice of pragmatism in his head told him that if the police found him collapsed here he would be arrested, that they'd find out about his status, they'd link him to Gebre's escape and suicide, they'd link him to Quentin and Molly too, and he would be done for. He should turn off his phone to avoid being tracked, use the quid in his pocket for a chocolate bar, and get straight on a train. *A train where?* North. *Where north?* Somewhere. Elsewhere.

Gebre is dead, Gebre is dead, Gebre is dead, buildings, fields, trees, buildings, fields, trees, buildings, fields, trees, Peterborough, Newark North Gate, Doncaster, York, Northallerton, Darlington, Durham, Newcastle... New. Castle. Newcastle. What was it about Newcastle that made Yonas fixate on the name?

And then he remembered: Tesfay. He should still have a text message on his phone, with Tesfay's address on it. This would mean turning the phone on again. Would the police be hunting for him yet? He doubted it, and in a way he didn't care, not now. He turned it on, ignored some new messages, scrolled down... yes, there it was. He had a pen in his pocket. Did he have paper? Yes – he had *that* paper, that newspaper article. Folded up in his pocket, next to his rooster. He unfolded it now. Was that headline still real? Too real. Much too real. Possibly the last asylum seeker headline he would ever collect, he thought. On the other side, in the margin, he wrote down Tesfay's address and phone number, but he had no credit left to call. He turned his phone off again.

There were barriers at Newcastle Station, but Yonas slipped easily through the luggage gate behind a quarrelling family. He had no idea where to go. But just down the main road he saw a sign saying the Literary and Philosophical Library, outside a grand-looking building. He couldn't resist going up the steps, remembering that moment when he'd discovered the Canning Town public library. Again, it seemed to be free to enter.

He walked through into a vast, gorgeous space with a high, curved ceiling and reams of books lining the walls on polished wooden shelves.

Compared to the libraries he'd seen so far, it felt as if he'd been going to church in a basement and had just found himself in a cathedral. The UK really was an incredible country, he thought. But why did British people deserve places like this, when he and Gebre didn't? He wished he could just sit in here and read for a while. But all he could think about was that Gebre should be here too, that if he'd only gone through with the escape they could have found a place to live up here and jobs in this city, and he could have started writing again, perhaps in this very library, and Gebre could have started drawing... If he only had a drawing of Gebre's to keep, as a memento. His chest started to constrict, and he turned to walk out.

But then he paused at the doorway. He still had no idea how to get to Tesfay's place. Should he ask a librarian if he could use the internet? But he'd need a special card for that, surely, and they'd ask his address.

'Can I help you?' a man at the desk asked. Yonas stopped. The man did look friendly.

'It is a beautiful library,' he said cautiously. 'I am actually trying to find a friend's address, and I do not know this city. Is it possible that you have a map?'

'Oh, sure,' the man said. 'Free Wi-Fi if you have a laptop?'

'No...'

'Not to worry. I can pull up a map for you here if you like, no worries. What's the postcode?'

He had a lilting accent, definitely different to London. Yonas stepped closer and told him the address, and the man typed it into his computer – and then, without even asking, printed out a map of the route, in colour, and got out a pencil, with which he carefully drew a snaky line from the library all the way to Tesfay's place. Yonas felt like crying as he took it, and thanked him. Why couldn't British people have been this kind to Gebre? Why didn't Gebre get a free map and a route to walk away from that detention centre to be with a friend?

It took him about half an hour to get to Tesfay's block of flats. Yonas hovered his finger over the buzzer for number 9, then retracted it and walked around the block.

What was he doing, coming here, with no money, giving no notice? It was a bit like that night he'd turned up at Molly's. But this was different: Tesfay didn't even like him. They'd parted on bad terms. It had got nasty. They fundamentally disagreed about politics. Tesfay would never want to see him again. But then, he had texted his address to Yonas's phone, and said to drop by. Why else would he have done that? But on the other hand, even if Tesfay was friendly, Yonas didn't know how he was going to manage to be friendly back, how he could act normally, hold a conversation, stop himself from crying, from raging. Since finding that newspaper, and reading the worst news imaginable, he hadn't yet talked to a single person apart from the kind receptionist at the library. He took the article out yet again to check it was real. It was still real. So real. And where else would he go now, if he didn't buzz Tesfay? He needed to see a friendly face, to eat, to sleep.

He came back to Tesfay's door and buzzed firmly.

Bounding footsteps. Yonas stood straight, preparing. The door opened. Tesfay's face transformed from confusion into a huge smile. 'No way! Yonas! This is... totally unexpected! *Selam!* What are you doing up here, brother?! You should have told me you were coming – but it is no problem, come in! You okay?'

Yonas tried to smile and make an affirmative sort of noise, and followed Tesfay. The flat was warm and he could smell cooking – a stew, the delicious sourness of *injera,* nourishment, love... 'Thanks. I – I need a place to stay,' he said, hearing his voice shake.

'Oh, to *stay* – er, you were thinking here?'

Yonas knew he should have waited until he'd at least had a cup of tea and made some small talk somehow before mentioning the idea. 'Don't worry,' he blurted. 'Please forget it – I expect you have no room. It is just that... my best friend from Eritrea, he was in a detention centre, and he got refused and he killed himself.' Saying this out loud for the first time, in a rush, hearing how concise and final it could sound in words, was almost physically painful. Yonas's head pulsed, his stomach burned acid.

But Tesfay reached out his arms. 'Hey, brother, I'm so sorry,' he said softly. 'Of course you can stay.' The hug felt so unexpectedly good that Yonas's eyes filled up again.

Several hours later, after a nap and a bath, he walked into a warm living room. It opened into a kitchen where Tesfay's wife Jamila was stirring a pot, reaching out for it beyond her swollen belly. 'You know, our second is due in two weeks now,' Tesfay said.

'Thank you for having me to stay,' Yonas said to Jamila, and she told him it was no problem, though didn't actually look at him when she said it. He reckoned she must be cross with Tesfay for agreeing he could stay without asking her first. 'I will not impose on you for long,' he added. 'I know that you are preparing for your new arrival.'

She smiled at him then, a smile that was clearly code for: *I'm glad that's understood.*

'Mummy, can you read this story?' Freweini said, coming into the living room.

'I'm busy now, can't you see I'm cooking? Go and play – I will read a story before you go to sleep.'

'I could read it to you,' Yonas suggested. The little girl gave him an appraising glance, then obviously figured this was the best offer she was going to get, so climbed next to him on the sofa with her book. '*The Enormous Crocodile,*' Yonas read grandly. It had been oddly moving saying goodbye to Clara with his own story – he hadn't realized how fond he'd become of the child until he was about to leave.

'So,' Tesfay interrupted, just as the crocodile seemed set to eat several small children. He was standing in the middle of the living room with a big smile on his face. 'I have good news, Yonas! I have got you a part-time job washing up in a hotel where my friend's brother works, and he says they are advertising some work in a nearby pub as well if you want. And you can stay here for another week, or even two, but then, like I said, Jamila is due, so hopefully you can find somewhere…'

'Thank you, thank you so much,' Yonas said.

The job turned out to be the perfect thing for his tangled brain, and the frequent impulses he felt to collapse into tears or start shouting at the universe. Nobody talked to him, music was always on in the background, he was always busy. The act of washing plates was repetitive, meditative, almost, which helped him not to think about the past or future, it was inherently cleansing, and his tears, when they flowed, could wash unnoticed down the plughole. There was only one moment when he got such a surge of anger he almost threw a plate at the wall, but he managed to hold back. Fortunately Tesfay seemed to sense his need not to engage with anything stressful, and there was no political talk in the evenings, or even any personal talk about Gebre or what had brought Yonas up north. The family just got on with their routine and let Yonas exist peacefully in the background.

The two weeks drifted past in a haze, until he sat up in bed one night with the realization that his time was up. In the morning, Jamila would give him the look that said: we had an understanding, did we not? But he had so successfully forced himself into this temporary retreat from reality that, again, he hadn't made a single plan for what to do next. He had his job now, but nowhere to stay, and he didn't have the energy to beg any more favours. But how would he say goodbye to Tesfay? He would be expected to say where was going. And if Tesfay found out he had no plan, he'd offer him to stay longer, when they really wanted him to go. He would just write them a letter, instead, like he'd done for Emil, and for Nina, to make it easier for everyone. He got up, pulled out his notebook, ripped out a page and hovered a pen over it, then wrote:

You have all been so kind to have me stay with you. Jamila, your cooking is spectacular, and good luck with the birth. Freweini, keep up the good work with your reading and you will inspire your baby brother or sister. Tesfay, you are a great friend, and I know that we have some differences, but for that reason your support has meant even more.

He went back to bed, but not to sleep, then rose early, before the sky had lightened, stuck the note to the fridge with a yellow smiley-face magnet, and left.

He walked down to the river path in the chill morning air. Tesfay had told him he should check out all the different bridges in Newcastle, and a building called the Sage, which he hadn't got round to doing yet. But that must be the one he was talking about: a huge structure that looked like a fat, silver caterpillar. Yes, it was a pretty spectacular cityscape, actually, especially with the lights still twinkling in the slate sky. And it felt good to be by water again.

He hung over the side of one of the bridges, looked down at the black shine of the river, broiling cold and mean beneath, and thought back to the day by the River Thames in London when he got his refusal letter. That feeling of being drawn towards losing himself in the current was even stronger now. He'd lost Gebre. He'd abandoned his appeal and his friends, and he would never get leave to remain, Lemlem could never come to join him and study here now... he had nothing left to offer the world.

But he wasn't ready to jump. Not yet. He had to walk, think clearly, face up to what had happened with Gebre, to his own actions – why he had ended up: here, in a cold, northern city in the UK, visa-less, bereaved, alone, on a road to... he had no idea where! When did he take the fatal path that got him to this bizarre place? And where would he rewind to, if he could do his life again differently? Could he ever get back on track from here? On track to where?

He couldn't think properly – he needed to walk. He set off on foot up the road that led north to the coast. There was nobody else around, and barely a car passed. The sky had lightened from slate to dove grey but the sun hadn't yet peeked through. Yonas let himself imagine that he was walking along with Gebre beside him, that the two of them were setting out to make a fresh start up here, incognito, under cover. Would they give each other new names, for their new identities? What ideas would Gebre have? Would they be cracking jokes and debating like the old days? Would they be summoning up all the other times they'd journeyed out for new starts? There were just so many memories of Gebre he didn't want to forget – now, he felt like sitting down at the side of the road to write them down. But who would ever read his scribbles? Who would care?

Picking up his pace, he wished he'd handled things differently. Gebre was far too fragile for an escape like that. Yonas should have paid him another authorised visit, to raise the idea with him, not just left him that note, and then ambushed him. What was he thinking, landing that plan on Gebre in such rushed excitement in the toilets, producing a wig from his pants, like a rabbit out of a hat, like some sort of caper you'd see in a film?

He shouldn't have planned an escape at all. Gebre was right: they should both have just submitted to the system, submitted to the humiliation of their interviews, trusted in Veata and waited for the process to work itself through, even though the odds were stacked against them. Against Gebre, anyway. Yonas had an appeal hearing all lined up, and now he'd thrown away his chance! Perhaps his impetuous determination to free them both from that shitty system was ultimately what killed Gebre. Was he the one responsible, then? Had he killed his friend? But all he'd wanted was to *save* Gebre! And would he really do it differently, if he had his chance again? He wasn't sure he would. He just couldn't bear standing by, watching his best friend, locked up in that place, in such despair after he'd struggled so hard for so long, but life had just thrown one hand grenade at him after another, until he had no options left.

Yonas turned off the main road, towards an empty-looking horizon to the east that must be the sea. Maybe it didn't matter any more. It was over now. Done. Finished. All he wanted was the chance to say sorry, to tell Gebre how important he was. That he loved him. Was it too much to bring him back for a day, an hour, a minute, just for that?

A little way down the minor road, he found himself in a village called Seahouses, tasted salt on the air, smelled frying food. He passed a fish and chip café, filled with feasters. When he first caught a glimpse of the sea, it had already darkened to asphalt, but the horizon was slashed with peach and bronze. And as he reached the harbour, and the wind hit his face, he was assaulted by the memory of that walk out of the factory, that first sight of the watery expanse, that sensation of space and freedom, that moment with Gebre at the top of the hill, the hilarity and delight, flopping down on the grass, Osman running off… He found his hands were clutching at his face.

He let out a long groan and carried on down onto the beach, his sore feet sinking into the soft bumps of windblown sand, scattered with bits of seaweed, a can, a bottle top, a crisp packet. He headed past a cluster of teenagers and a middle-aged couple sitting on the sand, tucking into portions of fish and chips wrapped in newspaper, and walked away from the village. The beach was sandy, and seemed to stretch ahead for miles. When the sound of chatter grew distant, he stopped at the boundary where the texture of the sand changed into a smooth, wet slope, descending to the water's edge. Boundary lines. His whole family might be alive now if it weren't for imaginary boundary lines and the stupid wars that were fought over them. Gebre would be alive. Because of boundary lines they were all doomed from the start.

He stood there and watched the sky intensify imperceptibly into its last embers. Gebre would have captured that nicely, if he'd been here with a canvas and some paints. But peaceful appreciation of this beauty was reserved for people lucky enough to have been born here, to live in comfortable houses, and to think nothing of pottering out together for a stroll and a takeaway meal at sunset, to have no reason to doubt that they could do so for every sunset if they felt like it, until they were old and passed away in their sleep. People like him, and Gebre, and Melat, they didn't have the luxury of picnicking. They were just born into the wrong country at the wrong time. Tough luck. Gebre was right: what was the point of struggling against the tide? Maybe he was right to end it his own way, to take control over his life at the end, when all other choices had been taken away from him. And what business did Yonas have, dreaming he might end up living a free and happy life here, not just with papers, a manual job and a roof over his head, but maybe even writing again, going out to galleries, buying expensive cappuccinos? Somewhere inside, he'd genuinely believed he might have a chance at all that. How deluded! And what was freedom here anyway, without his oldest friend? Who wouldn't even get a funeral, probably… Yonas seriously doubted they would have funerals for detainees who had nobody to pay funeral costs and no family to attend. That was possibly the worst part: not even having the chance to say a proper goodbye.

But he could at least say something right now for Gebre, just in case these burnished sunset colours had a magical, conductive force that could carry a message. And he knew the right poem: his friend, Amanual, had written it during the border war, before he was imprisoned, and Yonas had made a point of learning it, in tribute. He cleared his throat, as if he were on a stage again, looked up, and recited.

Something growled
Something boomed
Invading the calm
It echoed.
. . .
Where two brothers pass each other by
Where two brothers meet
Where two brothers join
In the piazza of life and death
In the gulf between calamity and culture
In the valley of anxiety and peace
Something boomed.
While the chia and seraw acacias spat at each other
Sorghum and millet cut each other down
With no one to collect them they feed on one another,
Until a single seed remains…
Brimming with tears
Being chopped – hacked
Sowed unto itself.
. . .planted
In earth yet to gush
In that indiscernible thing,
Stream of blood and water,
The seed…
Assailed by:
The freezing sun
Tempestuous nimbus cloud
Greyish lightning

Scalding rain…
Slipping through littered iron
Climbing onto the spirit of death
Shouldering its sterile life
Here, it has grasped at spring.
The seed…

He stopped. Silence. The clouds carried on drifting, expanding, blurring into each other, and slowly fading as the edge of the sun caramelized down and disappeared. Yonas sat on the pebbles, hugged his knees and scrunched his eyes.

After some time, he found he was shivering. When he looked up, it was dark. A few stars peeked out, nothing compared to the desert, but brighter here than in the city. The moon hovered, a thin crescent, like a tiny hammock you could float up to and lie in. He looked left and right: he was the only person still on the beach. He got to his feet, but his legs felt like sodden cotton wool. There were dunes at the back of the beach, and he walked into them and felt the cold wind drop a little. He pulled out two bin bags from his rucksack, lay down on them, and closed his eyes.

Chapter 29: Jude

You are weeping uncontrollably as you attempt to walk in a straight line along Fleet Street. Ridiculous: it's only a case. You've never even met the client! You should be getting the Tube home or you will miss Alec's bedtime, yet again; but you have to calm down first.

You pull a tissue out of your pocket, blow your nose, wipe your cheeks, but they're already wet again. You had been so ready for the hearing this morning, more invested in it than any other case you'd ever done, so to get a call from your solicitor at 9 a.m. to say that your client's best friend had committed suicide and that the client himself had now disappeared... it was a shock. You still went along to the tribunal, half expecting YK to show up after all. But he didn't. You had to request an adjournment, which was denied, and your solicitor said that YK had switched off his phone.

You went back to your room in chambers and sat there for a while, randomly doing internet searches about Eritrean asylum seekers. You turned up an interview with the President of Eritrea, who, when asked what he was planning to do about the thousands fleeing the country, said: 'They will come back. They are going for a picnic. They will come back one day.' Oddly, that was what had prompted this flood. You'd just gathered your stuff and left chambers before anyone heard you lose it.

A sharp wind cuts at your throat. You pull up your lapels, and attempt to use one of them to wipe your face. Where is YK? Why do you care so much? What the hell is wrong with you? You've just imagined such absurd amounts about him since you first picked up his case, from what he looks like to his fantasy foods; you felt like you knew him, you'd already started jotting ideas for writing about him in a spare legal notebook, and now you might never see him in the flesh. But he's just another client you'd never really have got to know anyway! How has his case got to you like this?

A blinding light. Pain. You've been whacked in the face. Assaulted! But no, as your vision returns, it becomes clear that you have just walked into a lamppost. You have – actually – just walked into a lamppost. How embarrassing! How bloody painful. You touch your forehead delicately. This won't look pretty tomorrow.

'You all right, love?' A kindly looking woman puts her hand on your arm, concerned.

You manage a laugh, wipe away more snotty tears. 'Thanks, yes I'm fine, was just distracted – I'll be okay.' You've really got to pull yourself together. You walk on, faster now, feeling a bit dizzy, keeping an eye out for rogue lampposts, and hoping you don't bump, literally or metaphorically, into someone you know… Is this some kind of early mid-life crisis? Are you just over-tired? But why did YK disappear? Is he actually still in London, devastated by his friend's death, holing himself up in whatever godawful room he probably lives in? Or has he fled? But where? He wouldn't kill himself as well, would he, before you've had a chance to fight his case? Could you go on an amateur detective hunt and find him? You're being ridiculous now.

As the road dips towards Ludgate Circus, you spot a QC you did some work for once, a misogynist slimeball who'd just love the opportunity to witness you upset and use it as an excuse to put a sleazy, BO-exuding arm around your shoulder. You veer off the pavement and start crossing the road. A taxi has to stop suddenly and honks at you, but you keep ploughing on. Several people are giving you weird looks now, so you cut away from the hubbub, up one of the little quiet roads towards Hatton Garden, where you and Max chose your engagement ring, at an absurd cost he swore he could stretch to, even though you knew he couldn't at the time, not really, and you didn't believe he *should* have to pay for it in an age of equal rights, but you weren't that strong about resisting, so here it is, on your finger, sparkling under the streetlight, reminding you that you are loved, that you are being silly, that you are probably just overworked, that you should call Max to tell him where you are, tell him the decision that's dawning on you... But you had better stop crying first.

As you were leaving chambers, the cleaners were coming in, a friendly bunch of Bulgarians, who always leave the communal areas spotless. And now, as you walk through the eerily empty cave of Smithfield Market, home of blood and butchery and bargaining and traditional English working-class men, you wonder how many asylum seekers are setting out to work, cleaning offices for peanuts, or selling their bodies, or doing whatever it takes to make a living and send money to their families, not moping about feeling sorry for themselves like you, not weeping pathetically and walking into lampposts. You have the chance to be with your little boy right now, and instead you're throwing all your time, energy and emotion on clients who don't even turn up to hearings. What's the point? You were stupid to think you could save the world by being a barrister, or even make a tiny fraction of a difference. You should just focus on being a better mother before Alec flies the nest. And maybe seeing some of your old friends before they give up on you for always bailing on nights out at the last minute in favour of work.

Yes, you'd better suck it up and quit the Bar.

You walk past the Barbican, looking up at the familiar brutalist ziggurat, remembering how you used to come here so often for films and exhibitions and concerts before you started this job and had a baby, and you're sure you read recently that it was voted the ugliest building in London, yet it's also listed and admired and beloved, and you try to imagine it when it was first unveiled here, as part of a utopian vision to rejuvenate the area after its pounding by bombs in the Second World War. It's so hard to imagine this city as a war zone, but it really wasn't that long ago – why couldn't it be again? You bet the fortunate elite who live in the tower – including a woman in chambers, actually – rarely contemplate the history of the ground below, as they pop down at will for a plate of three colourful salads in the restaurant, or a martini with a twist, or a shot of physical theatre. And why should they?

You wind around Finsbury Square and towards the City, dwarfed by the glass palaces of the world's richest bankers, and past the thrum of commuters around Liverpool Street, and through the incongruously narrow, irregularly paved medieval alleyways leading to Spitalfields and Brick Lane, and you think of all the migrant groups who've settled in this neighbourhood over the centuries and made it what it is now: the Jews, the Bangladeshis and, increasingly, the hipster artists, who are sort of migrants too if you think of them financially. They will end up getting pushed out by bankers and move elsewhere, further east, maybe even out to Leyton where you and Max could just about afford a place.

And what about the illegal immigrants, the recently arrived? Where are they all living? All over the place, probably, in attics and basements and random buildings above shops, an invisible crowd hiding away behind ordinary exteriors; could YK be hiding out in this derelict pub? In that council block? Above that nail salon? The Vietnamese-looking girls in there, intently painting their tiny fingertip canvases, could be trafficked too for all you know.

Your tide of tears has turned now, and it strikes you that you're not even sure which road you're on any more, thanks to your emotional speculating spree. You'd better get your bearings and find the nearest Tube – you must be somewhere north of Whitechapel – and you can't walk all the way home or you'll arrive in the middle of the night to an angry, clucking husband. But when you pull out your phone to call Max you find your battery's dead. Maybe you'll end up walking all the way home after all, because your legs and your mind just keep on going, going, going…

Chapter 30: Melat

Dear Yonas,

I don't know if you will get this letter, but if you do, you have Saba to thank - you remember, my friend who documents Eritrean history, who had a daughter Lemlem's age? Well, she got an invitation to go to Scotland for a fellowship. And because of her father's connections she was actually granted a visa. Amazing, no? She said she would bring this and post it to you when she arrives in UK. I really hope you get it, now that your appeal is coming up. If you do, you should also find other things in the envelope.

Two are signed letters. One is from the owner of the Blue Balloon internet café you used to go to, and the other is from Mariam from the British Council office, both confirming that you used to use the computers there regularly to send articles about the situation to the UK, using your pen name. I had to use all my persuasion skills to get them to risk signing, because they both remembered you but denied knowing you did anything like that. At the other internet cafés you went to, they said no. But this is better than nothing, I think. I wish I had some evidence to help Gebre too. Please send him my love.

I did find one thing of Gebre's, though: a cartoon he did of you two when you were kids that had been pinned to your wall and slipped behind the bed, so they did not find it when they took all your things. I've included that in the envelope too. You can give it to him when you see him.

You will also find a drawing of a flower Lemlem made for you, with a poem she wrote underneath. She wants to be a poet, now, you know, though I am sure she will change her mind and want to be an astronaut again next week. She misses you a lot, but she is still doing well in school, even though the education here gets worse every week. Sheshy helps her more these days, as well as me. He is in a much happier mood most of the time, you will be pleased to hear.

Which reminds me: another thing you should have is a photograph of Lemlem, grandmother and me – three out of four generations, standing together in the garden, which Sheshy took with his camera. Camera? I can hear you thinking! A family from the UK sent a box of second-hand cameras to the disabled martyrs group he belongs to, and he was lucky enough to get one. It keeps him occupied, and gets him out of the house, wheeling around the streets, snapping. A silver lining of having no legs is that people always pose for you, he says.

Grandmother is frail now, but still recognizes me, usually. I started taking her to a local group where she can go to drink coffee with other old people – they never remember each other, and usually have exactly the same conversations each week. I met someone there recently who was caring for his grandfather - a widower, a little older than me, not much. You'd like him. He did a literature degree too, but in Addis - his mother was Ethiopian. He avoided military service because he can't see out of one eye. He is handsome, though, and he has a good singing voice and makes me laugh.

So, life is hard here still, and every day I fear them coming for me again, but we try our best to live in hope.

On which note, good luck with your appeal - and next time be honest with me earlier, okay? I know we are far away and I am always telling you about our problems and asking for your help, but we are still your family and you can count on us too, for support if not for money. You don't have to go through everything on your own, all right?

Call soon. We miss you. We are all rooting for you to be allowed to stay there, even though we are jealous and would like you back here with us.

Your loving sister,
Melat

Chapter 31: Yonas

Sunshine woke him. Soft swishes of wind. Seagulls at their daily antics, coasting and flapping and screeching at each other. He'd slept through the dawn, more deeply than he had in a long while. He got up, stiff as a robot, and stretched. The sea! He felt a little bit glad that he'd lived one more day, just so he could wake up to this huge, surging, endless vista, all his own.

But practicalities quickly nagged. He couldn't stay here. Should he continue north? The vague plan at the back of his blurry mind had been to walk all the way to the top of the UK, and then finally throw himself off the rocks and into the sea. Not that there would be anyone to witness it. That seemed like an absurd, melodramatic gesture now. But he supposed he might as well walk on for a bit. He set off up the beach.

His legs felt light and hollow. He pulled his penultimate slice of bread out of his rucksack and munched as he walked. He tipped up his water bottle afterwards, but all that came out was a trickle. He would have to beg a favour from a café somewhere if he was going make it more than five miles. How had he and Gebre done this in the desert? Through that relentless heat, with the acacia thorns, the rocks, the wilderness, all roads to safety heaving with soldiers? He couldn't imagine, now. He was a younger man then, a more desperate man, a more fearful man, a more hopeful man.

A dog dashed past him, hell for leather, chasing a seagull, knowing full well that the bird could swoop out of the way as easily as it liked, but the dog didn't care – it was just running out of sheer energy, for thrills. A couple followed it, its owners, Yonas supposed, arm in arm. They smiled and said hello to him as they passed, as if he were just another normal person out for a stroll. Apart from them, the beach was empty.

A looming structure appeared ahead. It looked like a castle. He carried on towards it, curious. Yes, it was definitely a castle – huge, tall and fierce, towering over the sea, the land, a testament to human assertiveness, human ingenuity, human creativity. He stood at the base, looking up, and felt tiny and insignificant. He wondered about the tiny, insignificant men who built it centuries earlier. Did they have any inkling that the thing they were creating would be appreciated by tiny, insignificant people from across the world so far into the future? Did anyone still live there?

His reverie was broken by the sight of a woman emerging onto the beach from behind the castle. A red-haired woman. His breath shortened. *Nina.* But it wasn't of course. She looked nothing like Nina, actually – apart from its colour, her hair was totally different, all wispy and messy – and although she was short, she was stocky, and dressed in hardy walker's gear, with a sporty-looking pole. She lifted a friendly hand to greet him. He lifted his in return, and watched her proceeding south along the beach. *Nina.* What if it had been her, with her long skein of hair, and her elfin, freckled face? What would he say to her? He wished it was Nina. It struck him that he was an idiot to have ditched her and Molly, to have run off in his grief without telling them, turning his phone off and abandoning his appeal, despite all they'd done for him. But how could they help now? They couldn't do anything about Gebre, or the police who must now be on his trail, and they wouldn't want to get mixed up in all that. They couldn't change the fact that he hadn't shown up for his tribunal hearing. And they certainly couldn't change the asylum system.

Still, he missed Nina now, with a sudden pang. For whatever reason, she had really seemed to like him. Yes, she and Molly – and Clara, in fact – had genuinely been happy to have him around. He remembered the feeling of Nina putting her hands gently on his cheeks, pulling his face towards hers, and his heart tugged, like it used to do when he thought about Sarama, back when his memory of her was more vivid, when the sensation of her warm skin was more tangible. So much time had passed now, that thinking about Sarama these days was less of a pain, more of a dull ache. It was difficult even to picture her face properly. Nina's face, on the other hand, was as crisp as a close-up photo when he called it to mind. Her greenish eyes. Her mass of freckles. Her delicate lips blurting out that sudden, silvery laugh.

But he couldn't go back to Nina, not now. It would be wrong to put her in that position anyway. She'd be angry with him. He'd not only cut them all off and missed his appeal, he'd broken into an immigration facility and would probably be arrested and jailed if they found out. He'd made his choices – his cowardly, impulsive, stupid choices. He was alone now, completely alone, with nothing and no one left. Free!

He turned back to the sea, kicked off his shoes, felt the sand between his toes, flung off his coat, ripped off his jumper and T-shirt, tugged off his trousers, and ran across the beach, towards the water, closer and closer, faster and faster as the sand firmed up, then splashed straight in. The icy cold made his heart race, even just around his feet and calves. He slowed, stood still for a moment, felt the waves splash hungrily up his thighs and tug at his feet, felt his toes turn numb, his muscles start to tremble, wished the cold liquid could just spread up through him and purge him of all his mistakes, all his memories, everything he'd done, everyone he'd loved. He clenched his teeth and threw his whole body into the water, and the cold took his breath away, but he thrashed his legs and arms as hard as he could until he breathed again, hard and fast, and it was as exhilarating as anything he'd experienced – until he started losing feeling in his fingers. He splashed out of the water and began to jump around on the sand. He flung his arms around in circles, circling round and round. Finally, tired out, he walked back over to his bag, blood pumping through every vein.

As he shook out his trousers, something fell out of the pocket and clinked on a shell before landing on its side in the sand, regarding him with a beady eye. His rooster. He picked it up. 'You're still here, then,' he said aloud. He remembered how captivated Clara had been by his little lion story. How would Nina have explained his disappearance to her?

It dawned on him that, right now, she and Nina and Molly might not just be concerned and angry that he'd disappeared on them – they might be upset. Really upset. He'd been thoughtless and cruel. They'd cared about him. And even hearing some of the horrible memories that would always be boiling away in his head hadn't put Nina off wanting to spend time with him, or even letting him look after her only daughter. On the contrary, she'd started to rely on him. And she'd changed too, since he'd met her, not only by opening up to him, but by getting her new life together without her husband, and volunteering to help other people in his position. But he'd just abandoned her.

Veata, too. She'd worked so hard for him. And he'd let her sit in that waiting room while he attempted to get Gebre out. Maybe they suspected her of conspiracy. He hoped she wasn't in trouble. He should at least have told her he was leaving London and abandoning his appeal. She deserved that much. He couldn't get another hearing now, surely, especially after disappearing, when he was supposed to stay put and be closely monitored.

How he wished he could see his family. Maybe could give himself up for deportation and fly home to Eritrea to be with them for a brief, sweet day or two until he got found out by the authorities. But they probably wouldn't let him past the airport. He'd already be on a blacklist. They would put him straight into another prison and get back to torturing. It would be more upsetting for Melat and the family to know he had come back, only to be taken away before he got to see them.

But then, what would Melat think if she found out he'd died over here? That he'd just thrown away his chance to get legal leave to remain? And how would they all manage if he wasn't alive, sending them money, even if he had to work illegally to do it?

Pocketing his rooster, he walked up and down the sand, along the wet rim of it by the water's edge, feeling it squidge under his soles, reassuringly soft and simultaneously firm under his weight. Maybe the police wouldn't be searching for him right now after all. It wasn't as if Gebre's escape from detention had been successful, in the sense of him disappearing, so maybe they wouldn't bother investigating it any more. Also, what would Gebre say if he heard Yonas had given up everything because of him? *Good luck*, he'd said, before that bus drove away. *This was meant to work out for you.*

Was it? Could he make it work? He pulled out the rooster again, flipped it over, stared at its tiny black eye.

He took out his phone – Nina's old phone – and tried to turn it on, but the battery was dead. He brushed the excess sand off his feet, put his shoes back on and walked fast up the track past the castle and into the village behind.

The light was on in what looked like a café. He looked in the door: yes, definitely a café, with just one elderly couple inside, drinking tea, and a newspaper rack on the wall. He probably had enough change left for a cup of tea – and a cup of tea suddenly seemed like the most appealing thing in the world. He walked in, ordered one, and asked if he could plug in his phone to charge. The lady pointed him to a table near a socket.

He plugged in his phone, then took a couple of newspapers from the rack and sat down. He read:

ILLEGAL IMMIGRANT WHO KILLED PENSIONER, 91, IN CAR CRASH FINALLY CAUGHT AFTER FOUR YEARS... HIDING IN CUPBOARD

He looked at the lady behind the counter, and wondered if she'd mind him ripping this article out, looked back again, and noticed the date on the paper: 2 March. His birthday! It was actually his birthday today. Well, happy birthday, he thought to himself bitterly. Nobody else would say it to him now. Melat might be thinking of it. Perhaps she was hoping to hear from him today, maybe telling Lemlem it was her uncle's birthday, maybe looking at old photographs of the family with Sheshy and Grandmother... and he'd let her down. She didn't deserve such a failure for a brother. And he couldn't bear to tell her about Gebre. But the more he thought about his sister, the more he wanted to hear her voice again.

And he still could. He and she were both still alive, after all, in the same spinning world, even if he'd never get to see her in the flesh again. And he wasn't completely alone in the UK, either. He had some friends now – at least until he disappeared. Tesfay. Emil. Molly. Nina. Were any of them thinking of him?

He turned on his phone, and a stream of texts came through.

Molly:

> Dear Yonas, we are all very worried about you and hope you will come back soon. Love from Molly

Tesfay:

> Where did you go? You better not be sleeping rough, bro. Get in touch, okay?

Emil:

> You got a letter, a packet, could be important... Where are you, Prof?

Veata:

> Devastated about Gebre. But I have news. Please contact me as soon as you get this. Do reverse charges if need be.

Nina:

> Yonas, where are you? I miss you so much. Please, please call. Xxx

He imagined Nina saying those words aloud. *I miss you so much.* No, *I missed you*; past tense, it would have to be, if he were to hear her say it. He really wished he could hear her say it.

Oh, he was such an idiot to have run off and left her like that without any explanation, the one person he cared about the most – not to mention his one chance at a relationship, however improbable. What a stupid,

stupid decision. She would probably be furious with him, and disgusted with herself for having invested so much time and emotion in him for him just to chuck it all away.

But perhaps – perhaps it wasn't too late. Perhaps she was still missing him.

And perhaps it wasn't even too late for his appeal to be re-listed. If it wasn't, he owed it to Veata to try; she'd worked so hard on his case already. And he owed it to Gebre, to fight for his rights, to make their journey worthwhile. And to Melat, to Lemlem, to Sheshy and Grandmother – even to his parents, to Tekle and his grandfather and Sarama. Everyone who'd loved him, who would want him to keep going, not to give up.

And this was his birthday. Another new year of his life. It could be another new start.

He picked up his phone again, and dialled. *Nina, Nina, Nina.* As the ringtone sounded, he realized he was almost trembling in anticipation of her answering. But then he got her recorded voice anyway. *You've reached Nina. Please leave me a message.* Her tone was so bright, so promising, but he couldn't find the right words. He hung up. Who next?

He tried Molly, and she answered after just one ring. 'Oh, Joe – I mean, Yonas!' He'd expected her to be politely cross, to give him a schoolteacherly scolding, even, but she just sounded delighted.

'I am very sorry—' he began.

'No no no, I'm just so *relieved* to hear from you! We were so worried when you missed your appeal. I can't imagine what you must have been feeling, after your friend Gebre, oh it's just *appalling*. You must be heartbroken. But come here, now; where are you calling from? In fact, can you just give me your number to write down so I can call you back? Oh, Nina will be so happy to know you're okay! And Veata too – she's been trying to get hold of you – she has some news.'

'About Gebre?' he asked. She was going to say they'd linked him to the escape attempt after all, he knew it.

'No, no – it's about the factory!'

'The factory? You mean, where I worked?' He wasn't sure he'd ever told Molly about that.

'Yes! The police raided it!' she continued excitedly. 'There's *new evidence*. About smugglers, or traffickers. Veata thinks you can use it for something called a *fresh* claim?' His brain started fizzing. Had the police got Aziz? Had they found Osman? 'But where are you now?' Molly asked.

'I am not sure,' he confessed. 'Somewhere north of Newcastle, actually right next to a castle, a very tall, red one, right by the sea...' As he said it, it sounded ridiculously implausible and vague, like a fairy tale. *A fairy tale you've just made up...*

'Oh, it must be Bamburgh!' Molly said. 'I know it well. How marvellous. Nina will be thrilled – I'm sure she'll want to drive up and get you. She'll be back soon and I know she was just planning to take Clara swimming, but I can do that. She can drive up for you this afternoon. You just sit tight there, okay?'

He walked back to the dunes. The landscape looked exactly the same, the weather, the sky – but now everything had shifted. There he'd been, imagining himself like one of the tiny, lone figures in Gebre's war paintings, when all along, people – friends – had been right behind him. And now Nina was coming for him. As he waited, his excitement mounting, he wrote down some random thoughts in his notebook, whatever words came into his mind.

He was walking back, past the castle, when he saw her. Nina. She was waiting outside, looking at her mobile phone, with that crease down her forehead, just like that day at the Serpentine. Flooded with relief and longing, he remembered the very first night they'd met, when she wished he'd disappear – and now she'd driven all this way up the country, just to bring him back. Her red hair was going wild in the sea wind, like flames being stoked. She looked up as he approached, and he started to apologize but she put her fingers to her lips, and reached out. Her arms around him. He thought he should pull away, but he wasn't going to make that mistake again, and as she clung closer, he clung back.

They stopped off at Tesfay's flat in Newcastle on the way down to London. Yonas knocked, expecting the familiar bound to the door – but after a long pause there sounded a slow tread, and Tesfay answered, looking bleary-eyed, carrying a bundle of laundry. Then Yonas noticed that the bundle appeared to have a face. 'Heyyyy, little Lula,' Tesfay crooned down at it, 'meet your Uncle Yonas!' The baby started to shriek between fast, desperate gasps, which made them all laugh.

'Congratulations! She arrived – I'm so happy for you!' Yonas said. 'This is my friend, Nina.'

'Oh, she's so gorgeous!' Nina said. 'Look at those tiny fingers!'

'Come in, come in, both of you!' Tesfay said expansively. 'Jamila is sleeping and Freweini is at school, but they will be happy to see you. We were worried after you left – we could not contact you. Is everything okay?'

'Yes, please do not worry,' Yonas said. 'But we cannot stay now – Nina is driving us back to London. I just wanted to say thank you so, so much. Really, you saved me.'

'Any time for an Eri brother in need,' Tesfay said, and then gave a side glance at Nina while she was doing up her coat and slipped Yonas a wink. When Yonas explained he was going to appeal his refusal after all, and that there was some fresh evidence now, Tesfay slapped him on the back and laughed out loud, prompting the baby to squeak. 'Good for you! I knew it. Now go, *believe*, and do not thank me again, okay? Just come visit us again some time.'

Back in the car, Yonas and Nina didn't talk that much, but it felt good to be sitting next to her again, as if they were a standard couple who were just driving back home from a normal day out by the beach. Nina had brought a stack of CDs, and he flipped through them. Nina Simone… that Bereket Mengistab CD… and a Bob Dylan album that included 'Like a Rolling Stone'. Nina was happy to listen to that too, especially when he told her the story of where he'd last heard it, and they both sang along with the windows down.

They stopped at a motorway services, and Nina bought sandwiches. They sat on the bench out front, facing the crowd of cars, the hordes of people coming in and going out, one mother leading a grandmother by the arm, another rushing a child quickly to the toilets, a son asking his dad if he could have a burger, a girl complaining that she wanted to go to the pub later, that all her friends were going, that it wasn't fair, that her dad was *ruining her life*... and Nina grinned. 'I can just hear Clara saying that to me in ten years' time – less, probably,' she said.

Yonas tucked into his sandwich. 'Mmm, what is this again – smoked salmon? It is salty and sweet and slimy at the same time. I like it.' Nina put her arm around him and laid her head on his shoulder. She didn't open her sandwich, so after he'd finished his, he opened hers, and fed it to her gently, waiting for her to chew each bite and swallow, as if he were feeding Clara but without the aeroplane effects.

When they finally arrived back at Molly's house, the teapot was already on the table, and Clara was jumping up and down, shouting his name. It felt a bit like coming home.

After tea, Yonas called Emil, expecting a terse or indifferent reply. But he let out a kind of happy caterwaul sound. 'Professor Jojo! You are back! I thought you had run off to join circus, doing book juggling act on back of donkey reciting Shakespeare. Wait, that is my idea. You cannot steal it. You are not allowed to join circus without bringing me to play violin, okay?'

The next day he went to see Veata, who wasn't so welcoming. For the first time, she bristled like the lawyer he'd feared before he met her, and rebuked him soundly for disappearing. 'You're very lucky this evidence has come up to give you another chance. But if you run off like that again, it could all be over. I know how you were feeling after what happened to Gebre, but it does nobody any good if you just give up and cut people off. Next time you have any silly ideas like that, call your lawyer first. Okay?'

Yonas agreed, chastened.

'But you know how sorry I am for your loss. Gebre was a lovely man. I was honoured to meet and represent him. I am going to make sure that we make a claim against the detention centre for breach of Article 2 – that's the right to life – I'll discuss it with you in due course.'

'Thank you,' Yonas said. 'It would be good to get justice for him.'

'It would. Now, the factory raid—' she began.

'Did they get Aziz?'

'I am afraid Aziz Hussain evaded capture. Petros Solomon was found, but he claims to know nothing about the larger operation and to have been trafficked too.'

Yonas felt a stone sink inside him. 'How did Aziz get away?'

'We don't know that much yet. He must have anticipated it, somehow. The police only found two other workers there: Rashid and—'

'Osman?' Yonas asked hopefully.

'No – Samuel, I think.'

Yonas closed his eyes. What had they done to Osman then?

'But Osman is in London!'

'In London?!' Yonas nearly laughed. 'How. . .'

'I've just taken on his case. He's in hospital but doing well. Says he hitched a ride with a bin man and got on a train, just like you and Gebre, but reported himself to the authorities when he arrived here.'

'He is okay, then, physically?'

'He's still finding it hard to walk, but they've just operated to reset some bones and he's on the mend now. They're busy lining up a foster family for him as he's not quite eighteen – I'm hoping the local authority won't follow through on the threat to challenge his age. I've got the details if you want to visit. He was so disappointed to hear that you'd disappeared – he'll be thrilled to see you.'

Yonas got straight on a bus after the meeting, texting Nina the news on the way. He found Osman lying in a room in St Thomas's, right by the river, with a view across to the Houses of Parliament that was so direct it seemed as if this room were Osman's own luxury apartment and Westminster was an oversized playhouse. Yonas realized he must have walked right past this hospital that day with his unopened refusal letter, never imagining this could be the place he would see Osman again. Lying as if in state in the narrow hospital bed, yet still scrawny and malnourished enough to be swamped by it, the kid looked almost more fragile than Yonas remembered, but older too. He smiled lopsidedly at the sight of Yonas and waved an arm in greeting. His eyes looked different. Brighter. And not red any more. 'You came back! I knew you would. I can already walk around now!' he bragged. 'I have a phy-si-o-the-ra-pist.'

'Amazing. We will get you running the one hundred metres in the next Olympics,' Yonas said, and patted his head, wondering if he'd been told about Gebre yet. Probably not, or he'd have said something. He didn't have to know straight away. 'It is so great to see you! Nice place you have here. Give me a hi-five… yes! Hey, do you want to do some reading practice? You must have been slacking since I left. I brought a newspaper for you. How about you start from the top? And when you get out of here we will get you up to speed for going to a British school and passing all your exams with top marks. Okay?'

'Give me a break!' Osman laughed, but he leaned forward eagerly and grasped the paper.

When visiting hours were over Yonas went to find Nina in a café where she'd been meeting with a gallerist. She flipped her laptop shut and got up, before he could sit down. 'How was he?' she asked.

'Great,' Yonas said. 'I was so happy to see him. You will have to meet him soon. How was your meeting?'

'It was okay, I think. We'll see if she follows up or not, but she sounded keen. And how about now, do you have any plans, or can I take you somewhere?'

'I was going to go to the squat, to see Emil and thank him for passing on the letter,' he said, but registered her disappointment. 'I can go later though. I will probably take all my things back there tonight, if they still have my bed…'

'Are you sure? You're welcome to stay at Mum's…'

'You and your mother are very kind, but I am happy living there. At least until we all get evicted again. I will not disappear again, okay? I promise.'

'You'd better not. Okay, let's go then.'

'Where are we going?

'You'll see.'

They took the Northern Line up to Hampstead, then Nina led him down through some grand, leafy streets, before climbing up a steep street that opened onto a large green space. 'The Heath,' Nina said. 'You haven't been here before, have you?'

He hadn't. The sky was splotchy like a filthy car window, but the sun was cracking through ahead, and blue shapes were emerging in the grey. They climbed further uphill, and headed for a summit which was busy with silhouettes of children playing, kites drifting and darting, adults shielding their eyes and looking out.

From the top, London was a huge basin full of geometric shapes, criss-cross patterns and pinhead windows, and millions of people swarming around doing their thing, so tiny that all their successes and failures seemed no more significant than a colony of ants lugging grains of soil to an anthill. 'I used to come here with my dad,' Nina said, and took him over to a silver plaque engraved with little outlines of buildings. She pointed out the tiny image of St Paul's, then led his eye with her finger to where it stood in the distance, dwarfed by skyscrapers. Osman was probably looking out at this at the same time from the other side of the river, Yonas thought. Nina told him it was built after the Great Fire of London, and survived through the Blitz. She pointed out the London Eye, which she said was built for the new millennium, but nobody had expected it would end up as a permanent icon. Yonas remembered his prickling fear at the sound of the fireworks from that wheel on the TV, and tried to think back to where he was when the new millennium arrived. Probably trying to sleep on his cell floor as cockroaches crawled over his face. It seemed so impossible, here, now, that this was the same life, that he had come all this way and had remained the same person – or a person in the same body. He found he'd tuned out of what Nina was saying and his gaze was fixated on a needle-like tower that looked like it could give you a lethal injection. 'Sorry, what was that?'

'Don't worry,' Nina laughed. She took his arm and tugged it gently. He followed her along a path into the woods behind. Knotted tree trunks drew criss-cross stripes across the ground. Birdsong tinkled like bells. He liked the way that the trees here were all wild and bent and curled like old people dancing. They emerged into an open space, and Nina beckoned him to sit with her on a bench with a view of a green valley rising up to a hill, topped by a village and crowned with a church spire. Emil had told him houses near Hampstead Heath cost millions.

'If you read the papers,' Yonas said, 'you probably think that all the big houses around here are full of asylum seekers lying on velvet sofas, watching giant-screen TVs, sniffing expensive drugs or plotting robberies.' This made Nina laugh. 'Actually, I have got a bag full of headlines like that,' Yonas added. 'I rip them out and keep them.'

'Really? Why?'

'Something to think about. I guess some day I thought I might use them for something.'

'Maybe we could use them to make art!' Nina said. 'Come to my studio again one day. We could paste them onto a board with images, make a collage...'

'Gebre would like that,' he said, and felt the loss again sharply, in the pit of his stomach.

'Oh Yonas. You must be missing him so badly. Maybe we could make it a tribute to him?'

'That is a nice idea.'

'What kind of thing would you like to make? And actually, if you could write or create or do anything you like here, after you get leave to remain, what would it be?'

'If,' he said.

'Okay, if.'

'Well,' he said, 'when I arrived, I thought the biggest challenge would be to earn just enough money to survive and send some home to Melat. But if I got to choose... You really want to know?'

'Of course!'

'Well... I would still want to let people know about the situation of my country, just like I tried to do from inside. Especially about all the journalists and writers who are still in prison. So I would write some more articles. I read about an organization that campaigns for writers, so maybe I could talk to them.'

'That is a great idea.'

'And I would like to write something for Gebre. Maybe just a story of his life. I am not sure. Actually, years ago, back home, I started to write a novel. But I got stuck. It was more difficult than I expected. It was no good at all! I threw it all away. But after I began lessons with your mother here, I started thinking, maybe I can try to write a book again. Fiction, or non-fiction, I am not sure. Another idea I had was that I could maybe open an Eritrean restaurant or café and display art in there, music, even put on small plays or poetry nights, with Eritrean artists. Crazy, right?'

'It sounds brilliant!'

'I could serve asylum seekers cheap meals, like, twice a week, even free or in exchange for time helping out. But you need money to start up something like that.'

'You can get small business loans. I could help you apply for funding. People would donate. And what about plays? Could Melat find any of your old scripts, do you think?'

'No! They raided my room at home, and probably most published copies were destroyed. I doubt that audiences here would appreciate plays about Eritrean liberation fighters anyway. But I have never actually seen a play in a theatre here so...'

'Well, that's easy, we'll go to the theatre one day soon! I'll look at the listings.'

Putting these vague, secret, half-baked aspirations into words, and hearing Nina respond as if they were all possible – simple to achieve, even – made Yonas feel like perhaps they were. If only he were lucky enough to get leave to remain. Without papers, his hands were as tied as ever. But there were some things he could get going with. 'Of course I am going to look after Osman now,' he added. 'I want to make sure he gets a good place to live and studies hard and does well in the UK. And for him, and also for me, I am going to try to connect with more people from the Eritrean community here. I avoided doing that for a long time, but I miss my culture too much.'

'I bet.'

'One day, all being well, I would like to bring my family over, if the situation in my country does not improve,' he said. 'And start a family of my own… But that is all just dreaming.'

'No harm in dreaming.' Nina smiled, then shook her head.

'What are you thinking?' he asked.

'Nothing much. Well, I was just thinking how someone I know, another friend (who's also friends with Quentin so probably on his side), said to me the other day that I should be wary of spending so much time and energy helping you out because you'd just cause me huge amounts of stress and money and you were probably teeing things up for a marriage visa! I told her she had the wrong end of the stick. That it was more likely to be the other way round.'

Yonas wasn't sure he was understanding her properly.

'Oh look, I shouldn't even have mentioned it,' she said. 'I just hope you can make some or all those things happen.'

'Thank you,' he said, embarrassed, and got up, a bit too quickly. 'Shall we go back?'

Nina got up too and took his hand. It was nice to feel her palm against his, steady, despite the syncopated rhythm of their strides.

By the time they approached the road to the station, it was already dusk. In Asmara, three hours later, it would be almost bedtime. Yonas resolved to phone Melat in the morning. He had left it far too long without calling. She would be cross, and he would have to apologize. But then he would tell her he'd got her letter, that it could well make all the difference, that she might have saved him. He might not tell her that he nearly didn't receive it – that he had nearly made himself disappear. And he would have to break the news to her about Gebre. That would be hard. She would probably cry. He would probably cry. Would he tell her about their mad escape attempt? He owed her the truth. Truth that wouldn't unnecessarily hurt her, anyway. He would definitely tell her that his lawyer was going to claim against the detention centre, to seek justice for Gebre's death. And of course he could now tell her the good news about the factory raid! She would be so happy to hear that Osman was safe, even though she had never met him. And he should tell her about Nina, too. He had hardly told her anything about Nina yet.

He looked over. 'Actually,' he said to Nina, 'when I was up in the north, I started to write a little bit. I even finished something short, but I am not sure if it is any good.'

'Would you let me read it?'

He pulled out his notebook, and handed it over.

Chapter 32: Jude

**HOW TEN HUMAN RIGHTS CASES CLOG
UP OUR COURTS EVERY DAY**

'Mr Kelati, would you like to swear on a holy book or take the oath?' the judge asks.

YK chooses the oath, and swears solemnly to tell the truth, the whole truth, and nothing but the truth, sounding as if he means it. He looks so calm up there, tall and slim and as striking as a Giacometti, that you relax, a little – but you're still gripping the lectern hard. There is so much more evidence for this fresh claim hearing than there was for the no-show appeal a year ago – the letters Melat sent confirming his internet use as well as their persecution by the authorities because of his escape, the police evidence of the fish factory raid, the letter from the human rights organization that published his reports and others he emailed – but still. You never know. The pressure of standing up to give evidence at a hearing with such weighty consequences can inject poisonous stress into even the most measured person. Plus, this is Judge Gratchet. *Bad luck!* your old pupil supervisor said, when you told him. *She's basically the Home Office mascot.* Her jowls do actually remind you of the Churchill bulldog.

'May I have permission to do a brief examination in chief,' you ask the judge, as a courtesy, turning the pages of your blue notebook to the list of questions you intend to kick off with.

'You may not,' she snaps. 'It should all be in the witness statement.' YK flashes a quick glance in your direction – you had assured him that you would get to examine him first – but as you cringe, nod at the judge and sit down again, his face remains as unreadable as the *Mona Lisa's*.

He should have been the anxious one this morning, but he'd almost seemed to be the one putting you at ease. You'd been so psyched about meeting him today, after all this time, anticipating and imagining, and after his non-appearance last time made you go to pieces, that you had to restrain yourself from reaching out to kiss him on both cheeks, and make an effort to remain professional. But he seemed to have no trouble. And, once you sat down in conference to discuss the proceedings, you found that he was polite, quietly spoken and reassuringly articulate, even in English. You cross your fingers behind your back.

'Mr Kelati,' the judge says, 'Mr Eastly may have some questions for you.'

Your opponent, a Home Office Presenting Officer called Gavin Eastly, jumps to his feet, almost slobbering with excitement, but props himself on the lectern on one elbow, in a faux-casual pose he might adopt to initiate a flirtatious chat with an unobtainable woman over a pint. From his balloon paunch you'd say he spends a lot of time drinking pints. You feel like maliciously sticking a pin in it to see if it pops. You knew you couldn't stand the guy when the first thing he said to you outside the consultation room this morning was: 'So, Miss Munroe,' (*it's Ms*), 'I see you're only just out of pupillage. Is this your *very first* appeal?' He smirked, revealing a whole extra chin, before handing you his skeleton argument and a pile of comparable cases, as if you'd have time to read them in the five minutes before the hearing started. 'Uphill struggle for you here,' he said. 'But you'll soon learn when to advise those instructing you to back down in these kinds of cases.' *At least I'm a proper barrister, not a HOPO*, you'd felt like retorting. Guys like that weren't worth wasting energy over – but he'd still managed to get you rattled. *Was your case really that bad?*

'Mr Kelati,' Gavin Eastly says, 'you entered this country illegally and you proceeded to work here without a visa for *nearly a year* before seeking asylum.'

'Yes, but I was trafficked here, and forced to work—'

'Well, hang on a minute, you say you *first* worked in a *shellfish factory* run by a man named Mr Aziz Hussain, whom you describe as a *gangmaster*.'

'That's right.'

'Who was never found there, or anywhere.'

'Maybe not, but he ran it. The police found his documents—'

'You worked there for *four months*.'

'Just under that, yes.'

'Without a visa.'

'We had no papers at all, it was impossible to—'

'And there was nothing stopping you leaving the factory, was there? No handcuffs, no locked doors, no wall.'

'Aziz told us—'

'Mr Kelati, the question is, there was *no* physical barrier of *any kind* stopping you from leaving, was there?'

'No.'

'So when you claim that you were engaged in *forced labour*, that's incorrect, isn't it? You're not *forced* to do something if you're free to leave.'

'But Aziz had a gun—'

'Now, now, Mr Kelati, you have made much of this *gun* in your *new* witness statement, but you failed to mention it in your original statement.'

This was true – you couldn't believe Veata had left it out before.

'I did tell my caseworker,' YK said.

'Hold on. Now, *you* signed your first witness statement, didn't you, Mr Kelati? Signed to affirm that it was true.'

'Yes. It was.'

'But you omitted to mention a gun. Now, if you had known of a gun or perceived it as a genuine threat, Mr Kelati, you would have mentioned it originally, wouldn't you? It would have been a very *important* thing to mention.'

'Well...'

'So I suggest to you that there was *no gun* either in your mind or on the premises before you *decided* to move on, Mr Kelati. So surely, as a man who *claims* to be educated to *university* level, you *must* have received *some* cash payment for your work there, or you would not have stayed in the job voluntarily for so long.'

'We were not even paid one pound. Aziz told us we were in debt for being smuggled, and if we left before it was paid his men would get us, or the police would lock us up, and we would be too late to claim asylum, and he tortured the workers, it is in the fresh evidence...' YK is rushing, now, speaking too fast.

Don't panic, you whisper.

'Let us leave evidential burdens to the *lawyers*, shall we, Mr Kelati?' Gavin Eastly says, pulling his signature smirk as he glances at the judge. 'You are making several *assertions* here. You assert that Mr Hussain was a trafficker, but you've provided *no* evidence that he was involved in your journey here, or that *any debts* were owed by you to him for services related to that journey – apart from the shared assumption of your fellow worker, Osman Zekarias.'

'Objection,' you pipe up. 'There *is* evidence that the workers at the factory were trafficked and not paid: if I may refer you, Madam, to the police statement at Tab 3 of the bundle...'

'Well...' Gavin Eastly says, reddening a little, 'you certainly did work illegally for cash for nearly a year after that, before you finally *did* decide to claim asylum, didn't you? And somehow you knew it wasn't too late *then*.'

'Because they advised me. The Refugee Legal Centre.'

'Advice you could have obtained earlier. Advice that illegal friends of yours must surely have discussed.'

'I was scared of being deported.'

'Mr Kelati, I put it to you that you delayed seeking asylum for so long because you knew you didn't have a case for it.'

'Objection – speculation!' you butt in, more squeakily than you mean to.

'Yes. Could you move onto another line of questioning, Mr Eastly,' the judge says, irritably, you are pleased to note.

'Indeed, madam…'

Gavin Eastly starts asking about YK's illegal work in Molly Muldoon's house. You suspected he'd make that connection with the story in the papers, even though neither of them was named – he probably just wants the gossip to spread around his HOPO buddies. Seems pointless, as they will both flatly deny it, just as Quentin Lambourne did. But the possibility will still be raised in the judge's mind, and that must be Gavin Eastly's purpose. The other witnesses are sitting outside the hearing room still, waiting to give their evidence, and you wonder what Quentin Lambourne – Quentin Lambourne *MP* now – thinks about his wife coming along here. They've separated, apparently, so perhaps he doesn't know or care. It was interesting to put another face to a name, this morning, meeting Nina. She's kind of pretty, in a skinny, angular way, more so than in the pictures you'd seen of her with her husband, and her red hair is even more striking, almost unnaturally so; you suspect she's dyed it to conceal greys. She's quirkily dressed, with a vintage cardigan, but she looks almost childish, she's such a featherweight. You had your eyes peeled for chemistry between her and YK this morning in conference, and she was certainly gazing at him a lot. You couldn't be sure – nothing was overt. But now you're the one speculating…

'Now, back in Eritrea, you *claim* to have been persecuted,' Gavin Eastly says.

'Yes, I was put in prison because they found out that I was writing critical things about the regime, and I was tortured, but I escaped—'

'Now hang on a second. You have *said* that you were a political prisoner and you escaped. But you don't have any *evidence* of that *either*, do you?' Gavin Eastly is clearly preparing himself to suggest next that your client's whole story of making his way across a thorny desert and a militarized border is inherently improbable…

But then Veata taps you on the shoulder, and passes you a note.

AZIZ HAS BEEN FOUND!

You re-read it. You turn around to check she's serious. She brandishes her Blackberry at you, which seems to have an email on it. The font is too small... *Suicide?* You could not have made this up.

You get to your feet, heart thumping. 'Madam, I apologize for the interruption, but I must request a short adjournment. I have just been informed by my instructing solicitor that...' You look over at YK, and it crosses your mind that he should hear this privately first, but you need to explain to the judge now and you want it to make an impact. 'Aziz Hussain has just been found,' you say, leaving a short pause afterwards, in which everything in the room goes deadly silent, before adding, with appropriate emphasis: 'Our contact informs us that all signs point to him having shot himself shortly before the police arrived. I submit that evidence in connection with the incident is reasonably likely to be relevant to this case, madam, and propose to seek further information about it accordingly, for the benefit of the tribunal.'

YK is staring at me as if I'd just pulled Aziz's corpse out of my suitcase and started waltzing with it.

'Madam I submit that it is for too late to introduce this information and I cannot see how it is in any way relevant,' Gavin Eastly pipes up, unconvincingly, while turning purple around the edges. 'The mental state of a former *employer* of the appellant has no bearing on—'

'Adjournment granted,' the judge barks, ignoring him. 'Tribunal rise.'

Outside the tribunal, you invite YK and the witnesses to come to the conference room, while Veata scurries off to make more calls. You all gather around the table.

'What's happened?' Nina asks.

When you tell her, she and Molly gasp in unison, then Nina leans over to put her arm around YK. And, from the way she looks at him – well, then you just know.

'This is good, isn't it?' Nina asks him. 'I mean, suicide is tantamount to a confession.'

YK gives her a one-sided smile, but doesn't look quite so thrilled.

'Understandably that news was a huge shock,' you say. 'But I think—'

'I wanted him to die,' YK bursts out, 'but I didn't want him to *kill himself*. Especially after... I just thought there would be... justice.' He looks down at his lap for a moment. Then up again, and puts his palms firmly on the table. 'I wanted to watch him admit what he *did* to Osman and to all of us, and explain... I wanted...' This is the first time today that he has seemed hesitant, lost for words. He retracts his palms, clasps his hands.

'Closure?' you ask, thinking, as it pops out of your mouth, what an inane word that is. 'Of course you did.'

Veata comes back into the room. 'So,' she says, 'it seems that Aziz was found working as part of a different operation, connected with the same smuggler chain, but involving the "protection" of women working in prostitution above a massage parlour. An informant came forward and the police raided the place, but it seems Aziz had been tipped off and killed himself rather than handing himself in. I just can't believe the timing.'

'I know. Thanks.' You look over at Yonas. 'Well, I could ask the judge to adjourn until the investigation is complete so that we can take the evidence into account. She might refuse. Or we could elect to continue and hope she draws the appropriate inferences, and makes the right decision on the basis of the body of evidence we already have...'

Yonas looks at the table, thinking it over. Nina puts her hand on his arm. 'You want to maximize your chances, don't you?' she asks him.

He nods at her slowly, but then looks back to me and says, 'Maybe. But I also want this to be decided. It has gone on too long now, and I think we have enough evidence. Especially with the documents my sister sent. And Osman with us, able to give his evidence in such good English.' You watch Osman smile delightedly, and stare down at his lap. 'And I think the judge is on our side,' YK adds.

You are taken aback by his confidence. But as it happens, you agree. Judge Gratchet has been impatient with Gavin Eastly so far, though you wonder now whether to mention to YK how notoriously pro-government she is reputed to be in these cases, so perhaps it's all an act. But what would that achieve? He seems so sure about his case, now. As he should be. Yes: YK *should* win this appeal hands down, even with a fraction of the evidence you have now. Especially thanks to the documents his sister sent through. You wish you could fly her over to witness his victory, and get her leave to remain too. 'Let's carry on, then,' you say, re-enthused, looking at Veata for confirmation.

Veata nods and smiles slightly. She's such a petite lady, and so polite, compared to most of your instructing solicitors, but somehow closed, private, remote. You wonder, briefly, how she came to be doing this work.

Back in the tribunal, you pass on the information about Aziz and propose proceeding. The judge agrees, and Gavin Eastly resumes his cross-examination.

In bullish fashion, he does his best to paint YK as a devious interloper – but you're not overawed by Gavin Eastly any more. And you don't think YK is either. He isn't rushing his answers now. He's speaking fluently but at a measured pace, replete with self-assurance, making it harder for Gavin Eastly to interrupt convincingly, or maintain the pace of his previous quick-fire attack.

And when you get to re-examine YK, you feel a calm confidence float up in your chest as you ask him clarifying questions. The bizarre timing of the news about Aziz arriving during this hearing a year after the factory raid might make it too late to count for much as evidence, but it does feel like a sign, a good omen, an early vindication of sorts that seems to give every word you utter a renewed boost of validity. And Yonas's answers seem to sing back to you across the tribunal now, in harmony with what you want to hear, never scrambled, never going off on tangents, never extending unnecessarily. The two of you are perfectly in sync, at this moment, just as you were when you first arrived in different corners of the world. And it's a foreign sensation, this smooth control you seem to have gained over the hearing; it feels a bit like the time you and Max landed a jammy new Mercedes on your first holiday together to France due to an error on the hire company's part, when the only car you'd ever driven before was your old, beaten-up Mini with its spongy gears and grunting engine.

Judge Grachet listens to both sets of closing submissions, then pauses to finish some scribbles. Every muscle in your body clenches. Then she looks up.

'I am going to reserve judgment,' she announces tartly.

You let out a sigh, which you hope she didn't hear. It's obviously disappointing not to hear her declare your victory immediately and unreservedly, and proclaim how uniquely deserving YK is as a candidate for leave to remain in this country and what excellent representation he's had – but at least she's not making a quick decision to boot him out. It's probably a good sign that she needs more time, isn't it?

'Tribunal rise,' the clerk crows. You mirror the judge as she stands, then watch her take her leave. You can't help tingling with optimism, and find you have to stifle a smile.

Outside the hearing room, Emil is ecstatic, clapping like you've already won, but YK laughs at him, saying you'll all have to wait and see. He's right, of course. You thank all the witnesses. YK shakes your hand and tells you how grateful he is, which means more than you could possibly express at this moment, and you wonder if this is the last time you'll ever see him.

'Pleasure,' you say. 'Also – happy birthday for next week!'

'Oh! Thank you,' he says, surprised.

'I only noticed because it'll be mine the same day. We're even the same age, as it happens.'

'Really?'

And now you've said it, and seen the look on his face, you realize it sounds like you've stalked him, or made it up. But it's only because you saw you shared a birthday that you started imagining switching places, that you got so caught up in his case. Still, you briefly imagine receiving a formal letter saying: *Dear Ms Munroe, The Secretary of State finds your assertion that you and the appellant share a birthday to lack credibility...* 'Let's hope we have good news by then, so we can doubly celebrate,' you tell him.

'Yes, let us hope!' he says.

You want to ask him to keep in touch, to see if he'd like to meet for a coffee, to let you know where he is by next year's birthday, to say you'd like to send him a card... You want at least to say something about how his case has affected you, to tell him that you've since thought about his life so hard that you've imagined details like his favourite dish, the music his parents listened to, the objects he carries around in his pockets... But you just smile, wish him the best of luck, and watch them turn and walk away: Nina, threading her arm through his, and Molly, placing her hand on his back from other side, then falling into step with Emil and Osman.

You lose sight of them, but stay staring down the corridor for a few more moments, before you notice that Veata has appeared next to you, and is looking at you oddly. You grin at her, collecting yourself, as if you'd just been spaced out for a second, and have a short wrap-up chat about the case. After you've thanked each other, you walk back to the robing room alone.

You feel bereft at parting with YK, even though you've only just met. Exhaustion descends like a thick curtain. Your limbs are leaden, and you want to curl up on the floor... but Gavin Eastly would inevitably come in and mock you. You sigh, pull out your phone, switch it on, and find a text from Max that he must have sent this morning.

Good luck smooch. And one from Alec, whose entire face is smeared with yoghurt xxx

Yuck! you imagine saying with maximum disgust, to your son's hilarity. You should head home and make it in time for bedtime, for once. And then, once Alec is asleep, you should crack open a bottle of wine and fess up to Max that you've been having an elaborate fantasy about a client; but that it's not how it sounds – that it's made you realize what's important: home, family, love...

He'd probably think you were being flippant, or having an over-emotional case come-down. But you could insist you meant it. And maybe he's been wishing for ages that you'd not only be around occasionally, but would express some genuine affection. Yes, you will try to tell Max from the heart what he means to you. And then break it to him that you're not quite ready to quit being a barrister after all.

All you need now is a quick sugar hit to summon up the energy to pack up your stuff and head home via chambers, so you reach into your handbag for your emergency Snickers, and pull out…

A postcard. *Where did this come from?* The picture is of the Queen's Royal Guards marching outside Buckingham Palace in their furry hats. Is this a joke?

Thank you for fighting to save a bear
from extinction.

Yours,
Yonas Kelati

Epilogue

The morning sun bathes my skin, bee-eaters chirp in the bushes, and our hens cluck lazily from the shade. 'Come on, Yonas, or we'll be late for school,' my mother calls from the kitchen.

'Okay,' I yell back, and head over to our mango tree to look for some fallen fruit that she can chop up for breakfast, just like any other day. But it's not just any other day. For the past year, which feels like for ever, I have been walking with my mother and sister to school filled with envy, wishing I could go in too, sit by Melat at a desk, learn what she's learning. We used to be as good as each other at reading, but now she shows off with her writing, all neat with perfectly curly letters. When I tried to copy, it looked like a cockroach had lurched across the page, so I gave up and pretended I didn't care. Being the younger one is so unfair! But now I'm going to catch her. By the end of the first term I'll be able to write any word in the whole dictionary.

A fallen mango glistens in the grass, perfectly fat, and I pick it up to confirm the soft give of its skin, then place it in my basket. I head on to the hens' coop and open the door at the top, provoking the usual flustered clucking. Russom is looking at me silently with a beady eye, reminding me to say hello to him too. I feel around the hens' fussing, feathered bodies, and… yes! An egg, perfectly smooth and warm. Two eggs. Three! This is a great sign for my first day. I place them gently in my basket next to the mango, and walk back towards the house, diverting around the pile of bricks…

But my foot catches – oh, no, no, no – I fly through the air, then smack down onto my knees, putting out my hands to protect my face and jarring my wrists, while the basket continues floating on in space, spraying out the three precious eggs and the mango which seem to hover, intact and tantalizing, before smashing to the ground.

My knees sting. I sit up to inspect them. Blood and dirt mingled together, flaps of skin hanging off. I start to cry. My mother is going to be cross. She was already cross that I got up late, and now I've ruined everyone's breakfast. So much for my first day of school.

'Well then, little man.' It's my grandfather. He's standing over me, eyebrows tangled in a frown. I look up at him, miserable.

'I smashed three eggs,' I confess, quaking – as if it wasn't obvious. Grandfather swears that eggs from happy hens are the key to good health, and built our poultry palace himself from cut-off bits of timber, complete with special walkways and nesting corners.

'Never mind about that.' He chuckles. 'Give me your hand.' He pulls me to my feet. 'Let's have a look at those knees. Hmm, in the wars, just like our country. Well, there'll be more scratches along the way, but you'll come out all right. You're a lucky one, you know.' I look at him, confused, as I scrub away my tears with a filthy hand. How am I *lucky* when I've just fallen over on my first day and ruined my knees and smashed all the fresh eggs? But my grandfather is smiling. 'And just so you remember that, I've got something for you.' He holds out a clenched fist.

'What is it?' I ask.

'It's something you can carry in your pocket, to keep you safe.' I reach out for it. 'Wait,' he says gruffly. Reluctantly, I retract my arm. 'It will also remind you, like Russom over there each dawn, that you need to get up on time and work hard if you want to do well. Always strive for what you wish for, and never give up. Got that?'

I nod eagerly. I can't imagine what he could have in there. A watch, maybe? 'Can I see now?' I ask. He lets me peel back his fingers, one by one. In his deeply creased palm lies a tiny wooden rooster with a perfectly curved tail, smooth ridges for feathers, and black pinpoint eyes that

Grandfather must have burned on with a hot wire. Nobody else at school will have anything like this. 'Cockadoodledoo!' I call out gleefully, for a moment forgetting all about my mangled knees. Carefully, as if it were a real live chick, I take it.

Afterword

Like Jude, I used to be a barrister specializing in human rights. Early on, before the current refugee crisis exploded, I worked on an Eritrean asylum appeal. Reading the legal documents and precedent cases made a huge impression on me; I knew nothing about Eritrea and its extraordinary history before, and I was fascinated by the journeys and experiences of the appellants. I was particularly struck with how inherently dramatic their stories were in 'plot' terms, and yet how much individual experience must have been lost in translation to arrive at the dry, legal language in my papers. I also felt angered by the gulf between the factual realities of the lives I was reading about and the sensationalist tabloid headlines about asylum seekers. It reminded me of the potent power of language to distort and exclude – and yet how language can have at least as much power to forge empathy and bridge gulfs of experience or narrative, particularly in fiction. So I looked around for novels that were telling these sorts of stories, but at that time there didn't seem to be many. I decided to experiment with writing one myself.

It wasn't just about a message, though. No good novel is. Story is always queen. And I wanted to write fiction anyway. One of my earliest memories is cowriting a fairy tale with my dad on his old Amstrad word processor with its bright green Courier font, and I already had a few failed novel attempts in the desk drawer, but this was the first one that compelled me to keep going until the end. So, while I hope people read *The Invisible Crowd* as a contribution to the growing body of stories about refugee, asylum and migrant experiences, which are sorely needed in these times, most of all I hope they will enjoy it as a yarn about humans.

Acknowledgements

This book simmered sporadically over the course of nearly a decade around barrister work, adventures in Myanmar, a PhD, an experimental live literature project, and two beautiful, bombastic babies. It owes its finished form to a multitude of sources, places and people.

For those interested in finding out more about Eritrea, key sources include articles by exiled journalists Abraham T. Zere, Eyob Ghilazgy and other writers whose work can be found on the PEN Eritrea website; Christine Matzke's research on Eritrean theatre culture, and *Three Eritrean Plays* by Musgun Zerai, Isaias Tsegay, Solomon Dirar edited by Jane Plastow; Ghirmai Negash's work on Tigrinya literature and the fiction of Beyene Heile in particular; Lesley Gottesman's work on literacy in Eritrea; wider-ranging histories and non-fiction accounts of Eritrea, including Michela Wrong's powerful book *I Didn't Do it for You,* Martin Plaut's *Understanding Eritrea,* Edward Denison and Edward Plaice's *Eritrea: The Bradt Travel Guide* and writings on Asmara's architecture, and Alemseged Tesfai's work on Eritrean history. Novels about Eritrea include Thomas Keneally's *Towards Asmara* set during the liberation struggle and Nadifa Mohamed's *Black Mamba Boy* about her father's journey to the UK. Michela Wrong's *Borderlines* is a novel set around a border dispute between fictional countries that are strikingly comparable to Eritrea and Ethiopia. Notable memoirs about Eritrea are Hannah Pool's *My Fathers' Daughter,* Justin Hill's *Ciao Asmara,* and Senait Mehari's controversial *Heart of Fire.* Texts on the asylum experiences of Eritreans in the UK include Rachel Warner's *Voices from Eritrea,* as well as online articles published by the Refugee Council, AVID (Association of Visitors to Immigration

Detainees) and others. For those keen to read more fiction about refugee, asylum seeker and immigrant experiences, some that I have enjoyed are Viet Than Nguyen's collection *The Refugees* and Jamaica Kincaird's *Lucy*, Caryl Phillips's *A Distant Shore*, Lloyd Jones's *Hand Me Down World*, Zadie Smith's *White Teeth*, NoViolet Bulaweyo's *We Need New Names*, Chris Cleave's *The Other Hand*, Dave Eggers' *What Is the What*, Benjamin Zephaniah's *Refugee Boy*, Stephen Kelman's *Pigeon English*, Rose Tremain's *The Road Home* and Sunjeev Sahota's *The Year of the Runaways*. Warsan Shire's moving poem 'Home' deserves a special mention for its poignant plea for understanding the reasons why people leave theirs. Thank you to the family of Amanuel Asrat and for granting me permission to include in the novel part of the text of Asrat's powerful poem 'The Scourge of War', translated by Tedros Abraham. One of the most rich, beautiful and humane books I have come across on migration is Ruth Padel's *The Mara Crossing: Poems and Prose on Migration*.

I have spoken to many Eritreans about their experiences of seeking asylum in the UK, most of whom do not wish to be named, but all of whom I am incredibly grateful to. In particular, Eyob Ghilazgy and Abraham T. Zere were both very generous with their time in talking about their experiences as exiled journalists, and one member of an Eritrean church in London, who knows who he is, spoke to me at great length with insight and sensitivity about his and his community's experiences. Volunteering with asylum seekers and refugees at the Refugee Council and at an immigration removal centre in the UK has been profoundly moving and illuminating. There are just so many heartrending and astonishing stories out there to be told and to be listened to. If more of them were, then surely more voices would be raised in protest, and oppressive policies like the indefinite detention of asylum seekers in the UK and cuts to legal aid would change. Organizations like Counterpoints Arts, PositiveNegatives and Refugee Tales are now working hard to convey these messages through the arts, and The Refugee Council, Refugees at Home and numerous other organizations do fantastic work to ensure that communication leads to action. There are always many sides to a story, and thank you also to the Home Office interviewer who took the time to tell me his.

Two bookish havens for my research and writing have been the British Library and Gladstone's Library. I have a host of wonderful people to thank for supporting me on this journey and reading drafts along the way, in particular Christine Green and Clio Cornish, for believing in the book and offering many excellent suggestions for improving it, but also to David Wiles, Sarah Polcz and Rachel Louis for taking the time to read drafts. Last but not least, my stoic and supportive husband Sydney Nash has not only read numerous versions of this story but has looked after our two tots during vital writing retreats so that I could take a break from reading picture books and focus on finishing this one.

References

Chapter 1: Jude
Page 3: 'Welcome to heaven, how about a cup of tea? The cold facts about immigration – why so many asylum seekers head for Britain.' *Daily Mail*, 14 November 2009

Chapter 2: Yonas
Page 10: 'Cereal offenders: Asylum seeker gang collected £24 million drug money in Special K boxes' *Daily Mail*, 9 February 2010

Chapter 3: Joe
Page 17: 'Asylum seeker travels 50 miles to Britain strapped under school trip coach . . . and emerges with a grin and thumbs-up' *Daily Mail*, 14 April 2010

Chapter 4: Yonas
Page 24: 'MIGRANT SHAMBLES: EU "has surrendered complete control of its borders to people smugglers"' *The Sun*, 22 June 2016

Page 24: 'Tortured asylum seeker fraudulently claimed £21,000 in benefits while earning £2,000 a month' *Daily Mail*, 28 February 2011

Chapter 5: Quentin
Page 34: 'BARE-FACED CHEEK: Fury as German nudists are ordered to cover up after a migrant shelter arrives near their lake' *The Sun*, 23 June 2016

Chapter 6: Yonas

Page 39: 'Rapist asylum seeker who dumped victim on rubbish tip is released after being TWO hours away from deportation' *Daily Mail*, 15 December 2011

Page 45: 'Smuggling gangs want to sneak Calais migrants into Britain to commit crimes HERE' *Daily Express*, 21 August 2015

Chapter 7: Emil

Page 59: 'UK IMMIGRATION SHOCK 150,000 illegal immigrants enter UK each year, says whistleblower ex-Home Office boss' *The Sun*, 16 June 2017

Chapter 8: Yonas

Page 71: 'MIGRANTS CLASH: French cops use tear gas in running battles with hundreds of migrants trying to clamber on lorries bound for Britain' *The Sun*, 21 June 2016

Page 83: 'Stowaway shambles: asylum seeker who keeps trying to return to Morocco sues Britain for STOPPING him' *Daily Mail*, 4 January 2011

Chapter 9: Jude

Page 87: 'Who knows what horrors he has been through?' Swedish police chief sparks anger by SYMPATHISING with Somali boy, 15, charged with social worker's murder' *Daily Mail*, 27 January 2016

Chapter 10: Molly

Page 91: 'Asylum seeker who paralysed a pensioner in car crash escapes jail' *Daily Mail*, 17 September 2006

Chapter 11: Yonas

Page 99: 'Taking us for a ride: £100k of your cash blown by charity on days out to help refugees "integrate"' *The Sun*, 19 December 2015

Chapter 12: Meg

Page 120: 'Lying asylum seeker can stay here – because she had two children by an HIV alcoholic' *Daily Mail*, 1 February 2011

Chapter 13: Yonas

Page 128: '"I was possessed by ancestral African spirit": Asylum seeker's astonishing defence over noise complaints' *Daily Mail*, 21 January 2011

Chapter 14: Veata

Page 149: 'Lawyers "play the system on asylum"' *Daily Mail*, 19 November 2008

Chapter 15: Yonas

Page 159: 'Former asylum seeker living for free in £1.2m taxpayer-funded mansion is charged with benefit fraud' *Daily Mail*, 25 January 2011

Chapter 16: Jude

Page 168: 'One-legged Albanian killer who pretended to be a Kosovan asylum seeker to gain UK citizenship will finally be deported after 14 YEARS of living on handouts' *Daily Mail*, 1 July 2016

Chapter 17: Gavin

Page 171: 'Migration officer sang Um Bongo song to an asylum seeker from Congo' *Daily Mail*, 4 March 2010

Chapter 18: Yonas

Page 178: 'Asylum "chaos" allowed ricin plotter to kill' *Daily Mail*, 14 April 2005

Chapter 19: Tesfay

Page 186: 'Failed asylum seeker who has dodged deportation for a decade told he can stay . . . because he goes to the GYM' *Daily Mail*, 24 October 2011

Chapter 28: Yonas
Page 278: 'Bogus asylum seeker accused of murdering teenager attempts suicide in prison' *Daily Express*, 16 March 2017

Chapter 29: Jude
Page 291: '"Let's clear asylum backlog": Tough new rules to deport foreign crooks FAST' *Daily Express*, 18 April 2017

Chapter 30: Melat
Page 295: 'Failed asylum seeker who raped a teenager in a park as she had an epileptic fit is jailed for ten years' *Daily Mail*, 28 June 2011

Chapter 31: Yonas
Page 298: 'Asylum seeker jailed for hour-long HAMMER attack on wife he used for visa' *Daily Express*, 1 May 2017

Page 303: 'Illegal immigrant who killed pensioner, 91, in car crash finally caught after FOUR years . . . hiding in cupboard' *Daily Mail*, 27 April 2010

Chapter 32: Jude
Page 315: 'How ten human rights cases clog up our courts EVERY DAY' *Daily Mail*, 13 February 2011

ONE PLACE. MANY STORIES

Bold, innovative and
empowering publishing.

FOLLOW US ON:

@HQStories